## ABOUT THE AUTHOR

Peter Gray has been writing in various guises since he was twelve years old and he has never been able to stop. From plays to magazine articles Peter has produced a plethora of work.

His first 'Sam Series' book "A Certain Summer" has had excellent reviews, one from TV presenter and ex England soccer coach Bob Wilson who grew up in the same area and could easily identify with the character in the book.

With many short stories, articles and celebrated Mummers Plays plus many touring productions under his belt. Peter is always busy writing something or other. He has also acted in and directed some of those productions and one such production played at Warwick Castle for six full seasons. He has also written several scripts for advertisements, mostly with a humorous theme as well as several live shows for the stage. He has now embarked on a new series of Adventure Novels of which more details can be found on this website at www.petergrayauthor.co.uk.

He currently lives in the Highlands of Scotland.

ALSO BY PETER GRAY

A Certain Summer
Sam's Kingdom
With Feeling

FROM THE AVALON SERIES

The Drums of Drumnadrochit
Auld Clootie
The Brollachan
The Black Clan
Caledonian Flame - out 2019

# The
# Black Clan

by
Peter Gray

Tricky Imp Publishing

# The Black Clan

First edition first published November 2018

Tricky Imp Publishers
Highlands, Scotland.
Email: books@trickyimppublishing.co.uk

A CIP catalogue record for this title is available from
The British Library.

ISBN 978-0-9572668-6-5

Cover artwork by the author.
Cover photography by Barbara Jane Gray

More Information at:
www.petergrayauthor.co.uk
www.trickyimppublishing.co.uk

Printed and bound in the UK by 4 Edge.

Once again, thanks go to
Jonathan McColl for his
tireless work on the manuscript.

"Sadness and sorrow cut deep and permanently, and if the savage scars they leave are what prove we have been alive, I have already lived a thousand years."

The inscription on the back of Avalon's motorcycle key fob.

# Chapter One

DS Ross was crouched over the body checking the pockets, but could find no clue or information that could have given him an idea who had committed the murder. He was determined that he would crack this problem before his boss, Detective Inspector James Avalon, though that same man had already intimated he knew who had done it. The room was busy with people and a few were glancing at what Ross was doing. He tried his best to cover the gaze of the other eyes in the room by positioning his body to shield his actions, but finding nothing of importance on the victim he sighed and stood. He placed his hands on his hips and looked down then around the room. There was no obvious murder weapon and there was no injury save a red patch on the base of the skull. He sighed again and walked over to the drinks cabinet where he noticed it had a mirror on its rear and he cautiously looked through it to see if Avalon was in the room. He wasn't. This was his opportunity to have a word with Rory Mackinnon and he made his way towards him. Mackinnon was speaking with a pretty young girl in her late teens. Ross smiled at her briefly and then put his face close to Rory's ear.

"Any ideas?" he whispered.

"Not a clue," smiled Rory, "though I have suspected Mrs Weir, I did think her statement was inconsistent with what we know to be true."

"Hmm, I never considered her," mused Ross with a frown, "I was under the impression she didn't know the victim and that would leave no motive."

"Motive?" asked Rory with alarm, "I never expected there to be a motive." This was a surprise to Ross, he stood looking into space for a moment, Rory became bored and returned his interest to the young lady. Ross returned to the drinks cabinet, he wasn't considering a drink, after all, he already had one though he couldn't remember where he had put it.

"Ef I'm gonna have tae carry you around I'm off home," hissed a voice in a broad accent to his left. It was Megan Frazer and she was handing him his drink.

"Oh, I forgot where it was," said Ross raising his eyebrows.

"Aye, a' know, but next time et goes down the sink," she insisted. Ross drank the lager greedily and then stopped and asked,

"Have you any idea who the murderer is then?" Frazer shrugged.

"No an' tae be honest, I don't much care."

"I thought once you had downed a few you'd be a little more sociable," frowned Ross taking another drink.

"Sociable?" she replied raising the tone of her voice, "et's nothin' tae do with being sociable or not, I mean, what sort of muppet organises a party for coppers and then makes et into a murder mystery?"

"Well, it's an odd one I'll grant you that, seeing as most of the assembled are detectives, but," continued

Ross, "it's been a bit of fun and it's nice to meet some of the other people away from work," smiled Ross.

"Well et's not my idea o' fun, it's like a bunch of surgeons going out to a night club and then deciding to do an appendectomy on the dance floor," frowned Frazer sipping from a dainty crystal glass.

"Well yes," grinned Ross, "I suppose it is but on the other hand, I've never seen you in a posh frock before."

"An' don't get ideas above y'r station," she insisted pointing a single slim finger at him from under the glass, "I only agreed tae come with you so y' didnae look like a lemon turnin' up on yer own."

"Well the boss arrived on his own," explained Ross with yet another lifting of his brows.

"He's got the right tae look like a lemon, he's the boss," she insisted and took another sip of the drink.

"So who are you putting down for the murder?" asked Ross again before taking another gulp of lager. Frazer looked at him with a deep frown.

"Are y' serious?" she asked, "do I look like I give a shit?"

"Don't be such a grouch, just guess if you don't know," insisted Ross taking a look around the room.

"Guess, es that how you usually crack a case?" she asked raising her eyebrows, "no wonder y' don't have a very good 'solve rate',"

"Very funny," replied Ross still looking at the people in the room, "why didn't your man come with you then?" Frazer made a noise that was a cross between a stifled laugh and a cough.

"Et's not his kind o' thing, he's more comfortable with his own company," she paused, "an' I can't fault his

9

reasoning at the moment."

"Have you spoken to Mack?" asked Ross with no warning, it was a touchy subject still. Frazer was caught off guard for a moment.

"No," she replied and then finished off her drink, "I don't know what tae say t' him." Ross turned to her.

"Why? He's not a leper, just be yourself," insisted Ross then amended the statement, "no on second thoughts, try to be nice for a change." She scowled at him and held up the dainty glass.

"Et's a good job this es empty or you would be wearing the contents by now." She gave a long pause and then shrugged, "I know et's still the old Mack but I can't get over seeing him as a civilian, I mean it's just not right." Ross looked into her eyes, he could see something burning in there, something he hadn't seen in Frazer before and it took some time to recognise it for what it was. Compassion, compassion for someone she liked and it was such a hidden emotion of Frazer's that she didn't know how to control it and it made her afraid of the whole thing. "I mean, what do you say to him, 'hey Mack, how are you doin', well except for the fact that you can't walk properly any more', es that et?"

"I had never got you down for this," said Ross with a slight smile on his lips.

"For what?" frowned Frazer.

"Total selfishness, denial, fear..." Ross trailed off expecting some verbal abuse to begin, but it didn't. She just sighed and in that moment Ross began to feel sorry for her, he never thought he would ever feel that for Frazer but here she was, out of her depth, at a meeting of many people, in an environment that was completely anathema to her, having to deal with an emotion that she rarely showed and he thought she was incapable of. He looked into her eyes again, watching them flit around the room, defensive and slightly ill at ease. He wondered what had happened in her past to make her so insecure. He looked again at those eyes, enhanced by the mascara that defined them, not the usual, slightly red-rimmed eyes devoid of make-up, but a more gentle, womanly look that Ross had seen on so few occasions. Since her work on surveillance some months before, she had gained a little weight and it suited her and though she complained that she was fat, she had kept the look rather than the 'pinched', previous incarnation. With the gentle make-up and the wearing of a dress, Frazer had become some different species of the detective constable that everyone knew - and generally stayed clear of. Ross looked at her deeply, why was she so against talking to Mack? He had been very seriously injured in a collision with a truck, Wilson had saved his life with quick thinking, but even the doctors couldn't fully repair his leg. It had left Mack able to walk but suffering with a pronounced limp that meant he was unable to continue as a detective. He had been moved to lighter work but the young lad had pride and had decided to leave the police force rather than become something he had never intended to be. Everyone was sympathetic, he was popular even with the uniform branch at the station but he had wanted to be a successful detective, not some desk officer doing a clerical job. The scars were not just on Mack's body, Wilson who had been in the crash with Mack had suffered deeply, and though not physically he had been off work for some weeks. He was having trouble sleeping and in some crazy way he constantly thought he hadn't done enough to help Mack, he still wondered if he had done the right thing cutting into Mack's leg to stop the bleeding. It was clear from the reports that Wilson had done everything and more at the scene of the accident. A piece of steel from the smashed door of the car had speared Mack's leg, cutting the femoral artery and it had been Wilson's quick thinking that had saved Mack's life. Mack knew this, everyone knew it, but Wilson felt guilty as it was possible that the limp that Mack now had was due to those few life-saving seconds.

"Come on," said Ross, "let's go and talk to him."

"No!" she spat and then calmed, "not yet, I'll have a word when I'm ready." Ross was taken aback. It was some odd kind of fear that she was experiencing, much more than denial but Ross once again felt something he never thought he would for Megan Frazer and he decided that they were at a party and a party it should be.

"Okay," he said holding up his hand, "let's go and get your glass filled." Ross made his way to the drinks area in the conservatory once more with Frazer following on and as he passed through the hallway of the house he noticed Avalon sitting with Mack and it looked like they were having a serious conversation. He poured himself and Frazer a drink and then looked around the room. There was a broad mix of people, other detectives, uniform officers and a couple of faces he didn't know but what was now glaringly obvious was that all the people that had come to the occasion alone, were detectives. There were plenty of couples, but the ones who were there alone were inevitably from the CID. He looked back to Frazer and pointed his observation out to her.

"Aye," she nodded after taking a sip of her drink,

"I'd already noticed that." She took another sip and then added, "an' the few that are here as couples are struggling with their private lives." Ross knew what she was hinting at. Since DS Wilson had gone through the horror of the accident, he had changed, he wasn't the easy-going man he had once been and it was taking its toll on his marriage. Ross had been the most recent victim of the divorce curse, he and his wife had split up the previous year and he was just about settled into the idea of a single life. Unlike his boss DI Avalon, Ross was enjoying the freedom - for now. A dark shadow suddenly swept over Ross and Frazer in the shape of DC Rutherford. He was a very large individual who seemed completely out of context inside a house. The police station down at Inverness was large enough to accommodate his huge frame but here in a roomy, but normal middle-class house, he looked like a bridge troll in a dog kennel.

"You two look like you've just dropped a pound coin en a cow pat," he said with a straight face. Rutherford had proved to be a reasonable addition to the team, even if his size did mean his assignments had to be chosen well. He also had a dry and somewhat clinical sense of humour, he and Ross had become a bit of a 'double act'. Strangely, Frazer seemed to get on with the big man but the young DC Mackinnon and DC Boyd were less enthusiastic about his character.

"Aye, well, I had to put off a meeting of the sock darning club to be here," hissed Frazer.

"You are such a miserable person," said Ross frowning at her.

"Well you look no better," insisted Rutherford, "you've got a face like a Paisley Pug." Ross had no idea what he meant but shrugged, it seemed *he* was the only one that had attempted to try and solve the murder mystery as everyone else seemed thoroughly uninterested.

"Solved the case yet hot-shot?" he asked glancing up at Rutherford. He made a sound that was halfway between a laugh and a sigh.

"Not tried that hard, there doesnae seem much point, your man from B Section," he nodded towards Tom Murrey who was talking to DC Boyd, "has organised this I believe, an' he doesnae seem like the type tae have put much effort into et."

"Ah, well," began Ross with a smirk, "that just means you're a bad judge of character," he then raised his eyebrows and looked over towards DS Murrey, "Tommy is one of the best." He took a quick drink from the bottle of lager he was holding. "Don't let his quiet and unassuming ways fool you, he's thorough and he doesn't miss anything in the fine detail."

"He's a good copper," nodded Frazer in a rare moment of compliment, "even if he is a bit too 'old school'," she concluded. Rutherford shrugged and reached for another drink from the table and then the three of them moved off, meeting Avalon coming the other way.

"Having fun?" asked Ross with a hint of sarcasm.

"Yeah it's quite successful," nodded Avalon disarming Ross's possible, humorous riposte, "it's good to see people getting together away from the office." He glanced around the room to the left as he pushed his hands into his pockets. Rutherford noticed Avalon didn't have a drink.

"Can I get y' a drink Boss?" Avalon looked up to

the big man about to tell him that he wasn't the boss at a social gathering, but paused as he didn't quite know how they should address him.

"Yeah, why not?" he said instead.

"What d' y' want, sherry?" Rutherford paused and then shrugged before adding, "Mead?" Avalon gave a slight frown.

"Mead?"

"Well, a' don't know what English people drink," insisted Rutherford with an innocent look on his face.

"This man here," interrupted Ross pointing to Avalon with a free finger of the hand which was holding the bottle, "is the cause of several head distillers, demise." He paused for a moment then continued, "He once suggested was he was going to drink a little less and two Speyside and one Highland distiller took their own lives unable to accept the possibility of such a loss of profit."

"I like a dram or two but nothing untoward," insisted Avalon.

"Hard stuff hey?" nodded Rutherford then said, "okay I'll get you a Baileys and Absinthe," and he headed back to the drinks area.

"He's an odd one," commented Avalon shaking his head.

"How's Mack?" asked Ross with more than a little interest in what Avalon had been discussing with him.

"Oh, he's…" began Avalon but it was clear the DI thought Mack was troubled, "well, ask him yourself," he added with a weak smile. Frazer seemed to become slightly uneasy and said,

"I'll see you in a mo," and she left to walk over to

the other female DC in C section, Alison Boyd.

"She alright?" asked Avalon when she was out of earshot.

"Yeah why?"

"Dunno," shrugged Avalon, "she just seemed eager to get away."

"You know women, if they don't symbiotically connect with another female every thirty minutes they run out of inane chit-chat and have to go for a refill." Avalon didn't react, he just reached for the single malt that Rutherford handed him as he returned. "So," continued Ross, "have you solved the murder then?" and he took a gulp of lager as if he wasn't really interested.

"Sort of as I said earlier," nodded Avalon.

"Go on then, who is it?" asked Ross puzzled how Avalon could have possibly worked it out without looking for the clues. Avalon shrugged a little as if he didn't care if the others knew his idea.

"Julie Murrey," concluded Avalon taking a sip of his drink.

"Tom's wife, how the hell do you reckon that one?" smiled Ross.

"I have tae agree boss, et's pretty unlikely seeing as she has no real motive," interrupted Rutherford, "though I'm probably expecting too much to think he may have included 'motives'."

"I don't get how your mind works, even after this long working with you. So where are the clues, where was the opportunity?" asked Ross his frown deepening as he realised he was admitting to trying to solve the problem himself.

"Clues? Motive?" asked Avalon opening his eyes wide, "I didn't look for clues, I just used logic."

"Here we go, more bullshit," said Ross shaking his head.

"It's quite simple, I just-" began Avalon but Ross held up his hand and interrupted.

"I don't want to hear it, when you come up with logic it always sounds more akin to some old witch throwing bones onto a gravestone to predict the weather." Avalon shrugged again and took another drink.

"Well *I* want to know," insisted Rutherford with a questioning look. Avalon gave a slight grin and then pushed his free hand into his trouser pocket.

"Look around the room, what do you see?" Rutherford looked and raised his wide shoulders then slowly lowered them with a long sigh.

"Drunks mostly," Rutherford answered.

"And beyond that?"

"Constables, sergeants, detective inspectors, strangers..." Rutherford trailed off as he looked at a few people he didn't know. Avalon stared at him tilting his head to one side and raising his eyebrows. "Coppers mainly," nodded Rutherford eventually but still missing Avalon's main point. Ross was beginning to see Avalon's thinking now though and he slowly shook his head as he grinned.

"And what does almost every copper in here have in his pocket?" asked Avalon taking another drink.

"Phones and pagers," nodded Ross, "talk about making shortcuts," he added. Rutherford's wide open eyes began to steadily close down as he saw some significance in the theory and as Avalon watched he saw the conclusion gradually dawn on Rutherford's face. The big man then began to nod slowly.

"That kinda' makes the whole point of this

redundant," he said and then added, "if you're right o' course." Avalon nodded as if he admitted that the theory could be flawed. Frazer returned and asked,

"What's so interesting over here?"

"The boss has solved the murder," explained Rutherford.

"Possibly," added Avalon as Frazer came closer.

"Go on, I'll buy et," frowned Frazer expecting she had been drawn into some elaborate joke devised by the three of them. It was Ross who explained as he wasn't all that sure that Rutherford had picked up all the details of the theory.

"The Detective Inspector," he began giving a slight sarcastic edge to the moniker for effect, "is working on the theory that the murderer has to be someone who can't be called away during the evening as that would spoil the fun for those left behind." Frazer nodded and jutted out her bottom lip slightly.

"Aye sound theory, go on," she said.

"Well, he thinks the murderer is Tom's wife, probably as Tom doesn't know the other wives and husbands all that well," and he ended with a blank expression.

"I can see et makes sense en some ways, but equally et could be Alistair Nicholls's wife, he knows *her* well as he and his wife spend some time with them as I recall." As Frazer finished, the two men turned to Avalon to see his reaction.

"True," he admitted, "that is equally plausible," but he offered no further explanation. To Ross, it was clear that Avalon hadn't seen that possibility but he had to concede that it was unlikely for the murderer to be any of the police officers present. Ross took another large gulp of lager and watched Avalon react to his surroundings. Ross was a good detective, he knew he was too but over the short time he had known Avalon, he had begun to see his boss was something different, not the usual career copper with a point to prove. When he had first met the detective three years ago he had considered him cocky and manipulative but he had soon seen that it was just the Englishman trying to find his feet in a new job and a new country. Since then Avalon had become a friend and a trusted part of his private life, he even saw the man as role model though he found that hard to admit even to himself. It wasn't because he thought Avalon was a great detective, indeed, Ross thought he was pretty average, it was more to do with his compassion and his fairness, his handling of the team and the way he looked after them. Avalon was the sort of copper that would put his own career on the line to protect his colleagues, certainly if he believed they were in the right. Avalon seemed able to balance problems of the job with the problems of the personal lives of his team. Most of the time the team were happy, if they weren't it wasn't due to the boss. DS Ross smiled inwardly as he thought about Avalon's arrival at the station, he was probably the sole reason Ross was still a detective, he wasn't going to tell him that however, no, he was going to keep his boss on his toes by being a pain in the arse. Ross was considering another drink when Tom Murrey came up to them with some small squares of paper.

"Okay people," he began in his usual soft voice, "it's time to decide who the murderer is, put your name on there and the name of the person you suspect." The scraps of paper were taken unenthusiastically and each person wrote their own name and the person they suspected of being the murderer. Tom Murrey then gathered up all the notes. It took little time for Tom and his wife to sort through them and then he coughed and began to announce the winner.

"First," began DS Murrey, "I want to thank you all for coming, it's rare that we can all get together and rarer still that none of us get called away on some call-out or other," he said. There were a few murmurs around the room confirming the truth of it. "I have to say," he continued, "that I thought I may have been a little too cryptic with the clues but I see two people got it right." His eyes gave nothing away and he looked at no one directly. "Some answers are a little strange," he continued as he broke into a smile, "but I suspect most of you were more interested in the booze than the clues." There were a few muffled laughs. "So, the two who got the murderer correct are both from C Section to my horror," he smiled again, "DI Avalon and DC Rutherford," Ross was shocked for a moment, "who both deduced correctly that Mack was the murderer," continued Murrey as a few people clapped and others called out well done.

In the corner Mack smiled and raised his glass to those looking over. Ross was puzzled and a little angry at first but then he realised that Avalon was as crafty as he was good at his job, he had thrown everyone off the scent.

"Well done," he said as he closed in on Avalon.

"It was pure guesswork," he smiled.

"So what was that bullshit about Mrs Murrey then? It was a great way to put us all off the real suspect I suppose?" continued Ross.

"Not at all, I did think it was her but when Tom came up to us with the little bits of paper, something struck me." He paused for a second. "Tom Murrey is a real nice chap, I knew he had probably picked someone who wouldn't get called away but I also considered that he would include Mack in there some way. I was right, he did," and he sipped the dregs from his glass.

"Or were you getting inside information when you spoke to him earlier?" frowned Ross.

"Come on you dozy sod," spat Frazer, "do y' really think Mack would be party tae cheatin'?"

"No, I suppose not," replied Ross shaking his head, "it just seems odd that he got it right."

"What about Martin?" Avalon said pointing to Rutherford.

"Aye, that's true," nodded Frazer, "how did you work et out?" she asked him as she turned to face the big man.

"Pure skill," demanded Rutherford, then after the jibes of the others he added, "and though I don't know Mack or DS Murrey very well, I did overhear him talking to his wife and saying that Mack would miss being in the thick of things more than anything else, I just put two and two together..." he tailed off with a slight shrug of his wide shoulders.

Three weeks later, Ross found himself standing on a rocky promontory looking up a cliff towards DI Avalon, who was obviously uncomfortable with the height of it. Avalon was shouting down something but Ross couldn't hear above the sounds of the waves crashing onto the rocks. Ross and his boss DI Avalon had been returning from a routine follow-up visit in

Dornoch and heard about an incident nearby on the radio. A body had been seen on the rocks near the lighthouse at Tarbat Ness and the local police had been dispatched to investigate. Ross and Avalon arrived soon after the uniform police and parked near the three police cars in the car park. Ross had quickly made his way over a wooden stile and along the cliff to find the site of the reported body. Avalon had held back to change his footwear. He had soon learned that having a change of shoes was a good idea in the Highlands of Scotland and his walking shoes were a wise decision he thought, if not the ideal pedial accompaniment to a dark suit and tie. By the time Avalon was on the top of the cliff, Ross had already reached the massive, brown slab of rock below and was standing near two uniform officers. Avalon hated heights and though the cliff was only twenty or thirty feet high, his toes were beginning to tingle. Ross took out his phone and pointed to it. It soon rang.

"I can't hear a thing down here," he said into it.

*"I'm guessing there is no body,"* replied Avalon.

"The PC says that the body was reported just here but the tide is coming in, so it could have been washed further along. The other officers are looking further round the end of the rocks."

*"Okay, I'll have a walk down the path,"* and Avalon ended the call. He looked up at the tall lighthouse with its two red stripes and moved off, retracing his steps back over the stile. He walked the length of the car park and turned right past the lighthouse and down the damp path that ran along the spit of land beyond. The lighthouse was almost right on the end of the peninsula just past the coastal village of Portmahomack. It was bleak and barren with a multitude

22

of jagged rocks at the water's edge, heather and gorse growing where soil had managed to keep its grip to the land. Many of the rocks had an odd look to them with holes worn here and there as if the whole area was made of a brown Swiss cheese. Several sea birds scurried past and Avalon noticed a seal poke its head out of the water to see what was happening. As he neared the end of the path, which sloped steadily down to the rocks, he noticed two more uniformed officers to his left looking along the broken rocks to the west. Two more could be seen further down in the distance. Avalon decided to move forward onto the rocks but it was difficult underfoot and he moved slowly to the water's edge, or at least as close as it was safe to go. If there was a body floating about in the sea, it was going to be difficult to find in that surf. The water wasn't as rough as he had seen previously on this coast but still, waves crashed into the jagged edge with a dull thud and splashed just in front of him. After an hour of fruitless searching, Avalon was shivering. The breeze was coming from the north and was piercing his suit jacket and a damp feel was evident. He made his way back to the path where Ross was talking to a man in a blue and red weatherproof coat. He had a dog by his side and Avalon assumed this must be the man who reported the body. Ross saw Avalon and approached but with the helicopter buzzing overhead now and then, they had to raise their voices to be heard over the noise.

"This is the man who reported the body," informed Ross pointing a thumb in the rough direction of the man. Avalon nodded and was going to ask a question but the helicopter flew over and he waited, looking up at the white and red monster as it hovered over the rocks. Eventually, Avalon touched Ross's elbow and motioned with his head towards the lighthouse and Ross followed his boss up the path. As they reached the lighthouse the helicopter flew back along the coast down the southern edge and it became quiet once more, the only sound left was the distant crashing of waves and the 'squeaky-toy' sound of the sandpipers.

"So what's the story?" asked Avalon.

"Man walking his dog down the same route he comes every day, sees what he is sure is a body on the water's edge. He then climbs up the rocks and makes his way to the exact place but the body has gone." Ross finished and looked up at the lighthouse as if he had only just noticed it.

"So is he reliable, could he have been mistaken?" asked Avalon.

"Of course he could but he walks this area almost every day and sees lots of jetsam but this is the first time he's reported seeing a body." Ross wasn't intending to be sarcastic but Avalon felt he was.

"Okay," he nodded, "he could be reliable but what the hell happened to it?"

"Dunno," shrugged Ross, "maybe the sea dragged it back out." Avalon thought for a moment.

"We need to get a salty sea-dog type," began Avalon, "someone who can tell us about the tides and currents in this area. We need to know where the body might have started and where it could end up. It's pretty obvious that it didn't fall from the cliff, being that far away," insisted Avalon, Ross nodded and replied.

"Dowd does a bit of sailing I believe."

"Yes but we need an expert, not a part time fisherman," insisted Avalon.

"I just thought he may know someone, but I'll

find us an 'expert'," he concluded with a slight emphasis on the final word. He looked back out to sea. "I don't think there's any point in getting forensics out here?" there was a hint of a question in his voice.

"Not really, the sea will obliterate any evidence and we're not even sure it *was* a body until we find one," insisted Avalon. Ross walked back to the rocks to speak with the uniformed officers and then he returned to the car park where Avalon was already seated in the car, his previous footwear returned to his feet. Ross went through his usual ritual of cleaning his shoes with tissue.

"The PC on the rocks has been in touch with the coastguard and they are going back to base," he said as he busied himself with his shoes, "they haven't seen any sign of a body."

"It seems odd, you would think it would still be in the area," replied Avalon.

"If it was a body," added Ross.

"Is there a pub near here?" asked Avalon.

"Early for a drink isn't it?"

"I was just wondering if the man with the dog had been drinking."

"I couldn't smell anything on him but the wind is so strong here I don't suppose the smell would stay around for long," Ross replied looking at his now reasonably clean shoes. Avalon had the window wound down and was taking great gulps of air.

"It's lovely though, so clean and fresh," he said.

"Aye, but then again, the air in the rest of the Highlands isn't exactly toxic," shrugged Ross placing the used tissues in Avalon's glove box. The DI noticed and looked over at Ross. "I'll take them out when we get back," he proclaimed before Avalon could say anything.

Avalon raised his eyebrows for a second and then took another breath out of the window.

"There's something special about sea air," he concluded, "but |I suppose we'd better get back." Ross nodded and Avalon turned the car around and headed off back along the same single-track road that had brought them there.

"Ever been down to Portmahomack?" he asked.

"Nope," replied Ross.

"Let's have a look then," and he turned right, into the village, at the junction. He parked in a small car park on the seafront where the village was stacked up on the hillside, a pretty place with most of the houses painted white. The tide was in but it was clear that there was a nice beach and to the right a small but pleasant harbour. They walked past the shop and on towards the harbour noticing a pub nestled in the side street but Avalon was making a beeline for the jetty where the boats were moored.

"I love these little villages," he smiled.

"I know," nodded Ross seemingly unimpressed, "you made that clear up in Golspie last year."

"That's your problem my friend, you have nothing in your soul that allows you to partake of this finery."

"Why does it always sound like a Shakespeare soliloquy when you talk about the coast?" asked Ross with a half frown.

"It's called 'waxing lyrical' and I didn't realise I did," replied the DI.

"Well you do, we have to go through this crap each and every time," insisted Ross, "and you seem to forget, I was born in Inverness, the sea has always been there and as far as I'm concerned it smells of rotting seaweed." Avalon smiled as Ross continued, "and for god's sake, don't start quoting some damn poem about the sea." Avalon turned to him with a fake look of shock and then returned his gaze to the water where a few scattered rocks jutted from the sand and the waves swamped and frothed them every few seconds. There was a moment's pause and then he began,

*"I must go down to the seas again, for the call of the running tide, it's a wild call and clear call-"*

"I'll see you back at the car," interrupted Ross with a scowl and he walked back down the road. Avalon raised his brows and thrust his hands into his pockets, then, he looked back out to sea.

*"which cannot be denied,"* he continued. He noticed a wooden seat to the right and so he perched on its edge. It was late in the afternoon and the sun was low in the sky ahead of him. Over the wall of the harbour the mountains of Ross and Sutherland rose up across the bay to kiss the clouds. Ahead of him over a small pile of lobster creels, the small fishing boats bobbed lazily, tugging now and then on their moorings, and in the far distance the still snowy peak of Beinn Tharsuinn. Avalon felt at peace, behind him the white painted village sat in rows on a terraced hillside with the protection of that hill keeping the northerly wind from biting his face. Above and around him, seagulls hovered almost motionless on the breeze and the ever-present call of the oystercatchers echoed off the buildings. Avalon wasn't a bird watcher by any stretch of the imagination but he loved to watch them and he noticed a dark bird sat on a rock jutting from the waves, he guessed it was a cormorant. He took in a deep breath and sucked in the cool sea air and

sighed with pleasure. At that moment he could have thrown all in and stayed there, rented a house and forgotten all about police work, watching the birds and the seasons dance over those far mountains.

*"And all I ask is a windy day, and the white clouds flying, and the sea spray and the blown spume and the seagulls crying."* He looked down the road and with a lighter heart he stood and headed towards the car park.

As he strolled on he looked up to the pub, which was called the Castle Hotel and saw what looked like a Detective Sergeant sitting on a bench. As he neared Ross he called.

"I thought you were heading back to the car?"

"I was but I decided I was thirsty," he announced holding up a glass with what looked like orange juice.

"Do you want one?" he continued as Avalon reached him. Avalon just shrugged and followed Ross inside to where the landlord of the hostelry was stoking up the fire.

"What can I get you?" he asked as he made his way back to the bar. There were a few other people in the pub, mostly sitting in the main part of the room and so Avalon stayed at the bar and perched on a stool.

"Whatever he had please," replied Avalon pointing to Ross's glass and as the landlord went off to pour the drink he turned to Ross. "The irony isn't lost on me," he said. Ross looked puzzled.

"What irony?" he asked.

"The fact that the pub is called the Castle Hotel," explained Avalon as the landlord placed the drink on the bar.

"I hadn't thought of that," smiled Ross handing

the man some coins, "maybe we should do a tour of Scotland but only going into pubs with 'castle' in their name. Avalon looked to the landlord dropping the coins in the till.

"Your name isn't John is it?"

"Yeah, it is. How'd you know?" he asked with a slight bemused look.

"Well, it seems we can only go in pubs called the Castle with landlords whose name is John," shrugged Avalon picking up the drink and taking a sip.

"Be careful John," began Ross, "he may subject you to a poem about coincidences or the nature of chaos."

"I'm from Lancashire," shrugged the landlord, "so unless it's the one that starts with, 'There was a young man from Sale', it'll probably not mean a thing to me."

"Don't worry," frowned Avalon replacing his glass on the bar, "I know neither a poem about two castles or two pub landlords with the same name."

"Well, that's good to know," smiled Ross finishing off his drink. Avalon looked up at the shelf with the single malts and smiled inwardly, thinking about his earlier idea of settling at a seaside village, but he lifted himself from his dream and looked at his watch. It was time they made a move and he downed his drink which turned out to be orange and lemonade and said,

"Right, we better get on, thanks John." The landlord nodded and told them they were welcome. Just as they were about to exit the pub Avalon stopped and turned to the landlord as if he had remembered something.

"*There was a young man from Sale, whoes wife looked just like a whale, she had skin like a shark so that*

29

*even at dark, he could find his way round her in brail*,"
he said in limerick style and then tuned and left. Outside
Ross walked at his side towards the car park.

"Did you know that limerick?" he asked with a
puzzled look.

"No," shrugged Avalon, pushing his hands into
his trouser pockets, "I just made it up." Ross creased up
his eyes for a moment and then shook his head slowly.

## Chapter Two

Avalon hated meetings with his boss. DCI Croker had the capability to be a good boss, he just chose not to be. The meeting hadn't been all that long and it hadn't been particularly stressful but he was glad to get back to 'The Cave'. That was the name C Section gave to their office and Avalon had his own glass-panelled booth at one end. Most people aren't particularly fond of their place of work but Avalon liked the Cave, it was as comfortable as a workplace could be and even had its own coffee machine, which Avalon had provided. It wasn't the original one as that had broken down through overuse but the DI had provided a brand new one. As he opened the door there was already some lively discussion going on between the occupants but Avalon ignored it and strolled to his desk in the booth. He took off his jacket and placed it on the back of his chair and sat, looking up into the main office to see Ross, Rutherford, Mackinnon and Frazer working, but busily discussing some subject or other. The team had seen a few changes over the last year, losing DC Macdonald from the team was a big blow. Mack wasn't just the regular partner of DS Wilson, he was an essential part of

31

the team, he did a great deal of work behind the scenes. True, they had DC Rutherford but the big man was so different to Mack in methods, approach and appearance that Mack was going to be impossible to replace. Wilson had changed too, he still got through an immense amount of work but his demeanour was different. No longer the ebullient and jovial character that burst through the door in the morning with the usual, "Morning all," he entered quietly and just nodded to everyone. Avalon had considered teaming him with DC Rory Mackinnon but decided against it thinking that a total change of partner style may be a better option. He had settled on DC Boyd as his partner. Boyd had a quick mind and a seasoned head on her shoulders and would be a good balance for Wilson. It seemed to be working, the two of them got on well and they certainly got results though even Boyd admitted that Wilson had become even quieter over the recent weeks. This pairing however had left Ross without a regular partner and gave Avalon another problem, he didn't think Frazer was ideal to work with Ross and the confident DS would overshadow Mackinnon in a negative way and so Ross generally worked with the newest recruit. DC Rutherford had a similar sense of humour to Ross and yet together they seemed to cancel each other out. Ross had made it plain that he didn't want Rutherford as a partner, not because he didn't like the man but because Rutherford gave Ross limitations due to his appearance and his size. Ross had tried to get the DC to join him at rugby training nights, he would have been a real asset in the scrum but Rutherford always declined saying he hated rugby. This left Frazer with Mackinnon and to Avalon's surprise the combination was working well. Frazer and the young

DC made a great team and complemented each other in every aspect of their work. Three teams were never enough though, there was always too much work for such a small collective and though there were always promises of new staff, this rarely came true. B Section had seen a new face and the anti-drug section had two new people but C Section saw nothing after Rutherford. Maybe Croker thought Rutherford was worth two or three people, he was certainly large enough for three. One of the main problems recently was an actual 'lack' of crime. Through the start of 2018 there had been very few incidents and in February, no crimes were reported in Inverness, not even a stolen bicycle. March had been much the same, which was allowing more time to look at 'Cold Cases' but Avalon was sure that the quiet wouldn't continue and it certainly wasn't helping their case for more new staff. He looked through the reports that had gathered on his desk while he was away, they were mainly updates of old cases so he stood and walked into the Cave to see what the conversation was about.

"But apart from my size, what else would make you think that?" Rutherford was asking Ross.

"What else does a wrestler need for Christ's sake?" was Ross's reply.

"What's this about?" asked Avalon pushing his hands into his pockets and leaning on the wall by the coffee machine. Rory Mackinnon stopped typing for a moment and looked over his computer screen.

"We were talking about what jobs we had done before joining the force, Martin suggested we wouldn't guess what he did." Avalon gave a slight smile.

"So what did everyone else do then?" he asked. Ross looked up and explained.

"Frazer won't tell us but Rory was at college doing some part-time work including pizza deliveries, as you know I worked for the Post Office for a while and Rutherford was a professional wrestler." Rutherford shook his head at this.

"Just because he's a big man doesn't mean he worked in something where his size was important," offered Avalon. "So," he continued, "what do you two think?" Rory smiled and said,

"I suggested farmer, I could just see him walking over the fields with a sheep under each arm." Rutherford gave a questioning look to Avalon.

"I said he worked in a building society," added Frazer without looking up from her screen.

"Building society, why that?" asked Avalon and Frazer stopped typing and looked up. She shrugged and frowned before speaking.

"I dunno, I could just see him working in an ordinary environment," and she looked back down to her screen then back up to Avalon, "which es a point boss, I've no idea what you did before you became undead," she added. Ross smiled and said,

"He had no previous life, he was grown from a walnut at the police hatchery in Oxford."

"You mean after all the time you two spend at the pub you never brought the subject up?" frowned Frazer.

"Oh we did," nodded Ross, "but he," he nodded towards Avalon as if he wasn't in the room, "only tells you what he wants you to hear."

"Not true," insisted Avalon, "I told you the truth, university, dispatch rider, copper in that order."

"Dispatch rider?" exclaimed Frazer raising her narrow brows, "so you became a bike cop?" she asked.

"No," frowned Avalon, "that's what I wanted but I didn't realise how difficult it was to get into that."

"You should have come up here then, no one wants to do that up here," interrupted Ross.

"So I realise now but I ended up in the Scenes of Crime Office, and I enjoyed that for a while," Avalon explained, "it was almost a natural progression to CID."

"So it wasn't what you wanted to do then?" asked Rory.

"Not at all," shrugged Avalon, "I wanted to be a musician but I'm crap at that. If I hadn't been into bikes, I would have probably ended up in the building trade or something." Avalon saw Frazer smile at this as if she was imagining him with a wheelbarrow. He brought her out of her dream by asking why she wouldn't say what she had done. Avalon knew she had been in the police force for some time, he had seen her record and also knew parts of her past that he would never tell a soul about, even Frazer still didn't know that *he* knew about her.

"Et's boring and I don't think et has any relevance," she admitted.

"Don't be so tedious, just tell us," said Ross. She went back to her typing and seemed to ignore Ross but after a few heartbeats simply said,

"I worked en a shop."

"Is that it, no revelation or dark past in a secret society?" frowned Ross theatrically.

"That's the trouble," replied Frazer looking directly at him, "I'd love tae have some kind o' legend but the truth es that I worked en a café and then a florist shop." The door opened and in walked DS Wilson and DC Boyd.

35

"Just in time to hear about Frazer's dark past," began Ross but before he could continue Boyd called back,

"Not half as dark as yours I'm guessing," and she made her way to her desk. Wilson just nodded to Avalon with a weak smile and also sat removing his coat first.

"But what about Martin?" put in Frazer trying to deflect the conversation from herself, "what do you thenk he did boss?" she asked. Avalon looked at Rutherford, his large face looking back with a half grin and his large arms crossed over his massive chest.

"I'm not sure, he certainly has the build for a wrestler but I think that it was something more straight-forward." He paused and held his hand to his chin and thought for a moment. "I reckon he worked in the oil industry or something to do with engineering," Avalon eventually said and he turned to pour himself a coffee.

"No, you're all wrong, no one's even close," Rutherford grinned.

"Go on then, you have to tell us now," smiled Ross.

"I was a chef," he said, the grin broadening. Most people raised their eyebrows at this and someone said they would have never have thought it. Boyd looked over and said,

"You know, now I think about it I can really see you in your black and whites, it does make sense."

"I bet he was like the mad chef from Monty Python," frowned Ross.

"Et's true though, an' afore that I was still en the food industry," he nodded to Boyd.

"Aye, probably eating most of it," replied Ross.

"I like my scran certainly," he said looking round

36

to Ross, "but I worked en a canning factory where they filled the tins with fruit an' baked beans."

"In the same tin?" frowned Ross, "no wonder they got rid of you."

"I had a specialist job en that plant," insisted Rutherford with a more serious face.

"Doing what?" asked Boyd.

"Well," Rutherford explained, "y' know when you open a tin o' baked beans and no matter how hard you try tae empty all the beans en the pan there are always a few stuck tae the side?" he pause a moment to let the image sink in.

"I do," nodded Boyd, "I always end up getting a spoon to clear them all out." Rutherford nodded then continued.

"Well et was my job tae stick those beans to the side o' the tin," There were a few smiles at this until he continued, "an' they left it tae us tae think of ways o' achievin' that," he concluded raising his eyebrows.

"Too much information," cut in Boyd screwing her face up with disgust, "change the subject now," she demanded.

"Beans on toast for tea is it?" asked Ross with a grin. Avalon returned to his booth with his coffee and waited for Wilson to bring him a report on his morning. He knew Wilson would be in a sombre mood but he was winding up a case and would be wishing to give Avalon an update. This he did and as he spoke Avalon wondered if the man would ever get over his doubts, for no matter how much everyone applauded his actions he just nodded and walked away. Avalon had spoken to his wife about it on two occasions and she was just as troubled by his behaviour but was trying to bring him out of his depression. She knew him best so Avalon left it at that and as long as Wilson continued to do his job, there was little Avalon could do.

The DI leaned back in his chair and reviewed the work once more, it had been several days since the incident at Tarbat Ness lighthouse and nothing more had come of it. No body had been found anywhere on the coast and no one had been reported missing and so he archived the incident file and forgot about it. Without any major current cases the atmosphere seemed relaxed and even the selection of court appearances and meetings at the Procurator Fiscal's office didn't seem particularly taxing though as always Avalon and the team were constantly on edge when the phones began to ring. He picked up the only file that was causing any consternation, an assault that had happened in Inverness under the gaze of a CCTV camera. It had happened some months ago and the perpetrator could be recognised but the victim was refusing to formally identify the man. Maybe he was scared, maybe he was confused but it meant that the best they could do was prosecute for breach of the peace. Cases like that were frustrating, the police had the man on bail, they knew it was him and they had the incident on camera but unless the victim testified there was little chance of a conviction and meant the Fiscal would refuse to take it forward. He sighed and dropped the file on the desk and took a drink of the cooling coffee. There was a slight knock at the office door and it opened to reveal a uniformed officer, it was PC Neil Dowd and he was carrying a sheet, which usually meant some kind of incident. He came to Avalon's booth.

"Hello Neil, get a coffee and take a seat," he said.

Avalon liked Dowd, they had worked together on previous occasions and though Dowd worked as a uniformed officer, he had intelligence and awareness that brought a great deal to an investigation.

"I'd love to Inspector but I have t' get back, some halfwit has put me in for promotion and that's worrying," he frowned. Dowd was unusual when it came to such things. Avalon had suggested that Dowd should be in the CID but Dowd had almost laughed at the idea.

"So, Sergeant Dowd doesn't appeal?" asked Avalon.

"Not at all, I like the job and I do et to the best of my capabilities, but sergeant?" he asked frowning deeply, "I like my free time, fishing, sailing and going down the pub."

"And the odd Saturday at the Jags I'm guessing?" smiled Avalon.

"Exactly, what kind o' life would it be without footba'?" Avalon nodded at this, though he wasn't much into watching sport himself, he understood Dowd's commitment to it. Dowd was unfathomable to Avalon. He was the most ordinary man you could wish to meet, he did ordinary things, had an ordinary job, an ordinary wife and lived in an ordinary house. He even had an ordinary car and had ordinary hobbies but inside, he was anything but ordinary. Avalon had known very few people who had intelligence, insight, compassion and understanding of the world in degrees that elevated them so high above their fellow man, but Dowd was one of them. Even the people he worked with understood Dowd was different, they called him 'sage' and 'The Oracle' in jest, but they also believed he had a further understanding of the world than they did. Avalon too loved to chat with the man. He found that they could begin a conversation about the price of diesel and end up wrapped deep in a discussion about the personal life of Aristotle. That was how Dowd was. He always brought something to a gathering, yet he was humble too. To the untrained eye he could seem staid and boring.

"This one just came en," he said placing the sheet on Avalon's desk, "right," he continued, "I better get off and find out who thinks I want promotion," and he left with a slightly puzzled look. Avalon smiled and shook his head slightly and then looked down at the sheet. It was a theft, but no ordinary theft. Avalon read through the details. Several classic motorcycles had been stolen from a lock-up garage in the Drummond area of Inverness. Avalon owned a 1956 Triumph Thunderbird and so it was of interest to him but the more he thought about it, the crime would be a difficult one to secure a happy ending to as the bikes were probably already stripped down and being moved. He looked over what his team was working on and decided that everyone was busy enough. He decided he would look into it himself and stood pulling his coat from the back of his chair. He decided to exit the building through the foyer to see if Dowd was any happier, but as he descended the stairs he could hear shouting and a noise like a scuffle. He saw that a man, who was still shouting, was pinned to the ground by two officers and a third was forcing cuffs onto his wrists. It was strange to see something like this in the foyer, downstairs in the cells maybe but this was new. He decided to ignore it and walk out not even looking who the three officers were. They were more than capable of handling the situation and he didn't see the point in creating more paperwork for himself.

It was good to get out of the office and he was fairly upbeat about his life at the moment. He thought back to Dowd and his dislike of the idea of promotion. Promotion wasn't a thing that came easy. Avalon was forty-three and had only recently been promoted to inspector, he doubted he would ever rise higher, but then again, like Dowd, was that what he wanted? His time as a detective constable had been reasonably happy and his time as a detective sergeant hadn't always been good, but that had been caused by other factors. He had enjoyed the relative freedom as a DS but as an inspector, there was a far more rigid path to follow, and that wasn't really how Avalon worked at his best. He snatched his free time where and when he could get it and a case like a few missing motorcycles gave him that opportunity whilst still being able to run the section from a distance. It was early in the year but the sun was out, for how long he couldn't tell as there had been a severe storm some weeks previous though Inverness had missed most of it. Some villages had been cut off due to the snow and another 'beast from the east' had blown through but not with quite the severity of the previous one. It was still cold and the wind seemed ever present but for now Avalon turned the car heater up and opened the window to breath in the air, it smelled of freedom.

He found the fingerprint team had arrived and they were busy dusting the area of the garage and so Avalon got on with the task of informing the owner of the machines that there was a likelihood that it may not be a happy ending. It helped that Avalon owned a classic machine himself and could be empathic with the man's loss, but as Avalon left, he knew it was unlikely the man would see his bikes again. As he returned to the station he felt his phone vibrate in his pocket, so he pulled it out and quickly looked at the last few digits before tossing it onto the passenger seat. He scanned his mental phone book and realised it was Sarah Underwood from forensics so he looked for somewhere to pull in. He was nearly back at the station but he was always eager to speak with Miss Underwood and he turned into Kingsmills Gardens and parked up. As he rang her back he remembered how he had gone to her house with his guitar to play her a song he had written and how euphoric he had been when she had told him she liked it. He also remembered it was just as he received the call about Mack's accident. He considered what may have been if not for the timing of that incident, but then again, no further opportunity had arisen since, so he raised his eyebrows to himself in the rear view mirror as the phone connected.

"Hello, it's Avalon, I think someone tried to ring me," he said into the phone. It was a male voice who answered, probably Hendry.

*"Oh, she's on the other phone detective, shall I get her to ring back?"*

"Can do," replied Avalon, "I'll be back in the office in ten minutes," he added and ended the call. For a few moments he looked out of the window wondering if he ought to take the initiative with Sarah, it just wasn't his style to be pushy, and if the truth were known, he didn't like the idea of rejection. He shrugged and started the car and returned to the office but as soon as he entered the main flow of traffic the phone rang again. He looked down for an instant but couldn't see the screen and so he waited until he could get back to the office.

42

"Sarah Underwood's been after you," said Ross as ambivalent as he could as Avalon entered the Cave.

"Yeah she tried my mobile but I was driving." Avalon began to wonder why she would be in a hurry to contact him, was she trying to... No, he remembered, he was expecting some results from a break-in near Balvraid She must have found something and as she was aware that the investigation had stalled, she was probably eager to get the information to them. There had been a spate of house break-ins in isolated settlements and at one, a house owner had discharged a shotgun at the thieves and traces of blood found there had shown no DNA matches on the database. The thieves were still at large but one of them was probably injured. Maybe something had happened to one of the perpetrators and a blood match had come onto the database.

"Anything I should know about?" asked Avalon as he removed his jacket.

"Well," begun Ross, "a new ice age has started, the Russians and the Americans are about to start a world war, the cost of living is-"

"Just the information pertaining to Inverness will suffice," interrupted Avalon.

"Oh, no then," shrugged Ross, "same shit, different depression." Avalon returned to his booth and sat at his desk hanging his jacket on the chair. He then remembered he had missed another call and so he reached back into his jacket pocket for his phone. As he read the number he realised it was his ex-wife, Carol. It was odd for her to ring in the day. For some time, Avalon had harboured the hope that they would get back together but Carol now had her own life and though he didn't think it was going as she had planned, he had now come to the realisation that they would never be together again. They were friends, but that was all. Now and then, one or the other would ring to keep in touch but the conversations were short and more difficult as time went on. Not for any particular reason, it was just that their lives had diverged so much that they simply had nothing to talk about that the other would be interested in. Avalon had realised that there would probably be a time when the calls would stop and for that reason he was surprised that she had called him in the day. He was about to call her back but then considered that Sarah may try to ring him. He swallowed hard as he realised that Sarah now took precedence over Carol. That never would have been the case just twelve months ago. Times had changed, Avalon had changed. He put down the phone justifying his actions with the thought that he shouldn't be making personal calls in office hours. He almost laughed at his poor excuse. Another phone rang, this time it was in the main office, Rutherford answered it. He was a man of few words and Avalon watched him listen without answering until he eventually put down the phone, then he lifted his large frame from the chair and after speaking briefly with Ross, made his way to the office.

"That was a call from the tidal expert that DS Ross contacted," he said.

"Oh?" replied Avalon motioning to the chair opposite.

"The man says that he doubts anything would wash up at Tarbat Ness lighthouse that had entered the water on or near the coast."

"What's that mean?" asked Avalon with a frown.

"Dunno exactly," shrugged Rutherford, "he seems tae think that if anythen' the size o' a body landed on the rocks at that point, it probably came from a source out t' sea."

"So it's likely that what the man saw on the rocks was some crap thrown off a ship rather than a body?" asked Avalon.

"Aye, maybe," the big man shrugged again, "or a body thrown off a boat."

"Did he say where such an object may resurface again?" Rutherford looked vague at this question, he suddenly realised he should have asked but he knew nothing about the oceans, currents or even boats.

"No, I suppose I should find out," he admitted and rose to leave. Avalon watched him go back to his desk and pick up the phone. Ross spoke to him, then Rutherford replaced the phone and Ross picked up his own desk phone. Was it the case that Rutherford wasn't thorough enough? Was Ross doubting the man's abilities? It was a simple mistake, Avalon considered that there was no point in dwelling on something so slight, in other areas Rutherford was coming along fine. He wasn't Rory Mackinnon and he wasn't Mack but it was early days. Ross came to the booth, he was carrying a map.

"I had a word with the tidal expert, he says if the object entered the water on the coast it would have to be around here," he pointed to the northern coastline, "but he says it's more likely whatever it was hit the wet stuff from this direction." He pointed at the map from the north-east, from out to sea. "He says he can't be sure where an object starting at Tarbat Ness would move to," continued Ross, "he was blathering on about a 'tidal stream atlas' and tidal gates."

"The short explanation will do," insisted Avalon.

"His best guess at this time of year would be Burghead or Lossiemouth," shrugged Ross.

"We'll just have to wait and see if anything washes up around there then," admitted Avalon, he didn't want to spend time and resources on something that could simply be some vessel dumping waste overboard. Ross nodded and returned to his desk and as he sat, spoke briefly with Rutherford. Avalon could read nothing on either man's face.

By the late afternoon Avalon looked up from his computer screen and glanced at his watch, it was ten minutes past six and Sarah Underwood had not returned the call. It obviously wasn't as important as he had thought.

There was just Ross and Rutherford left in the Cave and they were chatting about something to do with a case they were on. Avalon reached for his phone and gave Carol a try.

"Hello, it's me," he said with a slight amount of trepidation.

"*Oh, James, I rang earlier but I forgot you would be at work, sorry,*" she replied apologetically.

"It's okay, I was driving anyway," he said, "how are you?" There was a slight pause and hesitation, then she said,

"*Oh, it's nothing, I was just feeling sorry for myself,*" she replied. Avalon was well aware that wasn't what he had asked so he knew there was something wrong.

"So you're not fine then?"

"*Oh, sorry, that's not what you asked, my head's*

*in a bit of a muddle at the moment."*

"Why?" he asked with a good idea what it was about.

*"Nothing to concern yourself with, just a few issues I have to sort out,"* she promptly replied. Avalon sighed as silently as he could and glanced over to Ross and Rutherford, they hadn't even noticed he was on the phone. He spoke a little quieter into the phone to keep the conversation private.

"Unless you've changed, you having a muddle in your head means you are up to the neck in it."

*"Just a temporary glitch, I was feeling sorry for myself and I wanted to hear a friendly voice."*

"Relationship problems?" he asked.

*"Sort of, well yes,"* she replied, *"we argued so much I walked out and so I've lost my home and my job."*

"What has your job got to do with it?"

*"I moved back to Wolverhampton... well to Merry Hill actually, I'm sharing a flat with Denise Lowe, you know the girl you never liked."*

"It's unfair to say I didn't like her, there were times I positively loathed her," Avalon insisted. He heard her give a fake laugh.

*"She was good enough to offer a roof over my head, there was no question about it."*

"Yeah, she likes you, she likes you a lot, anyway," he continued, "what're you going to do?"

*"I'm not sure yet, I have to take stock of my life, I was thinking..."* there was a pause, a pause which lasted far too long in Avalon's opinion, *"I may go and see my parents."* Avalon looked back towards Ross, it seemed their conversation had finished and Rutherford was leaving, Ross was pulling on his jacket and saw Avalon

watching him.

"I suppose that's not a bad idea," he admitted still looking at Ross.

"*No, it will give me time to think things over,*" she said. Rutherford raised his hand to Avalon and he reciprocated, he then glanced back at Ross who was leaning on a desk with his arms folded. He was obviously waiting for his DI to finish the call.

"Will you tell them?" Avalon asked rolling his eyes to Ross in a theatrical manner.

"*What, that I've made a complete cock up of my life again?*" For a moment, Avalon felt some bitterness, did the 'again' mean she was referring to their previous life together. She was quiet for a moment, she was obviously conscious of the implications of the statement too. Avalon decided a break would be in order and so he said,

"Just one second, I have to talk to someone, then I can speak."

"*Oh, you're still at work?*"

"Yeah, I'm the last one again," he replied.

"*Nothing changes,*" he heard her say as he clutched the phone to his chest and beckoned Ross into the booth.

"You want to see me?" he asked as Ross entered.

"Just wondering if you fancied a wee dram later?" smiled Ross.

"Maybe," nodded Avalon, he thought that he may need one after the conversation he was having, "Where?" he asked.

"Castle?" asked Ross.

"Which one, Inverness or Portmahomack?"

"Inverness of course, unless you want to drive."

"About nine?" asked Avalon raising his eyebrows. Ross nodded and left Avalon alone in the Cave. In his usual playful manner, he turned the lights out, all of them. Avalon reached into his jacket and found the small flashlight he always carried and made his way over to the light switch as he spoke into the phone.

"Sorry about that," he said, "I'm alone now."

"*While you were talking, I was wondering,*" she said, Avalon knew what was coming, "*can you maybe get away to come and visit when I'm up in Edinburgh?*"

Two things immediately struck Avalon, the first was how people in England think that Scotland is only twenty miles from one end to the other. There seemed to be the general opinion that once you crossed the border into Scotland, every part of it was instantly accessible. Inverness was just up the road from Edinburgh after all, wasn't it? He knew this was the case because he had thought it too, that was until he had to traverse the everlasting A9. The second thing was that she would have a good idea that he wouldn't be able to get the time off, that meant that she was expecting him to invite her northward. He was now in a muddle himself. He had finally managed to detach himself from her apron strings and now he wondered how he would feel if they were to meet. Would those strings start to wrap themselves around him once more?

"If you give me the dates, I'll see what I can sort out but you know I can't promise," he said, trying to fill the silence that he suddenly became aware of.

"*I know it's difficult, but it would be nice to see a friendly face again,*" she admitted. He was trying to think quickly, he didn't want his brain to get bogged down with thoughts that he knew would cause him to lose sleep.

"*I suppose I could come up to see you, it can't be far,*" she offered.

"You may be disappointed, we are busy here as usual, I wouldn't be able to get away that much." He knew her so well, he knew that was where she had been going all along. He did want to see her but under *his* conditions, he didn't want complications in his life at the moment. He knew it was pure cowardice but Carol had been so much to him, he had been like a schoolboy that had just broken his favourite toy when she was around.

"*I could book in a bed and breakfast, I'm guessing you are still sharing that flat?*" it was more of a question. He wasn't, Avalon had finally purchased a house on Fairfield Road, he liked it too though even after six months he still hadn't made it into a home.

"Er, well I've bought a little house, but..." why had he admitted that? He couldn't tell her a lie but did he have to tell her the whole truth? "I suppose you could stay there but I haven't even finished moving in yet."

"*I couldn't do that, I would be happy in a guest house, I'm sure you can find me a number.*"

"Yes, I'm sure I can find somewhere close by," he admitted, slightly relieved but trying not to sound it.

"*That's great, I'll look forward to it, I'll ring later in the week to arrange some dates if that's okay with you?*"

~~~~~~

Avalon took some considerable time to get dressed. He was troubled, not by anything major but by many niggling little things. As he pulled on his jacket and picked up his house keys he headed for the door and began the ten-minute walk to the Castle Tavern. Inside, Ross was having a slightly heated conversation with one of the customers they knew as Harry the Hat. It sounded like a gangsters name but Harry was quite the opposite. He was mild mannered and easy going, until he was confronted by Ross that was. He was always seen with a hat, a trilby usually but on this particular evening it was a cap. Avalon walked to the bar and nodded to the landlord who pulled him the half of bitter he usually ordered.

"What's with the new hat Harry?" asked Avalon trying to defuse the situation. Harry turned on the bar stool and faced Avalon.

"Evening Jim, och et's thes bloody wind, a' keep losen me hat en thes constant sou' easter that wunna go awa'." His thick accent was high pitched but slow.

"Aye, it's blown his brains away with it," added Ross finishing his drink and handing the landlord his glass.

"Will y' tell thes young arse o' a man that y' cannae mak' a cake without breakin' eggs," frowned Harry. He wasn't much older than Ross but his nature made everyone think that he was in his sixties.

"Harry thinks it's okay and fine for the Highland Council to charge what tax they like," insisted Ross as he paid for the round.

"A didnae say that at all, a' said that y' can appeal and they will look intae it f'r yous," insisted Harry, "an ef they got et wrong y' get a rebate."

"My point is that they should get it right the first time instead of stealing from us and hoping we don't pursue it," demanded Ross. As usual, he was making waves in what was, under normal circumstances, a mill pond. Avalon took a sip of his drink and then shook his head.

"I'm sorry Harry but this is one of those rare cases where I have to agree with Ross," he began, "I just got my council tax bill and I reckon they came up with a random number, multiplied it by the age of the chief executive's cat and then added the date of a famous Scottish battle. They have got me two bands too high by my calculation." Harry looked dejected, he was sure Avalon would be the voice of reason and it showed on his face.

"A' thought coppers were supposed tae have no opinion?" he eventually asked.

"Not when it comes to being ripped off," smiled Avalon and he motioned to a couple of seats that had just been vacated. "You shouldn't wind Harry up, he'll be giving John some earache now."

"Maybe, but the council are my pet hate at the moment, he walked straight into it," he shrugged as he sat. Back at the bar, as Avalon had guessed correctly, he could hear Harry trying to bring others into his conversation but he could find no one to endorse his way of thinking. "Talking of council tax," continued Ross, "are you settled in yet?"

"What's to settle?" shrugged Avalon, "the bed is in, my chair and stereo are in and there is a dining table in the conservatory. I'm living a pretty minimalist life at the moment." He took a drink and continued, "the bike is in the garage which is fantastic and the kitchen cupboards have some food in them."

"It's been noticed that no house warming has

been forthcoming," said Ross making a start of his drink.

"House warming? God no," replied Avalon shaking his head, "you know damn well I'm not a fan of parties"

"But everyone wants to see your new home," smiled Ross.

"Everyone? does that include Donald Trump and Kim Jong-un because I would have thought that they would have more-"

"You know what I mean," interrupted Ross with a laboured voice, "people are interested, particularly the females."

"It's not up to 'inviting people round' quality yet," insisted Avalon.

"Oh?" said Ross questioningly.

"In fact," added Avalon looking at him, "I could do with some advice."

"From me? On houses?" laughed Ross, "you've seen my place, bed, coffee table, rugby ball on old sideboard, picture of me stood at the side of a McLaren F1 on a Gothic triptych mirror and the ubiquitous Lonely Detective's chair in front of the television."

"I suppose so, I forgot how 'empty' your place looks," nodded Avalon.

"Thanks for the compliment," sighed Ross taking another drink. "So what's wrong with the place?" he asked resting his glass down on the table.

"Well, your place is minimalist right?" Ross nodded at this, "and it's a one-bedroom flat?" Ross nodded again, "well my place is a four-bedroom house and I've got less stuff than you," it was Avalon's turn to take a drink. "I put the guitar in the corner of the bedroom and it looked so alone I shoved it in the wardrobe."

"So why did you buy a four-bedroom house then?" asked Ross with a frown.

"It was a no brainer, close to the city centre and a garage for the bike," he looked at Ross, "and I thought it was cheap for what it was."

"Well does it matter if some of the rooms are empty?" questioned Ross leaning back in his chair, "you could take in a lodger."

"No, well..." there was hesitation in his reply, "no I don't suppose so, and there's no chance of a lodger," he concluded with a slight sigh. Ross instinctively saw something in Avalon's face.

"There's something you have chosen to omit," he insisted with a frown, "have you got someone coming over, have you found a female who feels sorry for you and..." Ross stopped as his smirk-riddled face became first serious and then slightly shocked. "It's not? No it can't be," he spluttered.

"Who?" asked Avalon a little self-consciously."

"The lovely Miss Sarah Underwood?"

"No, course not," smiled Avalon, "it's certainly not her."

"So there is someone?" he questioned taking another quick gulp of lager. Avalon realised he was trapped, but then again he would probably have to tell Ross anyway.

"Carol's coming up to stay." Ross nearly spit out his lager but he managed to control himself and swallowed it before asking,

"You mean Carol, as in the ex-wife?" Avalon nodded with a sheepish expression. Ross took this in and then blew out a long gust of air as he shook his head slowly.

"She's just coming up for a visit, it's nothing serious," insisted Avalon defensively. Ross held up his hands as in submission.

"Hey, it's nothing to do with me," he insisted. There was silence for some moments until Ross continued, "so you're not trying to impress her then?"

"No, why?"

"So why do you want advice on the house?"

"Because she's still a close friend and if she sees my house is like a disused chapel she'll worry."

"And you don't want her to think that you are a husk of a person that lives like a vampire," grinned Ross.

"That too," nodded Avalon.

"But you don't want to impress her?" asked Ross again looking round at Avalon. Avalon pinched his lips tight and frowned. "Okay," nodded Ross, I'm not the person to help, you need a woman's touch I would think."

"Like who?" asked Avalon reaching for his glass. Ross gave a little shrug and thought for a moment.

"Ollie," he eventually said.

"Kirk?" asked Avalon knowing Ross was suggesting the female PC from downstairs.

"Why not?" asked Ross, "she's ideal and she likes you."

"She likes me? How do you come to that conclusion?" asked Avalon hesitating with his glass to his lips.

"I just know she does, the poor deluded fool," he answered, "but I think she could help you with your problem." Avalon considered this. PC Olivia Kirk was certainly thorough and had an eye for detail. She was also a practical joker and that side of her character troubled Avalon, particularly if he was to hand her the keys to his house.

"Right, I'll ask her," he eventually said and he finished his drink. "Another?" he asked holding up his empty glass.

## Chapter Three

Avalon's ex-wife Carol had decided that she would visit Inverness after she had been to see her parents in Eyemouth and though Avalon had suggested a suitable Bed and Breakfast, he capitulated and told her she could stay at his house. To his surprise she had refused but in some ways it came as a relief as Avalon had done little to make it into a 'home'. He decided that he ought to make an effort and try to make the place more comfortable and after some soul searching, he decided to ask PC Kirk her advice on making the house more pleasing. She had arranged to visit the house along with Ross who had yet to set foot through the door and was insistent that he wanted to see the place. On one particular Sunday afternoon in May, Avalon waited pensively for the two of them, they arrived almost together and he showed them in through the front door and into the lounge.

"So what do you think?" asked Avalon as he went to boil a kettle. Kirk looked around the main room and Ross strolled into the conservatory.

"It's big for an end terrace," he said glancing around.

"I told you," called back Avalon from the kitchen, "it used to be a Bed and Breakfast."

"I like it," insisted Ross, "it's way better than my place and you even have plenty of parking space round the back."

"But your place is good," frowned Avalon carrying a plate with biscuits on it, "I mean, it's well laid out."

"I hate it," scowled Ross, "it's a recent build and everything is wrong about it."

"I don't see that," added Avalon, "I like the modernity of it,"

"That's what I don't like about it, I mean, the shit-box is square," he said with exasperation, "last time I looked, my arse was round and sitting on a square seat is a pain in the arse, literally." Avalon smiled and nodded. "And, continued Ross, "all the doors are short, there's so much of a gap that the Inverness and District Limbo Dancing Club come to my house to practise." Avalon smiled again and said,

"And I thought you were the king of modern convenience?"

"I am usually but..." he trailed off and they both turned as Kirk entered.

"Et's a bit sparse, have ye been burgled?" she asked.

"I never really got around to doing a job on it," Avalon explained with an embarrassed expression.

"A job?" she asked raising her voice, "the cells at the nick are better furnished than this place."

"So can you do anything with it?" he asked standing as he heard the kettle click off.

"That depends on whether you want t' buy any

furniture," she insisted, "though a' have tae say, I do like the house." Avalon nodded and went to sort out the drinks. He returned and placed the cups on the small coffee table that stood forlorn at the edge of the room. He considered moving it to the centre but there was only one seat in the main room so he suggested they move into the conservatory and the small dining table that had four chairs clustered around it.

"Just get what you think," suggested Avalon.

"Then have you got some sort o' a budget?" she asked. Avalon shrugged.

"Just make it right and tell me what you need," he replied, "just don't make it too... well, girlie," he added as an afterthought.

"There's no television I notice," put in Ross.

"Neither do I require one," insisted Avalon and then he looked around, "oh," he said and he left the room to return a minute later holding two keys on a key ring.

"You better take these, the small one is the back door," he explained handing them to Kirk and he sat once more.

"What about seating, d' you want a couch or a three piece or somethen'?" she asked nodding to the living room.

"And what would he do with the LDC?" asked Ross.

"The LD what?" asked Kirk with a frown.

"The patent, Lonely Detectives Chair," replied Ross raising his eyebrows. She shook her head at Ross and then turned to Avalon.

"I have to admit, that is the saddest thing I have seen, one seat facing nothing in particular," she admitted, "we have to get rid of that."

"So where will he sit and drink his booze and think of the things that have passed him by?" asked Ross.

"I'm guessing you have one o' those?" she said.

"Of course," smiled Ross lifting his cup, "what self-respecting lonely detective doesn't?"

"You two need to get a life, y' know that?" she said finishing the tea, "and now a' need tae be awa'," and she took a quick glance at her watch. "I'll give et some thought and let y' know what a' need," she added. Avalon nodded and Kirk left to carry on with her hectic life.

"I told you she was the one for the job," said Ross crunching into one of the biscuits.

"Hmm," sighed Avalon, "I'm guessing this is going to be painful to the wallet."

On Monday morning, Avalon cast his eye over the work list, he sighed and walked into the main part of the Cave.

"Well people," he began as he leaned on a desk folding his arms, "it's still pretty quiet so, if anyone is severely behind on time off, now would be a good time to take a couple of days." All the faces looked up but no one was eager to volunteer, that was the way of things, if you had time off, you put extra pressure on the rest of the team. It was the culture of the detective to pull your weight and not heap work onto your colleagues. Avalon knew this so he sounded out the feelings of the team by dropping a few hints. He looked over to DS Wilson but the detective shook his head.

"I've been off a lot over the past few months, not me boss." Avalon moved his gaze to Mackinnon, he couldn't remember the last time the young detective had time off.

"You then Rory, it must be months since you've had some time away from this place?" Rory shrugged.

"Aye, it is but I'm fine if someone else wants time," he insisted. Avalon then looked at Ross.

"And you," he announced, "I'm guessing Christmas was the last time you took days off?"

"Probably," nodded Ross, "I was thinking of having a trip to Edinburgh at sometime this year so yeah," he shrugged. Avalon then looked at Frazer but he knew she had been off for three days recently so the next target was Boyd. The problem was, she was doing a really fine job of keeping Wilson from his dark thoughts and he considered that maybe the time wasn't right for DS Wilson to be working alone. Rutherford was fairly new to the team so the decision was made.

"Okay, Ross and Mackinnon," he announced unfolding his arms, "rest of the week off unless something big comes in." Rory and Ross nodded and Avalon was about to return to his booth when there was a slight knock at the door and PC Dowd entered, it was clear he was carrying at least one report sheet.

"Neil," smiled Avalon, "it looks like you have some trade for us," he added glancing at the paper.

"Aye, two o' them," he admitted holding them up. He handed them to Avalon explaining briefly what they were.

"One is a reported suicide up near the golf course and the other is a report of body parts found in a bin down on the Longman Estate." He looked around the room and then added, "we've sent cars out but we've had nothin' back yet." Avalon nodded as he looked at the two sheets and then looked up as Dowd quietly left the room.

"I'm guessing our holidays are cancelled?" said

Ross raising his brows.

"Not necessarily," announced Avalon, "let's find out more before we commit." He then looked up to Wilson and Boyd, "are you two still on catch up?" he asked. Wilson nodded and then replied.

"Aye but nothin' urgent, we can go over if y' want."

"No," replied Avalon, "stay put on that for now," and he looked at Ross, "take Martin with you and look at the suicide, Megan and Rory check on the body parts incident." He handed the teams the sheets and glanced at Rory Mackinnon's face. To his knowledge, Rory hadn't worked on any kind of 'unpleasant' case and Avalon thought that it was time to face the grim reality of the job, yet Rory didn't show any doubts as he read the incident sheet. The two teams gathered their coats, phones and keys and left for their assignments. Soon after, Wilson and Boyd left the Cave to continue their probing into some old 'cold cases' they were working on. Avalon sat in his office looking into the main room through the glass wall. It was strangely quiet in there. Gone was the sound of phones ringing, the conversation between flurried taps at keyboards, the occasional spat of laughter or the constant opening and closing of the office door. It could certainly be eerily quiet late in the evening but this was lunchtime, and it seemed very odd. He leaned back and sighed before walking to fill his cup from the coffee machine. He then moved over to the windows near Ross's desk and looked out towards the road below, sipping from his cup and thinking about Carol, and what they would talk about after all this time. There had once been a time when he would have been excited about her coming to see him, but now, there was an element of dread. His life had changed, *he* had changed. Through the window he watched a young mother pushing a child's buggy down the pavement, whilst another child walked alongside. It was an image he couldn't delve into that deeply, he knew if he did, he would see *her* face, that face that haunted him and he would have to relive the whole nightmare. Instead, he thought about Carol again, how she may have changed, how she would look and would he still be attracted to her? A phone rang in the Cave and brought him out of his dreams, it was Ross's desk phone.

"Avalon," he said in a level tone placing his cup on the desk.

"*Hello inspector,*" it was Dowd's voice, "*there's a...*" there was a slight hesitation, "*character down here wants tae have a word with DS Ross, he says he's known to him.*"

"Who is he?" asked Avalon.

"*His name es Robert Darrow, he's been brought in suspected of stealing a bicycle.*" Avalon afforded himself a slight smile, it wasn't exactly a 'big time' crime, but it may relieve the tension he was feeling.

"I'll come down and see him," replied Avalon. When he reached the front desk PC Kirk informed him that Dowd had taken the young man into one of the interview rooms. It was obviously an informal interview as the door was wide open, Dowd had probably taken him in there for a place to sit out of the way and write out the report.

"So you're now saying et wasn't you on the bike?" Avalon heard Dowd ask. As Avalon entered the man looked up, he was in his early twenties and had short-cropped hair with a mass of tattoos on his arms. He kept his eyes on Avalon for a moment and then said,

"No, am no' sayin' that, I was on the bike but I didnae steal et." He had an accent that was somewhat broader than Inverness but Avalon had no idea of its origin. Dowd looked over to Avalon who was now leaning on the wall by the door.

"This is DI Avalon," explained Dowd pointing with his pen.

"A detective," spluttered the man, "for a nicked pushbike?"

"Yes," nodded Avalon, "there's so little going on at the moment they've roped us in on stolen bikes." The man frowned at Dowd and made his mouth slightly crooked,

"That's just wrong," replied the exasperated man, "when there's murderers and drug dealers on the streets, the polis have got et all wrong," he continued.

"That's just it," explained Avalon, he was already reading the man as not as bright as he might have been, "we've taken all the serious villains off the streets, we *were* living in a crime-free city until you came along." Dowd was keeping a very straight face.

"But I've already told this cop," he nodded to Dowd, "that I didnae nick anythen'." Dowd looked down at the notes in front of him.

"So," he began, "you maintain that you 'found' the bike as ef et had been abandoned?"

"Aye, that's et, abandoned," insisted the man looking pleased with the word.

"So," continued Dowd, "an abandoned bike in your eyes is one that is leaning on a fence?"

"Aye, that's right, no one was with et, et was abandoned," he confirmed and folded his arms.

64

"So et was *abandoned*," continued Dowd, obviously playing for the benefit of Avalon, "leaning on a fence of a house on Lochalsh Road?"

"Aye that's et," nodded the man.

"The fence of the house of Steven Woodley?"

"Aye," shrugged the man.

"A person known to you I believe?"

"Aye, a' know Stevie, he's no' a bad bloke," insisted the man.

"And were you aware," asked Dowd looking up from the notes, "that Mr Woodley owned a similar bicycle?" The man thought for a moment.

"I thenk he might, aye," he eventually concluded.

"A bike that may be very similar to the one you were seen riding away from that address?" The man looked up for a moment and then placed his hands on the desk saying,

"Et doesn't mean et's the same bike though does et? I mean, when somebody abandons a bike et's just abandoned," and he shrugged.

"So at no point did you consider that the bike you thought was *abandoned* was the one and same bicycle that was owned by the man whose house you found it at?"

"No a' never," shrugged the man and he folded his arms once more.

"Not even," and at this point Dowd paused a moment, Avalon thought he knew what was coming, "when Mr Woodley ran after you?"

"Och, come on officer," sighed the man unfolding his arms to open them wide, "he could o' just been going for a jog down the shop."

"He was shouting..." Dowd looked down at his

notes to read the quote, "*Oi y' wee bastard, that's my bike?*"

"I didnae hear that officer," sniffed the man and he folded his arms again.

"But you weren't alone were you?" asked Dowd as the man gave a quick glance up at Avalon, "your brother Ian was with you was he not?" The man simply shrugged, "and he explained to you that the bike you were..." Dowd looked down at the notes once more, "*peddling like your arse was on fire*, shouted to you that the bicycle did indeed belong to Mr Woodley and that you should give et back."

"He did aye, but a' never mind him, he's no' right in the head all the time," and after a slight pause he pointed to Avalon with his thumb and added, "he doesnae say much does he?" Dowd looked around to Avalon who seemed to be transfixed by the conversation and said,

"He's more a man of action."

"So why did you wish to see DS Ross?" Avalon asked.

"Detective Ross knows me, he'll put in a good word for me, tell them I'm no' a bike thief," he said giving a slight sign of a confident grin.

"DS Ross is off long term sick, I'm taking on his cases," insisted Avalon.

"Shite," said the man moving uncomfortably in his chair.

"So Robert, are you still maintaining you didn't take the bicycle without consent of the owner?" asked Dowd.

"Aye a' did that, but I didnae nick et," insisted Darrow. Dowd noticed out of the corner of his eye that

Avalon gave a slight shake of his head, Dowd gave him a glance.

"I'll see you later PC Dowd," he said and rolled his eyes, "I can see you have your hands full."

Avalon hadn't been back in the Cave all that long when Frazer and Mackinnon walked in and the look on Frazer's face told Avalon all had not gone well.

"That didn't take long," he asked. Frazer slumped into her chair and looked over to Avalon.

"Just ten percent less incompetence would make this job fifty percent easier."

"Go on," replied Avalon folding his arms.

"Well," she sighed, "when we arrived the uniform lads had already found out that the dismembered body was just a shop dummy and radioed en to say as much, but nobody had thought tae let us know," she looked round at Mackinnon as much as to say 'it's your turn'. Mackinnon got the hint and continued.

"There was a bit of a mix up," began Rory in a less belligerent tone and Avalon heard Frazer make a sound as if she would have put it more succinctly, "but the main problem came much earlier than that." Frazer soon became impatient with Rory's gentle tones and wrestled the explanation from him.

"Almighty cock up es more like et," she began, "the so called 'body' was spotted by a certain Derek Alan Stoars, a person known to everyone at the nick but under the name of 'Mad Larry'," Avalon raised his brows at this.

"Go on," he said folding his arms and leaning on the wall.

"Derek Stoars es a paranoid schizophrenic who,

67

on top of his prescription drugs, takes the non-prescription variety too," Avalon nodded slowly, "which en itself es the natural state of affairs of several of his friends. Et's not ideal but apart from the occasional, odd time he thinks Napoleon, Stalin or God talks to him, the man is fairly harmless." She paused and then stood to finally remove her jacket. "Derek saw parts of an old shop mannequin that'd been put en bin liners and dropped en a skip and with the help of the voices en his head, decided et was a real body. Again, not a vast problem as this sort of thing happens tae Derek every day o' the week."

"Can I have the short version?" asked Avalon.

"Aye, sorry," apologised Frazer taking her seat, "et's just that our trip out was a waste o' time and if we had been busy as we usually are..." she trailed off and took a breath. "Anyways," she continued, "whoever took the call didn't put the name Derek Stoars and 'Mad Larry' together and so they got us involved."

"That is an issue with disparaging nicknames," announced Avalon, "is there nothing that can be done with him?"

"Not really," said Frazer shaking her head, "people have tried but he's a wino, an addict and he's not that bright even when he's lucid so apart from a section order..." Avalon saw the dilemma. Derek wasn't a problem to the public or the police, at least not a serious problem and so it was probably easier to leave things as they were until there was reason to believe he was a danger to others or himself.

"Put that one down to experience," smiled Avalon and he returned to his booth.

"Aye, an experience I could do without," replied

Frazer in a more subdued voice. Avalon was sympathetic, he knew that most officers, no matter how many gruesome scenes they have witness, never take it in their stride. The amount of buildup needed to attend what could potentially be an horrific crime scene took a great deal out of a person. Even after much preparation, you could still be taken by surprise. Frazer was now feeling that sense of relief but also the frustration of having to 'psych' herself up on the journey there. He sat and looked back into the Cave, for some moments, Frazer just stared at her blank computer screen. Rory, on the other hand, had already begun typing as if nothing had happened. Rory was a much more complicated character than he first seemed. One minute he was young and innocent, the next he could just brush off a possible sighting of a dismembered body as part of a day's work.

Less than an hour later, Ross and Rutherford returned and they too looked a little frustrated. Avalon once again walked into the Cave as Ross and Frazer were talking.

"Problems?" he asked.

"No, no," replied Ross turning from Frazer to look at Avalon, "just a suicide without a body."

"Meaning?"

"Suicide note but no body, we've set forensics to work but I doubt they'll find anything, the rooms look untouched," he shrugged.

"Seems odd?" replied Avalon.

"Odd yes, not the first time though, I bet this turns out to be an insurance scam," Ross insisted, "and what's going on around here lately?" he continued, "a suicide without a body, a dismembered corpse that turns out not to be a body and some weeks ago a body washes up on the beach and yet there is no body?"

"At least you can still take a few days off," smiled Avalon.

"Hmm, to be honest," sighed Ross, "at the moment all this on-off stuff is driving me crazy."

"Et could be the calm before the storm," added Frazer.

"Let's hope not," said Avalon raising his brows and he turned to his booth.

"No, just more sodding paperwork," he heard Ross say. Paperwork had become part of the job, even in this modern age of technology and computers, there was still a great deal of real paper in the work. That in itself didn't bother Avalon, he found the intrinsic feel of the hard copies rather than the ethereal nature of computer data easier to work with, what he didn't like was the fact that every move they made had to be recorded. It was the curse of the job. Avalon remembered something so he turned and walked back into the Cave.

"Oh, do you know a character called Robert Darrow?" he questioned. Ross looked up with a doubtful gaze.

"Yeah, I know of him, why?" he asked.

"He's downstairs, brought in suspected of nicking a push bike."

"It sounds like him, he's a bit of a kleptomaniac when it comes to transport items."

"What, buses and trains you mean?" asked Rutherford, but Ross ignored him.

"He seemed to think you might help him out," added Avalon with a slight smirk.

"He's got the idea that I like him, I once settled an altercation he was involved in and now he seems to think I'm his guardian angel."

"Es he the one who has a sister who's a model?" asked Frazer in a tone that meant she knew a story.

"Er..." hesitated Ross, "I think she does some modelling, or at least I think I heard that she does."

"And es that why you played the knight errant?" she asked, Rutherford began to grin, he could sense a Frazer-Ross argument brewing, Avalon smiled and went back to the booth to the sounds of Ross saying,

"Knight errant is a bit flamboyant, I was just doing my job."

~~~~~~

The next day, Avalon sat in the quiet office, making his way through the paperwork he had to complete and for the first time in many months seeing light at the end of the tunnel. The period of quiet had helped so much but Avalon knew it wouldn't last and so he did what he could while he had the time. Wilson and Boyd were in the Cave working on one of their cold cases with Rutherford assisting down in the archive. Frazer was doing the same as Avalon, paperwork catch up and with Mackinnon and Ross enjoying a few days off, Avalon didn't expect to see either of them until the following Monday. He stopped for a moment to rest his eyes and looked around the Cave. It was only now when two people were taking a break did he see how severely under staffed they were. It was only Wednesday yet already, the unfamiliar quiet of the Cave was becoming unnerving. Frazer looked comfortable with the situation however, though Avalon knew she preferred to work alone but Rutherford seemed slightly at odds with the situation, which was why Avalon had put him with Wilson and Boyd. He knew if something came in that Rutherford was there when needed. Around the time that normal people have lunch, Avalon suggested that the Cave could do with a few sandwiches and offered to go out for something but Frazer said, as she needed to go downstairs, she would be happy to go to the sandwich shop. An order was made up quickly scrawled on a scrap of paper and off she went. Avalon glanced over at the coffee machine and saw there was plenty left for all of them, then he leaned back and stretched his legs. He was slightly worried that his ex-wife Carol had not rung yet to confirm any dates for her visit. He didn't want to ring her in case she thought he was eager to see her, though he didn't know why he felt that way. Maybe she was still trying to sort out dates with her parents, so why hadn't she rung and explained that? He sighed and looked over to the windows, the sun was shining but he knew it wasn't very warm out there. Down south, England was enjoying hot weather but here in Inverness, the wind was ever present and it was a cold wind at that.

"Better than rain," he thought to himself and he sighed, regretting that he had let Frazer fetch the sandwiches, he would have valued a walk out there. The door opened and brought him out of his thoughts, it was Ross who looked around the room and then came to Avalon's booth.

"Where's Rutherford?" he asked.

"What are you doing here?"

"Oh, er, just an itch I can't scratch," replied Ross and he looked through the glass into the Cave, "so where's Martin?"

"He's down in the archive, doing some research

for Gordon and Alison."

"Oh," said Ross sitting in the chair opposite the DI. He looked slightly ill at ease.

"So what's wrong?" Avalon asked. Ross shrugged and kept silent for a moment, then he said,

"I got the forensics report from that suicide note this morning," he paused, "I asked them to email me a copy when it was ready."

"They did that one quick," admitted Avalon raising his eyebrows.

"It was easy, they found nothing, the report says the house was as clean as a hermit's conscience."

"And you think they missed something?"

"No," said Ross abruptly and shaking his head, "they didn't even find fingerprints or DNA from the man in the whole house, it was as if he didn't live there."

"You should know by now," shrugged Avalon, "not everyone lives in what is considered a normal relationship, they may not have lived together on a regular basis." Ross made no comment, he was leaning forward in his chair, his forearms resting on his knees and he was looking at the floor. "Maybe he has been gone for years, the wife may be trying it on for the insurance," suggested Avalon eventually.

"No, I thought it had all the smells of that to start with but I doubt that now," answered Ross sitting up and looking at his boss, "a few comments she made at the interview makes me think this isn't an insurance scam at all," he paused before continuing, standing and pacing the little space, "even forensics have their doubts."

"Explain?" said Avalon. Ross returned to the chair.

"I rang Hendry down at the lab and he said it's

too unusual to find so little, he says that they found absolutely nothing," insisted Ross opening his eyes wide, "as if the house and particularly the husband's rooms were recently, forensically cleaned."

"Well, I admit, it sounds fishy, did they conduct-"

"All tests, yes," interrupted Ross knowing the way Avalon thought, "they even went all round the house with Luminol but nothing showed up."

"So what do you want to do?"

"I want to open this up," insisted Ross, "the more I thought about it this morning, the more my doubts manifested."

"Does the wife of the man work?" asked Avalon.

"I've no idea, I can find out," replied Ross standing.

"Give her a call, I'll finish up here and come with you," said Avalon nodding to his computer screen.
They climbed into Ross's car and Avalon pulled on the seatbelt.

"You better give me the full story then," he suggested as they drove off.

"It's pretty straightforward on the surface," began Ross as he pulled out onto the main road, "successful couple, nice house, he's made money in electronics, she owns some kind of hairdressing business." Ross paused to manoeuvre on the road. "His wife said her husband had been acting odd before the suicide note appeared but he was secretive anyway and I have the distinct feeling that the two of them didn't get on at all well," he insisted as he glanced over to Avalon.

"Name?" asked Avalon.

"Jason Buchanan," answered Ross checking his rear view mirror, "he doesn't have any 'real' previous but his name has cropped up several times before."

"In what way?" Avalon inquired.

"Three years ago a girl reported that Buchanan tried to rape her at a party and only stopped because the girl vomited," explained Ross.

"It wouldn't stop most rapists," frowned Avalon.

"Well, he was never held to book for it because although the girl was insistent the incident took place, no one at the party would corroborate the fact that he was left alone with her. Eventually, the girl withdrew all complaints against him."

"So she was making it up?" asked Avalon expecting Ross was holding something back.

"I don't think so, not long after, the girl had access to money she hadn't had previous to the accusations."

"That just means she could have been a gold digger," suggested the DI.

"To me it means she was paid off yes, but would he pay her off if he was truly innocent?" insisted Ross glancing over again.

"It's a point to consider," nodded Avalon, "but there could be many other reasons."

"The more serious case his name cropped up in was an incident some years before that," continued Ross, "a girl was attacked outside a nightclub, she was dragged into an alley and stunned with a Taser type of instrument, when her boyfriend came out just after, he looked around for her and eventually saw someone undressing his girlfriend in the alley. Boyfriend tries to stop it and got his head staved in for his trouble."

"Nasty," frowned Avalon again.

"Very, he was in hospital for eight months and

never fully recovered," agreed Ross.

"And I'm guessing Jason Buchanan was implicated and got away with it?"

"Sort of," nodded Ross, "the doorman at the club said that at the time, he recognised Buchanan leaving the nightclub with the same group as the girl, but Buchanan denied even being at the club that night and the doorman changed his story soon after."

"So what possible reason could Buchanan have for leaving a suicide note and cleaning his house to a degree that it seems like he never lived there?" asked Avalon.

"I'm not sure," shrugged Ross bringing the car to a halt, "but he clearly wants to disappear."

"So what are the odds of a body turning up anytime soon?" asked Avalon to himself more than Ross.

"Pretty high I would say, but probably not the body of Mr Buchanan," sighed Ross and then added, "this is it." The two of them got out of the car and looked at the large house.

"Well money issues weren't the reason for a suicide by the look of it," offered Avalon.

"Not all that glitters is gold," replied Ross with a smirk.


"Thanks for seeing us again Mrs Buchanan," said Ross as the two of them entered, "this is Detective Inspector Avalon," he added holding his hand slightly towards his boss.

"Have you found anything out?" she asked. She was in her early to mid-thirties by the look of her, well dressed and with perfect make-up and probably attractive, but Avalon was too focused on her body language. Her accent was Scottish but not at all broad, more like the gentle timbre of Edinburgh or similar and he suspected she was hiding a much broader dialect. The house was much like her, tidy, clean and with an edge of modern simplicity about it wrapped in an expensive lustre that spoke of class not brashness. They were shown into what she described as the 'drawing room' though Avalon had seen libraries with fewer books than the shelves held. Glancing at a few of the titles, he guessed that they had been chosen to decorate the shelves, rather than slake the avid thirst for knowledge. As they sat in the sumptuous chairs, Ross spoke.

"We have nothing new for you yet Mrs Buchanan but it's early days of course, we have really come to ask a few questions."

"Of course," she nodded intertwining her fingers of both hands and laying them on her lap, "I'll help if I can."

"Do you have a cleaner?" was his first question.

"Yes, she comes in three times each week," replied the woman.

"Is she a good cleaner, I mean, is she fastidious about her work?" asked Ross. The woman gave a surprised look as if she didn't understand the question and then shook the doubt free.

"She's okay, but I..." she paused, "let's say she does what she gets paid for, nothing more." Ross nodded and then asked,

"Is your husband a tidy man, or at least would you consider him a tidy person?"

"Not particularly, indeed as I said on our previous interview, I was surprised to find his room so spick and span," she informed him.

"Would it surprise you then Mrs Buchanan," cut in Avalon, "that the house has no forensic record of him ever being here?"

"Yes it would," she nodded, "he was here two nights before I found the note."

"So he wasn't here the night *before* you found the note?" asked Avalon.

"No he stayed with friends," she replied, "he must have left the note the previous day." Avalon looked over to Ross who asked another question.

"As well as there being no record of your husband in the house, there is little evidence of you either, items collected from your bedroom supplied us with fingerprints and hair, but nothing in the rest of the house, can you explain that?"

"Not at all," she replied shaking her head, she looked quite dumbfounded.

"So, can you tell us your actions from two days previous?" asked Avalon and Ross took out his notepad.

~~~~~~

Avalon and Ross leaned on the wall looking over the river, enjoying the sun, but keeping out of the biting breeze.

"So what are your thoughts?" asked Ross as he pushed more food into his mouth.

"As Scottish chips go, these are quite good," nodded Avalon picking out a long, thin example.

"I meant Mrs Buchanan," frowned Ross, "anyway, what's wrong with Scottish chips?"

"Nothing wrong with these, but some of the chip shops up here..." Avalon trailed off and shrugged but then continued with, "her story holds water, though I don't quite see how anyone could have cleaned the house in such a short time without her knowing."

"That's what's getting to me. Fine she says he stayed out that night," explained Ross, "but if she's being truthful about the hours she was out in the day I don't see how Jason Buchanan, or anyone else for that matter, could have done such a job in the time available." Avalon chewed his food for a moment and then turned to Ross.

"We have to interview the cleaner, the people he's supposed to have stayed with and the people who work for him," he looked back to his chips, "we can't do anything until that's done."

"I'll nip back and get Martin and we'll get onto it," nodded Ross.

"Okay, you and Martin go and see these friends he's supposed to have stayed with, I'll go and see the cleaner and have a word." Ross nodded again and screwed what was left of his lunch into a ball. Avalon emptied what he had left onto the bank and watched the gulls swoop into the fray.

"The locals will give you some grief if they see you do that," said Ross taking the empty paper from the DI.

"I don't really care, I just hope the gulls enjoy them as much as I did."

"I've never known you go for chips before," smiled Ross.

"I was looking forward to the sandwich Frazer was bringing and I just got hungry," shrugged Avalon. Ross found a litterbin close by and put the papers into it, he turned and looked to Avalon.

"Well, I'm sure I can polish the sandwich off for you when we get back," he smiled and began walking away.

"No wonder you're putting weight on," frowned Avalon as he followed. Ross held up his hand as he walked.

"And you can't wind me up on a full stomach," he replied.


The Cave was reasonably populated when they arrived back and Rutherford showed some surprise to see Ross with Avalon.

"Bored already?" he asked raising his heavy brows.

"Bored?" cut in Frazer glancing up, "his life is so empty he's probably already started writing on the walls of his flat." Ross removed his jacket as he reached his desk and turned to Rutherford.

"I'm back because if I'm away too long Miss Sexy here gets withdrawal symptoms and becomes unbearable to work with," he was pointing to Frazer with his thumb, "and the term 'unbearable to work with' is relative." Frazer was already holding up the slim middle finger of her right hand even before Ross began his reply, the left hand however continued to type away merrily on the keyboard. "Anyway, we've got some trade," he added. Avalon closed in on Frazer's desk.

"You better give them a hand too Megan, it looks like there'll be quite a bit of legwork on this one," he explained. Avalon saw Boyd look up from her desk but he ignored the reaction and moved over to the windows before he continued. "Ross will fill you in with the details but it comes down to a suicide note, lack of a body and a man who seems to have never existed. Apart from that it's cut and dry," and he turned and headed back to his booth as Ross began to dig out all the information he had. Back in the booth, Avalon checked his phone, she still hadn't rung and he was now starting to think that Carol had become one of those people who sever contact once they don't need you. He was beginning to feel slightly angry about it. He checked his emails and then walked back into the Cave. Frazer had been reading up on the previous cases that may or may not have been connected, Ross was preparing a whiteboard with what they knew and Rutherford was looking through Ross's previous notes on the interview. Avalon glanced at the whiteboard and then walked back to the windows looking out, his hands linked in the small of his back.

"Why didn't the attack on the girl at the nightclub crop up in the cold cases?" he suddenly asked.

"Because someone confessed," admitted Ross and Avalon spun on his heal.

"So you have to discount that one then," he insisted.

"Well, yes, or we could have another look at the case." Ross sounded slightly sheepish about it but Avalon maintained that you have to have a completely open mind, untainted by what you think may have happened.

"No, unless there is reason to connect that case, leave it out of the inquiry." Avalon sounded adamant and so Ross gave a curt nod and continued writing on the whiteboard. Avalon turned slowly back to gaze out of the window.

"So," began Ross when he was ready, "we have

to interview the woman who cleaned the house for the Buchanan's and the people who the missing man was supposed to have stayed with the night previous," and he took a pause as if waiting for volunteers. It was Avalon who made the suggestion.

"You and Martin visit the friends, me and Megan will pay the cleaner a visit." Ross looked to the whiteboard and pointed to a name with his marker pen.

"Mrs Ailsa McIntyre, the address is in the notes." Avalon was about to move to look through the notes but Frazer was up and copying them into her notebook.

"Do we know anythin' about her?" she asked as she wrote.

"Not much," explained Avalon, "she just cleaned for them three times a week and there is a mild possibility that they didn't get on all that well, probably to do with money."

"Money?" asked Frazer opening her eyes slightly wider than the usual slits she wore.

"It's just a guess," explained Avalon, "but it may be a way to unlock the gossip box," he concluded raising his brows.

"Any other questions?" asked Ross. There was silence and so they set off to their targets.

As usual, Frazer was quiet on the journey, Avalon had learned long ago that trying to engage her in chitchat was pointless and so he sat in silence. To Avalon's surprise, it was she who actually broke it.

"Can I ask you a question Boss?" she said quietly.

"Yes, of course," he replied with a slight amount of astonishment.

"Es et true that your wife..." she amended it,

"your ex-wife es coming tae visit you?" she suddenly turned to him and added, "I don't mean tae pry boss..." there was a pause, "et's just what a' heard."

"It's no secret, yes she's supposed to be coming up but I've heard nothing to confirm it, so..." There was silence once more. "Any particular reason for the question?" he asked glancing over to her. He turned his gaze back to the road but he could see her turn to face him in his peripheral vision.

"Not really," she paused and he noticed her gaze return to the front, "a' was just wonderin'," there was another pause, "no it doesnae matter, it's none o' my business."

"Come on Megan, we all live in each other's pockets, what's on your mind?" he insisted.

"Well... how's that work, I mean, you get married, you get divorced and then you still see each other?"

"We split up but we didn't hate each other, we just grew apart," he explained.

"Grew apart? I hear people say that but a' don't know how that would work," she insisted fidgeting in her seat.

"Not everyone splits up in a destructive way, you must know that," he glanced over to her, she was an intelligent woman, what part of the explanation wasn't she getting? And then it struck him. This wasn't about *his* relationship, it was about hers. He recoiled slightly, this was a minefield, particularly where Frazer was involved. He knew much more about her than she realised, DI Lasiter had explained much of Frazer's past life and it wasn't pretty. There were things he knew about her that he couldn't ever tell a soul about and never would, but how could he have a sympathetic conversation with her and discount all he knew about her troubled past? His decision was the only one he could think of, he had to pretend he knew nothing about her and the rest of his explanation reflected this. "Take Ross's break up, that was pretty explosive, with Carol and me, we just sort of decided to part company."

"So what?" she asked, "you just sat down with a bottle o' wine and said, 'hey let's not live together any more'?" Avalon then had all the information he needed. It was clear Frazer was unhappy with her own relationship. He had already considered that they may not be the perfect couple, her boyfriend was ex-special forces or something similar and he didn't seem any more stable than Frazer in some ways.

"Sort of," was his answer, "though we did have arguments, I mean, living with a detective is a nightmare for the partner," he made a slight pause, "as you must realise," he added. She didn't reply, Avalon decided that he was too unprepared for further investigation into Frazer's troubles and so he left it for the time being. He did consider though that at some stage this particular piece of information would be of some importance, knowing Frazer, she had something buzzing around in her head and the conclusion could produce fireworks, and Avalon hated bonfire night.

# Chapter Four

"Mrs Hopwood?" asked Frazer as the door to the bungalow swung open.

"Yes love," replied the English voice, "I 'spect you've come about his nibs," she nodded in no particular direction but Frazer caught her meaning and was surprised by her directness.

"We want to ask you a few questions about Mr Buchanan, I believe you work as a cleaner for them?"

"A do, y' better come in," and she turned, walking away leaving the door open, "no point in standin' ont' door step," she continued. Avalon followed Frazer into the hall and closed the door. He recognised the accent as probably east midlands, maybe Lincolnshire or Nottinghamshire. She was difficult to age, maybe in her sixties, plain but with a pleasing manner. There were photographs of children everywhere, which likely meant she had a large family and an even larger extended family. That in itself would be at odds with her, and the sort of people the Buchanans' were. She invited them to sit and offered tea but Frazer politely refused.

"This es Detective Inspector Avalon and I'm Detective Constable Frazer," she informed the woman taking out her notepad.

"We just want to clear a few things up Mrs Hopwood, it shouldn't take us very long," explained Avalon.

"We believe you go up to the house three times each week," began Frazer. The woman nodded.

"Most weeks a' do yeah, not that it always need it."

"You mean et doesn't need cleaning?" asked Frazer.

"That's right, a' mean, they're not there all that much are they?" she replied with a slight edge to her voice.

"What do you mean by that, do y' mean they are away a lot?" asked Frazer.

"Just not there," shrugged the woman.

"We were under the impression Mr Buchanan was away last Sunday night," asked Avalon.

"A' couldn't say 'bout that love, but it's likely, he's never there that much anyway," she replied as Frazer wrote down some notes.

"Do you know where he goes?" asked Avalon.

"Sorry," began the woman shaking her head, "he's a bit secretive that one."

"You say Mrs Buchanan is away a great deal too?" asked Frazer looking up from her pad.

"She is, but then again, I 'spose she has to have her fun as well," she replied, Avalon caught the slightest hint of a smile.

"I see," he nodded, "so you think Mr Buchanan was having an affair?"

"Well, he wouldn't be the first man to do so would he love?" she raised her eyebrows to him, "an' she's a bit of a stuffy..." she paused trying to find more appropriate words, "so and so."

"So," began Avalon in an effort to separate the woman from her speculation, "you say the house was reasonably tidy, due to the couple not being there very much?"

"That's right," she nodded and was about to add something but Avalon continued.

"And you can't give us any idea where either of them may be staying when not at home?"

"She says she sometimes goes off t' see her cousin but a' don't know," shrugged the woman.

"Were you at the house on Monday when Mrs Buchanan found the suicide note?" he then asked. The woman looked at him for a few moments.

"That note had been on the dresser some days, she found it Sunday, but a' saw it there on the previous Friday."

"Friday, are you sure?" asked Avalon sensing Frazer glance over to him.

"Well, yeah, a' was there Friday and I haven't been since, I was supposed to be there Monday but she told me what had happened and she'd phoned the police," explained the woman.

"And you didn't inform her of the note?" asked Avalon with a frown.

"I don't go looking at my customers' private stuff, what sort of person do y' take me for?" she frowned back indignantly.

"So it might not have been the actual note then?" demanded Avalon.

"Oh it was the note," she insisted nodding her head.

"But Mrs Hopwood, if you didn't read the note and yet you are sure it was the note...?" began Avalon but she shrugged and said,

"I didn't read it, not all of it, it was on the dressin' table and I went in there to tidy up and that had been left on the dresser." Avalon jutted out his bottom lip and glared at her and then asked,

"But you can say for sure it was the same note Mrs Buchanan showed you when you were waiting for the police to arrive?" The woman simply nodded with a determined glare. Avalon looked over to Frazer who raised her eyebrows.

"Was Mr Buchanan's room ever untidy?" she asked the woman. The woman looked to Frazer and replied.

"Sometimes," she shrugged, "like I said, he weren't there all that much, on occasions I had a bit to do in there but it were mostly a bit of dustin'."

"Mrs Buchanan has the opinion that her husband is untidy," offered Frazer looking from the notes Avalon had given her.

"That depends on who you're judging it against, my Ronny is as scruffy as a moulting hen so I wouldn't say Mr Buchanan's any worse than other man in that regard," she insisted.

"So to your knowledge," cut in Avalon, "Mr Buchanan had used the room in fairly recent times?"

"Oh yeah, about a week or so ago," she nodded. Avalon stood, thanked her and explained they may have to interview her again at some time, and then they left.

"Why did Mrs Buchanan take several days tae inform the police?" asked Frazer.

"I suspect," began Avalon as he pulled away in the car, "that she rarely went in the room, which sort of backs up what the cleaner told us."

"So what was the difference on Monday," asked Frazer, "what made her go in there on Monday morning if she knew the cleaner was due in?"

"I really don't know," shrugged Avalon, "at the moment, the more immediate question is why did the room contain no DNA evidence of Mr Buchanan, or anyone else for that matter?"

"Because he doesn't want his DNA finding?" she shrugged.

"That crossed my mind I have to admit," nodded Avalon, "we have to do some deep digging into the affairs of Mr Buchanan when we get back, I suspect he has a very dark past."

"Maybe both of them," added Frazer.

"Probably, but after my short interview with Mrs Buchanan, it seems like the money was more important than the man."

"I thought you didn't stereotype?" asked Frazer with a rare grin. Avalon glanced at her and smiled a little himself, it was good to see her back in her element.

"It wasn't stereotyping," Avalon insisted, "he's well into his fifties and if the photograph that his wife has given us is an accurate representation, not great shakes in the 'looks' department. She, on the other hand, is in her early thirties, good looking and with a great figure. He divorced a wife to be with her - she probably gave up a mediocre career in a shop to help him spend his money." shrugged Avalon, "not stereotyping, just observation."

"Well boss, I think you're spending too much

time with Ross," she grinned again, "you're beginning to sound like him."

"Holy Christ," he sighed, "okay, point taken, I'll book myself into a clinic." Frazer's grin grew into a full-blown smirk, Avalon could just about make it out in his peripheral vision. It gave him an idea.

Back at the Cave, Avalon and Frazer arrived just after Ross and Rutherford, the room had been previously empty.

"So what do you have?" asked Avalon as he removed his jacket and placed it on an empty chair.

"Not much, the friend says that they hadn't seen him for several weeks but they did say that he's not the sort of person to take his own life," frowned Ross.

"Yes, I've come to that conclusion myself, had they any idea where he may have been?"

"No," replied Ross shaking his head, "they did however provide an interesting name," Ross paused for a second, "Lawrence Hilliard." Avalon stared blankly at him for a moment. "You've never heard of Lawrence Hilliard?" Ross asked with wide eyes.

"Nope," replied Avalon still staring.

"A true gold-plated slime ball," interjected Frazer with a slight amount of venom in her voice. Avalon looked at her and shrugged.

"So is anyone going to fill me in with relevant information?" he asked looking back to Ross.

"Hilliard has his slimy fingers into most things, horse racing, property development, internet security and politics," explained Ross.

"So he has the credentials, why should he be of interest us?" asked Avalon.

"This man is so sleazy," interrupted Frazer, "even the SNP threw him out of their ranks."

"And he ran straight to the Tories, it's not about politics it's about contacts and business deals," added Ross.

"Hell people, that covers every politician in the world, you know that," hissed Avalon scornfully, "you can't base an investigation on a person being 'a bad egg' for Christ's sake." He stood and walked over to the coffee machine, he seemed agitated.

"He's also been connected to insurance fraud," added Ross.

"Now I'm interested," frowned Avalon pouring himself a coffee, "convicted?"

"No," replied Ross with a sigh, "and I say 'connected' loosely, he was implicated in setting up a scam for one of his friends but as usual he pulled in favours and got off with it." Avalon shook his head and sat again.

"Okay forget people he knew, let's start from the bottom," insisted Avalon holding up a hand, "Buchanan is probably not dead, the evidence as it stands points to the man being involved with something where his DNA may implicate him in a crime. He clears his whole house or has someone to do it and fakes a suicide note so he can disappear." Avalon paused for a moment, "Anyone think differently?" No one spoke, "So," continued Avalon, "unless forensics find something on their second pass we will have to look elsewhere for clues to where he has run."

"Shall we inform airports and ports?" asked Rutherford.

"There isn't much point, it seems that Mr

Buchanan left the note several days earlier."

"So how come-" spluttered Ross but Avalon interrupted.

"I'll fill you in later, at the moment we need to get on the phones and track down everyone who knew him and everyone he dealt with." He paused to take a sip of his drink and then added, "I'm only running with this until we get busier, it's just a missing person and unless something crops up that he may be connected to, it's just speculation." Rutherford and Frazer nodded, Ross just sighed and leaned back in his chair.

"Do you wish you had stayed off now?" smiled Avalon. Ross folded his hands behind his head.

"You know when you say 'instinct' and I say bullshit?" he asked, Avalon just smiled. "well, this time it's my turn to say 'instinct', I can feel something bad is hidden in this one."

"Let's hope you're wrong," said Avalon dropping the smile and standing, "though I think you're not," he eventually added and he returned to the booth.


Thursday was the first day that Avalon put resources into the 'Suicide Note Case' as he began calling it. His reasoning was based on something that Frazer had found the previous evening after their return to the Cave. She had trawled through files that had been collected as part of the investigations into the two cases that Buchanan's name had appeared in. It was the name of the solicitor that dealt with the cases. He seemed to appear every time Buchanan's name was involved with any incident and 'Trevor Cameron' was known to the police in connection with other cases too. He had a reputation for defending people who had no defence. He was a specialist in getting people acquitted due to technicalities or simply by an overwhelming amount of 'jury-friendly' rhetoric. To the police, he was known as the 'criminal's friend' as he was quite capable of making a concrete conviction go away, so he was hated. He was also very expensive to hire and the whole Cameron connection told Avalon there was indeed something dodgy about Jason Buchanan.

On a different subject, Avalon was also beginning to see that he had the capability to get the best out of DC Frazer in a way no one else could. He wasn't sure why, but he could see that there was a great deal of potential in the woman that had not yet been unleashed. If he could tap into that, she would be unstoppable. She also seemed happier when she was working directly for him, and yet, he didn't see what was really important, what was actually happening to Frazer. The problem that Avalon had at the moment was two-fold, Ross was the one who had first found reason to delve into the case and indeed he considered it was *his* case. That meant that Ross and Rutherford should be the ones to work on it but if he put Frazer on the job, Rory Mackinnon would be left out in the cold. It was so slack with anything major, he couldn't even excuse himself by a reshuffle of the staff. For the time being he let Ross continue heading the investigation and used Frazer and Mackinnon to mop up around the edges, until something bigger came across the table. At that point he would have to re-organise.

"What d' y' want tae do about these burglaries?" It was DS Wilson's voice and it brought Avalon out of his thoughts. Wilson was leaning on the edge of the booth waving two sheets around.

"Are those the two from Culloden Street?" asked

Avalon looking up.

"Aye, do y' want us tae drop back onto them?"

"As far as I can see, we have nothing new to work with, what do you think?"

"Well aye," shrugged Wilson, "there's nothin' new but Alison wondered if there was any connection with the ones last week at Culduthel."

"And she thinks that these all may be connected to the rural break-ins down at Balvraid?" asked Avalon expectantly.

"Well, she may have a point, B Section are on the Culduthel ones, d' y' want us tae go an' see DI Lasiter?"

"Why not, I'll leave it to you to say if you think they are worth following up."

"Okay boss," said Wilson and he turned and left. Wilson was looking more upbeat in recent days, Avalon hoped he would soon return to the old DS that everyone knew and loved. He watched as Wilson returned to his desk at the rear of the room and spoke to Boyd, she nodded and the two of them stood, then left the office. Avalon also stood and walked to the coffee machine.

"Anything on Cameron yet?" he asked to anyone who would answer.

"Nothing yet," said Ross without taking his gaze from his computer screen, "but I doubt we will ever find a paper trail on that slimy git," he eventually looked up, "I'm more interested in finding a weak link."

"Meaning?" asked Avalon.

"Meaning, I'm looking into people he works with," replied Ross as he turned back to his machine, "if I can find anything, we may stand a chance."

"Not a bad idea but I doubt he would leave chinks in his armour as you said," frowned Avalon lifting his cup.

"Oh," cut in Frazer, "the handwriting expert says et's definitely Buchanan's handwriting on the suicide note, she says there's only a two percent chance of error." Avalon nodded.

"Any duress in the hand?" he asked.

"She doubts that's possible, the hand writing is a perfect match," she replied with a deep frown.

"What is it?" asked Avalon.

"Oh, I don't know," she suddenly sighed, "we know he wrote et so why aren't his dabs on the note?"

"It just confirms to me that his DNA is at some crime scene and he doesn't want it connecting, he probably wrote it with rubber gloves on," replied Avalon.

"Have we found his car yet?" asked Rutherford.

"No," replied Ross shaking his head, "but I'll bet six months gold membership to the Caledonian Gentleman's Club that we find no DNA in it.

"What make of car es et?" asked Rutherford, Ross was quick with the answer.

"BMW Alpina, D5." It meant nothing to Avalon but Rutherford pursed his lips and said,

"Hmm, expensive taste, I wonder ef et has a tracker?" There was stunned silence in the room until Avalon asked,

"Why have we not thought of that?"

"It's a good idea but even if it has one, if it's not factory fitted we'll struggle to find the company who fitted it," explained Ross.

"His insurance company might have details," was Rutherford's reply.

"Get to it," growled Avalon and he made his way back to the booth. As he sat, he felt his personal phone vibrate. He pulled it from his pocket and placed it on the desk casually looking for the text that had just come in. It was from Carol.

"*Please give me a call when you get time.*" He looked up into the Cave and then back, down to the phone. He would ring later, though, as the minutes ticked by, he considered phoning her straight away. As he reached down and picked up the phone he noticed Ross walking to the booth and so he placed it back into his pocket.

"Found something?" he asked.

"Nothing ground-breaking but I'm going down to Buchanan's unit to talk to the employees."

"Okay," nodded Avalon, "taking Rutherford?"

"Yeah," Ross confirmed, "we've just got off the phone to them, they're still working normally until they're told otherwise so I want to question them while they're all together."

"What's Megan doing?" asked Avalon.

"She's still digging around trying to find out if Buchanan's car had a tracker," explained Ross as Avalon nodded, "right, we'll get off," he added, he turned to collect Rutherford and left the Cave. Avalon forgot about the phone call he had considered making and walked into the Cave to talk with Frazer. She was speaking on the phone and nodded every now and then.

"Okay, thanks for that anyway," and she put down the phone. "Not much luck with the tracker boss. I found the insurance company but though they confirmed the car had a tracker, they don't have any details about et."

"I would have thought it would be in their interests to know the details," replied the DI.

"Insurance companies," shrugged Frazer then added, "their only interest es ripping us off for our coin," she paused and glanced at the computer screen, "I still have the main dealer to contact, they should know ef et had a factory fitted system." Avalon nodded.

"Keep at it, I might have a word with Buchanan's solicitor."

"Trevor Cameron?" she asked widening her eyes, "good luck with that one."

Avalon was surprised to get to speak with the solicitor so easily, he was shown into a large wood panelled room by a very nice looking receptionist. An elegantly suited man in his early forties stood and approached Avalon with his arm outstretched, his handshake was strong and confident and the man had a broad smile on his face.

"Detective Inspector Avalon, we haven't met as yet," he beamed, "welcome and please take a seat," he pointed to the large chair in front of his equally large desk. As Avalon sat, the man returned to his own seat and asked, "So to what do I owe the pleasure?" His accent was English with a slight 'tint' of Scots lingering in some of the vowels.

"I believe you once acted for a client by the name of Jason Buchanan?" The man seemed to scan his memory and it was obvious he found the name there, his face lost some of the smile.

"Yes, I do recall him, it's unfortunate that in this profession we are called to work for people who normally we wouldn't pass the time of day with."

"You didn't like him I assume?" asked Avalon.

"That little statement," smiled Cameron, "is as far

97

as I'm prepared to go on my client confidentiality ethic Detective Inspector." Avalon raised his brows a little.

"When were you last in contact with him?" he asked.

"Oh, not since I represented him," assured the man. Avalon gave a slight nod, there was no point in asking any leading questions, he knew the solicitor wouldn't give any more away, "so you have not set eyes on him since, in any capacity?"

"Not at all, I'm sure of it," insisted Cameron.

"Then I'm sorry to have wasted your time," announced Avalon standing, he noticed the man press something on the desk and a buzzer sounded in the distance.

"Not at all," smiled the man as he stood, "I'm sure we will meet again considering our respective professions," and the door to the office opened to reveal the receptionist once more. As Avalon reached the door he turned and looked over to Cameron in his throne.

"Oh, did you know he has disappeared?"

"No, I didn't," he replied.

"A suspected suicide," added Avalon - there was a pause.

"Suspected?" asked the man but Avalon turned and left, it hadn't been the most successful of meetings but he had a snippet of information he hadn't previously known.

~~~~~~

"Hello, it's Av..." he paused to correct himself, "James."

"*Oh, thanks for ringing back,*" said Carol, "*I*

*didn't know if you would have time during the day.*"

"It's a bit quieter than normal and I managed to get out of the office for an hour."

"*Crikey, it must be quiet,*" she said with a playful tone, "*I was wondering if sometime next week would be good for me to come up?*"

"Yeah," replied Avalon trying to think if there was anywhere he had to be, "I don't think I have any specific appointments."

"*Okay, so what about Tuesday?*"

"Yeah, Tuesday should be fine, but I thought you were spending some time at your parents first?"

"*I am,*" she replied, "*I'm spending the weekend with them, and then I'll catch the train up to Inverness.*"

"Oh, okay," replied Avalon but inside he was thinking that the weekend wasn't long to see her parents, was she so eager to get up to Inverness?

"*I'm looking forward to it.*"

"Don't get your hopes up, we're not having the weather you are enjoying down there," he replied.

"*The weather doesn't matter, I've never seen Inverness and I'm looking forward to seeing you too.*" Avalon swallowed, he really could do without any complications in his life, *work* was his life, there was hardly any room for any distractions.

"Okay," he eventually said, "text me when you know which train you'll be on and I'll try and meet you at the station."

"*I can manage you know.*"

"I know but I can drop you off at the house and then we can get you in at the B and B later, it's just down the street."

"*I can go straight to the bed and breakfast, it*

*would be easier for you, I'm sure Inverness has taxis."*
There was an element of playfulness in her voice.

"Plenty of taxis but I'll meet you anyway," he insisted.

*"Still trying to play the chivalry card I see,"* she gave a slight laugh, *"okay, I'll see you at the station."* He said his goodbyes and dropped the phone back in his pocket. He was glad he had remembered to phone her before he went back, he was beginning to wonder if there had been a problem at her end. He looked out of the car window to get his bearings, he had pulled off the road at the roundabout and was parked opposite the Travellodge, he noticed the sign for the Kart Raceway and realised he was close to the golf course. That meant he wasn't far from the Buchanans' house. He decided to have a drive past the house, just to have a look around. Inside, Avalon likened himself to a performer, maybe it was the fact that he had failed as a musician but he sometimes saw that being a detective was akin to being on stage and he liked to get a sense of the occasion by taking in the surroundings. He usually only performed this ritual on major cases but like Ross, he was considering that there was something hidden in this inquiry. He turned the car around and set off to the Buchanans' house thinking his way through the interview at the solicitors and wondering if he was blowing the whole issue up out of normal proportions. As he passed the house he noticed a car in the drive, he didn't slow down but he remembered the first part of the registration. It was a very new Mercedes and Avalon wondered who might have called on the Buchanans' so soon after the suicide note. At the top of the road he turned the car and slowly passed the house once more

noting the rest of the registration and jotting it down when he was out of sight of the house. His phone rang.

"Avalon."

"*Boss, we may have found Buchanan's car,*" it was Frazer.

"Where?" he asked.

"*At a storage company, et could be in a container by all accounts.*"

"So did it have a tracker?"

"*I don't know, I found it through his credit card transactions, a few phone calls later...*" she trailed off.

"We need to apply for permission to open the container-" began Avalon.

"*Already started the process,*" she cut in.

"Good girl," he smiled but then wondered if he was being patronising, he shook off the doubt and added, "Listen, I'm going to text you a vehicle ID, I want someone to check who the owner is."

"*Okay, send it over, I'll get on et.*" Avalon sent the text and opened the window of the car. He knew that Buchanan's car wouldn't reveal anything, it was likely it wouldn't further their pursuit in any way but Avalon knew that if the car had been so easy to find, maybe Jason Buchanan wouldn't be able to stay hidden for very long either.


For some reason Frazer was wearing a wide smile as he walked into the Cave. He ignored it for a moment, it was too late in the afternoon to get embroiled in some joke she had devised. He quickly scanned the room, Wilson and Boyd were busy at the rear but the surprise was that Rory had returned.

"Can't you stay away, a young man like you

should have lots of things to do with a few days off?" he smiled.

"Aye, if I was back home, I'd have plenty going on but here?" he shrugged. Avalon found it interesting that Mackinnon still considered the west coast 'home', where as Avalon saw Inverness as *his* home, not England.

"Et's my fault boss, he rang to see if there was anythen' happening..." she shrugged but the smile was still on her lips. The curiosity got the better of him and the unusual sight of Frazer smiling unnerved him slightly.

"Go on, what's the joke?" he asked.

"Joke boss?" the smile suddenly vanished, "I'm... not sure..." she looked puzzled.

"Well, I'm sure that the shape your lips made when I entered was an actual smile, and though it warms my heart to see you enjoying your work," he paused for a moment, "if Ross comes in and sees it, we may have a problem."

"Aye boss," the smile returned for a moment, "it won't happen again."

"So unless Rory has told you an amusing story, I'm thinking you might have some news for me?" Avalon asked as he sat the wrong way in the chair in front of Frazer's desk.

"Aye, sort of," she began, "The car you wanted identifying belongs tae none other than Trevor Cameron," she allowed the information to sink in. Avalon's face didn't alter, "and by my calculations, he must have left for the Buchanans' house soon after you left his office." Avalon nodded slowly and his eyes drifted to the floor. Frazer saw the mechanical working

102

of the inspector's brain in his features, he looked up to her and then back to the floor.

"That makes sense," he eventually said.

"Care to share?" asked Frazer tentatively.

"Oh, yeah, sorry," smiled Avalon, "When I told Cameron his ex-client had gone missing, there was little reaction, he responded quickly as if he already knew, but when I told him there was a suicide note, he seemed a little..." he paused as if looking for the word, "hesitant," he concluded.

"And so he went tae see Mrs Buchanan tae find out what had happened?" she asked.

"It's likely, if he didn't know about the note, yes he probably did," nodded Avalon.

"So why not just ring her?" asked Rory. Avalon looked at the young DC.

"Cameron is a wily character by all accounts," explained Avalon, "telephones can be tapped and tracked as you know but going over to the house..." Rory began to nod slowly as he said,

"Going over there, no one knows what was said and he's just a concerned solicitor looking out for his client."

"Oxymoron," said Frazer.

"Pardon?" was Rory's reaction.

"Oxymoron, 'concerned solicitor'," she explained.

"An' I thought the boss had a monopoly on big words,"

"That's not totally correct," insisted Avalon, "and in any case it's more of a habitude than a monopoly." He stood and poured a coffee as Rory raised his eyebrows to Frazer. "How are we doing with the application to open the container?" he continued.

"The storage company are fine with et, they just want something official before they'll open it up," explained Frazer, "we're trying to fast track et but we'll have to wait for the PF office to let us know." Avalon nodded and sipped the coffee.

"Anything you want me to do boss?" asked Rory. He was young, he was eager but in some ways he had slightly altered Avalon's plans for Frazer. Avalon was sure, given some time working with her, he could get more out of her abilities, she was good at her job but her insular attitude was preventing her progressing. Maybe she just wasn't cut out for responsibility, but unless he tried, no one would know either way. He was about to answer Mackinnon when the door opened and Ross and then the man-mountain Rutherford came into the Cave.

"Found anything?" asked Avalon as he leaned on the wall by the coffee machine. Ross walked up to him and poured two cups.

"Not much," he replied, "apart from everyone who worked for Buchanan disliking him, we found very little from the employees."

"Well he was their boss, nothing new there," shrugged Avalon.

"No," insisted Ross looking straight at Avalon, "they hated his guts," he turned and offered a cup to Rutherford before they both sat.

"Any particular reason?" asked the DI.

"Not really, everyone has different reasons, mostly because the guy is a complete knob by the sound of it," insisted Ross.

"We did get a bit o' something though," added Rutherford.

"Go on," frowned Avalon.

"One of them," continued Ross, "a sort of foreman there took us aside and told us that recently they had been building some odd surveillance kit for a particular customer," he paused to take a drink, "I couldn't make out what he was trying to tell us, not even sure *why* he told us but to humour him I asked him who the customer was. That's when things got interesting."

"Why is everything you explain like a radio play?" frowned Frazer.

"What's made a nest in your knickers?" retorted Ross.

"More like a story from James Hogg," added Avalon looking at Frazer.

"Who?" asked Ross with a half frown.

"Typical that you, a Scotsman wouldn't know about one of your most outspoken poets," sighed Avalon.

"Sod poets, do you want this info or not?" asked Ross raising the tone of his voice.

"Yeah but not the life story o' everyone you met today," nodded Frazer.

"Right," said Ross displaying a little anger in his voice, "cut to the chase then, the butler did it," he turned away and continued drinking.

"What my excitable friend es trying to say," smiled Rutherford, "es that there es no real customer, the invoices are for Butler Electronics, and there es no such company."

"So what? It's a scam?" asked Avalon not quite sure why it would be important.

"I don't think so," replied Ross coming back to the conversation, "the goods were made and shipped out, the money came in and was recorded."

"So why is it significant?" was Avalon's next

question.

"It might not be but the delivery address was never recorded, Buchanan took the stuff in the company van." Avalon shrugged.

"I can't see anything all that important here but maybe we should get a forensic tech to go and see the foreman to try and find out what the 'kit' was?"

"I think it's worth looking into," insisted Ross. Avalon nodded and looked down at Frazer.

"Bring everyone up to speed with what we know and find out if the storage company have a way of knowing if their containers are accessed."

"Already done that," she said and she looked down at her notepad, "they can only check after the fact, they have CCTV but nothing tae stop people entering at night t' remove stuff."

"Crap!" exclaimed Avalon, "we can't really put surveillance on this yet," he sighed as he thought, "well we'll have to hope that no one moves the car before the PF office gets us the paperwork."

"You've found the car?" asked Ross.

"Yeah, Megan will fill you in," nodded Avalon and he returned to the booth.

~~~~~~

Avalon and Ross entered the pub almost together, of late, Avalon hadn't been the regular at the Castle Tavern he once was. It was nothing to do with the pub, or the company, it was Avalon. He was beginning to feel as if life was passing him by and spending time at the pub seemed such a waste of it. So he sat in the house looking at the space where normal people would have a television until boredom took over and he reached for the guitar. He would then end up reading with a glass of something at his side sitting, in what Ross described as, the Lonely Detective's Chair. On occasions, the boredom would be such that he would drag out his laptop and do some work on a case he might be working on at the time. Before depression took hold of him he vowed that the odd night at the pub was the better of available options.

"You're late tonight," pointed out Avalon as they stood at the bar. Indeed Ross was invariably the first in but tonight he only achieved that by a minute.

"I forgot I hadn't ironed my shirt for tomorrow," frowned Ross paying for the drinks.

"A woman's work is never done," replied Avalon and he took a sip of the beer.

"That's why I wear tee shirts more often than not," cut in the landlord, "I used to iron stuff but it always ended up looking worse than when I started. I came to the conclusion that if I dropped it on Castle Street and let the traffic run over it for half an hour it would probably look better than my ironing."

"That sounds like a plan," grinned Ross.

"What, throwing your washing on the Queens highway?" frowned Avalon.

"No, tee shirts for detectives," replied Ross pausing to drink, "we could have a logo on the front saying 'Snatch Squad'."

"Don't even go down there," interrupted the landlord pointing at Ross, "this is a respectable establishment," and he went off to serve another customer. Avalon and Ross made their way to a seat on the higher level in the bar and slumped in unison.

"So," began Ross, "is anything confirmed about

Carol?"

"Yeah, it is actually, we sorted it today. She's coming up on Tuesday."

"I'm looking forward to meeting her," smiled Ross. Avalon's heart almost stopped. He hadn't considered that part of the visit, everyone would probably want to meet her.

"Well, er..." he spluttered, "she's not here for long and, well..."

"Don't panic, I'm fully house trained," Ross grinned, "has OK sorted out your house yet?"

"She says she wants to put it all together at the same time," shrugged Avalon.

"What's that mean?"

"Well, she's sorted most things out but she wants them all delivered on Monday, for 'full impact' she says. She's even having the day off for it."

"I told you she likes you," smiled Ross.

"What... you mean," Avalon hesitated, "you mean like that?" he spluttered with a look of doubt on his face.

"For some reason I just can't fathom, *most* of the female uniforms see you like that, I think it must be their training, you know, look after those in dire need and all that," explained Ross with a serious look.

"Really?" frowned Avalon then the frown changed to a slight smile and he repeated the word. "I don't think I'm her type," he added self-consciously.

"I don't think you're anyone's type but back to the plot, is Carol staying at your place then?"

"No," replied Avalon with a slight shake of the head, "she's staying at a bed and breakfast a few doors away but I doubt I'll have much time to spend with her, you know, I'm not planning any meet and greets with people from the nick either," replied Avalon in a stilted manner.

"She's not coming all this way for you to say 'there you are Carol, this is Inverness'," Ross swept his arm about in a theatrical manner, speaking in a perfect English voice, "now bugger off back to cider land so I can get on with my miserable life."

"You didn't get the subtleties of my accent," frowned Avalon as he took another sip of his beer.

"What accent? you sound like Martin Freeman to me."

"Who?"

"Martin Freeman, the guy that played Bilbo Baggins."

"I thought that was Ian Holm?"

"That was in the first film, I'm on about-"

"There was more than one film?" asked Avalon with surprise.

"No," insisted Ross shaking his head, "I know you too well, you're not drawing me in with that one." Avalon tilted his head to one side.

"You're no fun anymore," he said.

"You're too old to be having fun," insisted Ross and he took another heavy gulp of lager, "oh and talking of fun, there isn't going to be any with the luscious Miss Sarah Underwood."

"What do you mean?" asked a surprised Avalon.

"Didn't you hear? she's getting engaged," replied Ross. For a moment Avalon was speechless.

"Do you know, I thought I heard you say she was getting engaged?" he frowned.

"She is, some doctor from Edinburgh."

"That's come out of the blue hasn't it?" said

Avalon as upbeat as his tightening stomach would allow.

"It seems she met him when she was at a seminar last year," explained Ross turning to Avalon, "he's a vegan from what the girls downstairs have told me and..." Ross cut his explanation short as he saw the look on Avalon's face, "you knew didn't you?" he added glaring at Avalon.

"No," said Avalon dumbly shaking his head, "until you just said I had no idea, I-"

"Not about the engagement, I mean about the vegan thing, you knew, you bloody well knew. All this time you knew she was vegan, that's why you asked me about it, what...?" Ross looked up at the ceiling trying to remember something, "two years ago was it?" Avalon just stared into space, he wasn't really listening to Ross. "All this time you somehow knew she was vegan and told no one. Craftier than a box of bishops." Avalon came from his thoughts.

"And what exactly pray tell would you have done with that information?" he asked.

"Well nothing I suppose," shrugged Ross, "it's just the principal of it, no! It's a trust thing." Avalon lifted his glass and finished it in one. He made a half-hearted attempt to point to Ross's glass and said,

"Do you want another or are you going to refill it with your tears?"

"Of course I want one," he said and emptied the glass in a single gulp. As Avalon stood waiting at the bar he thought about Sarah Underwood, he thought about the night he had been at her house to play his song to her, and the feeling he had seeing her pleasure that evening. Had he missed out on something? Had one possible timeline been cut from his grasp forever. As he

110

considered it he realised that was probably not the case, Ross had said she met the doctor a year ago. She was probably in touch with him even when Avalon played his song to her, that stupid song. He felt foolish, to think that he could have impressed her with something so simple. He ordered the drinks and the landlord filled the glasses.

"Is it still hectic at the office?" he asked as he pulled the drinks.

"It's not bad at the moment, bound to get busy again soon though," replied Avalon. The landlord rolled his eyes as if he was going to say something but thought better of it so Avalon turned to move back to the table but Ross had joined him at the bar.

"What's wrong, don't like sitting on your own?" he asked passing Ross his glass.

"At your age I didn't think you would make it back with two full glasses without spilling it," frowned Ross. Avalon sighed but not from Ross's comment.

"I can't believe she's getting engaged," he said shaking his head slowly.

"Well, you should have moved on the information," said Ross taking a sip.

"What information?"

"The fact that she was vegan, although I do remember you considering going vegan when we worked on the Drumnadrochit case."

"Yes, to my embarrassment a pretty shallow gesture."

"Yes, it was," admitted Ross, "nothing wrong with shallow when it involves a good-looking woman."

"That statement is shallow too," insisted Avalon leaning on the bar.

"Have you considered that she might not have

111

fancied you even if you had gone vegan?" asked Ross raising his brows, "though for the life of me I can't see why veganism has anything to do with it?"

"It's pretty straight forward," explained Avalon, "why would a vegan want to have a relationship with a non-vegan?" Ross shrugged so Avalon tried to explain, "well, think of mealtimes and how difficult it would be."

"But if you fall in love, surely that comes before 'what's for tea tonight dear?'"

"Then consider the act of kissing," offered Avalon, "I suppose for a vegan, sticking their tongue into a meat-eaters mouth must be like..." Avalon couldn't think of any comparison.

"If you stick your tongue into any living things mouth then you are already breaking your religion, the transfer of skin cells guarantees that," said Ross in a matter of fact way.

"Firstly, I think you'll find it's not a religion and secondly, it's a moot point as everyone consumes their own skin cells anyway."

"Can you two change the subject back to violent robberies and gruesome murders," cut in the landlord, "people are trying to eat."

"Sorry John," smiled Ross, "it's just that this numpty missed out on his ideal woman."

"Ah, didn't we all," shrugged the landlord, "Kate Beckinsale used to come in here all the time asking for me to take her out, I told her straight, I've already got the perfect woman at home." Avalon glanced over to Ross and then back to the landlord who noticed a customer waiting to be served the end of the bar. "She's too old for me anyway," he added as he went. Avalon lifted his glass up high and said,

"Oh, well, here's to Sarah Underwood, may she find happiness."

"And missed opportunities," added Ross as he raised his own glass.

## Chapter Five

For the first time in his life, Ross was the first one in the office, he was so shocked that he looked at his watch. Had someone forgotten to tell him there was a meeting somewhere and he was the only one not there? He soon found the problem however when he checked the time on his watch against the office clock. He picked up his internal phone and called the front desk.

"Morning PC Kirk, do you happen to know what the correct time is?" he asked when the phone was answered.

"*Er, et's ten to eight,*" she replied. There wasn't much of a response from Ross and so she continued, "*an' et's Friday,*" she paused but the silence was still there, "*the eighteenth of May?*" she concluded the conversation as a question.

"Thanks OK, I think I need to lie down," he eventually replied and put down the phone. So what the hell had gone wrong with his watch? It was quartz so it couldn't really go faster could it? But it had. He stared glassy eyed out of the window for a moment thinking how much sleep he had missed by being there early. He shook his head as the door opened. It was Frazer and she stopped in her tracks when she saw Ross, turned and then walked out closing the door behind her. Ross frowned and was thinking about getting the coffee machine set up but then the door opened again and Frazer came back in, stepping just over the threshold. She looked around the room as if she was getting her bearings and then looked back to Ross.

"Are you really here or am I hallucinating?"

"Surely if you were hallucinating I would be standing here naked?" replied Ross.

"Jesus, that would be a nightmare not an hallucination," she frowned, "why are you here this early?" and she also checked her watch against the office clock.

"I really don't know," he replied removing his watch and placing it on his desk.

"This feels freaky," she said, finally plucking up the courage to move to her desk.

"You ought to be this side of my eyeballs," offered Ross with a puzzled look.

"So I'm guessing you need a new wrist watch," she added as she moved to start the process of bringing the coffee machine to life.

"I swear it was correct with my alarm clock, this is a real puzzler." The door opened again, it was PC Kirk followed by Rutherford.

"Careful Ollie," said Frazer raising her brows, "Ross isn't fit to be seen at the moment, but then again..."

"So et *was* you?" Kirk began, "I thought when I heard your voice you must have called from home but I checked the number and realised et was internal."

"Aye, Ollie said there might be a surprise waiting in the Cave," added Rutherford, "but this comes more

115

under the description of 'sublime'." The door opened again, this time it was Boyd.

"Holy Christ," she announced at the sight of Ross and made the sign of the cross."

"Will you lot behave, something strange has happened this morning," frowned Ross looking at the four of them in turn then the door opened once more. It was Avalon.

"Morning ladies," he announced and seemed not to notice Ross at all as he headed for the booth. Frazer stopped him saying,

"Boss, have y' not noticed anything strange?"

"Well yes I have actually," replied Avalon turning back to look at her, "the cooing that collared doves make, sounds like someone repeating, 'I'm forty' over and over."

"That's just weird," she said.

"Well you started it by bringing in an inflatable Ross to scare me," he frowned nodding to Ross, "I mean I know he's putting some weight on but I think you put too much air in that one."

"You can all bollocks, I'm early and it's strange I know but think how it feels to me," Ross replied with agitation in his voice.

"Good god, it's the real one," said Avalon with brief mock surprise and he continued to the booth as PC Kirk left. The next to enter was Wilson who saw Ross about the same time as he announced his 'morning all' and then added,

"Did your bed catch fire this morning Rossy?" Ross didn't reply, he just stared down at his watch, which was still on the desk. He pulled a sheet of paper from his drawer and wrote something on it with marker pen. He then stood, walked to the office door and went outside. Moments later he returned without any comment. Rory Mackinnon was the last to arrive as he was calling into the archive before going upstairs. When he finally arrived he was holding the paper that Ross had taken out earlier and was holding it up.

"Why is this on the door?" It said in angrily scrawled writing, 'DS Ross was early this morning – deal with it.'

"I think et was there tae warn anyone with a weak heart," answered Frazer raising her eyes to Rory.

"Sometimes I don't get the humour in here." shrugged the DC and he sat at his desk. There was a bang suddenly and all looked round to see Ross lifting his shoe from the desk, below it was the smashed wreckage of a wrist watch, Ross's wrist watch.

"You see," added Rory as Avalon came into the main office, "why is that funny?"

"It's not meant to be funny, it's meant to make sure I'm never early again."

"It's East Coast Highland humour Rory, I'm only just getting the hang of it," smiled Avalon walking into the main office.

"Scottish humour?" questioned Ross looking up from the crumpled wrist watch," when you get Scottish jokes you can truly call yourself a local," and he returned his gaze to the watch.

"Is there such a thing as a truly Scottish joke?" asked Avalon in a more serious tone.

"Yeah, course," nodded Ross, "Two cows in a field, how do you know which one is on holiday?"

"Go on," sighed Avalon.

"It's the one with a wee calf," replied Ross with a

straight face.

"Not particularly amusing but I do get it so am I a local now?" asked Avalon.

"Try this one boss," put in Rutherford, "A man goes into a baker's shop and asks, 'Is that a cake or a meringue?' The baker looks at the man an' says, 'No y'r right, et's a cake.'"

"Yeah, that's a good one," smiled Ross. Avalon stared blankly. He thought about it for a minute and Ross even saw him mouthing the joke back to himself but eventually he just thrust out his bottom lip and shrugged.

"Why did the chocolate bar melt?" asked Boyd. Avalon shrugged, "because it's Bounty." Avalon frowned, it took time to scan through the words turning anything he could find into Scottish, but he didn't get time, Rory got involved before he worked it out.

"What do you call a pigeon that goes for his holidays in Glencoe?" There was no answer so Rory eventually gave it, "skean dhu," he announced with a broad grin. All the other faces remained straight and Rory's grin also dissipated. "Oh come on, you must get that one?" insisted Rory.

"Nope, not me," shrugged Ross, "it must be an Island thing," he added. Rory guessed Ross was trying to wind him up, so he turned to his computer.

"Well now we've established that there *is* such a thing as a Scottish joke," announced Avalon, "can we see if there is a similar affirmation to 'is there such a thing as a Scottish detective?' we have a busy day." The team moved to their respective desks and began the toil of the morning. Avalon moved back to the booth and checked through his emails, one of which had some interest. He read though the rest and deleted anything of no use. He then checked his online diary and made a note that Carol would be arriving sometime on Tuesday. DS Wilson was making his way over and Avalon smiled to him as he entered the booth.

"Anything on the burglaries at Culloden Street" he asked as Wilson sat.

"A few bits of interest but we could do with someone on the ground who might know of this character." Wilson handed his boss a piece of paper, it had the name, 'Carlo the Cat' on it.

"Wasn't he on the front page of the Beano?" said Avalon light heartedly and then added, "I'm guessing when you say 'on the ground' you mean an informant?"

"Yeah, I've asked everyone I know and nothing rang any bells, I wondered if you know anyone?"

"I only know Antony Scobie and to be truthful he's provided me with very little over the last year," admitted Avalon handing back the paper. Wilson sighed and leaned back.

"Well it was worth a try," he said with another sigh.

"Have you asked Megan?"

"Yeah," nodded Wilson, "but she's never been very forthcoming in the past, she likes to keep her 'assets' for herself."

"I can sort of understand that," nodded Avalon, "but I can ask her if you like, who is this Carlo anyway?"

"His name crops up quite a bit, but no one seems to know much about him," explained Wilson, "some say he's Italian, some say he's Lithuanian." He leaned forward resting his forearms on his knees.

"I'll get in touch with Scobie, if he doesn't know anything he may be able to ask around?" Wilson nodded at the suggestion and stood.

"Thanks boss, anything would be good, I think this Carlo has put some sort of team together and finding him will tidy this investigation up pretty quick." Avalon nodded and Wilson left. It was now clear to see that Wilson was getting back to his former self, the hunger for the case was back in his eyes and his voice was more confident.

Avalon went back to the email he received, it was from the Procurator Fiscal's Office and instructed that the warrant was being processed and would be available in the afternoon. Avalon stood and entered the main part of the Cave.

"It looks like we'll get access to the storage unit this afternoon," he explained.

"That was quick, is it quiet down at the PF office?" asked Ross.

"Dunno," shrugged Avalon, "I was unsure they would grant it based on bank statements," added Avalon raising his brows, "it's not exactly a category A is it?"

"Danger to public?" shrugged Frazer, "and after all, there could be a body en the car, dead or alive." Avalon had considered that there could indeed be a body in the car but he hadn't read the warrant application and he was now wondering if Frazer had used wording to suggest that there could be a living person involved. If so, it was a good idea to ensure the warrant went through quickly.

"Shouldn't we have had the unit dusted?" asked Ross.

"Done," insisted Frazer.

"Megan was on the ball," explained Avalon, "she had the lock and the container door dusted for prints, she also asked the company for their CCTV records for the dates from the last time Buchanan was seen. As expected there were no prints on the part of the lock they could get at."

"We might get a look at who took the car there," she put in.

"Wouldn't the company know who delivered it?" asked Ross.

"Already spoken tae them about it," Megan explained, "the container was booked on the twentieth of April this year, nothing was put in there at the time but the guy at the company confirmed that Buchanan was the man who booked and paid for et."

"So the container could just be empty?" asked Ross.

"It's a possibility," admitted Avalon, "but the thing is, customers have access to the yard twenty-four seven so the vehicle could have been put in at a later date."

"Then wouldn't it have been safer to get the CCTV records and look through them first?" frowned Ross, "it's going to be embarrassing if the container is empty."

"Aye, we could have done et that way," nodded Frazer, "but et might take weeks tae get the PF to secure the footage, plus god knows how long tae look through it, then time t' get a further warrant tae open the container," she folded her arms and leaned back in her chair, "this way we get the footage and access tae the container and ef there es someone in there, they might still be alive."

"It makes sense," chipped in Rutherford.

"And it gets the container opened quickly," added

Avalon giving a quick glance to Frazer. "In the meantime," he continued, "I want DS Ross and DC Rutherford to continue looking into Buchanan's past, Megan," he looked at Frazer, "make sure the forensics team are booked in for this afternoon, we need them there when the container is opened." Avalon looked over to Mackinnon. "Rory, see what you can dig up on the politician, what's his name?"

"Lawrence Hilliard," suggested Frazer.

"Okay boss," nodded Rory and Avalon returned to the booth.

~~~~~~

There was a sizeable team at the storage yard by five o'clock when the warrant was to come into force. The area around the container was sealed off and the manager of the storage company was at hand with the second key. At one minute after five, the lock was opened and removed and the man stood back. Avalon and Frazer opened the two levers holding the doors and they were swung open. To his relief, Avalon was looking at a dark blue BMW that seemed shoehorned into the container. He looked around and under the car and could see no obstructions or problems that would prevent the car being removed. He put on rubber forensic gloves and felt the rear edge of the boot for a release and began to brace himself for what he might find. A sniff of the air in the container made him doubt a body being in there as there was just the background smell of the car. The boot popped open to his surprise and after a quick look inside he nodded to the forensics team.

"It looks clean," he said returning to the others.

"How the hell did they get it in there?" asked Ross.

"It looks like the driver's window is open, I suppose someone drove it up the ramps, which are in the boot I notice and got out of the car through the window," shrugged Avalon removing the gloves. "Right, we better collect the CCTV records and leave the forensics to get the vehicle out of there," he added.

Sarah Underwood wasn't at the scene, Avalon knew she had been called away to Aberdeen where her expertise was required on another case. He didn't know if he was glad about that or not. He was impressed by Miss Underwood, she was not just hugely skilled and professional, she was pleasant to be with once you got to know her. Certainly Avalon had fallen in love with her several times over but at the back of his mind he knew they were as incompatible as Ross and Frazer. Avalon considered Frazer too. Megan Frazer had changed a great deal since Avalon had first met her. She had been insular to a point where it was almost impossible to converse with her and yet now she was showing a remarkable talent within her profession, she was thorough and conscientious. She was now an invaluable part of C section and would be impossible to replace but Avalon still needed to keep her busy, it seemed that she thrived on the cut and thrust of the job. His main worry with Frazer was her private life, was she going through some crisis at home, it seemed so? There was nothing he could do about that though.

~~~~~~

The week seemed to be flying by, it was Saturday

123

morning and there was a feeling that the quiet period was over and Avalon would have to back off in the Buchanan case. He had been hearing from the forensics team that they were finding nothing significant in the car or the storage container and the only slight interest in the case came from the CCTV footage. Rory had spent a few hours in the screening room and had helped trawling through the endless hours of footage.

"It's a bit odd actually," admitted Rory.

"Go on," insisted Avalon.

"The footage shows the car arrive just before midnight on the twenty-sixth of April," continued the young DC, "the driver seemed heavily disguised and it's not easy to make out who it is, but the weird thing is, there is no record of the person leaving," Rory shrugged slightly. Avalon frowned and looked to his computer screen in thought. "I mean," continued Mackinnon, "the person would have had to have left through the same gate on foot and there is no record of that." Avalon looked at Rory again and said,

"That means that whoever it was stayed in the container until morning, probably until the gates were opened in the daytime. I'm guessing there was an arrangement to pick the driver up with another vehicle."

"Do you want us to check to see if a vehicle leaves with more in the car than when it arrived?" asked Rory. Avalon shook his head.

"No, it's doubtful they would have just sat in the passenger seat and I can't justify checking all vehicles that arrived that day based on what is still just a missing person case." Rory nodded, he could see that it would take some considerable time to check registrations and contact all the drivers. There wasn't really any case to answer, it didn't even seem like insurance fraud was going to be the reason for an investigation. Avalon knew that there was more to Buchanan going missing, but without evidence of a crime he would have to drop it. He explained the situation to Ross and he and Rutherford were put to work on an attempted robbery near Dingwall. Frazer and Mackinnon were moved on to two smaller priority cases in the city centre. Avalon began to write up the report for the PF office on the findings of the warrant. As he typed, he thought about Sarah Underwood and his ex-wife Carol, the first was just superficial dreaming, the latter wondering when she would text him with the ETA for Tuesday. He then remembered that he had promised Wilson he would contact his so-called informant Antony Scobie. Scobie, to his credit seemed to have 'gone straight', he still however lived on the fringes of his former life and on rare occasions had some snippet of information. He was a nervous man when it came to his 'grassing' however and a meeting with Scobie could be very cloak and dagger. He hated phones, so the system was for Avalon to text Scobie with the words, 'Happy Birthday' and Scobie would return a location for the meet. Avalon soon got a reply from Scobie, it said simply, 'Whin Park – 2.30'. Though it wasn't that far from the station, Avalon had never been to Whin Park but he checked where it was on Google maps and set off in plenty of time to meet Scobie.

The park was a wooded area which could be reached by bridge over what was known as Ness Islands and indeed Avalon passed over a footbridge to reach the islands. Scobie hadn't said where exactly to meet but Avalon guessed as the park wasn't busy it wouldn't take long to find him. He soon noticed Scobie leaning on a fence overlooking what seemed to be a miniature railway though the park, it was quiet and no trains seemed to be running. As Avalon approached he heard Scobie say,

"Afternoon Mr Avalon, I hope you're well."

"Scobie," nodded Avalon and he leaned on the fence besides the ferrety looking man. Scobie glanced at Avalon and gave a thin smile and then looked back towards the railway and nodded through a gap in the trees where a white but rusting bridge stood.

"Do y' know Mr Avalon, that wee bridge used tae cross the Ness until about 1988 when they moved et for a more modern structure, et's just a bridge tae nowhere now,"

"I didn't know you were into architectural archaeology Scobie," replied Avalon.

"I'm no' really Mr Avalon but I feel a bit like that wee bridge, I'm goin' nowhere."

"We all feel like that sometimes," nodded Avalon looking over towards the bridge.

"So what d' y' want Mr Avalon?" asked Scobie standing straight and glancing around the park. He leaned back on the fence but this time with his back to it.

"Ever heard of Carlos the Cat?"

"The name doesnae ring any bells," replied the man shaking his head.

"He might be running a gang doing house break-ins," suggested Avalon, "possibly Italian or Lithuanian."

"I can ask around but he's not known tae me ef y' know what I mean?" insisted Scobie.

"Anything would be appreciated," nodded Avalon as he too stood straight. For a moment the thought flew through his head to ask Scobie another question but he thought it would be out of the man's league. Then he considered he had nothing to lose so he asked him anyway.

"Ever come across a solicitor called Trevor Cameron?"

"Heard o' him Mr Avalon, I know he's expensive and that's all."

"How about Lawrence Hilliard?"

"Politician, seen him on the tele," offered Scobie.

"Jason Buchanan?" added Avalon. Scobie went quiet, his eyes looked around the park and he turned and leaned on the fence again.

"Heard o' him Mr Avalon, not a very nice man by all accounts, luckily never met him though."

"Any ideas where he might be?" asked Avalon not expecting an answer.

"No," replied Scobie shaking his head, "if I did know I wouldn't be keen on telling, he's got some serious friends ef y' know what I mean?"

"What have you heard?" asked Avalon turning to him.

"Nothin' honest," insisted Scobie holding up his hands, "I just know *of* him, if you're tryin' tae find him I would ask around at the club he's in."

"Club?"

"Aye, et's Freemasons, you know the sort o' thing, weird hats and funny handshakes."

"Are you sure?" asked Avalon.

"No I'm no'" sighed Scobie, "et's what I heard," and he returned his back to the fence. "You could ask someone you have been en touch with a'fore," he added.

"Who's that?" asked Avalon with an intense stare.

"Ef I tell yous' you have tae promise not tae mention my name." Avalon gave a single curt nod.

"Charlie Sands," Scobie said and then added, "he'll tear ma' nuts off ef he knows I told yous'."

"Sands?" questioned Avalon with a frown.

"Aye," nodded Scobie, "he used tae be in the Masons at one time, he's your best man tae talk to."

Back at the office, Avalon was wondering about the veracity of Scobie's information. If Buchanan was in the Masons then a whole new world could open up in the case, but would Sands play ball, was he even in the Masons? Only an interview would sort that out. He looked up Sands number and picked up the phone. A high pitched female voice answered.

*"Hello, Sands residence,"* but in the background he heard a man's voice complaining and there was a muffled scuffle before another voice spoke.

*"Hello, Charlie Sands."* This voice seemed agitated.

"It's Detective Inspector Avalon from Inverness."

*"Oh,"* there was the female voice in the background sounding as if she was doing her best to start an argument, *"interesting you called detective as I was just thinking of,"* the volume changed as the phrase turned into a shout but was aimed away from the phone, *"committing a murder!"* There was the sound of a door slamming in the distance.

" I can call later if it's a bad time," added Avalon.

*"It's always a bad time, anyway, what do you want?"*

"I was wondering if I could call round and have a word?" explained Avalon, there was a moment's silence and then Sands asked,

*"What's this about?"* There was an air of uncertainty in his voice.

"Oh, nothing to concern yourself about," insisted Avalon trying to put Sands at ease, "I just want to ask you about Freemasonry, I heard you may have been involved at some time."

*"Take my advice detective, join a golf club, you'll have more fun and the friends you make there will be much more genuine."*

"I don't wish to join Mr Sands, I want a little inside knowledge," suggested Avalon.

*"Normally I would tell you to shove your inside knowledge up your arse but it sounds like you have some dirt on one of those back stabbers,"* there was a rustle of paper and Sands continued, *"tomorrow, around eleven? Oh and don't bring DS Ross with you, staff are difficult enough to come by without your man mutilating them as they go about their duties."*


Avalon rang the bell of the palatial home of Charlie Sands. He had interviewed Sands on a previous occasion in connection with a murder near Golspie the previous year. As he stood on the doorstep, looking across to some sort of sports car that Ross would have identified immediately, he wondered about what approach to use with Sands. The door opened and a somewhat overdressed woman stood there. A tight skirt hugged her form and an off-the-shoulder top was held in place by a fake tiger skin blouson. She was heavily made up and her bleached blonde hair was piled up on her head. She reminded Avalon of the television character called Marlene from the *Only Fools and Horses* television series but she was much taller, given that she had high heels on, she stood an inch or so taller than Avalon.

"Hello sweetheart, what can we do for you?" To Avalon's amusement, the accent was English, not dissimilar to the Marlene character. Her smile seemed genuine though as if she was constantly happy with the slightest thing.

"I'm here to see Mr Sands."

"Oh Mr Grumpy?" she gave a short laugh, more akin to the sound a Zebra made, "come in sweetheart, who shall I say is here?"

"Detective Inspector Avalon."

"Ooo," she cooed more like a pantomime dame than a real woman, "we *are* lucky, we usually only get trash visiting," and she showed him into the hall where he had stood once before, when Ross had almost emasculated one of Sands' muscle boys. He noticed the old fashioned phone Ross was going to use as a weapon had gone, now replaced by a vase with flowers in it. "Wait here love, I'll see if I can pull the frown off his eyes." As 'caricature' as the woman was, Avalon was beginning to like her, even the odd way her lips seemed to return to a pursed condition after every sentence. She soon returned with her odd gait caused by wearing the tight skirt and came close to him. "He's waiting for you in his dungeon," she smiled and then sniffed Avalon which he found unnerving then she added, "you smell nice, don't let him taint you," and she touched the end of his nose with her long finger and walked off in the other direction. Avalon watched her as he crossed the room. She was odd, but her ability to give everyone the benefit of the doubt was pleasing, yes, he liked her. One of the two doors was ajar, so Avalon knocked and walked in. Sands was in his usual place, behind his desk, in front of the cathedral windows overlooking the garden.

"Detective, please, come in," said Sands holding his arm out towards the chair by the desk, "take a seat, I hear you've met Celine."

"Er, yes," nodded Avalon thinking the name suited her, "is she..." he held his thumb towards the door.

"New?" asked Sands guessing what Avalon was hinting at, "not by any stretch of the imagination but yes she's new to the house." He turned in his seat and glanced across the garden. "She'll probably end up in the rockery with the others," he added and then turned back. Avalon considered that maybe Sands didn't ought to joke about such things to a detective, if he was indeed joking. "So you want to know about the Freemasons?"

"Not as such," replied Avalon, "I want to know about one of its members."

"Oh?" said Sands lifting his brows.

"I'm under the impression that a certain Jason Buchanan is a member of a local lodge," said Avalon but Sands expression went back to a frown at this then he asked,

"Who gave you that information?" Avalon stayed stock still and said nothing. "Ah, of course, you can't say, well the informant was incorrect," insisted Sands. Jason Buchanan has never been a member of the Masons, not locally at any rate." Avalon stared for a moment and then said,

"Oh, well it seems I've wasted both our time with this, I'll not keep you any longer," and Avalon made to stand.

"Maybe not," said Sands looking up at Avalon,

there was a hint of something more to come. Avalon sat again. "Is this official detective?" he asked.

"No not really, no one even knows I'm here," replied Avalon. Sands sighed and then began a steady nod. He then looked directly at Avalon and said,

"Are you after Buchanan?"

"Sort of," nodded Avalon.

"As I said, he's never been in the Masons, but I don't like the man and as far as I know, you'll not find anyone who does," insisted Sands.

"I'd like to find him Mr Sands," said Avalon directly, "anything you can give me to locate him would be greatly appreciated."

"That I can't do," said Sands shaking his head, "I have no idea where he is, I'm guessing you have tried his business premises?"

"Is there anything else?" asked Avalon knowing Sands wanted to tell him something. Sands took a deep breath and placed his hands on the edge of his desk before exhaling.

"He's a member of a club, nothing to do with Freemasonry but it's easy to see how someone would confuse it."

"What's the name of the club?" asked Avalon.

"I've no idea, it's all pretty secret," insisted Sands.

"So how do you know about it?"

"Because Buchanan tried to get into the Lodge I was in, he was blackballed and he didn't take it well."

"Blackballed?" asked Avalon, "is that when one of the members votes no?"

"Exactly," nodded Sands, "and when Buchanan found out he went crazy, the master of the lodge emptied the whole bag on the floor to prove the point, there were two white tokens, all the others were black. Two weeks later he walked into the golf club and announced he was a member of a better club and shot his mouth off about it." Avalon nodded, Buchanan obviously had a temper and that was interesting.

"How long ago was this?" he asked.

"Oh, when I was still there, about five years or so ago," replied Sands.

"So why don't you like him?" asked Avalon wondering if there was something specific.

"I found him unpleasant in just about every way and his attitude to..." Sands looked a little shocked he was saying so much and Avalon felt the man draw back, "...well," he continued, "it doesn't matter what I think does it?" and he pulled open a drawer on his desk and popped a sweet into his mouth. "Would you like a drink DI Avalon?" the man asked, "I know we had our little moment but that was several months ago."

"No, er no thank you," Avalon replied holding up his hands.

"Tea, coffee?" asked Sands.

"No really, but thank you all the same."

"Well I need one," insisted Sands and he rang the small bell on his desk. It wasn't the same one as Avalon had seen before so he assumed the original had probably been broken in frustration. Sands seemed to have trouble getting his staff to react and this time it was no different.

"You were saying... about Jason Buchanan," reiterated Avalon.

"No I wasn't in fact," and Sands attempted a smile. It obviously wasn't something he did often as his face resisted it in every muscle and made him look like a creepy uncle from a nineteen sixties American comedy-horror sitcom.

"Then what about the other lodge?" said Avalon changing tack, "you said he told people he was in another lodge and yet earlier you said it was a club. Are we talking about a 'Hellfire' sort of club?"

"I have no idea what it is, I just know it has some serious sway in many different walks of life."

"Meaning?" asked Avalon. Sands looked over to the doors and rang his little bell once more.

"Just stories, things you hear along the way," replied Sands brushing off the question as he stood.

"Does it have a headquarters or a grand master?" asked Avalon as he watched Sands walk over to the door to the side of his desk. Sands looked back as he opened the door.

"I really have no idea about that as I said," and he turned to face the open doorway and shouted, "*Is there anyone else in this damn house or has everyone left?*" and he slammed the door shut before walking back to his desk, saying calmly, "it's just stories you hear over the years." Avalon began to see that even if Sands did know anything, he wasn't telling and so he stood.

"Well I've taken up enough of your time, but if you hear anything you know where I am." Sands nodded at this just as the small door opened, it was Celine.

"What is it, I'm trying to do my nails?" she frowned.

"Well I did want to offer our guest a drink but it seems I may as well sack the lot of you and get it myself," he raged.

"Oh I'm just one of the staff now am I?" scowled Celine.

"Yes, so get off your widening arse and show our

guest to the door," he continued.

"It's alright," explained Avalon quietly, "I can manage."

"I'll come with you sweetheart, anything to get away from the grumpy bear," she purred and showed Avalon to the hall. At the main door she opened it and turned to Avalon.

"He's not always like this," she explained, "sometimes he's positively horrible," she presented him with the Zebra impersonation once more and then a pouting smile. Avalon nodded and turned to leave and he felt a slight pat on his bottom as he did but by the time he had turned back to her, the door was closed and Celine had gone.

Avalon noticed that he had a text from Carol, it said she would arrive at Inverness Station at eleven fifty-eight on Tuesday morning. He had planned to have Sunday off, he had been considering taking his bike out for a ride, after all the weather was improving but having to meet Carol on Tuesday made him rethink the idea. He might have to take an hour out and get Ross or Wilson to hold the fort, since both Ross and Wilson were to be on call for Sunday, he decided to have a word with the former about it.

"I'll do your cover for Sunday if you like," he said.

"Why, what are you planning?" Ross asked.

"I have to meet Carol off the train on Tuesday so I'll have to have an hour or two off to take her to the house."

"I can do that ef y' want," put in Frazer. Avalon looked round towards her.

"I said I'd meet her at the station though," he explained.

"Well, ef we both meet her, then I can take her round t' the house and you can use those couple o' hours off later," she suggested, "I have to call at Burnet Road sometime on Tuesday anyway."

"Makes sense," agreed Ross, "you can leave early and I'll cover here." Avalon did think it was a better idea, it meant that he could go home in the early afternoon and he could sort out the bed and breakfast with Carol.

"Okay, that sounds like a plan," he nodded.

"I'll go tae Burnet Road in the morning and meet you in one o' the cafés after you pick Carol up at the station," nodded Frazer. Avalon still offered to cover for Ross on Sunday but he said it wasn't worth it, so Avalon could look forward to a bike ride, weather permitting.

As it happened the weather was good but early on Sunday morning Avalon received a text, it said simply, *"Got something, Ness Bank church - noon."* It was Scobie playing his cloak and dagger routine again. That meant his bike ride was off but at least he knew Ness Bank well, it was close to the Castle Tavern and if he had time he might call off there. He sent back a text saying 'happy birthday' and decided to get ready for the meeting.

Avalon made sure he was walking down the hill to Ness Bank at exactly twelve o' clock as he knew Scobie was a little paranoid and could scare off easily. As Avalon walked down towards the river, he could see Scobie sitting on a bench by the church. He casually walked to the bench and sat.

"Mr Avalon," nodded Scobie as he looked round,

"and not en uniform, I hardly recognised yous' ef y' know what a' mean?" he smiled. Smile was probably not an accurate description as Scobie had an irregular face by any standards, he had few teeth and those he had were in poor shape. His ferrety face creased along lines that faces didn't normally crease and the corners of his tiny eye sockets curved down.

"I don't wear a uniform Scobie, I'm a detective remember?" frowned Avalon conscious of his 'off duty' attire.

"You do tae me Mr Avalon," he said looking out towards the river.

"You've got something for me?" Avalon asked.

"Aye, et's not much but et may open a door or two ef y' get ma' drift?"

"Go on," insisted Avalon crossing his leg over his opposite knee.

"This Carlos, he is Lithuanian, but a' don't have a name, a' do have an address though," whispered Scobie and he looked up and down the street before passing a piece of crumpled paper to Avalon.

"Is this good intel Scobie?" Avalon asked glancing at the note.

"This es an address he's known to use ef y' know what a' mean?" and he pushed his hands into his jacket pocket. Avalon read the address again and placed the paper carefully into his own jacket inside pocket.

"If this turns out to be good, I'll owe you," said Avalon.

"You don't owe me Mr Avalon, you've done me a good turn o' two, et's just good tae know that ef 'a need somethin' sorted a' can count on yous'," grinned Scobie.

"To a degree Scobie, my benevolence isn't

boundless and you know where I stand." Scobie nodded and gave a quick glance around the street.

"How did y' go on with Mr Sands," he asked, "or have y' no' had time tae see him?"

"I've spoken with him but it seems Buchanan wasn't in the Masons lodge," explained Avalon with a slight sigh, "it seems he was in some other club." Scobie placed his hands under his knees and shuffled his feet. Avalon noticed he looked down the street rather than give eye contact. "I think you know some more don't you Antony Scobie?" There was no reply, the man kept his gaze towards the river. "Scobie?" growled Avalon.

"I cannae say more Mr Avalon 'cos ef a' did it would give away ma' identity," replied Scobie still not looking at Avalon.

"Why so?" asked Avalon sure he could sort the problem out.

"I worked for Mr Sands through a contact o' mine, he was just drivin' f' him an' I was helpin' out, that's all," explained Scobie.

"Go on," insisted Avalon, Scobie turned and looked at him, "Mr Sands was buying some kit in boxes from Buchanan, I don't know what et was," insisted Scobie, "a' mean I never saw Buchanan, we met a middle man at the unit late at night, my associate said his name was..." Scobie stalled as if he was trying to remember the name, "Gibbs or Gibson, no Gibson."

"First name?"

"A' never knew that," replied Scobie shaking his head, "but the thing es Mr Avalon, ef Sands gets wind o' this he's gonna know et was me or my associate who grassed him up."

"When was this?"

138

"Dunno," shrugged Scobie, "et must be three or four years ago," he paused, "aye definitely twenty-fifteen 'cos et was the same year o' the rugby world cup. A' remember 'cos we were still stingin' after that fiasco with the Aussies."

"And you have no idea what was in the boxes?"

"No," reconfirmed Scobie shaking his head again, "but a few o' them had the name 'Butler Electronics' on 'em, a' remember thinkin' that et was ma' first wife's maiden name." Avalon nodded, he could see Scobie's dilemma but he could also see that Sands knew more than he was saying. He looked out over the river and considered what to do. If he went back to Sands and told him he knew about the business arrangement he had with Buchanan, Sands would know that either Scobie or the driver had opened their mouths, and who was Gibson? His name hadn't appeared on the list of Buchanan's employees, but on the other hand he had nowhere else to go. He would have to give the matter some serious thought.

## Chapter Six

Monday morning meetings in C section were usually brief affairs, Avalon kept a close eye on all the cases running so he very often knew exactly what was going on. It was mainly a time for everyone to know how things were progressing and a chance for Avalon to formulate plans for the week ahead. This particular Monday, however, was to be different. Everyone was assembled and the first cases to go through had been two minor incidents that Frazer and Mackinnon had moved on to, next up was Ross and Rutherford and then Wilson and Boyd finished off. Their only real result on their case was from Antony Scobie's snippet of information, it had proved to be worthwhile indeed.

"So will it make a difference?" asked Avalon.

"We think et will, we're working with DS Murrey and DC King from B Section on a stakeout at the address and we have already identified a suspect we think could be this 'Carlos'," explained Wilson. Avalon gave a slight nod.

"Good," he said, "and finally the Buchanan case." Avalon looked down at the desk and then up to the whiteboard on the other side of the room. "Unless something crops up with any significance I think we'll have to shelve this one," he looked back to the team, "as far as I can see, there is still no crime as of yet to connect Jason Buchanan to, so though there are a few mysteries, we must continue to treat this as a missing person case."

"I had an email this morning," announced Ross, "from Hendry at forensics."

"And?" shrugged Avalon folding his arms.

"The deep sweep of the car found in the container has come up with a few items," explained Ross, "no DNA or at least not enough for a test but green fibres were found on the driver's door-card where someone had to squeeze out through the open window. There are also some signs of mud, a few pollen seeds and two partial finger prints."

"So nothing to further the investigation yet?" asked Avalon.

"Not as such," agreed Ross, "but a little note that Hendry included got me thinking. He put, 'obviously not cleaned by the same person that did the house', and though he was probably making a joke, it piqued my interest."

"You mean, if the car was cleaned by a different person to the people who did the house, there are several individuals involved?" suggested Avalon.

"Not just that," added Ross, "and I admit this is pure conjecture, if you really wanted to get rid of a car and any evidence within, you would do what most people do."

"Torch et," insisted Frazer.

"Exactly," agreed Ross turning to her for a moment, "but if I had a car like that, I wouldn't want to see it go up in flames, I might consider hiding it."

"Which means Buchanan was probably

responsible for cleaning and hiding it himself," nodded Avalon rubbing his chin.

"Which means that he probably didn't clean the house," concluded Ross.

"The wife?" suggested Frazer.

"No," said Ross shaking his head, "I doubt that, she doesn't seem bright enough to sustain a lie, I think she wasn't in the loop over this."

"So who does that leave?" asked Avalon refolding his arms.

"What ef someone else is running this?" suggested Wilson, he and Boyd hadn't been involved in the case but he was already picking up the pieces and putting the jigsaw together.

"You mean someone is pulling Buchanan's strings?" asked Avalon.

"Sounds a wee bit like et tae me," nodded Wilson. Avalon jutted out his jaw and raised his brows, he obviously saw that the pieces could fit.

"It looks possible but our problem is that, apart from Buchanan going missing, we have no real justification to follow this up, no crime - no time," insisted Avalon.

"Can't we find a small crime in this so we can keep it alive?" suggested Ross.

"We could try the electronics company, the records might stand a better going through?" put in Frazer. Avalon thought for a moment, maybe they could find something there but Avalon wanted to question Charlie Sands further, if Scobie had told him the true story, Sands had more to tell.

"Okay," he eventually said, "let's do a little more digging, nothing too obvious, we'll keep it 'as and when' we get time." He looked towards Frazer and Mackinnon. "Have a look through the company records, a bit deeper this time, particularly anything connected to Butler Electronics, and try to get the forensics computer tech to talk to the foreman there." Frazer nodded. Avalon remembered something. "Oh and see if anyone there knows an individual who goes by the name of Gibbs or Gibson." He turned to Ross. "You and Martin try and arrange a visit to Mrs Buchanan, ask her why she lied about her husband staying there two nights before the note was found. And then ask why the solicitor was seen there." Ross nodded and said,

"We'll try to get over this afternoon."

"Er boss," it was Frazer, she was looking at her computer screen.

"Megan?"

"John Mirriam Gibson, born third of September nineteen seventy-nine, got previous for receiving, shoplifting and fraud, all minor cases prior to nineteen ninety-eight. Worked for the Highland Council until he moved to Inverness where he took a position as Management Accountant." Frazer was reading through the record and obviously reading relevant information, "current address, Nevis Park, Kinmylies, current employer, Lawrence Hilliard." There was silence for a moment until Avalon asked,

"What would an accounts employee for Lawrence Hilliard be doing selling electronics for Jason Buchanan I wonder?"

"Who says he was?" asked Ross with surprise. For a moment Avalon was lost in thought and then shook free to answer the question.

"It's something I picked up, I heard the name

mentioned and if it *is* the same Gibson, then this opens things up a little."

"Well yes," nodded Ross, "a link between Buchanan, Hilliard and Cameron makes quite a difference."

"But the fact still remains," insisted Frazer, "there es no crime to investigate."

"Well," sighed Avalon unfolding his arms, "that's true so we have to dig around until something shows up," he raised his brows and added, "Megan, if there's an image of Gibson, print one off for me," and he paused, "okay, carry on," and then returned to the booth. He was soon followed by Frazer.

"I have a confession tae make," she said with a troubled look in her eyes. It worried Avalon for a moment.

"Go on I'm listening," he said tentatively.

"I know you said we had tae discount anything attached t' Buchanan's past but I did a bit o' pokin' about," she began to bite her bottom lip.

"I see," sighed Avalon staring right at her, "so I'm guessing by the fact that you are admitting this you have found something."

"Sort of," she frowned, "I'm just not sure we can do anything with et."

"Well, we better have a look at it then," said Avalon with an even deeper frown.

"Et's about the case where he was implicated in the attack in the alley near the nightclub," she began, I looked through the case and tae be honest it's a shambles."

"In what way?" asked Avalon.

"Tae start with, there was forensic evidence

found on the girl, a strand of hair, a tiny speck o' blood and a footprint on her skirt which had blood on et," she began to explain, "the problem es that the blood was mixed with that of the victim and couldn't be separated due tae the lack of et," she continued. Avalon saw excitement in her features, this was what Frazer did best. "the hair had the same problem, et was a broken stem and forensics couldn't extract enough DNA tae be a hundred percent sure."

"So I'm guessing you found something out or this conversation might be pointless?" asked Avalon.

"Last year," she continued, "the solicitor for Thomas McVie, the man who confessed to the crime, opened up the case saying his client was innocent and he had proof. He was insistent that his client was delusional at the time and new DNA techniques could prove him innocent."

"Sounds like he was clutching at straws," interrupted Avalon.

"Not at all," explained Frazer, "McVie has a less popular blood group, he was B, and as the blood found at the scene was B, et was seen as a good match. It was stated at the time that Buchanan had blood group O, so et put him out of the picture. But," she insisted, "and et es a big but, when the new technique was put under scrutiny, et was found that the process isn't perfected and as there was so little DNA material available, the police decided until the technique was proven to work en all cases the material should be preserved for the future."

"Sounds like a whitewash, didn't the solicitor appeal?" asked Avalon.

"He did but what es interesting, Cameron's office got involved and seem to put every spanner en the works they could, they even sent case studies done en the USA to discredit the new techniques."

"Interesting certainly, but is there a smoking gun?"

"Not really, but the doctor who examined the girl said that the instrument used to stun her left a very specific pattern on her skin, it seems Buchanan's company, MMS, were making a device similar for export," shrugged Frazer, "but ef Buchanan's blood group is O, why was the solicitor getting involved in this?"

"It looks like he doesn't want the case re-opening I would think."

"That's what I thought," nodded Frazer, "but is it possible to fake your blood group?"

"No," said Avalon with conviction, "but money greasing palms can get it altered I suppose."

"We need tae see his medical records then," insisted Frazer.

"Unless there is something concrete that is never going to be an option," sighed Avalon, "so we need to find something else."

"Aye, I realise that but I was wonderin' ef an interview with McVie and the victims may shed some light?"

"Possibly but I'd be more interested to know who the team was who worked on this."

"You mean from our end?" asked Frazer, "I know that, et was DSs McGill and Nicholls under DI Davies when he ran B Section."

"Obviously Davies and McGill have retired but DS Nicholls is still in B Section, we need to have a few words with him at some stage but we'll tuck it away for

146

now," insisted Avalon. Frazer nodded and returned to her desk. She was tenacious and Avalon knew she would probably dig further, whether he gave his blessing or not. For now, Avalon knew he needed to speak to Sands once more.

"I'll be out for a couple of hours," he called to Wilson pulling his jacket on. He noticed Ross looking up expectantly but he ignored it, he had to do this alone if he was to get Sands to open up.

~~~~~~

"Hello sweetheart," beamed Celine, "back again already?"

"Yes, I did call, he said he would see me," confirmed Avalon.

"Yes, come in love, he's with a..." she seemed to be choosing her words carefully, "a business associate I think, he'll not be long," she pouted pointing to a chair in the hall. "Would you like a drink while you wait sweetheart?" she asked bending over him slightly.

"No thanks," replied Avalon holding up a hand with a smile. He could see she wanted to fuss around him but Avalon just wanted to deal with the business at hand and leave.

"He asked me to look after you but if I can't get you anything..."

"No I'm fine really," insisted the DI, "I'll just wait for him if that's alright?"

"Course love," she purred, "mind you he'll probably be in a foul temper if he's with one of his 'business' interests," and she sat in, what looked to be, an original Louis the Fifteenth chair. "but then again he's always grumpy I suppose," she added wistfully looking at her nails.

"So what's the attraction then?" asked Avalon knowing that the answer was really the money.

"With Charlie?" she asked taken by surprise a little. She shrugged and said, "In those rare moments when he's content, he's kind, thoughtful and compassionate. That's rare in a man," she said as she looked into space but suddenly came to her senses and added, "no that's rude of me," she smiled and touched his knee, "I'm sure you are too sweetheart." She was about to ask him something but one of the double doors opened to Sands' quarters and a suited man walked out. The man looked over to the two of them, raised his brows, gave the briefest of smiles and left. Avalon didn't recognise him but kept a mental picture just in case.

"I'll see if he's ready love," said Celine and she waddled off to check. She soon came back and smiled at him holding her arm outstretched towards the open door. Avalon made his way to the door as Celine left by another route.

"You're spending more time here than me lately, what is it this time?" asked Sands pointing to the chair.

"I'll not sit Mr Sands, my visit will be brief, on our last meeting you told me you had nothing to do with Jason Buchanan and yet I find several people who swear you have done business with him in the past." Avalon was edging his bets with 'several people' to try and protect Scobie. Sands looked genuinely taken aback by the comment but Avalon saw a slight realisation creep over his face.

"It was the truth Detective Avalon, I have never directly done any sort of business with Buchanan," he

148

insisted.

"Somehow I don't believe you Mr Sands," frowned Avalon, "I did think after our last conversation you may have been ready to help but it seems your reputation is well founded."

"Reputation?" spat Sands, and he lurched forward in his seat, "reputation?" he called and banged his hands on the desk as he stood. "Let me tell you about reputation detective," and he seemed to calm slightly as he slowly sat again. Avalon wasn't fazed by the outburst but he considered that Sands may at last have had something to say and so he too sat. Sands was still glaring at Avalon but his scowl began to gradually subside as he spoke.

"I was born in Glasgow to parents that shared their home with another family. When I was thirteen we moved south to the Midlands to escape the poverty. My father went to work in the mines and when I was sixteen I joined him at the pit face." Sands seemed calm now and he swivelled his chair to look out of the windows,

"My dad developed a lung disease and died at the age of sixty, hardly able to speak or breathe at the end. Then came the miner's strike, I can't remember why but I decided to go on picket duty, I suppose because we got three quid if we turned up and apart from handouts that's all we got to live on. I had a wife and a young family and it was hard." Sands was shaking his head slowly as he looked through the windows. He then turned back to Avalon and his face was a picture of abstract anger.

"You probably won't believe me when I tell you we did nothing but peaceful picketing and yet we were persecuted by the police. The police, the courts and the government broke the laws they are supposed to uphold, 'win at any cost' was their mantra. Yet we weren't allowed to, it was a one-sided war. My temper broke when this copper punched me in the stomach, I was naive and I decided enough was enough so I retaliated and was arrested. When I went to court they already had witnesses ready and coppers working from a script. I was fitted up for things I didn't even know the name of. I spent ten months in the nick but by then my wife had gone. I don't blame her, she couldn't let the wean starve." He gave a big sigh and looked to the floor, after a few moments he looked up and seemed to compose himself. "With my life in tatters I decided that the 'system' was the enemy and there was no such thing as a good copper. I still believed that when I came back north to start a new life, and though I was far from being a crook, I hated the police so much any dealing with them ensured I got a bad reputation. My reputation was an invention by the police, just like the crimes I was supposed to have committed all those years ago." He stopped talking and pushed his hands into his pockets.

"I'm not a model citizen detective, not by any stretch of the imagination but for my one and only time in the nick, it was a complete fabrication by the police. That's how you get a reputation detective, by hating the system, not by committing crimes." He stood and walked to the windows.

"So now I've taken on the mantra that the system gave me, 'win at any cost'. Now get out and don't come back here unless you have a warrant." Avalon sighed, it hadn't gone as he expected. He noticed Sands take a handkerchief from his pocket and lift his spectacles. Avalon stood.

"I'm quite aware what went off during the miners

strike Mr Sands, but all coppers can't be held accountable for a corrupt government. I can at least promise you that under my small sphere of influence, no such injustice will ever happen."

"That's good to know, but it doesn't rid the rest of us of the scars," said Sands replacing the handkerchief to his pocket, "or an undeserved reputation," he added, "I started to live by the reputation they gave me, I've broken the law since, I've done things I regret, but I have never compromised my beliefs, I never killed, I never bullied. The police don't have the higher moral ground over me and never will."

"Possibly not, but without information we have our hands tied, we can only make a difference if we know the truth." There was silence and Avalon stared at Sands silhouetted in the large windows. He looked around the room, he didn't know if Sands had told him the truth but if he had, he had done well for himself yet the house, the cars and the money didn't seem to have made him a happy man, to Sands the loss of a life that might have been had broken him. Avalon walked towards the door.

"Is this meeting still off the record?" Sands asked.

"Of course," replied Avalon looking back, his hand already on the door handle. Sands replaced his spectacles and turned to face him.

"You better take a seat then detective."

~~~~~~

Avalon strolled up to Ross's desk as the DS leaned back in his chair.

"How's it going?" he asked.

"Pretty good but no leads on the Buchanan inquiry, the only thing we now know is the stuff Buchanan's company was making was micro cameras. They fit tiny video cameras into everyday objects like TV remote units and fountain pens. State-of-the-art tech for surveillance. They brand it as 'spy equipment' and sell most of it abroad," Ross then glanced over to Frazer's desk, "Frazer and Mackinnon are still out," he shrugged.

"I've got a snippet or two but nothing concrete," admitted Avalon.

"Really?" replied Ross leaning back, "let's hear then."

"This John Gibson was helping Buchanan cook his books, it seems that the company was making three to four times what it was declaring to the taxman and running with two sets of books. Gibson was freelancing that side as Buchanan wasn't too hot with accounts."

"He's not the only one with inventive accounting though is he?" suggested Ross.

"No he isn't," nodded Avalon as he perched on the edge of the desk, "but unknown to Buchanan, several people were ripping him off, one of them being Gibson. Gibson was selling some of the goods that were earmarked for Butler Electronics to other people, the foreman probably knew about it but as Buchanan is universally hated no one gave a damn."

"So Butler Electronics is a fake company made by Buchanan to help cook the books?" asked Ross.

"Yes, but it made it easy for people to rip him off while he was playing golf or spending time with prostitutes," explained Avalon.

"So does this help us?" asked Ross.

"Not much, it means we can officially bring all the accounts in that we can find and check through them but it's not going to lead us to Buchanan," frowned Avalon, "unless we lean on John Gibson."

"I would think that would be easy enough, by all accounts Buchanan has some nasty friends," said Ross raising his brows, "I would think Gibson wouldn't want this getting out."

"I'm not sure," replied Avalon still frowning, "Gibson had the balls to rip Buchanan off in the first place."

"We can find time to see him tomorrow if you like?" suggested Ross with a questioning look.

"Yeah, give it a go, bring him in though if you can, make it look a bit more serious than it is," said Avalon and he looked up at the clock.

"Eager for the off?" asked Ross with a slight grin.

"I was just wondering how the house looks now Ollie has been finishing off there," replied Avalon.

"Oh yeah, of course," nodded Ross, "it's today she makes your house into a home so to speak." Avalon nodded unenthusiastically and returned towards the booth just as Frazer and Mackinnon entered. Avalon paused and watched Frazer enter, she looked over to him and raised her brows.

"So what have you got?" he asked.

"Well I managed to get somethin' nearer the truth from Mrs Buchanan," she explained. Rory sat at his desk and Avalon noticed he wasn't quite as comfortable as he had been earlier, had Frazer used heavy-handed tactics with Mrs Buchanan? He hoped not.

"I'm all ears," said Avalon resting on one of the side tables.

"She told us that she hadn't been staying at the house on a regular basis, just now and then," Frazer began.

"Marital problems I'm guessing," nodded Avalon.

"Aye, y' could say that," continued Frazer, "though she says ef Buchanan was having an affair she didn't know who et was. She admitted she *was* though and after a wee bit of persuasion," Avalon glanced at Rory as she spoke but there was no sign that the 'persuasion' was dramatic, "she told us who et was." She ended for a moment and took out her notepad and read from it. "A guy called Connall Holmes, I don't think he has any links tae anyone, he once worked for Buchanan as a driver but Buchanan didn't like him so he was sacked," and she closed the notepad and pushed it back into her jacket pocket, "but the eye opener," she continued looking directly at Avalon, "es the fact that Mrs Buchanan had an affair with Cameron."

"The solicitor?" asked Avalon with some surprise.

"Aye the very same," she nodded and sat at her desk, "et seems she broke et off because she thought her husband had some suspicions."

"This inquiry certainly has its twist and turns," frowned Avalon looking back to Rory. The young DC felt the gaze and looked up, he took it as a sign that he ought to say something.

"She wants to make a full statement boss so we brought her in," he began a little uneasily, "she's downstairs."

"We'll get off and interview her ef that's okay?"

154

added Frazer.

"Yes fine," nodded Avalon, "I just want a word with Rory, he can meet you down there," Frazer nodded and left. Rory followed Avalon into the booth.

"How did the interview go?" asked Avalon pointing to the seat opposite his desk.

"Fine boss, I was surprised how easily we got the woman to talk," replied Mackinnon with a neutral look.

"So Megan didn't give her a hard time then?" he asked as subtly as he could.

"Well she's pretty plain talking," smiled Rory, "not the methods I would use but much more effective," the smile remained on his face and so Avalon felt that all must have gone well.

"I want you to give me an honest answer," said Avalon with a sterner face, "do you think you are learning from her and are you happy to stick with her for a while?" he asked making it seem like this was the point in the interview.

"Oh yeah," nodded Rory, "she's quiet most of the time, but I don't have a problem with that. She does things in a different way to anyone else and like I say, not the way I would work but it gives me a chance to see how someone with Megan's experience works their trade."

"Well that's good," nodded Avalon, "I just didn't want you to think I had forgotten about you," and he gave a brief smile, "well you better get off, you don't want to raise her ire."

"Certainly not boss," smiled Rory standing, "her anger is legendary," he announced and left. Her anger was legendary and that's what troubled him about Frazer, it was his only doubt and that's why he had to ask

Mackinnon about the interview. He also knew Frazer would ask Rory about the little interview *they* had just had and so he had to make it seem like he was checking on how the partnership was going, rather than him checking up on her methods.

Avalon decided to go and talk to Mrs Buchanan before she left the station. The interview was over, she had signed a statement and was drinking a coffee with PC MacLaine attending to her. Avalon knocked on the door to the interview room, which was wide open. MacLaine nodded to Avalon as he entered.

"I hear you wished to speak to me," she said as he came to the table.

"Yes, just a couple of questions," he said as upbeat as he could and sat opposite her and nodded to MacLaine. She understood that to mean 'wait in the corridor,' so she left.

"Thank you for making a statement," he said.

"In many ways I feel better for it detective, my life in recent times has been a mixed bag of pretending and lies," she explained placing the coffee cup on the table.

"Sometimes, shaking free of pretence can be very therapeutic."

"You had questions for me," she asked looking into his eyes for the first time.

"Yes," he nodded, "I understand you have stated that you really have no idea where your husband might be?"

"Yes, that's in the statement," she sighed.

"We think that he's been carving money from the business in order to create a sort of secret 'slush fund' and he's probably been doing it for some years," he let the statement sink in before continuing, "might you have any idea where this money had been kept, any other bank accounts or safe deposit boxes?"

"If you say he has then I can't argue, but I really don't know where he's put the money," she shook her head and then looked to the floor.

"One more question then Mrs Buchanan," he began and she looked up again, "we believe he was involved in some way with a club, a sort of secret society similar to the Freemasons," he saw a hint of recognition, "do you know anything about it?"

"He loves secrets, he always wanted to become a Mason, I thought it was ridiculous but it's so him," and she looked to the floor once again before adding, "I don't know what it was called or anything about it but he had some cufflinks made that were supposed to have the emblem of the club on them." She stared back to him, her eyes looked tired yet he could now see she was a very striking woman.

"Can you recall the emblem?" asked Avalon.

"Yes it was a thistle," she replied with conviction.

"That's quite a common emblem up here Mrs Buchanan," he shrugged.

"It was what you call..." she paused trying to think of the word, "sort of Celtic," she screwed up her nose slightly still not sure of the word she was thinking, "but not, sort of simple..." she trailed off.

"Stylised?" asked Avalon.

"Yes, that was the word," she seemed relieved Avalon had offered the suggestion.

"Could you sketch it for us?" he asked.

"I'm no artist," she demanded.

"It doesn't have to be accurate, just something we can work with," he gave a slight smile but she didn't return it.

"I could try."

Twenty minutes later Avalon had a pencil sketch by Mrs Buchanan and an improved version by Sergeant Gregory from the front desk who wasn't too shoddy with a pencil it seemed. Gregory had improved the sketch until Mrs Buchanan was sure it was a fairly close representation of what she had witness on her husband's cufflinks. He then made a short walk down two corridors and a flight of steps to the divisional office to ask if there was an expert on Scottish Insignia. He was told that a Professor Dale Thorburn, who lectured for the University of the Highlands and Islands, was probably the best bet. Avalon returned to the Cave and rang the man but there was no reply, so he left a message.

~~~~~~

Avalon felt slightly uneasy as he arrived home. It was late afternoon and as he slid out of the car and looked towards the house, it seemed just the same as it did when he left it that morning. The only sign that PC Olivia Kirk had been at work was that, as he looked into the conservatory, he could see a small vase on the table with some kind of flowers in it. That and the fact that he was several thousand pounds the poorer. He pushed the key into the lock of the back door and entered, the first thing that struck him was the smell. In place of a neutral 'carpet' sort of smell there was a stronger, harsher aroma, not unpleasant though, a mix between new clothes and the smell you get in a new car. He closed the door carefully behind him and looked into the conservatory where he noticed little had changed. He didn't know if the flowers in the vase were scented, as the other smells were prominent but he did notice the small rug had gone and the floor was just tiles and there was a shade around the light fitting. He then moved into the kitchen where, once again, the change wasn't great. Another vase of flowers stood in the windowsill and a new rack had been fitted to the wall with several utensils and items he didn't know the name of hung in regimented order. The biggest transformation was in the lounge where a huge looking sofa and an easy chair seemed to be relaxing themselves in the room. New curtains, with an ornate pelmet above, hugged the window and a substantial bookcase sat on the far wall. He then noticed that his box of poetry books had been removed and the books placed on the shelves in alphabetical order. Not how he would have stacked them but it looked tidy. The stereo was now on a proper rack and his guitar was on a guitar stand, not just leaning against the wall. There were several new ornaments, there was what looked like a brass oil lamp, a Newton's Cradle and several new pictures which included prints of poets. On the mantel above the fire was a box covered in wrapping paper. It had a note tied to it and he removed it and read it to himself.

"*I hope you don't mind but some of us chipped in and had this made as a house warming gift.*" Avalon gave a slight smile to himself and began to unwrap the gift. It was a fabulous piece, probably eight or nine inches across, that had a painted thumbprint on one side, and a carved hand growing out of the other. The hand was holding a real magnifying glass suspended above the thumbprint. Avalon grinned and shook his head when he saw it and he placed it back on the mantel. There was a new rug in front of the fireplace and an occasional table with a pretty lamp on it. He was amazed how the room had changed, he could see himself staying in at night much more. The rest of the house was well done too with a new double bed in the rear room, which Avalon took a shine to as soon as he saw it. It looked much more acceptable than his cheap single in the front room. He did the tour twice and then sent a text to Kirk saying,

"I love the house, fabulous, I'm not altering a thing, and the gift is excellent." Returning to the kitchen he noticed the kettle was new, after all the old one looked pretty shabby and there was a wooden wine rack, not that he had any wine. He pulled a bottle of beer out of the fridge and placed it on the rack just because he could. Something then occurred to him and for a moment he wondered why he hadn't noticed it. Kirk was a compulsive practical joker and he was considering that he hadn't come across anything out of the ordinary in that respect. It suddenly came to him that Kirk had both a sense of humour and a good memory and the two things together gave Avalon the clue he needed. At once he knew where to look and he scanned the kitchen units until he came to the one that he hadn't yet found a use for. He knew it would be there even before he opened the door and sure enough, there on the top shelf, standing alone in an otherwise empty space was a single tin of spaghetti hoops. He smiled again, shook his head and closed the cupboard, he then reached for the bottle of beer and a glass and went into the lounge to christen the new sofa. From his reclining position he felt at home at last and as his head swivelled around the room he smiled at how well Kirk had done, she seemed to know him better than he could have imagined and he suddenly thought about what Ross had said. Kirk liked him he already knew that and he liked her but was Ross anywhere near the truth about how the hard working PC felt about him. He didn't think so. Olivia Kirk was a 'driven' person, she loved her job and she liked her friends, all of them, not just Avalon, she was an intense person. If she liked you she loved you, if she didn't like you, well, you had to be careful. Thoughts about Kirk brought Avalon to a more immediate subject.

At around noon the following day, Avalon was to meet his ex-wife Carol for the first time in two years, he felt a little uncomfortable with it too. He then considered that although he was able to deal with criminals and murderers, he struggled with people he knew. Did he have some kind of flawed mental state that prevented him from connecting to decent people? Was that why he was a good detective? He finished the last of the beer and took the bottle and the glass back to the kitchen and looked out into the twilight. For some reason he knew he had reached a crossroads, he knew it was time to make some decisions about his life. He had changed drastically since he had last seen Carol, not just his lifestyle but the way he thought had changed. Maybe it was the job, maybe it was Scotland but the Avalon of the West Midlands was a very different animal to the Avalon of the Highlands. The more he thought about that, the more he knew he didn't want to reverse that course. He sighed and walked back to the lounge, dropping himself into the comfort of the sofa and tried to work out who he really was and what he wanted from life. It was obvious to him in many ways, he was now Scottish and he knew he would never be going back to England. No longer did he have to store away the old Avalon just in case he needed it, to revert back to the Avalon that everyone expected him to be. He was James Avalon, 'Detective Inspector James Avalon' and for the first time since he arrived in Scotland, that thought made him smile.

## Chapter Seven

The desk phone rang and both the detectives looked down at the source of the intrusion. Avalon reached for it.

"Just a mo," he said to Ross sitting opposite, "Avalon!"

"*DI Avalon, it's Dowd, there's a chap on the phone, say's you wanted to talk to him,*" said the voice.

"Who is it?"

"Say's his name is Dale Thorburn," replied Dowd. For a moment Avalon couldn't place the name and then it struck.

"Oh, yes, can you put him through Neil?"

"*Yeah, just a second,*" replied Dowd, there was a click and another voice spoke.

"*DI Avalon, it's Dale Thorburn, you wanted to speak with me I believe?*"

"Yes professor, it's about a Scottish insignia I would like you to try and identify, can I send it over to show you?" asked Avalon.

"*Of course, I can't guarantee that I can help but I'll take a look at it, I'm not far from you in actual fact, if you get time you could always bring it round,*" the voice said. Avalon jotted down the address, it was Inverness

Campus, he hadn't been but he knew where it was.

"Are you in at the moment," he asked, "it will only take me five minutes to reach you?"

"*Er, yes, of course. I'll look forward to seeing you.*" Avalon replaced the phone and looked up to Ross.

"We'll go through this later, I need to speak with an expert on insignia, it seems he's just round the corner," explained Avalon pointing to the case notes on his desk. Ross nodded and Avalon saw the expectant look. "Coming with?" he added as he pulled on his jacket. Ross gave a single nod and stood and they left for the car park.

The Professor met them at the door to the building on the Campus and led them to a small office as Avalon introduced Ross. He was much younger than Avalon expected, in his mind all professors looked like a cross between Albert Einstein and Emmett Brown from the 'Back to the Future' movies. This man was slightly younger than Avalon and looked more like a student than a professor.

"I lecture in military history," the man explained, "mainly Scottish history so I may not be able to help."

"If you would just cast your eye over it I would be grateful," smiled Avalon. The man had a gentle Scottish accent but had been flooded with so many other dialects over time, the original was almost wholly gone, replaced by that ubiquitous college dialect that Avalon had learned to identify from experience. Avalon unfolded the sketch of the insignia that Mrs Buchanan had overseen and laid it on a table for the professor to examine.

"Well, it's not military as such but I have seen it before," he said lifting the wire-rimmed spectacles to the top of his head.

"So you know what it is?" asked Avalon.

"I think so," nodded the man glancing down for a second, "it's not perfectly accurate but easy to see what it's supposed to be," he added. He pulled his spectacles back over his eyes and picked up the sketch. "The thistle is used as the basis for many Scottish clubs, regiments and groups but the stylised, Celtic knot work tells me this is a sketch of the badge of the 'Order of the Black Thistle'."

"I thought the Order of the Thistle was to do with royalty?" asked Ross.

"You're thinking of the order founded by King James the Seventh in 1687," replied Thorburn.

"Am I?" asked Ross with a frown.

"Er... yes," stuttered Thorburn for a moment, "it was an order he formed, probably as a whim to confirm his Scottish roots," he paused and then flattened out the sketch on the table once more, "*this* however is something very different," he added pointing to the sketch.

"It is military then?" asked Avalon.

"Not really, no," answered Thorburn shaking his head, "its origins come from a military background but in some ways it's the exact opposite."

"You better explain," sighed Avalon.

"It's a long story as I understand it but I'll try to keep it brief," said the professor as he sat and suggested they did the same. He pushed his spectacles back off his face and crossed his legs.

"The order was formed by an officer of the 79th Regiment of Foot, otherwise known as the Cameron Highlanders. They had an unblemished record all through their career but there was a little known incident during the Peninsular War that history has all but forgotten."

"So this is part of the Napoleonic Campaign?" asked Ross.

"Indeed, you could say that," agreed the professor, "the regiment was deployed to Portugal in 1808 and took part in the Battle of Corunna in 1809. The battle, and the retreat before it, was a complete failure and the morale of the British troops had broken on several occasions. It wasn't that the troops were cowards, they just saw that the poor management of the campaign was costing lives for no reason and the terrible attitude to the injured and dying started the ordinary foot soldier to think about his place in the army." Thorburn stopped for breath, "The regiment was evacuated with the rest of the army to England but returned to Portugal in 1810 and took part in the Battle of Bussaco and the year after, the Battle of Fuentes de Onoro. This was a disaster for the 79th Foot. The French wiped out two whole companies of the regiment and killed the regiment's commander, Lieutenant-Colonel Phillips Cameron and only a concerted counter attack relieved the situation." Thorburn noticed DS Ross fidget, he was obviously bored with the account and so the professor tried to speed it up.

"A popular Major of the 79th named Mortimer Hume, was so dismayed by the fact that the dead and dying were left where they dropped and the injured were left out in the open to die of their wounds, some without water, he decided that the time had come to act. Morale was still not fully recovered and he sensed unease throughout the army. He was so appalled by the poor treatment of injured men that he spoke to other officers about it. It didn't help that most of the army considered that Wellington had made a terrible miscalculation during the campaign prior to the battle. Several lower ranking officers under the leadership of Hume made official complaints about the treatment of the men soon after." Thorburn looked into Avalon's eyes, he could see even the DI was getting impatient. "To cut the story short gentlemen, some of the officers took to wearing black armbands, though at the time it was seen as an act of defiance. This escalated to the ordinary foot soldier and soon spread to other regiments, and though some reparations were meted out, the armbands continued to appear." Thorburn paused for a moment, he was thinking through the main points of the story he had read from letters written at the time.

"The senior officers knew something had to be done and action was eventually taken by one of the generals, who insisted that the matter was being addressed with promises of better conditions for injured men. It's doubtful anything was actually ever done to help the men but Hume was sent back to Scotland and four men from the 79th were singled out as ringleaders and flogged. They were returned to their regiments after being demoted of any rank they held. The matter was all but forgotten, the British Army managed to stop yet another mutiny and Hume was eventually dishonourably discharged to get him out of the way. He fought on however and formed the Order of the Black Thistle to try to help injured soldiers returning to Britain."

"So it was like the Chelsea pensioners?" asked Avalon.

"I suppose that's a good comparison," nodded

Thorburn, "but without any official support or patronage."

"How did Wellington view this, is there any record?" asked Avalon with a little more interest in the story than Ross.

"The dissension was only seen in a few regiments and never became an important issue, it's likely Wellington never even got to hear about it. It did however resurface after the Battle of Salamanca when black arm-bands were seen once more, though there is no record of any retribution."

"Was it just Scottish regiments that were affected?" asked Avalon.

"From what can be read from letters of the time it seems it wasn't, but as the whole thing originally stemmed from the 79th, the movement became known as The Black Clan due to the armbands and the Scottish connection."

"Not the Order of the Black Thistle?" asked Ross.

"Major Hume gave it that name," explained Thorburn, "at the time the soldiers probably knew it as the Black Clan, that was something they could identify with, Chivalric Orders were solely the domain of gentlemen not foot soldiers. There is also some evidence that the ideal of it continued to exist and the armbands appeared during the Crimean Campaign."

"So why would this insignia reappear here in Inverness so long after the men who were involved were long dead do you think?" inquired Avalon.

"Because the order still exists, would be my guess detective," shrugged Thorburn, "most of these kind of groups can exist for many years, or even be re-invented." Avalon glanced over to Ross who raised his brows, "It probably doesn't have the same aims as it did originally but I can see that there is a likelihood that something like this could even have resurfaced as late as the Great War," continued Thorburn.

"Do you have evidence of this Professor?" asked Ross.

"There are a few photographs," nodded Thorburn, "a famous one of the Seaforth Highlanders showing a stretcher-bearer wearing what looks like a black band on his sleeve."

"To what purpose could such an organisation be used for today do you think?" asked Avalon not sure if the professor was telling all.

"I really don't know," replied the man shaking his head, "it remained secret for all those years so you would have to ask someone who had been in it."

"Is there anything more you can tell us?" he asked.

"There is one thing but at the time I just shrugged it off as coincidental," frowned Thorburn, "but after your visit..." he broke off for a moment. "I was doing some research in Belgium five or so years ago and I decided to go and look at the war graves at Langemark. As I was strolling through reading the names of the fallen, I noticed two thistles laid on two separate headstones," he paused and seemed slightly unsure if he should mention it, "both headstones were from soldiers of the Queens Own Cameron Highlanders," he paused again then explained, "the 79th Foot's name during the Great War," he paused once more and sat up before he continued. "The two thistles were black, totally black and had obviously been dried and then dipped in ink or stain, but the whole thing was black."

"Thank you for the information professor Thorburn," began Avalon standing and holding out his hand, "you have been a great help," and they shook hands.

"I'm glad I could be of some service," smiled Thorburn.

"Am I correct in assuming that the 79th Foot was a local regiment then?" asked Avalon as an afterthought.

"Oh yes," nodded Thorburn removing his spectacles from his head and placing them in his jacket pocket, "it was originally raised at Fort George and the Cameron Barracks in Inverness was the depot of the regiment in many of its forms. It's just around the corner from here."

"Thank you once again and if you think of anything else, you know where to find us," smiled Avalon and they left. Once they were back in the car Avalon sat motionless glaring through the windscreen.

"Well at least we know the whole history of the British army," said Ross with a sigh.

"We know something else too," insisted Avalon looking round at Ross, "we know we're looking for an organisation called The Black Clan."

"Or the Order of the Black Thistle," added Ross.

"More likely the former," said Avalon starting the car, "it sounds more in keeping with a secret club."

"So Buchanan is a member and it's likely that Trevor Cameron is too," suggested Ross, "he even has the name for it."

"It's looking likely but let's not get ahead of ourselves just yet," insisted Avalon, "I think we should lean on Cameron and see what he does."

"Lean, how?" asked Ross.

"Ask him if we can have a chat about The Black Clan?" suggested Avalon glancing over with a grin.

"If you're sure?" replied Ross taking his phone from his pocket and he phoned Frazer to make an appointment with Trevor Cameron to discuss The Black Clan. As he put his phone away Avalon suddenly said,

"Shit!"

"What is it?" asked Ross with alarm.

"Carol, I have to meet her in three minutes," he retorted glancing at his watch.

"Light and horns?" asked Ross reaching for the switch for the siren and blue lights.

"No," replied the DI with a sigh, "we're not far off now, I'll stop at the car park and you take the car back," he suggested.

"You gonna walk back?" asked Ross with surprise.

"No, I'm meeting Megan at the café first so you get off back."

Avalon was three minutes late, luckily the train was five minutes late as he noticed looking up at the display board. Inverness Railway Station being a terminus has a broad waiting area and seeing the train from Edinburgh was scheduled to arrive at platform two he made his way there and waited for it to arrive. He leaned on the barrier and wondered if Carol would look any different, he wondered if he would look different to her. He suddenly felt self-conscious about his working suit and wished he had time to change to something more casual... and then he smiled. He shook his head to himself wondering why he was suddenly feeling that way and he took a turn

171

around the station area to relax himself. He didn't need to impress her but old habits die hard, he looked around at other people who were obviously also waiting for the Edinburgh train to arrive. Maybe parents, friends sweethearts and wives, waiting for loved ones whom they probably hadn't seen for some time. It sobered his thoughts, he didn't have that in his life, there was no worry about having to say goodbye to a loved one for extended periods, he was self-contained and at least for now, he was happy with that state of affairs. As he turned back to the platform he felt at ease, he felt ready to meet her.

He saw movement down the track in the distance, it was a train approaching and as some of the people around him readied themselves, he knew this must be it. The train eventually ground to a halt and the doors opened to let the people spill out. Avalon's eyes scanned the figures emptying onto the platform to catch an image that he should know well but she did take some finding. Only as she had turned and was walking towards him did he truly recognise her. She had different coloured hair in a different style and she was dressed in a manner not in keeping with her usual look, in short, she didn't look like he had expected. After all this time, did he really expect her to look like she did the last time he saw her? He smiled at this but kept the smile on his face as she closed in, she waved, he didn't return it. They gave each other a little kiss and Avalon said,

"Here, let me take the case," and he took the handle. It was the type of case with wheels but it looked a sizeable thing and so he took charge of it. "How was the journey?" he added looking down to her. He had forgotten she was so much shorter than he, how could he forget that?

"Oh, you know, boring but not as long as the first leg up to Edinburgh," she smiled.

"Shall we make a move?" asked Avalon wanting to be clear of the station.

"Yes," nodded Carol, "lead the way, I'm in your hands."

"We're meeting one of my colleagues at the cafe, she'll take you to the house and I'll see you later," he explained as he dragged the case behind.

"I didn't know if you would make it here," she said.

"It was close, I was at a meeting this morning," he replied, he thought 'meeting' sounded better than anything else he could come up with.

"Still busy then?" she added.

"Yes, busy enough," he replied but resisted the urge to elaborate.

"It looks like it suits you," she smiled but as they were negotiating the taxis and cars in the car park he didn't notice it.

"I like it here if that's what you mean," he said.

"I can see that, it's what I was trying to say," she explained. They stopped at the roadside waiting for the traffic lights to change.

"How do you mean?" he asked looking her as they waited.

"You look well," she shrugged, "really well."

"So do you," he smiled but he didn't fully mean it and considered that she was just being kind and he probably looked tired. She seemed to have aged, much more than just a couple of years and he thought that her change of hairstyle didn't help. "I have a slightly healthier lifestyle than I used to," he continued to get his mind off the subject, "I mean I haven't gone mad and bought a bicycle or anything, I just eat healthier than I used to and I think the air up here is better for me." The lights changed and the traffic stopped so they crossed the road and entered Union Street.

"You don't have to try and convince me James, and I'm not trying to make you feel better. You look great," she was still smiling, "I didn't expect you to look so different, but you do."

"Really?" he asked with a sort of friendly frown. He glanced down at her as they walked and she seemed genuine, "I sleep better, I suppose that helps."

"Of course it will but you're..." she seemed to lose the words for the description, "well I don't know, you look leaner, stronger if that makes sense." It didn't, Avalon felt good health-wise but stronger, leaner? Did she mean he had lost weight? He didn't think he had. "It's difficult to explain," she continued, "you just look..." she paused and shrugged emphasising the final word, "*good*." He glanced back to her again and gave a slight laugh.

"Well I suppose I should take it as a compliment then," he smiled.

"Well that's how it's meant," she replied. Avalon thought that he should return the sentiment, he thought that he should say something about Carol, but what? 'You look older' or 'I don't like what you've done with your hair' was never going to get him brownie points and so he changed the whole subject by saying,

"The café is just round this corner, we're meeting DC Frazer, Megan," he added her first name as an afterthought. "I've got a few things still to do so she's going to take you to the house."

"You mentioned the bed and breakfast is close by," she said.

"Yes, it is," nodded Avalon.

"Then she can take me there just as easily can't she?" This took Avalon by surprise.

"Well... yes if that's what you want."

"It makes sense, I can unpack my things, have a shower and have a walk up to see you later," she suggested.

"Okay," nodded Avalon as they reached the cafe, "I suppose it does make sense."

Avalon introduced Carol to Frazer and there was a little bit of the friendly chit-chat between the three of them over a coffee but then Avalon looked at his watch and explained his plans.

"I've got things to do so I'll get off," and he looked at Carol, "I'm knocking off a few hours early so I'll send you a text when I'm back if that's okay?" Carol nodded with a broad smile and Avalon stood.

"Boss, can I have a wee word?" asked Frazer also standing. Avalon realised it was something she wanted to say privately so they both excused themselves and exited the cafe.

"What is it?" he asked.

"I contacted Cameron and asked if we could speak t' him about an organisation called The Black Clan," she said softly.

"And?"

"He denied knowing anything about et and said et would be a pointless interview."

"So what do you think?"

"Well," sighed Frazer, "I don't know for sure but I

would think et jarred his spine a wee bit."

"So he may know something about it," replied Avalon nodding slowly.

"Oh an' did y' know you're being followed?" she added as an afterthought, as casually as if she was asking about the weather.

"Followed?" he frowned.

"Aye, dunna look round, I saw him arrive just after you," she said looking straight at Avalon.

"Are you sure?" he asked, a little confused.

"Boss, et's what I was trained tae do," she raised her brows a little, "He's not very good at et but he's certainly following you or Carol and I'm thinkin' et's probably more likely tae be you." Avalon nodded.

"What's he wearing?" he asked.

"Black jacket with a green shirt under it, he stands out like an angel in a brothel," she hissed and then, "shall I pull him?"

"No," replied Avalon, "let's see how determined he is, make sure it's me he's following before you take Carol back."

"Aye, course," nodded Frazer and Avalon stepped inside the door, waved to Carol then turned to Frazer.

"See you later," and he left. Avalon walked down Church Street and into the Victorian Market so he could glance around the stalls and try to catch sight of his pursuer. He saw the man out of the corner of his eye some distance away as he browsed a shop window. He then continued out of the market and onto Queensgate where he pulled out his phone. He knew it would take him a good thirty minutes to walk to the station and he wondered if he should act on his pursuer. As he walked, it gave him time to think. He made his way around the

Eastgate Centre and onto Crown Street where he dialled and explained his plan to Ross. By the time he reached Kingsmill Road he saw the police car drive past him and pull up. Avalon didn't even look back, he knew the officers involved would be fully briefed and he knew a hundred yards further down the road the car pulling to a halt would be a black BMW with Ross in the driver's seat.

"So who's following you I wonder?" asked Ross as he drove back to the police station.

"I don't know his name but I bet he has connections to Buchanan or Cameron," replied Avalon.

"Never heard of him," insisted Avalon when he was back in the Cave.

"We don't have him on the database either," explained Dowd looking down at the sheet of paper in his hands.

"So what's his address?" asked Ross.

"Nairn, lived there for twelve years, got a management job with a rental car company," replied Dowd.

"So you've let him go I assume?" asked Avalon.

"Aye," nodded Dowd, "as soon as we confirmed his ID we told him we had made a mistake and let him go."

"Odd that he seems to have no connections to anyone though," announced Ross.

"We have tae consider ef there es no obvious links then this Black Clan could be the connection," added Frazer. Dowd looked up from the paper and with a slight grin asked,

"Y' havnae been fishin' en another man's pond

have y' Detective Inspector?" Ross laughed at the suggestion but Avalon looked at Dowd and said,

"If this were only that simple, we have disturbed a wasps' nest here, there is much more to this than meets the eye."

"Meaning what exactly?" asked Ross the smile still on his face.

"Something that Gordon said yesterday morning, about Buchanan having his strings pulled," explained Avalon.

"To what ends?" asked Ross, "I still can't see anything but an odd missing person's case here." Avalon nodded, it was obvious he was going through something in his mind but it was clear he wasn't sharing those thoughts. Dowd looked as if he was going to add something but he abandoned the attempt. Ross noticed it however and stared at him. "What?" asked Ross still looking at him. Dowd raised his eyebrows and swallowed.

"Well, we told him we had lifted him because someone thought they saw him steal from one o' the traders en the market as you asked," explained Dowd glancing over to Avalon, "but he just took it in his stride, he obviously knew why we had picked him up and he wasn't anxious."

"He probably knew we'd let him go after," suggested Ross with a shrug.

"I doubt et," replied Dowd, "here's a man without a record and yet when we bring him en for questioning he doesn't complain or ask to see a solicitor, just as ef he had been told what to expect."

"So what are your thoughts?" asked Avalon, he valued Dowd's input and wanted to know what he was thinking.

"When we told him there had been a mistake and we handed him back his things, he just shrugged and said, 'mistakes happen' and smiled at me," continued Dowd, "not the usual experience I've had under those circumstances, particularly for a first timer."

"So either the records are wrong," suggested Ross, "or that isn't his real ID."

"Or he knew whoever put him on to this could get him out without bother," added Avalon. Everyone there gathered knew what Avalon was saying could have further implications for the case if he was correct.

"So why might he be following you DI Avalon?" asked Dowd.

"That I'm not sure about, we're not far enough into the case in any way to be putting pressure on anyone. We don't even know why Buchanan is missing." Dowd went quiet, now it was Avalon's turn to wonder what the PC was thinking.

"I'm guessing whatever we've stumbled on matters to someone," added Ross, "and that someone wants to know how far down the line we are."

"Could be," shrugged Avalon and then turned to Dowd, "come on Neil, what's going on in that atomic powered brain of yours?" Dowd looked over to Avalon and gave a muted laugh at the comment then he sighed.

"There's another option," he began, "what ef someone else es looking for him?" Avalon flashed his eyes at Ross and then back to Dowd.

"Are they still trying to promote you downstairs?" he asked.

"Aye, et's still on the cards so t' speak," he replied with a deep frown.

"I've just thought of a way you can get out of it," explained Avalon with wide eyes.

"Oh aye," replied Dowd folding his arms expecting a funny line, "what's that?"

"Take your exams for detective."

DC Frazer looked at Avalon expecting him to ask her about her meeting with Carol but she was totally wrong.

"Can you turn the tables on the man who was following me?"

"You mean follow him?" she asked with a little surprise in her voice.

"Exactly, it's enough reason to put resources into this so I want him watched twenty four hours a day without him knowing, can it be done?" Avalon had asked Frazer to walk down the corridor with him and even then he had lowered his voice.

"Yes Boss," she blinked, "ef we have the manpower."

"You've got Rory but I'll get some other personnel on this," nodded Avalon, "I want to know who he's doing this for, all his contacts all his meetings monitored until we find a name." Avalon seemed insistent so, as soon as they parted, she found Mackinnon and started work.

Avalon went to see DCI Croker to arrange for secondment of uniformed officers.

"How many are we talking about DI Avalon?" Croker asked with a deep frown.

"I think five or six would be enough, I need to put twenty-four-hour surveillance on a suspect," explained Avalon.

"Isn't this a missing person case?" asked Croker.

Avalon nodded carefully, he couldn't remember previously apprising the Detective Chief Inspector of the case, so how did he know?

"It is sir but there are details that make this much more than a simple missing person," replied Avalon thinking out his words before he spoke.

"Such as?" asked Croker. Avalon looked directly at the DCI who was returning the stare over his spectacles.

"I was being followed by a member of the public which I consider-"

"Can you find anything to link this incident to this case?" interrupted Croker.

"Not as such sir but-"

"Then it could be coincidence or even someone who you have troubled in a previous case," suggested Croker.

"With respect sir, I know my job," insisted Avalon allowing a little venom into his voice, "I believe the person following me was directly-"

"But you have no proof-" interrupted Croker again but Avalon was angry now and he threw the interruption back in Croker's face.

"Was directly involved in this case and quite frankly, I fail to see how you could know enough details to make such a comment," insisted Avalon. Croker looked livid, he removed his spectacles and tried to calm himself.

"Firstly," began Croker, "I will not have a voice raised to me by one of my staff, secondly the interest in this case has been expressed by a senior officer," he continued.

"That surprises me as we have only just begun

any serious investigation, and until two hours ago I wouldn't even have described it as a case," Avalon now knew he had rattled the cage of a senior officer, that meant either collusion from on high or someone above Croker that had something to hide. For several seconds Croker stared hard at Avalon. The DI wondered what his boss was thinking but that soon became apparent.

"Is there a case here?" asked Croker then quickly added, "I mean, what exactly are you investigating?" The stare was icy, but Avalon could see Croker was testing him, he thought about what to say. His next few words could be crucial.

"Honestly sir," began Avalon in a calmer voice, "I'm not sure what we have but the simple fact that you heard about it from other sources means we are onto something someone doesn't want out in the open." Croker kept his gaze for a moment then leaned back in his chair and looked out of his small window. For a moment Avalon was thinking of giving up the idea of asking for staff and doing the surveillance himself but then Croker leaned forward and in a calm and quiet voice spoke.

"If you can't tell me what you have by Friday you drop this investigation." Avalon nodded, it wasn't long, he didn't even know what his next move should be. "I'll make arrangements to get you extra personnel," he added and replaced his spectacles and continued to look through the pile of papers on his desk. Avalon knew the interview was over.

"Thank you sir," he said then left. Back in the Cave he looked at Ross and nodded to the booth. Ross quickly joined him and sat opposite.

"Have we got anyone?" asked Ross.

"Yes, he's sorting it out," nodded Avalon with a blank stare.

"What is it?" asked Ross knowing there was something more.

"We've got until Friday to sort out what this is about."

"Shit!" exclaimed Ross, "that's pretty doubtful."

"The DCI knew about this before I reached his office," said Avalon still glassy eyed.

"How come?" asked Ross, "we've only done a little bit of digging around." Avalon nodded as his focus came back onto Ross.

"I'm well aware of that and quite frankly that's troubling. I previously said we had stirred up a wasps' nest, it seems this is much bigger than Buchanan going missing."

"I agree," shrugged Ross, "but what is it exactly we have stumbled into?"

"I don't know, but we better find out soon," sighed Avalon and he looked at his watch, "we have just four days to come up with something," and then he remembered something else, "crap," he announced with frustration.

"What?" asked Ross.

"Carol," he sighed again shaking his head, "I was going to finish early to spend some time with her." Ross tightened his lips and his face creased as he saw the dilemma.

"It's not going to be a great visit for her is it?" he said.

~~~~~~

"I'm really sorry this didn't quite work out as I planned," apologised Avalon to Carol.

"Don't worry about it," she smiled, "it's your job, we're here now and the meal is lovely."

"I've not been here before, one of the Sergeants down at the nick suggested it as a good place to eat," he returned the smile, "I just wasn't sure they would get us in at short notice."

"It's great, a bit of a rush but we can go for a drink after," she said still holding the smile.

"Unfortunately, Inverness is called a city but it doesn't particularly open late like some others you're used to."

"That doesn't matter," she replied, "it seems a really friendly place, and Megan is nice too."

"Megan can be..." Avalon wondered what description to give her and when he had found the word he continued, "impatient."

"I like her, she seems very helpful." Avalon gave a small laugh.

"I've never heard her described as helpful but I suppose under the circumstances she has been very helpful," agreed Avalon.

"What are the rest of the team like?" she asked. Avalon did his best to describe their characters from their personal sides rather than from a professional standpoint, after all, that's how he saw his team. They were colleagues in every way, not just at work but in his private life too.

"You seem happy up here," she said with a broad smile, she looked genuinely pleased for him.

"I am most of the time, the job can get on top of you now and then but..." he trailed off with a shrug.

"But that's always been the case," she said softly, "it's the nature of the job." He looked at her, he could now see why he had found her so attractive all those years ago. Yes, she looked a little older but he did too, unlike him, she still looked good.

"So what about you, it sounds like you've been through a rough time?" he asked changing the subject.

"It's my own fault, leaping into situations with my eyes closed," she shrugged, "but it's done with and I don't want to dwell on it really."

"That's fine," replied Avalon apologetically, "I understand." The conversation continued light heartedly for some time until they decided to leave to get a drink somewhere and Avalon suggested his house. As they entered, Carol was surprised that Avalon was living so close to the centre.

"Yeah, but it's not like Wolverhampton," he grinned closing the door behind her, "Inverness sprawls somewhat, but with housing estates, not industry. Living this close to the centre doesn't feel cramped or enclosed, it's just convenient." He showed her around the house, which she liked and then they went to the kitchen to make a drink. "It's single malt, cheap beer or gin and tonic I'm afraid." She went for the gin and tonic and they moved to the lounge.

"Do you have a thing about televisions?" she asked with a grin.

"I don't have one," he replied not quite understanding the question.

"I just recall you painted the screen of the last one you had, and," she paused, "and there was a tin of spaghetti hoops on top of it."

"Oh I still have a tin of spaghetti hoops in the

kitchen," he grinned, "probably the same one," he added and she laughed, shaking her head. After a moment she sipped on the drink and looked around the house.

"I do like the house, it's very nice," she eventually said.

"Thanks," smiled Avalon, "but I have to confess that Ollie, PC Kirk from the nick made it habitable, without her it would still look like a warehouse."

"Ah," nodded Carol raising her brows, "is this a romantic connection?" and she gave a genuine smile to disarm the question.

"Ollie?" coughed Avalon with a sound that was almost a laugh, "God no," and then he felt guilty and amended his response, "she's lovely in many ways but it would be a hard man who took to Olivia Kirk." He also had certain suspicions about her that he had never revealed to anyone.

"Of course you can just tell me to mind my own business," she added slightly embarrassed.

"No I'm fine discussing it, we know each other well enough to be honest," insisted Avalon, probably because he had nothing to hide and nothing to report in that area. He wasn't likely to tell her he had been terribly smitten by Sarah Underwood, particularly as that particular forensic-technician was 'spoken for'.

"So is there anyone?" she then asked with a slow shrug of the shoulders. Avalon then wished he had changed the subject. Did admitting the truth make him seem boring, then he realised he didn't care, he did still however wonder why she had asked the question.

"No," he smiled, "as usual I never get time, since the promotion it's become even harder to get time off."

"So how *do* you relax?" she asked noticing the

186

guitar on the stand.

"Reading, playing the guitar and I still have the bike," he explained.

"Well I didn't doubt you would still have that," she nodded taking another sip of the drink.

"I get out to the pub now and then too," he admitted with a slight grin.

"I was worried you may be attached, it never occurred to me until after I rang," she explained, "I was so embarrassed I was going to call it off but as you never said anything..." so tailed off the comment as she saw him holding back a snigger, "well, you're quite a catch," she added. This ceased his humour, the conversation was taking a different route, one he was unsure of.

"Me, a catch?" he shook his head.

"Yes, independent means, nice house," she insisted, "not bad looking for your age," she laughed.

"Thanks for that," he smiled.

"Seriously though you're in a great position, I'd..." she paused giving him a serious look then gave an embarrassed smile, "well, I did." Avalon noticed her demeanour change and to disarm a mutually uncomfortable moment, he said,

"I'm just about fully vegetarian now, I take my health a lot more seriously."

"There's a big difference in you as I said earlier, I don't know if it's the diet or the air but keep doing it would be my advice," and she continued to sip the drink. Avalon wanted to change the subject from himself, he wanted to talk about her but at every attempt she had manage to change the subject.

"So what about you?" he asked.

"Nothing really changes as I said earlier, I've got

a couple of interviews to go to early next month though."

"That's good," he nodded.

"Boring jobs, crap money," she replied, then added, "and you must be on good money now with the promotion?" She had steered the subject back to Avalon. He realised she didn't want to talk about herself, she just wanted to chat. He gave in trying to find any more out about her and they spent an hour or so catching up with stories about Wolverhampton and people they once knew. Eventually Carol decided she should return to the bed and breakfast and so Avalon walked her the few hundred yards to the door.

"Can we meet again before I go back?" she asked.

"Yeah," nodded Avalon doubtfully, "we've got a case on at the moment that we have to make progress on before the weekend," he frowned, "but I'll give you a call when I can get time off." After a peck on the cheek they said goodnight and Avalon returned home.

## Chapter Eight

DS Nicholls was an imposing man, not as large as DC Rutherford but heavier built than Ross and he had a deep, Invernessian voice that seemed to vibrate through the room. His close-cropped short hair gave him the look of an American soldier, his black suit and black tie brought memories of two movies to Avalon as he entered the room. One was The Blues Brothers, the other, Men in Black. He wasn't quite enough of a caricature to be humorous but Avalon found it hard to find anything but a bit of theatre about the man.

"Take a seat," said Avalon pointing to the chair opposite his desk. The man carefully lowered himself as if he didn't trust the strength of the furniture. "I just want to ask a few questions about a case involving Jason Buchanan."

"Aye," nodded Nicholls, "the DI said it was something about an old case."

"I know it's a few years ago but can you remember how Buchanan managed to get off the hook on the McVie case?"

"That's the one where the kid got knocked on the head in the alley?" asked Nicholls with a piercing stare. Avalon nodded. "It was a complete cock-up that's why, both Davies and McGill screwed up the case because they were getting some pressure from above."

"From above?" asked Avalon a little surprised.

"Aye, first from DCI Anderson and then from the Superintendent." Avalon raised his brows and leaned back in the chair.

"Why pressure?" he asked.

"I suppose because the *Super* plays golf with Buchanan's solicitor or is shagging Buchanan's wife," sighed Nicholls, "who cares, it's too late now?"

"I care, and it's never too late," insisted Avalon and he leaned forward again. "So did DI Davies and DS McGill supress evidence?"

"No," insisted Nicholls, "they're not bent, just cowards and incompetent. Because Anderson was dogging them they made mistakes and when someone like 'Crafty' Cameron is on the defence team, mistakes are something you can't afford."

"We always have pressure, what was so different on this case?"

"It's not my place to point any fingers DI Avalon, but..." he paused for a moment and then sighed, "DI Davies wasn't made of the right stuff to be a copper, his home life was a sham and he was constantly depressed, and McGill," his voice rose and his eyes opened wide at the mention of the name. There was quite a pause but Avalon stayed silent. "McGill was a good mate but during the investigation he was accused of touching a teenager 'in an inappropriate way'. It was tosh of course it wasn't his style but while the investigation was on, it put pressure on the whole team."

"And that was Buchanan's doing?" asked Avalon. Nicholls gave a little smile.

"You're catching on Detective Inspector."

"I've done some research on Buchanan and his solicitor and I'm starting to see how they work," frowned Avalon brushing his hand through his hair.

"What's he been up to now?"

"I don't know, he's disappeared leaving a suicide note," explained Avalon.

"Well let's hope something nasty has happened to the rotten bastard," replied Nicholls folding his arms.

"It's more complicated than that, there is something going on," added Avalon, "as of yet we just don't know what."

"I'm guessing you've done all your homework so I doubt I can help."

"Probably not," sighed Avalon but then he had a slight idea and asked, "I don't suppose you came across anything to do with The Black Clan or the Order of the Black Thistle?" Nicholls seemed to consider the question but eventually shook his head.

"No sorry, not heard that one, why?"

"It could be a club or society that Buchanan is involved with," explained Avalon.

"I heard he was a Freemason but I don't know how accurate the information was."

"We've checked that line of inquiry, he never joined the Masons, it was some other type of club." Avalon sighed again and then asked, "I still find it hard to believe that DI Davies and his staff would crumble over a bit of pressure from above."

"Like I said, not made of the right stuff," he shrugged, "and how many of them are still on the books?" He stared straight into Avalon's eyes as he added, "Davies retired, McGill retired and Anderson moved on."

"So how did you escape the onslaught?" asked Avalon. Nicholls dropped the stare and looked at the floor.

"I've been universally hated for years, I don't do things the way they like them done so pressure washes over me, and..." he added, "I don't give a damn," and looked up with a slight smile. Avalon thanked the DS for speaking with him.

"Anything?" asked Ross walking into the booth after Nicholls left. Avalon shook his head slowly, it was clear he was thinking things through.

"Is DS Nicholls a good copper?" he eventually asked.

"Yeah," nodded Ross, "old school but one of the best, why?"

"The McVie case, the one Buchanan was accused of assaulting the young man," Avalon paused trying to find the right words, "it seems the case was manipulated from within." There was a look of surprise from Ross, nothing dramatic but Avalon could see the implications taking hold of the DS.

"By who?"

"Possibly the superintendent."

"That could complicate things," replied Ross raising his eyebrows, "and it looks like Croker has already been tainted by his influence if he knew about our investigations."

"I'm not sure, I don't like the DCI but I doubt the man will bend to pressure from above," insisted Avalon. He tapped his fingers on the desk then continued, "We need to get moving on this, if we can't find something big soon, we will have to drop it and I really think Buchanan is worth pursuing."

"But there's still nothing to work on," insisted Ross with a frown, "the team are looking at every angle but nothing has shown up."

"And we'll not get anymore out of Cameron now he knows we're aware of The Black Clan."

"That's just Frazer's guess work," insisted Ross, "we don't know he's got anything to do with it."

"True, but I wish we had the resources to follow him," agreed the DI just as Frazer entered the booth.

"Boss, we've located an address that may be of interest."

"Where and why?" he asked turning to face her.

"Et's near Garve, an isolated property overlooking Loch Luichart," she explained reading from a notepad.

"Don't know it," insisted Avalon jutting out his bottom lip.

"Neither did I, we found et on satellite images."

"So why might it be of interest?" he asked.

"We found the address jotted down on an invoice from Buchanan's industrial unit," explained Frazer looking directly at him, "we've been en touch with the council, they say et belongs t' Lawrence Hilliard."

"Could be worth a look then," suggested Ross. Avalon bit his bottom lip as he thought it through. He turned to Frazer.

"Megan, any details about this property?"

"Probably a retreat or holiday let, et's not his regular address," she suggested.

"Okay, let's go and have a look at it," and he turned to Ross, "you better come with me."

"That's proper Teuchter country, shall I see if the four-by-four is available?"

"What? What are you talking about?" frowned Avalon not quite understanding the question.

"It's wild up there, they eat their own young and dance with their arms straight by their sides," insisted Ross pulling on his jacket.

"More Highland humour I'm guessing," sighed Avalon and he headed for the door.

The journey up to the address was quicker than Avalon had estimated and using the route on the satnav, took just over forty minutes. The house was down a short drive and couldn't been seen very clearly from the road. Ross knocked on the door and Avalon checked around the house for signs of habitation. There were a great deal of shrubs and trees surrounding the bungalow that had probably been a croft originally but so many extensions had been applied to the property that little of the original steading could be seen. There were a few garden tools around the rear of the house but no real sign of activity.

"Looks empty," announced Ross as he joined Avalon who was looking at the view over the loch.

"Nice place," he said.

"Aye in the summer but I doubt you would want to be up here in the winter."

"Have you got something against this part of the country?"

"No," insisted Ross thrusting his hands into his pockets, "apart from the midgies in the summer and the biting cold in the winter, nothing at all."

"I like it, it's not like living near the sea but the loch makes up for it."

"Aye okay," nodded Ross turning to leave, "but

let's get on before some poetry pops into your head."
Avalon had one last look at the view and he turned to
follow Ross but the DS was bending down looking at a
wheelbarrow.

"Not much good to you in the flat," said Avalon
but Ross was silent and was pulling out his biro.

"What have we got here?" he asked and he
moved some of the remaining soil in the base of the
barrow. Something slightly shiny caught the light and
Avalon bent down to look but Ross had caught the object
on the clip of the biro. With his free hand he reached for
a small evidence bag from his jacket pocket and Avalon
took it from him to open it for the object.

"Well, you don't need spectacles yet," mused
Avalon looking closer at the object in the bag.

"Is that what I think it is?" asked Ross replacing
his pen into his jacket.

"A woman's earring by the looks of it."

"Odd place to keep it in a wheelbarrow,"
shrugged Ross. Avalon was still inspecting the object,
holding it up and turning it around.

"I don't think it's been there all that long," he said
but Ross had found a small stick and was carefully
looking through the rest of the dusting of soil in the
barrow.

"Are we getting paranoid about this
investigation?" asked Ross as he stood straight, "after
all, it's just an earring. It may have been lost while
gardening."

"So why did you want to put it in an evidence
bag?" asked Avalon glaring over to him.

"Just instinct I suppose," shrugged Ross, "and the
fact that we know Buchanan has some connection to this

place." Instinct was also telling Avalon that he needed to make a better inspection of the property too and as he turned to walk to the back door he noticed a mark on the patio area, a scrape mark as if something had been dragged. There were some new dead leaves around but here and there a scuff mark could clearly be seen in the moss and debris.

"What do you make of this?" he asked. Ross walked over and looked around, he then knelt down trying his best not to kneel in the damp areas and carefully pushed a few leaves away and then stood again.

"I'd say it looks like something was dragged from the back door to about here," offered Ross pointing to a spot about five feet from the doorstep. Almost as one, the two detectives glanced back to the barrow and then to each other. Their faces were blank until Avalon said,

"We need to seal off this property and get someone over here," he looked back to the mark, "we can't afford not to, it could be innocent but it might not be."

"So you don't think we're over-reacting, it could be where they brought out the trash?"

"Yes, it could be," agreed Avalon looking back to the scuff mark, "but it could equally be where someone dragged out a body and placed it in a wheelbarrow."

"But if we're wrong-"

"Would you prefer it if I rang?" interrupted Avalon. Ross gave a sheepish expression and pulled out his phone.

"Your phone won't have a signal up here," he said making light of his reticence, "I'll get Megan to contact the PF office."

"No," demanded Avalon as he turned on Ross, "we need a warrant straight from the JP, it will take too long through the Sheriff's office." As Ross walked around to find a signal for his phone, Avalon looked around for other signs but there was little, he did, however, find a spot where the barrow had probably stood. It was some distance from its current location.

"I've got Frazer on it, she's got SOCO involved and is contacting the Sheriff's Office," explained Ross as he replaced his phone in his pocket.

"We had better wait in the car, no point in making a mess of this site," nodded Avalon.

It was well over an hour before a team of uniformed officers arrived to seal off the property, just about the same time that Avalon's phone rang.

"Avalon."

"*DI Avalon, it's DCI Croker, I hear you have something over near Garve.*"

"Yes sir," replied Avalon trying to think his way through the next few sentences and wondering why Croker was chasing him, "well at least we *may* have something."

"*I hope you do, the Scenes of Crime unit are not just your personal toy DI Avalon and you're going out on a limb with the warrant. What do you have?*" That was the question he was hoping Croker wouldn't ask, but there it was. Could he really tell his boss that they had found a woman's earring and a smudge on a mossy patio? But that was all he had.

"I think there are signs of a struggle at a property tied to an investigation we are currently working on," he replied, it sounded better that way and he knew Croker would understand the meaning of the words.

*"You have mobilised half of the Inverness Police Force on 'signs of a struggle'?"* Croker sounded irate, but then again he mostly did. *"I hope for your sake Detective Inspector that you really have something up there,"* and the phone went dead. Avalon looked at the phone for a moment and then shoved it into his pocket as he saw Ross watching him.

"Trouble?"

"Not really," shrugged Avalon, "just the DCI threatening to sack me."

"I don't know why, he can't do that," smiled Ross.

"Oh really?"

"No, he can suspend you until a further investigation into your actions is conducted and then the Superintendent can sack you but my best guess is that you'll still get paid for a few months yet," explained Ross, "but he can't sack you."

"Thanks for cheering me up," said Avalon without any emotion and he went to talk to the uniformed officers. Tape was placed to seal off most of the property and Avalon gave instructions to them, then he and Ross headed back to Inverness.

"Do y' want me tae inform Hilliard that we've sealed off his house?" asked Frazer as Avalon and Ross returned to the Cave. The DI had been walking to his booth but he stopped and thought for a moment.

"Not yet," he eventually replied, "let's get the warrant first, I'd rather not have the complications of an irate politician until we have something," and then he continued to the booth. It was then that his thoughts went back to Carol. If this investigation turned out to be serious, he would have no time to see her, on the other hand, if he was wrong, there would be all the time in the world. He checked his emails and had a cursory look through the work on his desk then removed his jacket and went to see Frazer.

"Anything on the person who was following me?" he asked.

"Nothin' yet boss, at least nothin' important."

"Okay," he nodded and walked across to the window near Ross's desk. Ross was examining the earring though the evidence bag.

"Know anything about jewellery?" he asked looking over to Frazer. She shrugged and said,

"I know what a diamond looks like but that's me done."

"That's a talent all women are born with," sighed Ross, "here take a look," and he handed her the bag. Frazer turned the evidence around and held it up to the light.

"White crystal clip-on," she began, "with a drop pearl pendant, nothing special, the sort o' thing a bridesmaid would wear."

"Can you translate that to 'man speak'?" asked Avalon turning from the window.

"Well, et's all white, y' know the sort of thing you see at weddings."

"You said clip-on?"

"Yeah," she nodded, "they clip-on rather than need pierced ears."

"Which means it could come off easily?" asked Avalon. She nodded again.

"They can come off ef they're not tight."

"Anything else?"

"Not really," she shrugged, "cost about twenty quid from a shop or off the internet." Avalon began to have doubts, it was something he hadn't noticed but if this type of earring could come off easily then it could have dropped off when someone was simply doing a bit of gardening, then she gave him hope. "They are a wee bit showy though," she added.

"Meaning?"

"Well, like I said, you'd expect tae see 'em at a wedding or with a posh dress, something like that."

"But not gardening?" smiled Avalon.

"I wouldnae think so," she replied, "though I'm sure there are some types that would." Avalon then thought of the type of woman that would, and the only image he could muster was Celine, the latest fling of George Sands. She certainly wore that type of jewellery and he could certainly see her tending flowerbeds dressed just as showy as he had seen her up at the house. The difference was, her earrings probably cost several months wages of the average copper. Sands had a habit of showering his ladies with expensive jewellery.

"So, not much chance of tracking the sale of these down?"

"Doubtful," replied Frazer, "but I'll give et a go ef y' want."

"We'll see what we find up at Hilliard's house first," said Avalon.

"If anything," added Ross with an expectant look. Avalon pulled in a deep breath and raised his brows before exhaling and Ross could see the doubt in his features. The DI walked to his usual spot by the window and looked out towards the road, his hands clasped in the small of his back. It was late on Wednesday afternoon and Croker had given him a very short time to find something worth pursuing and that time was running out fast. It was risky going direct to the Justice of the Peace but it could take several days to get the Procurator Fiscal to sanction the warrant. In Avalon's mind, the chance that a crime had been committed outweighed the consequences of him being wrong, and then more doubt came. What was he thinking? They needed evidence that a crime *had* been committed, as it stood, Avalon felt he had been suffering tunnel vision and there was a speeding train coming the other way. A phone rang and Avalon turned back to the source of the interruption, it was Frazer's desk phone.

"DC Frazer," she paused, "that's correct sir," another pause, "yes, he's here now, I'll let him know," and she covered the receiver with her hand and looked up to Avalon. "Et's the sheriff's office, they need someone down there for the warrant." Avalon nodded and reached for the phone. The warrant had to be very detailed as to what they were looking for and Avalon decided he would go and process the paperwork rather than have anyone else involved, just in case he was wrong. As he drove to the Sheriff's Office he began to wonder if he had made a fatal mistake, this could be the start of the end for Avalon. If he was wrong, not just his credibility would suffer, it would turn many people against him and make his job harder to do, if he still had a job. He pressed the button that wound down the window and breathed the Inverness air. It was cool, crisp and fresh enough to bring Avalon to his mental apex and he thought through every detail of the investigation. He saw it clearly, he could be wrong, of course he could, but he now knew he hadn't just jumped to any conclusion.

Both he and Ross had seen the same things and they had both come to the same conclusion, one could be wrong, but both of them? He had been in this position many times, it was the nature of the work. Every case could be the Magnum Opus of a detective's career, but it could just as easily be his undoing. As he opened the doors to the Sheriff's Office he looked at his watch, it was five thirty and he knew he wasn't going to be home until very late. He needed to let Carol know somehow.

"Jesus Christ on a stick!" exclaimed Ross as the powerful lights came on, "that's was straight in my bloody eyes," he continued covering his face with his hands.

"Sorry Sarge," apologised the uniformed PC who was holding the lighting stand.

"It's not even that dark yet," added Ross in a petulant mood.

"Stop complaining, let's see what we have," insisted Avalon pushing past the two of them. Ross and Avalon had been sitting in the car waiting for the Scene of Crimes team to check the outside of the house.

"DI Avalon," nodded the officer in charge.

"What have you got?" asked the DI, he didn't know the name of the man but he knew him by sight.

"Possibly blood, and if it is, there's a lot of it too."

"Possibly, what's that mean?" asked Ross still somewhat aggrieved.

"Well because it's outside, there are loads of things that can cause a reaction with luminol, such as copper or animal urine," explained the officer.

"Can we see it then?" asked Ross looking at the

ground.

"The effect only last for about half a minute but we have taken photographs of course," explained the officer, "we have contact from the door of the house, across the patio and in the wheelbarrow." Avalon almost breathed a sigh of relief at this news. The officer then added, "that's why I think it's blood, the soil could give false reading but the wheelbarrow?" Avalon understood and nodded.

"So we need a full forensics team up here?" he added.

"I would think so Inspector, if this is blood, then it leads from the house," nodded the officer, "I'll start an examination of the rest of the garden," he added and then left. Avalon looked towards the darkening horizon then to Ross.

"Let Megan know, we need access to the house so get someone to bring Hilliard up here but tell him nothing. Then tell Frazer when she's contacted forensics to get off home." Ross nodded and walked back to the car to get a better signal on his phone. Avalon then looked at his own phone, there was hardly any signal so he followed on, a short distance behind.

"Carol? it's James, something has cropped up, I'm sorry but I could be out all night. Send me a text when you get this message." He put the phone back in his pocket and sat in the driver's seat of the car. A few minutes later Ross joined him.

"Let's hope it's blood then and not pine marten piss," he said as he sat. It was dark now and the interior light came on. Avalon made a noise similar to a short laugh but he still looked stressed.

"To be honest, if it is blood, our troubles are just

starting."

"How so?" frowned Ross.

"Well, for starters, we have to try and link this to Buchanan going missing and then," he paused, "we have to wait for the Superintendent to get on the phone and I'm not looking forward to that."

"I see what you mean," nodded Ross, "but at least it would mean that our hunch was right."

"Yeah," nodded Avalon just as the interior light went out, "but at the moment, pine marten piss almost seems the better option."

Lawrence Hilliard was dressed in a casual suit but closer inspection showed he was wearing pyjamas under the jacket. Frazer was with him and she raised her eyebrows to Avalon as she closed. Hilliard looked stressed and it was doubtful it was just because he had been roused out of bed.

"This is Detective Inspector Avalon," explained Frazer to the man.

"What's this all about Detective, your colleagues seemed pretty insistent that I came here?" Avalon pulled out the warrant from his pocket and showed it to the man. Hilliard was, as Avalon expected, well groomed, in his forties and looked like every other politician he had had the misfortune to meet.

"Mr Hilliard, this is a warrant to search the grounds and house of this address which we are informed belongs to yourself."

"It does yes, but why all this activity?" the man ignored the warrant and was looking about as other officers, some in white forensics suits, came and went. Several lights were casting eerie shadows over the garden and a generator was running just inside the drive. Avalon ignored the question and asked,

"Have you brought the keys to the property Mr Hilliard, it would be more convenient to us both rather than breaking down the door?"

"Er yes... yes," stuttered the man turning from the activity and reaching into his jacket pocket. Avalon handed the keys to Ross who took them towards the house. The man looked to Avalon as if waiting for an explanation.

"We have reason to believe that a crime has taken place on the property, have you anything to say on that matter Mr Hilliard?" The man looked around again and then said,

"No, er... no I can't imagine how you could have come to that conclusion," he looked very stressed and genuinely confused. He stopped speaking and shook his head. "It's like some kind of nightmare..." he trailed off without finishing whatever he was trying to get across. He then gathered his thoughts and continued. "What has brought you to that conclusion? I mean has something happened here... I... I mean if there is something I should know..." he looked back to Avalon with pleading look.

"We have evidence that makes us believe that a crime was committed here but I cannot discuss any further details," said Avalon knowing he had an earring and that was all, "if there is something you need to tell us Mr Hilliard then now is the time to do it." Hilliard gave a pained expression and then asked,

"Am I under arrest?"

"Not at all, you're free to go if you have nothing to say," Avalon paused for a second, "but as I say, if there is something we should know then it's best you tell us now."

"I really know nothing about your claim Detective, I really don't." The stuttering had gone now and Avalon could see any opportunity for the man to talk had passed. He looked around until he saw a uniformed PC he knew.

"PC Drewer, make sure Mr Hilliard gets home will you?" The young PC nodded and closed in on them as Avalon returned to the house and almost bumped into Ross coming the other way.

"They've entered the house and at first glance the property looks clean," he admitted.

"If there's something there, they'll find it," replied Avalon with a blank stare just as his phone vibrated in his pocket. He pulled it out and read the message, it was from Carol.

"*Fine, let me know when you get back,*" it said. He placed the phone back in his pocket and wondered how their marriage had ever stayed together as long as it had. She had come all this way to see him and here he was stuck in the middle of a Scottish glen on a cold night at… He realised he hadn't a clue what time it was and he raised his arm to the glow of the lights to see the face of his wristwatch. He sighed when he saw how late it was.

"Problems?" asked Ross seeing his frustration.

"No, I just wish we had brought a flask or something." Ross didn't believe that was the only reason for the sigh but he didn't pursue it, he knew it would be about Carol.

It took almost another hour for Hendry of forensics to come to them with any conclusion.

"The house is showing positive sighs of blood,"

he began pulling the hood of the white suit from his head.

"Whereabouts?" asked Avalon.

"The kitchen area mainly but there are traces on the stairs and in the main bedroom."

"Is this just from luminol?" asked Ross.

"Yes unfortunately," nodded Hendry, "and I would guess that the place has undergone a thorough clean and the carpets have probably been changed, but I think we may be able to find DNA from the kitchen area." Avalon nodded but noticed one of the SOCO team from the garden approaching.

"Sir," began the officer, "I think you'd better come and look at this." Avalon and Ross followed the officer with Hendry tagging along behind. At the bottom of a slight slope was the rest of his team working under two lights. "We found significant positive luminol contacts in this area," continued the SOCO officer, "and we tested the surrounding area with no contacts. We think this area may be of interest." Avalon could see a well-defined area that looked the size of a grave. He knew it was so obvious that the others must have been thinking the same. "Do you want us to investigate?" asked the man.

"No," replied Avalon shaking his head, "the warrant was to search the house and grounds, I'll have to contact the Sheriff's Office before we start digging anything up."

"But there could be a corpse under here," added Ross.

"If there is, I'm sure it isn't going anywhere," replied Avalon with a sniff. His nose was beginning to drip with the cold air. He turned to Hendry.

"I suppose you need to get some samples for the lab now?" Hendry nodded.

"Yeah, we found some fibres and hairs already but it could take some time to collect everything," he turned and headed back to the house. Avalon looked back to the SOCO team.

"When you've done the rest of the grounds let me know, I think I have to get a few more people out of bed."

~~~~~~

Avalon had the distinct impression someone was trying to catch his attention. He felt like gravity had become more severe than normal, as if he had sunk into a vat of treacle. It was misty too, not the sort of sea mist that rolls up the Moray Firth but more like the curtain of fog that makes all the sounds seem distant. And there was a sound, he couldn't make out the words but he could hear a voice, Frazer's voice, as if they were both in a tunnel. It suddenly became clearer and he heard her saying,

"Boss, wake up, et's time." Avalon did his best to shake free of the sleep and looked up at Frazer but it was daylight and it stung his eyes.

"I must have nodded off," he announced taking a look at his surroundings. He was in the back seat of a car, not his or Ross's car and then he remembered. The previous night both he and Ross had driven back to Inverness to set a full investigation in motion and get warrants to thoroughly search the premises near Garve owned by one Lawrence Hilliard. It had been a long process and Avalon had suggested that Frazer went home to get some rest and DC Mackinnon would be brought in to assist. Frazer, as usual, had decided to be where the action was and had snatched a couple of hours sleep in the rest room and then jumped back into the fray. Ross had sent a text to Rutherford to be in the office early and then they had formulated plans for the whole of Thursday. Just before dawn, Avalon, Ross and Frazer had returned to the property near Garve and been met by the officer in charge of the location who informed him that SOCO and the forensics team had left for the night. The forensics team would continue with their lab work and SOCO would return when there was a warrant to excavate the garden and a second forensics team would presumably return to examine anything that the excavation produced. With the sky lightening to the east, Avalon had decided to take a short rest in the rear of a patrol car parked in the drive. It was from this location he was now desperately trying to revive himself. "Where's Ross?" he asked rubbing his sore eyes.

"He's just woken, he's trying t' blag a cup of tea from the Sergeant."

"Tea? I'm not sure I could face tea this early."

"How about this?" she replied offering him a large thermos flask. Avalon blinked and a slowly forming smile broke into his features.

"Is that what I think it is?" he asked.

"Aye et es, brewed in the Cave this very mornin'."

"Bless your totally organised soul Megan Frazer," he said reaching for the flask. He poured himself a drink and it made him shiver as he swallowed it, the cold seemed to have penetrated to his bones and he slid out of the car and stood. It was a reasonable morning and he quickly glanced at his watch. It was nine thirty and he could see activity in the garden. "Has anything happened?" he asked cradling the warm cup in his hands.

"Nothin' dramatic but the new forensics team have arrived, they're suiting up behind the house." Avalon saw Ross half staggering down the path from that very direction, he was holding a plastic cup.

"You look like I feel, do you want a sip of..." began Ross but he went silent at the sight of the mug in Avalon's hand. "Is that?" but he stopped once more as the fumes of the coffee reached his nostrils. "I didn't see you make that up earlier," he said a little dumbfounded.

"That's because I didn't, Megan was on the ball as usual," and he finished off the dregs of the cup. Ross turned to Frazer.

"So is there a reason you didn't tell me that there was coffee when you woke me up and I said I needed a drink?"

"Yeah," she nodded with a smile but didn't elaborate.

"So what was the reason?"

"I like tae see you uncomfortable."

"That's not nice," retorted Ross, "this isn't uncomfortable, this is positively unsettling, this is tea. Tea with a capital 'S'," he growled.

"Look," began Frazer, "when a pack of African Hunting Dogs pulls down a gazelle, the leader o' the pack gets tae eat first," and she opened the flask and topped up Avalon's cup, she then handed Ross the flask still smiling and walked towards the house. Ross stood holding the flask with a confused expression.

"Care to explain what she just said?" he asked still watching her walk off.

"I'm not sure myself," shrugged Avalon warming

on the fresh cup of coffee, "and I'm not sure I'm fully comfortable with the African Hunting Dog analogy." Ross was still looking up the path, Frazer had gone from view but he still watched where she had been.

"I'm not sure I'm fully comfortable with Frazer smiling," and he turned to Avalon as he tipped the remains of the tea on the floor and poured himself a coffee, "it's not normal and it goes against the laws of nature."


To Avalon's surprise, the new forensic team was headed by Sarah Underwood. He didn't know why but he hadn't expected to see her. She nodded and gave a slight smile when she saw him.

"DI Avalon, you seem to have a knack of finding these remote locations," she offered as she pulled the hood of the white suit over her head. He nodded and looked up to the sky.

"I think it's because we rarely went on holiday when I was a nipper." She smiled again and then added,

"Two of us are just going in the house to finish off in the other rooms, myself and Collins will go down to the garden site."

"We're just off down there too," explained Avalon and they moved off down the path. "I hear congratulations are in order," he added as they walked along.

"Yes, I think everyone knows about it by now," she smiled.

"Will you eventually be moving to Edinburgh?" he asked but considered he shouldn't have been so forward, it was none of his business.

"Of course not," she replied losing the smile, "I'm

not about to give my career up, no," there was determination in her voice. She glanced round to Avalon and concluded with, "we may look for a larger place though, you've seen my house..." Avalon took the statement to mean that the house wasn't large enough but he had seen the house and it looked adequate for two people. Unless she was considering... His thoughts would have to wait, they had reached the site of the dig where both he and Ross had considered a body was buried. He could see a shallow trench and two mounds of sifted earth. Several white suited technicians stood around.

"Ah, DI Avalon I presume," said a tall thin man with a dark complexion, "Donald Cruikshank," and the man held out his hand.

"So what have you found Mr Cruikshank?" asked Avalon refusing to use the familiar name.

"The greater surprise is what we haven't found detective," he replied and pointed to a small foldable table where several items were collected in evidence bags. Avalon glanced at the items but saw very little detail through the plastic.

"Here are all the items we have sifted from the soil which include several bones, all animal I may add," the man picked up a larger bag, "a lump of rusty iron, probably an old door hinge and two items that are more recent." When Avalon saw the man reach for two smaller bags he could see something that drew his attention immediately. "A button, probably from a blouse and an earring."

"A clip-on drop pearl type?" asked Avalon, Cruikshank raised his eyebrows.

"I assume you have its partner then," he said

holding up the bag. Avalon took it and examined it with a curt nod as his only reply.

"Is this everything?" he eventually asked.

"Yes, it's not much but that's everything."

"What about the body?" asked Ross.

"There isn't one," replied Cruikshank, "I don't doubt there was one here, but at some stage it must have been removed."

"We could test for the chemical signature of decay," suggested Sarah Underwood, "by measuring the soils' pH and the carbon dioxide levels we can at least get some idea of the state of the corpse, or even if there was one."

"Is that possible?" asked Avalon.

"It depends how long the body was here but yes the concentration of $CO_2$ in the soil can tell us a great deal. We can also check the pH changes based on a few other samples from the locality."

"It's worth a try at least," nodded Avalon as he turned back to the plastic evidence bags, "So what's in that remaining bag?" he asked looking directly at Cruikshank."

"That may turn out to be the smoking gun if Miss Underwood can make anything of it," and he handed it to her, missing out Avalon. Sarah flattened the bag and pulled out a small flashlight to examine its contents and her eyebrows lifted immediately.

"It's hair, looks like human hair too."

"That's what I thought too," agreed Cruickshank.

"There isn't much of it but we should be able to get a few answers from this," she explained to Avalon. He nodded and took a look at the bag, it did look like human hair but, until it was tested, they couldn't know for sure. He handed it back to Sarah.

"We'll make a start then," she said as she looked to her associate. Avalon retraced his steps back to the house with Ross and Frazer following on. He stopped and looked out across to the loch.

"Well, it looks like we have something here, even if it's not linked to Buchanan, at least the effort hasn't been in vain."

"And you still have a job," whispered Ross loud enough for Frazer to hear. Avalon looked round at him with a slight grin.

"Hell man, you look like shit," he said.

"Just imagine you're looking into a mirror," frowned Ross.

"We need some sleep I'm thinking," and he headed off to the car.

## Chapter Nine

Avalon was feeling guilty about Carol, he had sent several text messages to her to explain things but the replies had been concise to say the least. After returning home for a quick shower and a few hours' sleep he decided to ring her to say he was at home. He knew he had little time but at least he could try and patch things up by arranging an evening somewhere. When she arrived she was smiling broadly and, as he showed her into the lounge, she said,

"I'm guessing you have something big on?"

"Yes sort of, we've only been given a few days to make something of it and last night..." he trailed off, how could he explain? He had tried that early in their marriage, all it did was make things worse so he just shrugged and said, "well, you know." She did know, she had lived with the life long enough, but she seemed to have eventually accepted it.

"It's the nature of the job," she smiled, "I think I expected Inverness to be a sleepy backwater when it came to major crime."

"Just a month ago it was, in truth, the case we are working on is an old one, it's just that something new has cropped up." She just nodded at his explanation but said nothing. "Would you like a drink?" he added to try and change the subject.

"Yes please," she nodded again. Avalon stood and walked to the kitchen and raised his voice a little so she could hear his question.

"How are your parents?"

"Oh fine," she called back, "just the same as usual, mum's fretting over the slightest thing, dad's thinking up new excuses to get away to the pub." Avalon smiled to himself at this.

"I keep meaning to find time to go and see them," he said.

"You should, they always ask about you," and she caught sight of the carved ornament on the mantel. She stood and examined it.

"I was thinking of taking Rossy to Edinbourgh for his birthday, he's always wanted to visit."

"I didn't know you were friends with him." She called back still examining the object. Avalon was confused, he finished in the kitchen and returned.

"DS Ross in my team," he explained realising she hadn't met him. There was a puzzled expression on his face.

"Oh, I thought you meant the motorcycle rider," she mused placing the object back on the shelf.

"Rossi, not lost your sense of humour then?" he smiled but she just shrugged and sat down. "It was a gift, the carving on the mantel," he explained as he sat too.

"I love it, someone with an active mind I'm guessing." Avalon didn't explain any further, he was beginning to feel uncomfortable, he really didn't know what to say, there was nothing he could tell her. All he could do was make excuses why he couldn't spend much time with her, but that's all he had ever done and it bothered him. Not because it was Carol his ex-wife, more that she was still his friend and friends should find time for each other. He couldn't, that was that.

"Depending on when you are going back," he began, "we could probably arrange an evening out, I mean after this weekend-"

"You don't have to babysit me James," she interrupted.

"I know but there is so much to see up here and I would have liked to-"

"I'm going back Sunday." She had a fixed expression, no humour, no feeling, just the details as they were. Avalon then realised this hadn't worked out how she had imagined. Had she still harboured ideas of them getting back together as he once had? It seemed that way and some months ago it would have excited him but now, he knew any kind of meaningful relationship with *anyone* would always end with problems.

"Sunday? I thought you may be here a little longer than that."

"I have to get back and sort my life out," she sighed, "running away from problems never solves them."

"No, that's true, but having a break from them can give you a new perspective, even a new energy," he insisted. There was silence for a moment and then he stood, "I'll get the coffee," he said. He returned from the kitchen and sat again and handed her the cup, which she cradled in her hands. "Do you need anything, help, money?"

"No, but thank you," she smiled. He looked over to the carving on the mantel, not for any reason, he just didn't know what to say. She obviously had ideas buzzing around in her head but if she didn't share them there was little he could do. "Do you need to talk?" he eventually asked. She smiled again and took a sip of coffee then looked over to him.

"I came up here to see you and to talk," she began, "but since being up here that seems silly."

"Not at all, sometimes talking solves many things."

"Well, I've had a reality check and that's what matters."

"But I want to help-" he began but she interrupted once more.

"You have helped," she smiled.

"How?" he asked slightly bemused.

"Before you came up here you were a mess." Avalon tilted his head a little.

"Well I wouldn't have put it so succinctly but yes, I was mixed up I admit."

"But look at you now," she smiled holding her arms towards him, "you have *more* than sorted yourself out, you seem to have re-invented yourself."

"I wouldn't go that far," he laughed.

"Really, you have," she insisted, "you look different, you are stronger in body and mind and you've done that yourself."

"Not totally, I've had help working with a good team."

"Being happy at work goes a long way," she nodded.

"No not just work, these people are friends as well as colleagues and if they weren't who they were I couldn't have achieved anything." She was quiet for a moment, "everyone has to find some sort of balance, I haven't, by any stretch of the imagination but it's closer than I had before I came here."

"Maybe *I* should have a change of scenery then," she smiled but Avalon heard his phone vibrate on the table in the kitchen. He tried to ignore it.

"Maybe you should, once you move you can start again, you don't have to cling on to what you were or who you were. That's what I found anyway," he insisted as the damn phone shook again, he knew he had to answer it. "I have to get the phone, excuse me a moment," and he walked into the kitchen. It looked like it had come from one of the desk phones from the office, he dialled it, Rory Mackinnon answered.

"Hello Rory it's Avalon, has someone been trying to get me?"

"*Yes boss, it was me. The DCI is on the warpath and looking for you, he'll probably be ringing you soon.*"

"Okay, thanks for the heads up," replied Avalon, "is Ross or Frazer there?"

"*No boss, do you want me to get them in?*"

"No, no leave them to get a bit of rest, I'll be back as soon as I can." He turned off the phone and slipped it into his jacket pocket, he wasn't in the mood to talk to Croker yet, he would see him face to face. He returned to the lounge where Carol was pulling on her jacket.

"I'm not throwing you out," he said.

"No I know, but I must get on," she replied. Avalon knew she was being kind and making it easier for him to carry on with his job.

"We can meet before you leave can't we?" he asked.

"If you can find some time yes, but don't worry if

219

it's too difficult." She closed in on him and kissed him, not a peck on the cheek but a short, passionate kiss on the lips.

"Why does that feel like a goodbye?" he asked. She didn't reply to the question, she just gave him a wry smile and then opened the door.

"Look after yourself James Avalon," and she walked down the street towards the bed and breakfast.

~~~~~~

Avalon decided there was no point in beating about the bush, he would go straight to DCI Croker's office and find out what he had to say. To his astonishment the Superintendent was already with Croker and neither of them looked in a particularly good mood. Avalon gave the Superintendent a quick nod and then, still standing by the door of the office, said,

"I understand you wish to see me, Chief Inspector?"

"Yes DI Avalon, you take some tracking down I have to say," frowned Croker as he glanced over to the Superintendent. "We have been informed by Lawrence Hilliard's solicitor that you plan to bring him in for questioning today?"

"That's correct."

"Is this to do with your warrants?"

"Yes sir, we strongly believe that a serious crime has been committed on the property."

"Have you evidence DI Avalon?" interrupted the Superintendent.

"We have to analyse what we have found and that's in the hands of forensics at the moment," explained

Avalon.

"So as it stands," continued the Superintendent, "you have no real reason to question Mr Hilliard?"

"On the contrary," insisted Avalon, "there are several reasons to question Mr Hilliard, one of them being that blood has been found in the house and in the garden."

"Have you determined it is human blood?"

"As I said sir, we are awaiting the results from the forensics and until-"

"I have to point out detective," interrupted the Superintendent, "that Mr Hilliard has said, through his solicitor, that a few weeks ago he struck a deer with his car just outside his house, that may account for traces of blood."

"Unless Mr Hilliard is in the habit of taking dead wildlife to bed with him I would suggest that a deer is not-"

"I would strongly suggest that you do not take that impertinent tone with me," growled the man. Avalon was sick and tired of people interrupting him, it was something he had let slip on several occasions but now he was becoming angry. He held his tongue for a moment and just glared at the Superintendent, Croker saw the conflict and tried to disarm it.

"Could we say that until the results come in that there is no point in questioning Mr Hilliard?" Avalon turned to him.

"Are you taking me off this case?" he asked.

"No, I didn't say that," frowned Croker.

"Well that's the only way you'll stop me bringing him in, I have other evidence that I want Mr Hilliard to explain and-"

"I think John, that you may have to rethink this," interrupted the Superintendent again but this time Avalon wasn't standing for it, he raised his voice slightly.

"As I was saying, Mr Hilliard needs to explain why his house has large amounts of blood in several rooms and all around his garden." Avalon was stretching the truth somewhat but he was beginning to boil inside.

"I suggest, detective," glared the Superintendent, "that you remember your place and-" This time it was Avalon who interrupted.

"Mr Hilliard and his friends have spent far too long under the protection of Mr Cameron and his other associates, I am just setting the record straight and doing my best to bring criminals to book." He could see he was now in trouble, the Super was fuming. He turned to Croker.

"I want him off this case John," and he stood, his face so close to Avalon, he could tell what he'd had for breakfast. "You have overstepped the line Detective Avalon," and he left leaving the office door open. There was silence in the room as Croker wrung his hands as he looked at his computer screen.

"So?" Avalon began, "I better go and let the team know."

"Of course not," spat Croker.

"But I think the Super made it clear that-"

"I don't give a shit what that dickhead says," fumed Croker removing his spectacles, "all that bothers me now is, have you got something or have you not? I don't give a toss if you go down Avalon but I'll not be dragged down with you." Croker paused for a moment and then glared up at Avalon. "Have you got a case or not?"

"I can't be sure Hilliard is involved but I am as certain as I can be that a crime took place at that house." Croker nodded slowly, he stood and thrust his hands behind his back and paced the small area before sitting back down and looking back up at Avalon.

"The Superintendent has the ear of Hilliard, or his solicitor, I'm sure of that and in my book that is wrong," he sighed and looked away, "for Christ's sake Avalon, make sure whatever you find you make it stick for both our sakes." Croker replaced his spectacles and Avalon knew the interview was over.

~~~~~~

"Where's the boss?" asked Ross as he entered the Cave.

"He's interviewing Hilliard with Martin," replied Frazer looking up from her screen. Ross glanced over to the booth and around the room until his gaze fell on Mackinnon. "Where you been anyways?"

"Down the canal," Ross replied with a vague look in his eyes.

"So while we've been slaving away here, you've been taking in the sights?"

"Hey?" questioned Ross as if he was miles away, "er, oh aye, the sights, listen," and he pulled up a chair and sat the wrong way round on it. He crossed his arms on the back of it and rested his chin on his arms. "I've been thinking."

"That's not an accurate description of what goes on in your head," she retorted but he seemed not to have heard it, he just kept his eyes fixed on her.

"This Gibson whose name cropped up."

" John Mirriam Gibson you mean?"

"Aye whatever," nodded Ross, "why have we not questioned him?"

"Dunno," shrugged Frazer, "I thought the boss was going tae sort him but as we're not sure he's that same Gib-"

"We need to talk to him," interrupted Ross.

"Well mention it tae the boss."

"No, I mean *we* need to talk to him," insisted Ross and Frazer caught the meaning in the tone.

"You'll catch a shit storm ef the boss knows, y' realise that."

"I'll deal with the boss, you take Rory and put some pressure on this character."

"Not likely, I like this job now, I don't want tae-" Ross broke in again as he sat upright.

"*DC* Frazer, listen to what *DS* Ross is telling you." She stared at him for a moment as she took in what he was telling her, Ross was offering to take full blame for what they were about to do.

"Okay, but et's on your head," she said as she stood and looked to Rory, "you heard him, let's go."
Ross sat at his own desk and looked out of the window, he saw Frazer's car go round the roundabout in the distance and he wondered if his decision was worth the risk. Behind him the door to the office opened and in came Avalon with Rutherford behind him.

"Oh, you made it at last," frowned Avalon as he noticed Ross was alone, "where's Megan and Rory?"

"I asked them to check local shops about the earrings we found." Avalon looked at Ross for a moment and then nodded. "Found anything from Hilliard?"

"Bits, nothing profound but he's saying that he

hasn't been to the house for some time," began Avalon, "he admitted some of the carpets are new but he hasn't had them fitted so we need to track down all carpet fitters in the area. I asked him if anyone else had access to the house but his solicitor wouldn't let him answer that one."

"Which means they did," nodded Ross.

"I asked him specifically if Buchanan had access but that little arse wipe told me that his client declined to answer questions about Mr Buchanan."

"What's that mean?" asked Ross.

"Et means," answered Rutherford, "that he knows damn well that Buchanan es neck deep en shite."

"It also means that Hilliard is probably telling the truth but that's no reason to let the pressure up," added Avalon.

"So we're still stamping on Hilliard?" asked Ross with a slight grin.

"Yes, if only to make his life a misery," replied Avalon.

"It's a good idea," agreed Ross, "if he gets jumpy he may go over the head of his brief."

"That's the plan," nodded Avalon as he walked to the booth. Ross looked up to Rutherford as the big man said,

"You know you still look like shite."

"I'm tired, what's your excuse?" he replied.


It was too late in the afternoon to consider sending anyone else out to work on the incident up at Garve and Avalon sighed a deep breath as he realised that Hilliard was going to be little help while he had Cameron by his side. He looked at the screen of his

225

computer but he saw nothing, there were too many images and thoughts going through his head for him to see anything on the outside. He didn't even notice Ross slip quietly into the booth.

"That's the expression of a troubled mind," Ross said with a slight smile.

"What? Oh yeah," there was still a sign of humour in Avalon's croaky reply, "too right. They used to have a saying when I was a kid, they used to say 'it's a bobby's job' and it used to mean that it was easy. I'm not sure how that comparison came about."

"Probably stems from the time that coppers directed traffic and played bit parts in old Ealing comedies," grinned Ross, "anyway," he continued, "I thought they were still called 'Peelers' when you were a wean?"

"I feel that sort of age today," nodded Avalon. He leaned back in his chair and stretched his arms above him as Ross sunk into the chair opposite.

"I'm guessing you'll not want a quick pint this evening?" asked Ross.

"I don't think so, I'll be poor company tonight anyway."

"I just thought it may be good for you, bring Carol along." Avalon looked directly at Ross as he sat upright once more.

"That's a sore point," he frowned.

"You mean even when you're not married you're still filing for divorce?"

"It's not quite that bad," admitted Avalon, "but she's going back on Sunday, I think she's bored and I can't blame her."

"Then bring her to the pub for an hour, I'm sure

she'll enjoy that."

"She's not a pub person really and anyway, we could be here until midnight," insisted Avalon. He looked at his wristwatch, it was already late afternoon and the chance of them having time for a break was unlikely.

"If you consider the truth of it, until forensics has something to tell us, there is little we can do," said Ross widening his eyes. Avalon just shrugged, Ross was right of course but Avalon always found the frustration of a case stopped him relaxing and so he never tried to. Maybe that was a fault but it was his nature.

"We'll see," he eventually said.


Avalon was still feeling uncomfortable about the visit to the pub right up until the moment he met Carol at the door to the bed and breakfast, and then he felt fine. They walked down to the pub on Castle Street and Avalon did his best to explain a little of what Ross was like. He added the odd humorous comment here and there and so, by the time they entered the bar, she had already decided she liked him. Avalon introduced the two of them but when he got to Ross, he paused.

"... and Carol, this is Ross," he looked up to the ceiling for a moment and then continued, "tell me, what *is* your first name?"

"It's Ian," he directed to Carol and he took her hand and gave a slight bow of the head. Ross was quite taken aback with Carol and he became charming and so different that Avalon asked him if he was feeling the pressure of the case. Ross ignored him and continued to engage in chat with Carol, which left Avalon out of the conversation. They moved to a table with their drinks and Ross pulled the chair out for Carol to sit.

"Thank you, it's nice to have a gentleman around," she smiled.

"Oh this isn't normal," laughed Avalon lifting his drink, "and it won't last."

"Your ex-husband," began Ross, "is under the impression that we Scots don't have any traditional gentlemanly morals you see." He didn't take his eyes off Carol, he just nodded towards the DI in a casual fashion.

"That's not true, it's just you," replied Avalon after taking a drink.

"You notice he made a joke about my first name," Ross still looked at Carol, "but the truth is he has never called me by my first name all the time I have known him."

"Really?" smiled Carol glancing at Avalon.

"Never," continued Ross, "everyone else in the section gets called by their first names, but not I."

"That can't be true," insisted Avalon. Ross just glanced to him and raised his brows, Carol laughed. She could see how well the two of them got on, they were like a double act in many ways but she could also see the tired expressions they both had, tiredness held back by regular doses of humour and nights at the pub.

"He used to call me Wife," grinned Carol reaching for her drink.

"That doesn't surprise me, he's so uncouth," nodded Ross. Avalon folded his arms and stared with a blank face, he had resigned himself to the fact that he didn't stand a chance against the two of them and he sat back. It gave him chance to study Carol, he watched her reactions to Ross who was given her his full attention. Was he attracted to her? Probably, and as Avalon

228

watched her, he wouldn't blame him, enjoying herself and laughing and smiling she looked good. He could remember the first time he had seen her all those years ago across a crowded room. She had been with two of her friends at a wedding party for another mutual friend. Avalon had been ready to leave when he noticed her across the room and he fell in love with her at that moment. She had looked back at him and smiled and his heart had almost popped out through his chest. It took him three weeks of tracking down who she was but his detective mind had not only found her, but devised a way to meet her. From then on she had been the only woman for him and as he watched her laughing at Ross's poor jokes he could almost fall in love with her all over again.

"You were the same weren't you?" she asked Avalon with a broad grin. He realised he hadn't been privy to the conversation and stuttered so he was noncommittal and asked a question instead.

"What do you mean?"

"Your hairstyle, it was quite old fashioned," she laughed.

"Well I was never a follower of fashion."

"Not current fashion no," she said and turned back to Ross, "on our first date he looked like Nik Kershaw from 'The Riddle' video," and she laughed again. Avalon thought how ironic that they were talking about the same subject as he had been thinking, if not from the same perspective. He had remembered the romantic side of it and she? Well, she was amused by his hairstyle.

"Just like me," nodded Ross with a broad grin, "when my long hair could have been fashionable, I cut it short."

"You had long hair?" asked Avalon.

"Yeah, I cut it when I joined up," he grinned.

"That's something I never knew about you," replied Avalon with a slight grin.

"There's a great deal you don't know about me," said Ross and he turned his attention back to Carol, "and will never know if I have any say in it," he winked. Carol was enjoying herself and though Avalon thought Ross was trying to impress her at first, he now realised that wasn't the case. He wasn't using all the cheesy lines he heard him use when he met women for the first time, he wasn't plying her with the bravado and sleazy jokes he fed the females he sometimes chatted to in the pub. He was genuinely being attentive and friendly without any 'edge'. He was trying to ensure that not everything about her trip would be tedious and a let-down. In short, Ross was trying to help him out.

As Avalon walked Carol home she linked her arm in his and walked close to him, it brought back memories.

"I like Ian," she said quietly, "I can see why you get on with him." Avalon just made a 'humph' noise. "If the rest of the team are like Ian and Megan then I can see why you like it up here."

"There's more to it than that, it's about the place and its people not just about work, that's what I wanted to show you."

"Well, you never know, maybe we can arrange something next year," she said gripping his arm.

"Yeah, we could try and arrange something when I get some time off."

As they reached the door of the guesthouse it was

time to part company, Avalon had a big day in the morning and there was a great deal to do. They kissed, not the same sort of kiss that she had given him earlier but just a peck.

"I'm glad we went out tonight, I've enjoyed it," she said and walked inside.

~~~~~~

The Cave was busy on Friday morning, everyone seemed to be getting their information together ready for the meeting Avalon had called. He glanced up from inside the booth, he didn't want to rush them, he wanted them prepared and ready to give a balanced picture of what they had on the Buchanan case. Wilson and Boyd were the only ones not present, they were still working their own cases. Avalon looked through the preliminary forensic report and tried to feel optimistic about the meeting, then he took in a deep breath and walked into the main office.

"Okay team, I have a meeting this morning with the DCI so I need all information regarding the Buchanan case," he began, "I will first tell you what we have from the preliminary forensics report." He rested his backside on the edge of one of the desks and looked down at the sheet of notes in his hand. "Regarding the property we searched up near Garve, Miss Underwood has confirmed that the hair found in what we believe to be a shallow grave *is* human. It belonged to a female and DNA has been extracted but we have nothing on record about this person. There were traces of blood found in the hair too. One of the earrings has a partial print but it is too small to be of use and again there are microscopic traces of blood on it." He glanced up as he broke off for a breather.

"They have confirmed that the luminol contacts were indeed blood and forensics are still trying to match the samples to the DNA found in the hair but the upshot is that it looks like something catastrophic happened at the property. Mr Hilliard is claiming that he knows nothing about it so it's going to be tough going unless we can find a time for the incident and place him there," he broke off again and glanced out of the window. "I'm not sure an arrest would be in our best interests at this time," he added in a quieter voice. He looked at the assembled faces and then placed his notes on the side of the desk he was leaning on and folded his arms. "Does anyone have anything to add?" Mackinnon lifted his hand carefully into the air.

"Rory," nodded Avalon.

"Well boss," he began in a quiet voice, "I've been looking into the forensics process that McVie's defence were trying to use and it seems it is being used in the states to single out suspects where no DNA is available."

"Explain," insisted Avalon.

"Well, it's a bit complex but it boils down to finding close relatives, testing their DNA and running the results though a computer to see what possible DNA the suspect may have."

"It sounds a bit hit and miss," commented Ross.

"They use it in the States to make an arrest, then they can check the DNA legally and it does work, several criminals have been brought to justice already," insisted Rory.

"I'm guessing this is all assuming the close relatives give consent?" asked Avalon.

"Well yes," nodded Rory, "but it may be worth a try." Avalon nodded thoughtfully and then said,

"It might be worth checking with any relatives we can find, particularly any that are known not to get on with him." He turned to the others. "Anything else?"

"I've checked through missing persons and there seems tae be nothing that could match a female en this area," added Rutherford, "do you want to expand the area boss?" Avalon nodded.

"Yeah, may as well, we don't know anything about the possible victim except it's likely to be a female." Avalon noticed Ross looking over to Frazer but saying nothing. He then remembered something. "Has anyone done anything about finding the carpet company that supplied the new carpets to the house?"

"I'm still searchin' boss, nothing has cropped up yet," explained Frazer. Avalon nodded with a grim expression.

"Anything more?" he asked staring straight at Ross. Ross glanced back to Frazer and then said,

"Aye, there is something," and he adjusted his slouching position on the chair to something more upright. "This Gibson character."

"The one who may have been involved with both Hilliard and Buchanan?" asked Avalon. Ross just nodded and then continued.

"He does know both of them of course but he also knows a little more about this case."

"Go on," frowned Avalon wondering why Ross seemed reticent about revealing his information.

"He knows that Hilliard gave house keys to his friends, he had one himself but he gave it back as he never went up there."

"You sound as if you have spoken to him," said Avalon still frowning and spreading his hand onto the desk.

"Megan spoke to him," admitted Ross but he cut in immediately with, "but under my orders, she didn't want to go." Avalon kept his gaze on Ross for a second and then turned to Frazer.

"You realise that you could have made a cock up if Gibson had decided to keep quiet?" he asked. Ross cut in again.

"It's my fault, as I said-"

"We'll speak later," interrupted Avalon with a calm voice but everyone could see the flames leaping about in the boss's eyes. He turned back to Frazer.

"Well?"

"I know I should have refused-"

"I don't want excuses, I want to know what you found out." There was a menace in Avalon's voice. Frazer had never seen him quite like he was at that moment.

"Well," she paused to compose herself, "he was quite talkative, he said that Hilliard and Buchanan, along with a few others, used tae have parties up at the house."

"The one at Garve you mean?"

"Oh sorry, yes boss," explained Frazer, "he told me that close friends had keys t' the house and there were some wild goings on up there."

"You mean prostitutes?" asked Avalon.

"Aye, drugs, booze and wife swapping, all that sort of thing."

"Do we have names for any of the others?" asked the boss.

"Some aye," nodded Frazer, "Hilliard of course

and a few others I've checked out but only one with any form. He's been at Her Majesty's pleasure for some time though," she paused for a moment as she reached for her notepad, "two names rang alarm bells though, Ross Fleming and Malcolm Milne."

"Do we know them?" asked Avalon shrugging slightly.

"We know Fleming, he's got no form but we know him as a bodyguard for the rich and famous. In the past we've co-ordinated a few high-profile visits with him and his company."

"So why would he be mixing with the likes of Hilliard and Buchanan?" asked Avalon.

"That I don't know boss but Gibson says he wasn't one for the drugs or the women," added Frazer.

"He may have been there in a professional capacity," offered Ross. Avalon glanced at Ross and then back to Frazer.

"So who's the other face?"

"Malcolm Milne," announced Frazer checking the notepad, "he's odd because he's completely off the radar."

"Meaning?"

"There's hardly any record of him anywhere," shrugged Frazer as Ross added some detail.

"No form, no underworld connections, no known associates and doesn't appear anywhere on the internet except as the managing director of his company."

"Which is?" asked Avalon looking at Ross but Ross looked over to Frazer.

"Walker Consultancy," explained Frazer, "and as far as I can tell et's an internet cloud company with some other internet-based connections."

"So he runs porn sites?" asked Avalon folding his arms once more.

"Not as far as we can tell, Rory did a deep search but can't find much that they do." Rory tapped his keyboard and then read from it.

"Walker Consultancy Limited is a registered company supplying technology service activities and web portals."

"So he provides services for porn sites," amended Avalon.

"With respect boss, not everything on the internet is porn based," offered Rory. Ross wanted to make a humorous comment but thought better of it.

"Either way," sighed Avalon, "with that kind of company description his business is not particularly transparent."

"There's quite a growing internet gaming industry in Scotland these days," insisted Rory.

"Where is he based?"

"Thistle Street, Aberdeen," added the DC.

"Great," sighed Avalon again, "it couldn't be Inverness could it?" The room went quiet for a moment as Avalon looked through the implications of the news. "Well someone is going to have to go down there and have a nose around, we'll need to coordinate with the Aberdeen section too." He paused again and unfolded his arms and stood. "Rory, contact Aberdeen and tell them what we're after, they may help us out a little, Martin, you widen the search on missing people, you better include Aberdeen." Rutherford nodded and got to work. Avalon then looked at Ross and then Frazer.

"I hope you didn't stress Mr Gibson too much?"

"I just told him we knew he had some previous and we were investigating a murder, I just stretched the truth a wee bit," and then she looked down to her desk, "I've just had a thought boss."

"Go on," said Avalon staring at her.

"Well, the team watching the guy who followed you said he made a trip to Aberdeen two days ago."

"Follow it up, find out if they know where he went, you may need to coordinate with Aberdeen to search for any CCTV footage, we need something from this. Oh and widen the search for the carpet company." Frazer nodded and got straight on the phone. Avalon looked back to Ross. "And we need to have words," he looked at his watch, "but not now, I'm off to see the DCI."

~~~~~~

"No Ross tonight?" asked Carol with the beginning of a smile.

"No, I thought we would have a quiet evening together," replied Avalon as he sipped on the wine.

"Well it looks like a nice place," she said looking quickly around the restaurant.

"It's another one somebody recommended."

"So how come you got the night off?" she asked reaching for her glass.

"For a change we've had a good day, things are progressing and the Chief seems happy with what we have found so he's giving us some support."

"Which means he wasn't supporting you previously?"

"Sort of," nodded Avalon, "but it's complicated and there is an undercurrent of something internal going on."

"Oh, from what I remember, those are always dodgy cases to work on."

"They certainly are but let's not talk about work."

"If you don't want to, it's just that knowing you, it's all you'll be thinking about," she smiled, taking a sip of the wine.

"Not tonight, I've ignored you while this has been on, it's your turn this evening."

"Don't feel guilty, it's your job, if I had been more understanding..." she paused, "well anyway, that's water under the bridge," and she took another drink. Avalon raised his glass.

"Then let's toast to a good future for both of us."

"I'll drink to that," she said as her glass kissed his.

"Talking of which, are you still off back tomorrow?"

"Yes," she nodded placing the glass back on the table, "I rang my old place up earlier to see if they have any work for me, Dianna told me to go and see her on Monday."

"Well there you are, things could be looking up already."

"Yeah, but it's going to be a little odd going back there when they all know what happened."

"That sort of thing never used to bother you," he said raising his brows.

"No, but times change, and..." she cut off what she was about to say.

"What?" asked Avalon.

"I was going to ask you a question but it's not my business."

"Fire away, if I don't want to tell you I won't," smiled Avalon.

"I was wondering if you still had the nightmares." Avalon looked down at his glass then back up to her.

"Not as such, I think only when I get over tired or there is a build-up of stress they drift back, and then only as fleeting images, not the hell I used to go through." She reached for the glass but just played with the fine stem rather than pick it up.

"You never told me what that was about, to this day I still don't know."

"The same reason I didn't tell you still applies, I didn't want to bring the horrors of my world into yours, I tried to protect you from that."

"I know," she nodded, "and very admirable it was too but don't you think if you'd shared it, the impact on our relationship wouldn't have been so severe?"

"Yes, in hindsight it may have lessened the impact, but I made a decision early in my career that the cases don't come home with me," he insisted with a slight frown.

"But they came anyway, that's what I'm getting at."

"I made mistakes," sighed Avalon, "but it's as I said at the time, victims get counselling, even the crooks get it sometimes but coppers?" He tried not to sound too anguished, "they let us dry out emotionally and then throw us out with a pension when we're broken." He took a hard gulp of wine and Carol could see he was getting angry, he always did when it came down to that particular subject. She decided to change tack.

"Talking of pensions, I forgot to tell you, Dad's got a new hobby, brewing beer." Avalon gave a chuckle.

"Yeah, I can see him loving that, how did your mother take it?"

"Okay I suppose but she can't work out why he still goes down to the pub when he's brewing his own."

"I hope you didn't tell her the truth," he smiled.

"No, not at all, I just said he probably goes for the male conversation."

"Even I can't do that," laughed Avalon, "I don't know anything about football or cricket, and cars leave me cold."

"You do alright with women though," she grinned and Avalon saw a cheekiness in her eyes. For a moment he felt a little embarrassed but then he assumed she was talking about *their* past.

"I used to," he insisted, "I don't get time for anything like that now."

"Then you should make time, there will be someone out there for you."

"I don't doubt it, but..." he shrugged and fell silent.

"You have to let go of the guilt, not every woman wants a normal, happy-families sort of relationship," insisted Carol.

"This feels really odd, one minute it feels like you are chatting me up, the next you are selling me off to some loose woman from the Black Isle."

"Is that where loose women are from up here?" she grinned.

"Not at all, I just picked a random place name. It fits because it's not black and it's not an island." Carol laughed. Avalon saw the old Carol in those eyes and for a moment he wanted to kiss her, like the kiss she had given him when they first met. If she had said 'let's get back together' at that moment, he would have said 'yes'. As it was, he noticed the waiter approach with the bill and it brought him back to the real world. He walked her back to the Bed and Breakfast, they had agreed that it was late and as Avalon was at work early in the morning they would call it a night. As they said their fairwells they embraced and kissed, just a friendly kiss this time before she turned and walked inside.

Avalon walked back down the road towards his house, he looked up at the night sky, it was clear for once and here and there he saw the odd star. As he lowered his head back down, he felt a single tear in the corner of his eye. He quickly wiped it away as if it was offending his face and then he wondered if looking at stars could do that. Of course it couldn't but he couldn't think why it would be there, he wasn't sad, he wasn't ecstatically happy either, so why had it formed? Maybe it was the loss of the life he could have had with her that had caused it. Maybe it was that the last two hours that he had spent with her were some of the best he remembered and that was sad enough to form a tear. He stopped under the streetlamp near his house. What was he doing? For all this time in Scotland he had thought he had known what he was doing, but did he? The mention of the nightmares was on his mind too, he hoped that just thinking about them wouldn't bring them back.

He opened the door and went inside. He poured a large whisky, undressed and flopped onto his new sofa. The whisky warmed him, made his thoughts more pliable, made him relax, but was it enough to stop the images coming back? He didn't want to see *her* face again. He didn't want to travel back to that moment. He wanted to close his eyes and go straight to sleep and see nothing but a blank, black canvas. The glass was empty, his head felt empty and he made his way to bed. The sheets were cool and comforting but he left the light on and stared at the ceiling until his thoughts bent in the wind blowing through his mind and he drifted off to sleep thinking about himself and Sarah Underwood walking through Glen Affric.

# Chapter Ten

By Saturday afternoon, Ross was becoming a little worried. His boss hadn't, as yet, taken him aside and given him a dressing down as he had expected, either he had forgotten, or he was waiting until he cooled down. Whichever was the true reason it was disconcerting in many ways for if it was the former, the subject could easily raise its head at some inopportune moment in the future. If it was the latter, it meant that Avalon was furious with him. Ross hated not knowing what his boss was thinking and the frustration was becoming more important to him than the case. He then considered it could equally be Avalon's way of punishing him, Avalon knew Ross was the sort of person who disliked waiting for the action to unravel and his boss could simply be letting him stew in his own juices. Ross decided he would bring it to a head so he could concentrate on his work. As he entered the booth, Avalon was busy jotting notes on a sheet of paper that seemed to have a great deal of writing with long arrows pointing here and there.

"Got a minute?" he asked as he leaned on the partition.

"Yeah, take a seat," answered Avalon continuing to write on the paper. He hadn't even looked up, so Ross sat as he was bid.

"You wanted to see me."

"Did I?" asked Avalon glancing up for a moment before continuing with his work.

"Yeah, Friday, you said you were going to have words with me."

"I don't recall," replied Avalon this time not bothering to give eye contact. He seemed so engrossed with his scribbling that Ross became impatient and changed to a more belligerent tone.

"Well after the thing about Frazer interviewing Gibson, you made it clear you wanted to give me a bollocking." Avalon stopped sketching and writing for a moment and looked up. He then tossed his pen on the desk and leaned back in his chair.

"I don't think I said that," he then insisted.

"Not in so many words, but..." he shrugged.

"Obviously you must think you need a bollocking as you put it."

"You said we need to have words and you gave me a glare that would freeze the Ness."

"Just a bit of rhetoric," Avalon replied and reached for his sketch.

"Oh, rhetoric, of course it was. Rhetoric that everyone else in the room saw as 'Rossy has got his arse kicked for this one', that sort of rhetoric you mean?"

"It's never bothered you in the past," said Avalon concentrating on the image he was holding, "anyway, it's what *I* would have done," he added and sighed at the paper he was holding. Ross gave a sigh too, his was more to do with the fact that Avalon was almost ignoring him. He was about to leave when Avalon spoke again.

"What do you think of this?" and he handed Ross the sheet of scribble. Ross studied it for a few moments and made a quiet 'humph' sound and then turned the paper the other way up. He then handed it back saying,

"It's okay but I prefer Cézanne." Avalon frowned, he then pushed the paper back across the desk.

"Two aspects of that answer are annoying," he began, "firstly, you don't realise what you are reading therefore you're not as bright as I thought you were and secondly, you have no idea who Cézanne was."

"Paul Cézanne was a French painter," replied Ross.

"Well done, I'm surprised you knew that, did you know he was one of the most regarded post-impressionists?"

"I don't know about that," replied Ross folding his arms, "but he did a brilliant job of my sister's hallway." Avalon sighed and pointed down to the sheet of scribbling. Ross glanced down at it, there were notes written around areas of block text and arrows arcing across the page to link one block to another like a complicated cause-and-effect diagram. He didn't pick it up, he caught the gist of the sketch the first time, he did however think that Avalon had made it overcomplicated with links and notes.

"I know what you're getting at," he eventually said, "but you're always the one who tells us not to get bogged down with preconceptions."

"That's not what it is, *this*," insisted Avalon pointing to the sheet, "links up most of what we know in a logical manner. I'm not saying we should take it as a basis of how we should conduct the investigation, it just ties up the loose ends." Ross then picked up the sheet and read through some of the points and followed some of the arrows. He then tilted his head and jutted out his lip. He placed the sheet on the desk and folded his arms once more staring straight at Avalon.

"So," he began, "there is a party up at the house at Garve, probably with Hilliard and Buchanan in attendance, at least one prostitute there too and during the mayhem, something goes wrong. The body is buried in the garden until they can get someone to remove it. They get their 'club' involved to help sort out the problem and in the meantime they clean the house. Is that it so far?" Avalon gave a curt nod but said nothing. "So the 'club' send in their caretakers, remove the body and dispose of it but they insist that Buchanan, who is likely the one that did the deed, goes away. The 'club' cleans up his house too to remove any DNA from his house to match that of the crime scene and the note is left to seal the deal," Ross raised his brows for confirmation he was on the right track. Avalon just gave a slight smile. "So far so good," continued Ross, "then there is the problem of the house at Garve, carpets are changed and Cameron is brought in to cover anything they might have missed. Buchanan is sent off abroad to sunny climes and the 'club' keeps an eye on PC Plod to make sure they are going round in circles due to multiple red herrings. Is that about it?"

"So, what do you think?" asked Avalon again.

"I think you must be distracted," began Ross, "very little of it holds water and to be honest it doesn't even sound like your theory."

"I know some of it is hard to justify but which points bother you?"

"Well for starters," sighed Ross, "why would Hilliard agree to stay around when Buchanan is being handed a get-out-of-jail-free card?" Avalon pursed his lips. "And if he was to disappear for good, which would have to, why would he put his car in storage?"

"Hmm, the car is bothering me," nodded Avalon, "that part of it does make the theory problematic."

"Aye," nodded Ross, "but the main flaw is about the houses," he noticed Avalon wince as if he had seen the issue and not bothered to explain it. "Two houses are cleaned up but only one of them is done properly, that means, whoever did the Buchanan house didn't do the Garve house. The only answer is that the 'Clan' didn't organise the clean-up at the house at Garve." Avalon nodded at the statement, he knew exactly what Ross was saying but he looked up as Frazer approached the booth.

"Got something Megan?" he asked as she entered.

"Aye, a' think I have boss," she was carrying a sheet of notes, "I've found the carpet fitter who did the Garve house."

"Brilliant," announced Avalon sitting up straight.

"This guy says he got a phone call tae fit several carpets en the house but the problem es," she paused for a second, "he never saw the guy who owned the house. He was told where tae find the keys and let himself en. The money was left en an envelope and he was told tae lock the door and leave the keys afterwards."

"Did he have to remove the old carpets?" asked Ross.

"No, everything was gone, just the bare floors."

"So did he say who ordered the carpets?" asked Avalon.

"Aye, the guy said he was Lawrence Hilliard," replied Frazer turning back to Avalon.

"We need to know if he still has the envelope the money came in," added Avalon.

"I asked that, he hasn't, there was over four and a half grand en the envelope so the money went straight t' the bank."

"Okay, bring him in, we need his phone records so that we can find out where the call came from," insisted Avalon, "or rather *who* it came from." Frazer nodded and left. Avalon then looked back to Ross. "Did Buchanan have a van at his unit?"

"I think so," nodded Ross, "but I heard the unit has closed down now since we interviewed the staff."

"If there's a van we need to find it, we need to get it down to forensics and strip it down to the last nut and bolt."

"You think he may have moved the body in it?" asked Ross.

"It's possible but those carpets have gone somewhere and it's likely that van was used." Ross nodded and started to leave. "We have to go to Aberdeen at some stage too," added Avalon. Ross nodded once more and continued into the Cave. Avalon stared into space for a moment, he was trying to think through all angles of the case, making sure they were checking all leads and looking in the right places for the clues, he also tore up his page of notes. With no body however, it was going to be an uphill task and, unless one of his team stumbled on something important, it was going to drag on for some time.

A few hours later he walked into the Cave to talk to Frazer.

"I want you to contact this Malcolm Milne and make an appointment to see him. Invent some story to make him think we need his professional help and don't mention our real names. If it was him that sent out the man to follow me he will twig it straight away." Frazer nodded and looked back to her computer screen then Avalon looked to Mackinnon. "Rory, give her a hand to make some story up and then both of you go and see the other chap, er..." he tried to remember the name.

"Ross Fleming?" offered Frazer.

"Aye, that's the one," agreed Avalon pointing towards her.

"Hang on," put in Ross, "did I hear correctly there?"

"Probably, his name is Ross, like you," Avalon replied.

"I'm not on about that," continued Ross, "I'm sure I heard you say 'Aye' in fact I'm positive I did."

"I don't think I did, did I?" he asked turning to Frazer.

"I don't know boss, unlike some, I just listen to the important stuff," she shrugged.

"You did, you said 'Aye', not yes or yeah, aye," insisted Ross.

"You're mistaken, it happens when you get older," frowned Avalon, "anyway, more importantly you'll have to come to Aberdeen with me."

"Why me, that's a tedious road?"

"Because I don't want to drive," glared Avalon.

"You could get one of the lackeys to drive you," insisted Ross.

"Yeah, that's why I chose you," said Avalon and he returned to the booth. Frazer looked over to Ross and made a silent laugh. Ross glared at her for a moment and then blew her a kiss.

~~~~~~

Ross stared glassy eyed out of the car windscreen on a gloomy Monday morning as he turned off the A9 onto the Nairn road. He thought about switching on the radio but he didn't think his ears were ready for the verbal sludge that breakfast shows dished out. He glanced over to Avalon who seemed quieter than normal and he decided to try and open a gentle conversation.

"I assume Carol's gone home?"

"Yeah," replied Avalon blinking from his dream, "I took her down to the airport yesterday afternoon. It was nine hours on the train so she went for the one hour on the plane."

"Probably cheaper too," suggested Ross.

"Not far off," nodded Avalon and then he resumed the silence. Ross looked around outside and then back to the road in front.

"Did Frazer tell you about the van?" he asked.

"Yes, she said it was still parked at the unit, it's being taken down to forensics this morning." Silence again. Ross once more considered the radio but then he realised that white noise would probably be more pleasant.

"It's a long tedious trip this but if you're going to refrain from speech it's gonna be unbearable," insisted Ross glancing over to his boss.

"Sorry," replied Avalon giving a stretch of his legs, "I didn't realise I was."

"Something on your mind?"

"No not really, just tired I think," and as if to confirm it, he yawned, "so go on, what do you want to talk about?"

"Anything, any conversation would be better than the drone of the road noise."

"Okay," sighed Avalon, "what do you make of the final forensic report from the shallow grave?"

"It's not the sort of conversation I had in mind but as you ask, I think it sounds right and Miss Underwood and team are probably the best in Britain."

"So the victim is female, with red colouration to her natural hair and blue eyes. She is at risk of developing cystic fibrosis and her age is around thirty two, plus or minus three years," replied Avalon counting the points on his fingers.

"DNA can almost tell us what her favourite television soap opera was," nodded Ross.

"Everything except where her body is," replied Avalon bringing the subject down to earth. "It also says that it is doubtful the body was buried for long."

"You know," began Ross, "there is a rare possibility here that a lot of coincidences have come together to make it look like foul play."

"Do you believe that?" asked Avalon turning to face him.

"No," replied Ross shaking his head, "not at all but *you* always say don't assume."

"I do, but why would the carpets be changed, why would there be so much blood and how did the hair end up in what looks like a shallow grave?"

"I'm just saying," shrugged Ross.

"We have to follow what we know and from where I'm sitting this looks like someone killed a female and buried the body in the garden until they could move it," insisted Avalon a little edgily.

"But there again, why bury the body in the first place?" At this, Avalon turned to face Ross.

"There are so many reasons why that could have been done, are you being serious or can't you stand the silence?" Ross glanced back to him for a moment and then looked ahead once more.

"You must be tired," he said, "I've not known you this snappy since you last bought a round at the pub."

"I'm sorry," said Avalon rubbing his temples with his fingers, "sometimes lots of little things become a big thing and I forgot we coppers aren't supposed to have normal issues."

"So what's wrong, something to do with the meeting with Carol?"

"Not as such," sighed Avalon, "it's just..." he paused and then said with another deep sigh, "oh you know, you're just thinking that the bigger picture doesn't matter, you come to terms with who you are and what you should do, you even get to thinking that you've reached the end game. Then something very slight happens and you start to worry all over again that you have somehow got it wrong."

"Is this about the case?" asked Ross glancing over again, "or about life?"

"Both I suppose, the case keeps me doubting certainly but I can get over that, I know we have such a great team we *will* sort this one out, but, everything else just baffles me."

"You're not on your own there, I've looked deeply at what's going on for some time now, I mean, you see bodies now and then and you sometimes wonder, why them?" He paused, "well that's hard to explain, but to cut it short, when old Arty Struthers died in that puddle of mud it got me thinking about regrets."

"You're always going to have regrets, that's what proves you were ever alive," replied Avalon.

"Yeah, I know that but do you ever wake up one morning and think you are doing the wrong things and in the wrong order, even the wrong job?" Avalon glanced back to Ross and looked at his features, he saw that Ross was being serious.

"Yeah, I think that at night mainly, in the morning it doesn't bother me as much but at night..." Avalon tailed off and looked ahead. "So you thinking of jacking it in and becoming a postman or something?" he added.

"Not quite but a mate of mine asked me if I wanted to drive a tour bus for him, a mini bus, taking tourists around the Highlands."

"You'll still wake up in the morning and think 'what the hell am I doing?' that won't change. I think it's about the person not what job you do." Ross nodded and shrugged at the same time.

"Probably," he said and then there was silence for half a minute. It was Avalon who broke it this time.

"I've thought about it."

"Quitting the force you mean?" asked Ross.

"Yeah," nodded Avalon and stretching his legs into the floor-well again, "I have seriously thought about it. Just after Mack had his accident I was thinking that I would give it two years and then go."

"Do you still think that way?" asked Ross.

"In some ways I do, I mean I love the job but I would love to have a private life too and at the moment I'm afraid to commit to anything," Avalon altered what he was going to say, he thought the conversation had gotten too serious so he thought how he could lighten it. He needn't have bothered as Ross was thinking the same thing.

"I wish I'd put the radio on and left you to sit quietly now." Avalon laughed, he knew it wasn't good to talk about serious subjects on the way to an interview, he should be thinking of the approach he would use.

The rest of the journey was undertaken in silence. Both men were juggling thoughts about personal issues *and* the case. In the quiet moments, both of them allowed thoughts to mingle and knock against each other but before they reached Aberdeen they would have to separate them off once more.

As Ross turned off the A90 onto the A9012, he asked,

"So what's the story?"

"Rory booked us an appointment to see this Malcolm Milne about some sort of internet services," explained Avalon.

"What sort of services?"

"I don't know, Rory mentioned 'clouds' or something but it's irrelevant, we're just scamming our way in," he smiled, "Rory gave him false names, I'm Mr Dale and you're Mr Tubby."

"You're joking," insisted Ross with a shocked face, Avalon laughed a little and then added,

You're Mr McLeod." Ross nodded and turned onto Westburn Drive and continued along, he looked at his watch. They were just about on time, the journey had taken the best part of three hours. Once they were parked up they headed back to Thistle Street and into the offices of Walker Consultancies where a middle-aged secretary with a stern face took their names. She told them to take a seat and went into a side office for some seconds.

"Mr Milne will see you now," she said without any kind of niceties. Inside the office a smartly dressed man sat behind a plain desk but the office was far from plain. Avalon noticed several pieces of expensive looking, ancient furniture. The man himself stood as they approached the desk.

"Mr Dale and Mr McLeod," he said holding out his hand. He was a little younger than Avalon but incredibly well turned out. Avalon considered that if he was dressed in a dinner jacket he wouldn't look out of place on the set of Casino Royale. Though he was Scottish he didn't have the accent, probably the result of an English university education. "Please, take a seat and tell me what I can do for you." There was a hint of hesitation in his voice, as if he remembered he hadn't done something. Avalon was about to make up some story but before he could begin the man continued, "I'm guessing you are not Mr Dale or Mr McLeod are you?" and he frowned a little.

"No Mr Milne we're not," began Avalon, "I'm Detective Inspector Avalon and this is Detective Sergeant Ross of Inverness CID."

"Then why the subterfuge Detective Inspector?" asked the man steepling his hands in front of himself.

"I wasn't sure you would agree to speak to us if we told you who we were," replied Avalon.

"I don't see why you would think that, but as you have my attention now, what can I do for you?"

"Have you ever heard of a company called Butler Electronics?"

"No," replied the man calmly.

"Do you know Lawrence Hilliard?" asked Avalon.

"No, I don't though I have heard of him."

"Jason Buchanan?"

"No," he replied shaking his head.

"How about Trevor Cameron?"

"No, but seriously Detective, what is this about, we could continue in this way for hours?"

"We are pursuing a line of enquiry into the disappearance of Jason Buchanan," explained Avalon.

"And may I ask if this person is a resident of Inverness?"

"He is," replied Avalon.

"Then I may as well inform you that I do no business in Inverness so it's very doubtful that I will have any sort of acquaintance there, business or otherwise."

"Then you may know a man called Stuart Dunn," added Ross, "he is known to have connections in Aberdeen."

"No, sorry, the name means nothing to me," insisted Milne, "is there anything else?" Avalon noticed a large painting on the wall to the side as Ross continued.

"Can you explain to us why you were seen at an address near Garve at a house owned by Lawrence Hilliard if you don't know him?" he asked.

"I don't recall the incident, I have very few customers from that part of the Highlands so I think I would remember being there." Avalon stood and moved to the painting.

"Is this an original?" he asked.

"It is but not by any painter you would have heard of," replied Milne.

"He's a soldier from the Napoleonic Wars isn't he?" asked Avalon studying the picture.

"Yes indeed, one of the Scottish Regi-"

"79th Cameron Highlanders," interrupted Avalon, he didn't know for sure but it was an educated guess.

"Yes," continued Milne, "you certainly know your Napoleonic uniforms Detective."

"And I'm guessing this is..." he paused trying to remember the name, "Hume," he turned to Milne pointing at the image, "Major Mortimer Hume."

"It is," agreed Milne narrowing his eyes, "you seem to be quite the historian."

"Not really," replied Avalon with a frown, "it seems more than a coincidence that until a few days ago I hadn't heard of the man, and now I bump into an image of him hanging in an office in Aberdeen. What do you think the odds of that are Mr Milne?"

"I'm not a betting man Detective, never have been, I think that's why I've been so successful in business and in life."

"All men measure success in different ways I tend to think," added Avalon sitting down and staring straight at the man. He seemed stoic, unflinching and supremely confident. He wasn't going to be tricked or admit to something he didn't have to.

"Most men that aren't say that I'm sure, but rarely is it what they truly believe.

"Have you heard of the Black Clan Mr Milne?" asked Avalon. The man replied as if he had known the question was coming.

"Of course, it would be a nonsense not to have heard of it whilst having a painting of the man who some think devised it," replied Milne but he offered nothing more.

"Are you a member of it?"

"Just because I have a picture of Major Hume doesn't mean I'm at all linked to a protest movement that died out with the end of the Napoleonic wars," he replied with a playful smile on his lips.

"Many believe the organisation still exists," insisted Ross.

"And some believe in Aliens, God and Free speech but I have seen no evidence to show them as being real. Hume was a patriot in my eyes and a humanitarian, that's why his image hangs there, no other reason."

"A patriot, why so?" asked Avalon. The man gave a nod and a silent laugh then said,

"This country of ours has its heroes Detective, just like yours, but ours are make-believe, our heroes like Wallace and Bruce were nothing to do with patriotism, they did everything for selfish reasons, they wouldn't even understand the word, for then there wasn't patriotism as we know it," he paused and steepled his hands once more. "Major Hume acted out of pity for his fellow Scot, he had nothing to gain and everything to lose, which indeed is what happened. That is the true sign of a hero, that is why that portrait hangs there." Avalon nodded as he looked at the floor and then he stood.

"Do you believe in coincidences Mr Milne?" he asked as he nodded to Ross.

"As I understand the word, as in meaning a concurrence of events without apparent causal connection, yes I do."

"Well I don't Mr Milne," and he made his way to the door, "coincidences are in the mind, they are our perception of the events, not the reality. So you see," he paused, "that portrait hanging on your wall is going to help me sleep much more soundly tonight. Good afternoon."


"What was that about coincidences?" asked Ross as they travelled back to Inverness. Avalon seemed to shake himself free of thoughts and then replied.

"Oh, it's just the way I see things that people call coincidences, it's a long explanation and I'm too tired."

"Well you'll sleep well tonight," smiled Ross, "now you've seen that portrait."

"Well, it's pretty obvious, he may as well have hung a sign saying 'I'm the leader of the Black Clan' on the wall."

"Maybe, it doesn't do our case any favours though, even if he had admitted it, we have no proof he or the Clan are involved anywhere in this case," insisted Ross.

"I know, and it's not looking like we'll ever get anything out of Malcolm Milne," said Avalon and he yawned and stretched out in the seat. He closed his eyes and tried to work his way through what they knew about the case but by the time they had reached Elgin he was still no further forward. He sat up and looked at his watch. "There isn't much more we can do today, what do you say to the last ones in the pub tonight?"

"I was thinking about an early night," replied Ross.

"About nine o' clock be alright?" added Avalon.

"Hot cocoa and cuddling up with my teddy."

"In the Castle as usual?"

"Or better still with that new girl in the sandwich shop."

"First one there gets them in," said Avalon as he stretched back out in the seat.

"Or maybe just go straight to sleep so I can get a fresh start in the morning," continued Ross but Avalon had ignored him and closed his eyes again.

~~~~~~

"The phone records o' the carpet fitter are confirmed," began Frazer, "the phone number that rang to order the carpets was from the phone of Jason Buchanan."

"That's interesting, can we get a fix on the phone to see where it was last used?" asked Avalon sipping at his first cup of coffee of the morning.

"I can see what we can dig up but that phone seems tae be unused at the moment," she nodded.

"He's probably ditched it, it's likely at the bottom of the Ness now," offered Avalon as he looked over to Rutherford. "Anything on any missing persons?"

"Not yet boss," replied the big man, "the Aberdeen section are keeping their ear to the ground for us." Avalon nodded and sipped once more at the coffee.

"Did you find anything in Aberdeen boss?" asked Mackinnon.

"Not much," he replied.

"Except for the fact that we are pretty sure Malcolm Milne is a big wheel in the Black Clan," added Ross.

"How did y' find that out?" asked Frazer.

"We didn't," cut in Avalon, "he's guessing."

"Educated guess though," insisted Ross, "it didn't take him much more than ten seconds to realise we weren't true customers, he must have recognised the boss as soon as we walked in."

"It makes sense," nodded Frazer, "if he had you followed he would have seen a photograph of you."

"More to the point, he had a painting of the man that is credited with forming the Order of the Black Thistle, which probably became the Black Clan," explained Avalon.

"A bit of a giveaway then," added Rory. Avalon looked over to Mackinnon.

"I think he doubted anyone would know who the portrait was of," explained Avalon, "I was just guessing when I pointed it out."

"So do we know what this Black Clan is about?" asked Rutherford.

"I'm guessing it's just like the Masons," shrugged Avalon, "uniform, rules, mutual backscratching and some weird rites performed by the inner circle in the name of the brotherhood." There was a hard, single knock at the door and in came a Tommy Lee Jones lookalike. The man dressed in black with tight-cropped hair was surprised to see the room in a meeting and he glanced at several faces before saying,

"Oh, sorry, I didn't know…" then he looked at Avalon and held up a brown paper envelope approximately A4 size and shape.

"You have something for me DS Nicholls?" asked Avalon.

"Aye, I got you those tickets to the policeman's ball you were asking about," he passed the envelope to Avalon and walked out without another word.

"What was that about?" asked Frazer with a puzzled look. Ross was smiling.

"The policeman's ball, I like it." Avalon peered into the packet and noticed several sheets of paper and two photographs, one almost as large as the envelope. He tried to see what the image was without taking it out and when he saw what it was he pulled it from the packet and examined it.

"Someone caught you at Fishy Fiona's Massage parlour?" asked Ross. Frazer looked round at him with disgust.

"No," said Avalon with no emotion, "something a little more interesting," and he handed the photo to Ross. The image was black and white and very grainy as if taken from distance or in low light. It showed two males surrounded by large candles or torches, the individuals were dressed in kilts with full regalia but were naked on their top half. Ross didn't recognise either of the two men but the image wasn't of a high quality.

"It looks like a meeting of the Highland Vanity Club," mused Ross as he passed the image to Frazer.

"They're well-built guys," commented Frazer with wide open eyes.

"You into that look then?" asked Ross as Mackinnon looked over Frazer's shoulder at the image.

"You mean do I prefer the look of these two hunks than your flabby frame?" Ross frowned, "what do you think?" Frazer added as she looked back at the image. Avalon was busy reading through the notes as Frazer passed the image to Rutherford.

"They're a wee bit too fragile for my taste," he smiled and handed it back to Frazer.

"Is this supposed to represent this Black Clan boss?" asked Mackinnon.

"What?" asked Avalon looking up from the notes, "er, well it could be but there's nothing to confirm it," and he reached into the envelope to extricate the final image. It was a very blurred, blown-up image of what looked to be a section from the original photograph. Held to the back of it with a paper clip was a sketch of what the image may have showed. Avalon knew he had seen it before, it was almost identical to the image Mrs Buchanan had made some days ago.

"Do either of the two men appear to have tattoos on their chests in that image?" asked Avalon.

"Yeah, they both have somethin' but I cannae make out what et es." Avalon held up the photograph he had to Frazer.

"This maybe?" he asked and she looked down at the image she had.

"Aye. Et certainly looks like et."

"Then we have a way to identify members of the Black Clan," began Avalon, "that is as long as they *are* tattoos and they *all* have them."

"It doesn't take us any further though does it?" stated Ross with a frown.

"No, not unless we can make a direct link between Buchanan and the group," replied Avalon as he finished off his cooling coffee. His phone rang and he stood and walked to his booth.

"Avalon."

"*It's Sarah Underwood,*" the voice announced.

"Oh hello Sarah, have you got anything for us?"

"*I think so, we have completed all the analysis of the blood found at the house at Garve and everything except two small spots belong to the female.*"

"Right," was Avalon's cautious reply, "can you go further?"

"*There is no DNA match on record, but both spots are identical, male but that's all we know at the moment.*" Avalon thanked her and returned to the Cave.

"That was forensics," he interrupted the conversation, "we have confirmation of a second DNA contact at the house, not on record but it's what we need."

"It's not the breakthrough we could do with though is it?" added Ross.

"Not quite but we did speculate that Buchanan's DNA would be at a crime scene and this could be it." He turned to Frazer, "Megan, did we find any relatives of Buchanan?"

"I've found a cousin ready t' talk but I didnae think her DNA would be close enough."

"Maybe not but she might be able to tell us of other close relatives, or even help convince them."

"Okay, I'll get to it," she picked up her jacket and nodded to Mackinnon, the two of them left. Ross was now reading through the notes which were several passages relating to some of the surveillance work done on Buchanan in a previous case. It was mentioned that Buchanan was not one of the subjects in the photograph.

264

Avalon picked up the large image once more and looked at the faces, even if they had been people he knew, he doubted they were good enough images for a formal identification. Ross gave a deep sigh.

"There's nothing here we can use," and he dropped the notes on the desk.

"No but I need to have a chat with Nicholls, you and Martin contact Mrs Buchanan and see if you can get anything more from her," instructed Avalon and then he left the room.

DS Nicholls was waiting in a chair in the corridor to B Section's office.

"I thought you'd come to ask me questions," he said with a blank face.

"I can see that," frowned Avalon, uncomfortable with Nicholls' insight.

"Let's take a stroll into the car park," suggested Nicholls and they descended the stairs to the rear of the building. The sun was shining but it was cool, Avalon was grateful for the fresh air however.

"So where did they come from?" he asked as he leaned on one of the patrol cars.

"I don't know what you are talking about," replied Nicholls but before Avalon could remonstrate, he continued, "I didn't give you anything and I don't know where it came from. Even if it came from one of McGill's ex-snitches, I wouldn't admit to it. Neither would I be able to tell you why it wasn't used in the case or how the images were taken." Avalon folded his arms, he realised that Nicholls was waiting for questions and was not about volunteer information. Wherever Nicholls had got that envelope from, it was clear he didn't want to be associated with its retrieval.

"Who are the people in the image?" Nicholls looked around the car park in a casual manner.

"I can't tell, I haven't seen the images before, but based on the description you have just given me, I would say one is Lawrence Hilliard and the other is Nick Bell." The second name meant nothing to Avalon.

"It doesn't look like Hilliard," he pointed out.

"It's likely that it's some years ago, before he got the good life and became flabby," was the answer.

"Where was it taken?" asked Avalon.

"I can't say but I'm guessing if the snitch had been asked, he would probably say that it was taken at a guild meeting for new recruits at Gorrent House."

"Never heard of it," frowned Avalon, "where's that?" but Nicholls just stared at him. He seemed very reticent to elaborate with any of the information. "I can't react if I don't get all the details," insisted Avalon but Nicholls shrugged and then said,

"The people who found that information spent long nights and lonely days to get it, it doesn't all come free and it will cost me eventually," and Nicholls began to walk away, so Avalon tried to imprint the name onto his brain. Avalon turned to watch Nicholls walk to his car and shouted over,

"Thanks anyway," but just before Nicholls got inside the vehicle he called back,

"Oh, you might want to look closer at the darker sheet." Avalon didn't understand but went back to the Cave before he forgot the names of the house and the second man he had just been given.

"We can't find Mrs Buchanan so it will have to wait," explained Ross but Avalon ignored him and looked for a piece of paper in the booth, he then returned to the Cave and picked up the darker sheet of notes from the envelope. He looked at it but saw nothing significant.

"Martin check out an address called Gorrent House," Rutherford nodded and set to work on his computer, "can you see anything on this sheet that we have missed?" and he handed it to Ross. Ross looked at the notes.

"Nothing, just a few dates without the actual year and a few names of coppers who were on surveillance."

"Do you know any of those names?"

"A couple of them, Grant retired a few years ago and Dobson moved to Glasgow," explained Ross, "why?"

"I was told to have a close look at that sheet."

"If it was Nicholls who told you it might not be all that clear, he can be a bit cryptic at times." and he held the notes up to the light from the window. "There you go," smiled Ross, "something has been written over it, probably on another bit of paper that was resting on it."

"Can you transcribe it?"

"I'll give it a go," nodded Ross and he began work.

"Have you heard of a Nick Bell?" asked Avalon.

"Nope," replied Ross staring closely at the sheet of paper.

"Gorrent House boss, near Nairn, built around the time of Culloden, until a few years ago was the home of Sir Charles Mayland until his death and then his family sold it on to a French company."

"Okay," nodded Avalon, "find everything you can on Charles Mayland and his family, there must be something here," and he went to pour a coffee. For some moments he sipped at the cup staring into space until his phone rang in the booth.

"Avalon."

"*Boss, et's Megan, I've spoken to the relative of Buchanan and we have a problem.*" Avalon sighed, he just didn't need any more issues.

"Go on," he said.

"*Jason Buchanan was adopted, he's not a Buchanan so we can't-*"

"Second guess his DNA," nodded Avalon as he interrupted Frazer, "okay, get back here after you have got what you can," and he replaced the phone. He looked out of the glass partition, Rutherford was on the phone and Ross looked as if he had finished transcribing the impressions on the notes. "Got something?" he asked as he closed in on Ross's desk.

"Yeah, I think so, just a few words I can't be sure of but it goes like this," and he looked down at the pad he had written on. "*JB has got dirt on TS, he's gonna do exactly what he did to RB and LH if we don't move.*" Ross looked at Avalon and shrugged, "there's also something about needing to look at what has gone before but that's across several folds and difficult to work out."

"Well that's a load of bullshit," sighed Avalon again.

"I suppose JB is Buchanan, LH is Hilliard but who the other two are is anyone's guess," said Ross.

"There's nothing here we can use, we don't know who wrote this, when, or to whom, it's worse than useless," growled Avalon returning his empty cup to the shelf by the coffee machine. He turned back and added, "Oh and Buchanan is adopted." Both Ross and Rutherford saw the implications of this, without any DNA from Buchanan it would be impossible to implicate him. Rutherford finished on the phone and looked to Avalon.

"I've just spoken to one of Mayland's relatives, et seems the old man was a bit o' a rogue and had some weird parties up there, et could have been where the Black Clan used to meet or somethin'." Avalon nodded, that did seemed likely if the photograph they had was really taken there but the boss was more concerned with other aspects and problems of the case. He made a decision and it was a big risk.

"I'm going to see the Procurator Fiscal to see if we can force a testing of the DNA that was found during the McVie case, if it matches the specks of blood found up at Garve then at least we may be a little closer."

"And if it doesn't?" asked Ross as Avalon went to the booth for his jacket.

"Then McVie probably did the crime he is serving time for," he said pulling on the coat, "and you or Gordon get to be DI," he shrugged, then he left the Cave.

## Chapter Eleven

The phone was ringing as Ross entered the Cave and he heard Frazer answer it from Avalon's booth.

"He's no' here sir," she said and then looked up to Ross and motioned for him to come closer. "I don't know sir but DS Ross es here," she said. Ross had begun to shake his head but it was too late and she handed him the phone, mouthing "Croker". Ross sighed and took the phone.

"DS Ross," he said calmly.

*"Ah Ross, where is DI Avalon?"*

"He was down at the fiscal's office yesterday evening so I'm guessing he's probably back there this morning," he lied. Ross knew exactly where Avalon was.

*"Oh, er right, tell him to come and see me as soon as he arrives,"* insisted Croker and then added in a less stern tone, *"erm, this suicide-note case, how is it going?"*

"Oh, reasonably well sir," he lied again, "we've got a full team on it and the DI's progressing the investigation as we speak." Ross thought he could actually feel his nose growing.

"*Right, right,*" repeated Croker, then after a short pause, "*so you think there should be something concrete fairly soon do you?*" Croker's voice sounded unsure, he was quiet and hesitant and Ross could feel his tension.

"These sort of cases are never quick sir as you know but we're confident we're on the right track," Ross had learned long ago never to be precise to a senior officer and Croker recognised the rhetoric.

"*Good, good,*" he repeated again, "*carry on DS Ross.*" Ross walked out of the booth and over towards Frazer.

"Problems?" she asked.

"Not for me," replied Ross.

"So where *es* the boss?" she asked, Ross shrugged and leaned on his desk.

"He's up at-" began Ross but the door suddenly swung open and in came Rutherford with a smile on his wide face.

"Got et!" he announced holding up what looked like a report sheet.

"Promotion, the sack, exactly what have you got?" asked Ross.

"Missin' person," he said still smiling and he sat at his desk. Ross looked down at Frazer and said,

"I haven't seen him this excited since I let him drive my car," and then he looked back at Rutherford who was busy typing.

"So why es a missing person taking you back to your childhood?" asked Frazer turning in her seat to face him.

"This es our female, I'm sure of et," he grinned holding up the sheet. Ross and Frazer looked to each other and then both moved closer to Rutherford. Ross snatched up the record sheet and Frazer looked over Rutherford's wide shoulders to see what he was typing in.

"You might be right, the details fit," said Ross handing the sheet to Frazer. "So what are you doing?" he then asked.

"Recording the details," Rutherford replied.

"Don't bother with that you melon, get on the phone and arrange to bring in the person who reported it," and he took the sheet back from Frazer and read the name, "Melonie McInver, here's the contact," and he gave the sheet to Rutherford pointing to the phone number. Ross then looked at Frazer. "Do you want to do the interview?" Frazer shook her head.

"No, you're better at these sort," and she sat down at her desk once more. Ross wasn't sure what she meant by 'these sort' but he assumed she meant interviews that didn't need menace. Rutherford was on the phone and speaking to someone so Ross left him to it. He went and poured a coffee and waited by the door.

"So you were saying about the boss?" began Frazer.

"Oh, right, he's up at the Garve house, he's gone up with Hendry, now they have all the forensic details they are trying to recreate the possible sequence of events."

"That's a bit vague for the boss isn't et?"

"Probably," nodded Ross gulping the coffee, "but he's desperate, we all are, even Croker's getting jumpy."

"Well, he's bound tae be, he's got the Super breathing down his neck," she replied and for some reason a light came on in Ross's brain and he quickly strode to his desk and pulled out the A4 envelope from

272

his drawer. He pulled out the darker note and the transcription he had made, he read it quietly to himself and then again louder, looking over to Frazer as he did.

"*JB has got dirt on TS, he's going to do exactly what he did to RB and LH if we don't move.*" Frazer frowned as if to say, 'why are you reading that to me?' but then her memory began to see something too and she came to the same conclusion.

"The Superintendent?" she asked with a shocked face, "of course, et fits, his initials are TS and he's been very agitated about this case. Holy shit," she exclaimed looking off into the distance, "so what? Someone blackmailing him?" she asked.

"Could be," nodded Ross, "but it could be a coincidence." He looked out of the window, he was wondering what action to take next, should he tell Avalon? It was doubtful Avalon would get a signal on his phone up at the house near Garve so he continued to stare out of the window hoping something would pop into his head. It was the voice of Rutherford who interrupted his thoughts.

"I've arranged to bring her en, shall I go alone?"

"What?" asked Ross still considering his options, "oh, no, take someone with you, give Rory a buzz, he's down in the archive." Rutherford left, it was almost as quick to go and tell him as phone him. Ross turned back to the window.

"I thought you would have gone with him," said Frazer.

"It could be unconnected, we get missing persons like other people get junk mail," answered Ross turning back to her, "but this connection with the Super-"

"Could also be unconnected," she interrupted. Ross nodded.

"True, it could," and he sat in his chair and looked through the rest of the items in the envelope. Frazer had gone quiet and so Ross looked around. She was staring into space, which was unlike the DC and the more Ross thought about it, she had been doing that quite a bit recently.

"It looks like *you've* got something on your mind too." She blinked and looked at him with a vague expression.

"Och just tired, I'm not sleeping all that well at the moment," and Ross saw some regret that she had told him.

"Why, does your coffin need a refurb?" She didn't react but just began working once more. Ross watched her for a moment and he could see she was trying to ignore him, which meant there was a story. "Something you need to talk about?"

"You just keep your mind on your own problems," she answered abruptly and returned to the computer screen. Ross didn't give in, he watched her until she stopped and turned to him.

"Have you got nothin' tae do?" she asked with a glare, "I thought you were looking into a case?" Ross knew at that moment there was something wrong, her answers were so out of character, there was no sarcasm, no cutting riposte and she wasn't reacting as quickly as was normal for her.

"Yeah, okay," he said and he turned back to his computer screen before adding, "but if you want to talk…" After a few moments, Ross could feel that she was staring at *him* now and he glanced around. Her face

274

said it all, there was a look of doubt in her eyes that he hadn't noticed in all the time he had known her. He raised his brows a little and waited.

"We're no' getting on very well at the moment," she eventually said.

"We never have but that's no reason-"

"Not you and I, you halfwit," she spat, "me and him," and she nodded in a random direction. Ross knew she had meant her partner from the beginning but he was trying to lighten the mood. "I'm sleeping on the couch for now and et's no fun," she explained.

"I thought *he'd* be the one on the couch," replied Ross raising his brows in surprise.

"Et's not a big couch and he would never get on et. Anyway that's the way et es, I don't want any sympathy or advice," she insisted and turned back to her screen. Ross knew she didn't want sympathy, she wasn't that sort of person but he did feel she needed someone to talk to.

"You'll not get sympathy from me," he laughed, "and as for advice, I'm not exactly qualified for that am I?" He waited, she didn't react but she wasn't working either, she was just staring at her screen. "Why don't you move out, just for a while, see how it goes?"

"Et's my soddin' house," she spat with a lightening quick reaction, "I'll be damned if *I'm* gonna move out."

"I wasn't suggesting leaving the place to him, I just meant to give you time to think."

"That's givin' en and I'm not keen on that," she replied, turning back to the screen.

"No it's not giving in, it re-evaluating the situation, seeing how you feel away from him, that's all."

There was silence for a moment. "Call it a holiday if you want," he added.

"And where the hell would I go? I don't have anyone I can stay with even ef I wanted to."

"You could stay at mine, I'll sleep on the sofa. Or ask the boss, he's got enough bedrooms spare to accommodate the whole of the Inverness Police Pipe Band." She looked back over to him.

"That ain't gonna happen, I don't want the boss knowing, he's got enough problems without me burning out because I can't sleep," she insisted. She looked back to the screen and said, "I'll get et sorted, I'm just a wee bit tired, et'll pass." Ross was about to add something when the door opened. It was Rutherford, he opened it wide but didn't enter.

"I'm off with Rory, he's getting the car ready, let the boss know when he comes back, will ye? "

"Yes darling," answered Ross with an English accent, "give my love to mother and I'll feed the cat for you while you're gone, do write." Rutherford gave a puzzled frown and left. Frazer was smiling as she turned to him and said,

"Es there anyone you don't take the pish out of?" Ross thought for a moment and then held up his index finger, he frowned and then put the finger down again.

"No," he said shaking his head. She looked at him for some time, Ross felt uneasy, like he was being stalked by a predator.

"Did you mean that..." she paused for a second, "about staying over? Not that I would."

"Yeah of course," he nodded, "mind you, I'm having a bit of trouble with the council at the moment," and he leaned closer as if to keep it quiet.

"Oh," she said, "why's that?"

"I put a skylight in."

"What without planning permission or somethin'?" she asked, also leaning a little closer.

"It's not that, the chap in the upstairs flat complained." Frazer looked at him with a serious face for a moment and then laughed, making a snorting sound. That was another first, Ross had never seen her laugh. As the laugh reverted to a smile and the smile subsided, Ross noticed that stalking look again. In those few silent seconds he became worried, he became very worried. Her eyes bored right into his soul and yet again he saw a 'first' in Frazer, something he had never imagined he would see, and something he could never have thought would have excited him. He blinked and hoped she would stop, but she didn't and he was paralysed with indecision and doubt. Fortunately she saw sense and took a deep breath.

"Well, thanks anyway," and she turned back to her screen as if nothing had happened. Ross felt odd as he turned forward in his seat, as if someone had injected him with anti-climax solution. It was like being chased by a hungry lioness to then realise it was just a shadow. There was embarrassment and excitement too. He picked up the contents of the envelope once more and tried to continue with the investigation.

It wasn't long before Avalon returned, Ross turned to the opening door and nodded as his boss entered. Frazer said,

"Afternoon boss," the room being very quiet with just her and Ross present.

"Anything new?" Avalon asked as he strode off to the booth carrying some files.

"You first," replied Ross jokingly but he genuinely wanted to know what had transpired at the house near Garve. Avalon didn't reply at first, he was removing his jacket and then he seemed to fuss around with the files he had brought with him. Eventually he hung the jacket on the back of the chair and re-entered the room carrying a sheet from the files.

"Nothing profound, though Hendry was helpful forwarding some theories based on where evidence was found," explained Avalon as he leaned on the desk in front of Ross.

"Such as?" Ross asked. Avalon placed the sheet on the desk and folded his arms.

"Well, he says that there is a fairly obvious timescale for the events," explained Avalon, "and his theory is that the whole thing started in the bedroom."

"Doesn't it always?" commented Ross in a quiet voice. Avalon either didn't hear him or ignored it and continued.

"He also thinks that the male was the first to be attacked and then moved off to the kitchen. The female may have fled there and was attacked soon after." He stopped and passed the sheet to Ross. "This is a plan of the house and shows all the key points of forensic evidence." He let Ross have a quick look at the sheet then continued. "His theory is that it was probably a knife wound to the female due to the amount of blood that was deposited in the kitchen, they lifted the tiles and found pooled blood under there." Avalon paused and folded his arms again. "It's likely that the body was dragged outside soon after and that the female wasn't dead, she was probably left in the garden whilst he dug the grave, though it's likely she was deceased by the time she was buried. The house was then cleaned and the carpets removed, and here is where the interesting bit comes in."

"Interesting isn't a word I would have used," shrugged Ross. Once again Avalon ignored him and continued.

"They haven't quite completed the examination of the van from the unit yet but carpet fibres have already been found."

"Yes, okay, that's interesting," nodded Ross.

"Do they have a match boss?" asked Frazer.

"Yes, they match the carpet fibres found in the hallway of the house."

"I'm going to admit something now," interrupted Ross, "there were times when I thought all this was a setup. I thought we were being stitched up but this kind o' changes that." Avalon gave a slight smile.

"Well, I can see why you might think that but the car in the storage unit was the main problem with a 'stitch up' theory, it's still the main problem too but now we are getting somewhere at last."

"But," sighed Ross lifting the sheet up, "*this*, is still a theory."

"It is, but Hendry is quite the artist," insisted Avalon, "and his explanation is very compelling when you see him going through it. The evidence fits exactly and there is nothing out of place or left over when he's done."

"So," began Ross, "Buchanan takes a female to the house, at some stage she gets the hump and whacks him with something, he picks up a knife and stabs her.

He then takes the body outside to prevent any more blood pouring out and then buries her in case someone arrives. He then cleans the house, goes back for the van, returns and rips out the carpets from the house and takes them and the body..." he paused for effect, "where exactly?"

"I didn't say it was solved, we just have an idea what might have happened at the house," insisted Avalon reaching for the sheet. He passed it to Frazer and then stood near the windows looking out. "So, has anything come in since I've been gone?" he eventually asked.

"A bit," said Ross casually, "we may have a match for the TS."

"What TS?" asked Avalon as he turned to face Ross. The DS was holding up the paper that had the transcription on it. Avalon read it.

"Who do we know who has the initials TS?" asked Ross with wide eyes. For several moments Avalon jutted out his bottom lip and looked vague. Ross could see he was about to shake his head so he gave him a hint. "Think, close to home," he simply said. He watched as Avalon scanned initials in his mind until it stopped at one particular record.

"The Superintendent?" he hissed. There was silence in the room as Avalon turned back to the window and looked down at the sheet once more. He then stared outside for the best part of two minutes until he said, "It fits, but this is one hell of a crappy problem." Ross didn't need telling. He had thought about it since he realised the initials fit the Superintendent, and no matter how he saw the man, if the Super was involved, it was going to cause some serious waves.

"And there's something else," said Ross. Avalon turned slowly and frowned.

"Make it good news, we need good news."

"Martin may have found someone who knows the missing female, he's gone with Rory to bring her in." Avalon blinked and then ran his hand through his hair. "I took a look at the report of the missing person, reading between the lines the woman who reported her missing could be a prostitute so..." he let Avalon fill in the gaps for himself. His boss's eyes began to flit around the room, they weren't seeing anything, it was the tell-tale sign that Avalon was in overdrive, his brain was tearing the information to shreds and re-arranging it in an order that made sense. When the process was done, he sat in the nearest chair. "So what do you think?" asked Ross. Avalon's eyes had steadied but when they looked over to Ross they seemed to have electricity in them.

"Let's not go into what I think until we have interviewed this woman."

~~~~~~

Avalon sat opposite Melonie McInver in interview room two and Ross was by his side.

"Now then Melonie, we need you to tell us all you know," began Ross as he set a yellow folder on the table in front of him, "you say your housemate has gone missing?"

"Aye," nodded the woman with wide brown eyes, "I haven't see her for some time an' she didn't say she was going awa' or anythin'." She had a broad Inverness accent though she didn't look at all Scottish but then Avalon wondered what a 'Scottish look' might be? She had very smooth light-olive skin and jet-black hair, probably of Italian stock and very good looking even without makeup.

"So when was the last time you saw her?" asked Ross beginning to take notes.

"I reckon about the twelfth," she said and then added, "April that is." Ross stopped writing suddenly. He realised that with a date of the twelfth of April, the missing person could certainly be the one they were looking for, but Ross became angry and he actually voiced his chagrin whilst trying to stay calm.

"She's been missing over a month and you've only just decided to report it?"

"We're not joined at the hip, we have our own lives, we just live in the same house," she replied indignantly. She then looked over to Avalon and added, "she once pissed off to Sweden with some guy and she didn't tell me about that until she phoned a fortnight later." Avalon sat without any noise or movement, so she turned back to Ross. "She's just not been in touch at all so I'm sort o' worried," she added in a quieter voice. Ross nodded and repressed a sigh as he continued to make notes.

"What is her full name?" he asked.

"Margaret Elizabeth Storey, but she goes by the name 'Margo'," replied the woman watching Ross write. She didn't notice Avalon glance over to the two-way mirror and give a slight nod.

"Occupation?" inquired Ross, it was a question but it sounded more like moral indignation to Avalon's ears. It was clear Ross had made assumptions already.

"Entertainer," replied Melony looking down at her nails suddenly.

282

"Is Margo a prostitute Melony?" asked Avalon before Ross could dig any further. She glared at him for a moment.

"She worked as an escort, that's what she called herself an' that's another reason we don't come to you lot straight away. You always jump to conclusions."

"We are here to help everyone Miss McInver," replied Avalon sternly, "just because Miss Storey may have been a sex worker doesn't mean she'll get less than anyone else from us."

"What sort of 'entertainer' was she Melonie?" asked Ross before she had time to answer Avalon.

"Sex worker," sighed Melony, "but she wasnae your normal street scrubber," she suddenly insisted.

"We just want facts, nothing more, nothing less," explained Ross, "so can you give us a description of her please?" he continued. Melonie was very detailed and precise about the description, she was intelligent and observant, it was clear that her missing friend was likely to be the same woman who had lost so much blood at the house near Garve. Avalon had to be sure and though it was going to be awkward, he pulled out a photograph and slowly slid it across the table to the woman. It was a blown up photograph of one of the earrings. The woman put her hand to her mouth in shock and then looked over to Avalon.

"Oh my god, something's happened hasn't it?" Tears began to form in her eyes, "I knew it, I knew she wouldn't be away this long, oh god."

"We haven't found her yet," said Avalon softly, "but we found her earrings at, what we believe to be, a crime scene." The woman was choking back tears and

Ross passed her his handkerchief, she dried her eyes with it and then clenched it fast in her fist.

"They're not her earrings, they're mine," she said as her eyes began to redden.

"Yours?" asked Ross. She nodded as more tears ran down her nose and cheeks.

"Aye, I know they're the ones too, y' see I can't wear studs, and those are the clip on type," She pointed to the photograph, "I have type-one diabetes and any skin puncture can cause infection or cellulitis."

"So why was she wearing *your* earrings Melonie?" asked Ross.

"She wanted something a bit showy, I think she may have had a special meet."

"What do you mean?" asked Avalon.

"Margo makes a great deal of money, we don't rent the house, she's bought it, it's hers. She has some clients that pay a great deal for her particular..." she put the hanky to her eyes, "I told her no good would come of it," she said and broke into a full crying fit. Avalon rose to fetch her a drink but as he was leaving, Frazer was coming the other way. He closed the door behind him and took Frazer up the corridor.

"Got anything?" he asked. Frazer handed him a note, it said, "Margaret Elizabeth Storey, known prostitute, minor record for shoplifting, nothing since July 2004." Avalon nodded and placed the note in his pocket. "Can you get her a drink please?" he asked and as Frazer nodded, he returned to the interview room. Ross had calmed her down somewhat and Avalon took his seat saying, "I've sent someone to get you a drink." She nodded and he then asked another question.

"I have to ask this, Melonie, does Margo have any regular customers that you know of?" Her red-rimmed eyes searched his features, there was something she wanted to tell him he could see that but for some reason she seemed doubtful.

"A few I suppose, most of them have money so they wouldn't been seen where we live but I have seen her dropped off on occasions."

"Would you recognise them if you saw them?" he then asked.

"One of them I would, he used to drop her off quite a bit, I don't think he liked..." but she stopped, "well," she then said with a shrug, "Margo did some..." and then she ceased altogether.

"You need to tell us *all* you know Melonie," said Ross, "if something has happened to Margo we need to find her and the person responsible." The woman nodded. She looked at Avalon but then addressed Ross.

"Margo supplied a sort of special service. I told her no good would come of it but no one else would do it and she made serious money from it."

"What was that service?" asked Ross. The woman's eyes looked down as if she was ashamed, as if it was her fault.

"She would let the customer tie her up, you know a bit of rough stuff," Avalon saw Ross's eyes flick over to him, "nothing to mark, if you know what I mean but I have known her come home with bruises and scratches, I think she liked the money it brought." Ross nodded understandingly yet inside he didn't understand at all.

"So one of these customers would bring her home?"

"Yes," she nodded and looked down again, she shuffled her feet, then looked up and said, "I think he felt guilty after, you know, for what he had done."

"You think he went too far?" asked Ross.

"Not from what she said, like I say, it meant more money for her and this one paid well."

"So could you identify him from a photograph?" he asked.

"Yes, I would think so," she nodded again. Avalon reached into the envelope once more and pulled out a black and white image of Jason Buchanan and handed it to her. The woman studied the image and then shook her head saying, "No, it's not him, I don't recognise him." Ross looked over to Avalon who just raised his brows a little and then pulled out another image and slid it across the table. She picked it up and almost immediately said, "Yes that's him, I think she calls him Johnny." As she placed it back on the table, Ross could see it was Hilliard and he once again looked at Avalon but this time, there was no reaction, he just asked his own question.

"So this is the man you say probably felt guilty about what he did?"

"Yes, that's the one," she nodded still clutching Ross's handkerchief.

"Did she ever tell you the details of what they did together?"

"God no, we talked about nice things, not work. It's like you two going to the pub together and talking about work."

"If you only knew," smiled Ross trying to make her feel comfortable. Avalon passed her all the other images he had but Hilliard was the only one she identified. There was a knock at the door and PC Kirk entered with a tray of drinks and Avalon thanked Melonie. They were going to give her a break before they asked more questions but in the meantime Avalon and Ross took the air in the car park.

"So Hilliard was seeing her then, not Buchanan," said Ross as he leaned on one of the cars.

"We don't know Buchanan wasn't seeing her too though do we?"

"No, I suppose it just means Hilliard was the only one who took her back."

"Exactly, but knowing she did S and M for customers makes a bit of sense on Hendry's theory," explained Avalon, "he suggested that it could have been sex play that got too rough that started it off." Ross nodded but said nothing. After a couple of minutes of breathing the cool air, Avalon asked,

"So who's the weak link in this group of people do you think?"

"What do you mean?" asked Ross slightly puzzled.

"Who would you think would be the first to crack?" Ross thought for a moment, it was an easy answer to find.

"Hilliard of course."

"Why's that?" asked Avalon.

"Because when shit falls from the sky, Hilliard has an umbrella that only covers one."

"That's good, because I was thinking the same," smiled Avalon.

"So are we gonna bring the bastard in at last?" Ross asked with a slight smile. Avalon nodded.

"Yeah, you wind up here and I'll go and get the paperwork sorted," he said.

~~~~~~

"Very romantic, so what's the occasion?" asked Ross as he entered the kitchen. Candles were lit around the house and, on the table in the conservatory, were several bottles of alcohol.

"There isn't any real occasion, unless you want to celebrate three years of working together," smiled Avalon.

"I thought with all the candles you were finally about to propose to me," said Ross.

"You're not my type, I like a girl with a deep voice. I usually light the house with candles, I can put the main lights on if you like," suggested Avalon, "I realise at your age your eyes must be giving up."

"No it's fine as it is, I like low light."

"That's the sign of a vampire," nodded Avalon as Ross picked up one of the wine bottles and began to read the label.

"You may have something there, before I joined the force, I wore sunglasses all the time." Ross replied replacing the bottle and choosing another.

"So what's wrong with the wine, have you not seen red wine with corks instead of screw tops?" Ross put down the second bottle and looked at Avalon with an intense glare.

"Red wine is the only area of drinking I am particular about."

"Really? So we are saying that you're happy to drink ice-cold chemically based, homogenised lager, but you are particular about the red stuff?"

"I suppose you could call me a wine snob," nodded Ross.

"You know, the more I get to know about you, the less I know you."

"I'm complicated and interesting," agreed Ross picking up the last bottle of red wine. "I'll have a Glenmorangie," he said pointing to one of the whisky bottles and he reached for a glass.

"So the red isn't to your taste?"

"This first one I would serve to people I don't want to return, and that particular Rioja is labelled wrongly, it should say 'Cat Piss' but then again, most Spanish wine should only be used as fertiliser, and the last one, whatever it's supposed to be, should be poured down the sink and the bottle used as a lamp to give to some relation you don't like."

"Jesus, you're not wrong, wine snob doesn't tell the whole story though," frowned Avalon theatrically.

"I don't drink red wine unless it's French and no less quality than a Margaux from a decent house," insisted Ross taking the whisky from Avalon who smiled but shook his head.

"Well, it's not an area of expertise I have, I hope the aqua vitae is to your taste however," holding up his glass. Ross clinked his glass to it and said,

"Aye, you can't go far wrong with a single malt." Avalon nodded and motioned to the lounge.

"Shall we retire to the boudoir?" he said and they went to get comfortable. Ross noticed there were snacks on the small table as he sat.

"So what's wrong with the pub tonight?" he asked.

"Nothing, but I wanted to talk and the Castle isn't ideal if it's busy."

"Talk? What's on your mind?" asked Ross sipping at the whisky.

"This case," explained Avalon leaning back into the sofa, "as soon as we bring Lawrence Hilliard in I think that the Superintendent is going to hit the fan and I could get taken off it pretty quickly."

"He could but would he take that risk?" asked Ross.

"He already told Croker to pull me from the investigation," nodded Avalon with a smile.

"And what did Croker say?"

"He told me to ignore him and carry on."

"I'm warming to the Toad," smiled Ross taking a drink.

"But that's the problem, I think this time he'll kick Croker's arse for not taking me off."

"So what do you want to do?" asked Ross with a slightly concerned look.

"I'm not going to stop, I'll take time off and do it as a concerned citizen," explained Avalon, "but I need someone inside to keep me informed."

"That'll be Frazer then," nodded Ross.

"So you won't do it?"

"Course not, I'm due holidays too, we'll work on it together," smiled Ross lifting his glass. Avalon suddenly got a very emotional rush, Ross was saying that he was sticking by Avalon's side no matter what and it took him by surprise.

"It could cost you if you get found out," frowned Avalon.

"Think back to the conversation we had on the way down to Aberdeen, I don't want to throw away a good pension but I'll not run my whole life around it."

"It may not come to that anyway," added Avalon trying to think his way through why Ross had so much loyalty, "if we can play this craftily and press Hilliard enough, we may have enough to steamroller our way over the Superintendent."

"I wouldn't be so sure," replied Ross, "if the Super is up to his neck in middle-class shite, he has more to lose than us." Avalon nodded at this, he took a hard gulp at the whisky and it burned him into clear thought. Ross was right of course, the Superintendent wouldn't lie down and take it easily, he would use all the powers at his command to stop Avalon and his team. Then there was Croker, how far would the DCI stick his own neck out, Avalon knew the man had more integrity than most people thought, but would he risk his job for it? He had hinted that he wouldn't so Avalon would have to tread carefully when it came to his boss.

"Either way," continued Avalon, "you know my feelings now," and he stood, finishing his drink, "Top-up?" and he took Ross's glass. Ross followed him through the kitchen to the conservatory and leaned on the doorframe with his hands in his pockets. Avalon glanced to him and then poured the drinks saying,

"*I have strained the spider's thread, 'gainst the promise of a maid*," and he gave a slight smile and passed Ross the drink.

"Someone into poetry might know what you're rambling on about, but *I'm* not and *I* don't," frowned Ross taking the glass.

"*I have weighed a grain of sand 'gainst her plight of heart and hand,*" continued Avalon as he pulled out a chair and sat at the table.

"When you spout that tosh it usually means you have something on your mind, care to elaborate?" asked Ross joining him.

"It looked like *you* had something on *your* mind, not me, and I'm guessing that the puzzled look is to do with the fairer sex."

"How can you know that, it's not what you think but you're not far off the money."

"You have a particular look when the problem is woman based," smiled Avalon.

"What look is that?" frowned Ross.

"Oh, a sort of lost puppy look, anyway, I'm all ears," replied Avalon raising his brows. Ross let the comment go and his frown gradually faded.

"It's probably none of my business but..." Ross paused, he had to word the next part of the sentence very carefully, "well, have you noticed anything about Megan lately?" Avalon sighed, he knew that if Ross was using her first name he had concerns, but though Avalon had his suspicions, it wasn't right to voice them to anyone.

"I can tell she's got something on her mind, yes," he said toying with his glass on the table.

"So it's not just me then?"

"No," Avalon looked down at his drink and then back up to Ross, "she'll sort it out whatever it is." Ross nodded and Avalon could see that he had more information, he just didn't feel like pressing him about it.

Ross sat and thought for a moment, he then shrugged and took a large gulp of the whisky and slid the glass to Avalon.

"Is it on ration or what?" he asked. Avalon smiled.

"You can pour your own, I'm not your mother." So Ross did, he poured a large one and topped up Avalon's glass.

"I know we've got a busy day in the morning but tonight I don't feel like being sensible," said Ross and he held up his glass. "Sludge!" he announced.

"Sludge," agreed Avalon and he chinked the glasses together. Avalon watched Ross as he took a drink. He was a very complicated character and though Avalon thought a great deal about him, he was only just seeing the man that lived deep inside the crusty outer shell. The more he thought about it the more he realised that he trusted Ross more than anyone else alive. If he couldn't trust Ross, there was no one he could trust and he decided to add a little more information.

"I think Megan might be having a few issues at home."

"I know she is, she's sleeping on the couch at the moment," replied Ross grateful that he could now tell what he knew.

"Really?" said Avalon raising his brows, "I didn't know it was that serious."

"I told her she could stay over at my place but she's adamant it's her house and she's staying put."

"They'll probably work it out," suggested Avalon, "I expect it's not the first time they've argued, knowing Megan."

"I don't know," frowned Ross, "she's changed from when I first knew her, she's more..." Ross decided that maybe the whisky was loosening his tongue and he held back.

"She's more of a team player I admit," agreed Avalon, "but I never thought the day would come when DS Ross would invite DC Frazer to stay over at his," and he gave a muted laugh.

"Aye, well it's not like that, I just saw the confusion on her face and felt..." he broke off again. He couldn't imagine owning up to his boss what he had experienced back in the Cave. He didn't quite believe it himself but for the first time in his life he saw Frazer as 'attractive'. In his silence, Avalon was thinking similar things only he wasn't against sharing them with Ross.

"To be honest, I don't think he's the right sort of person for her," he shrugged, "I mean he might be a nice chap and all that but I find him slightly edgy."

"I suppose he has to be, living with Frazer," smiled Ross.

"Possibly," nodded Avalon, "but she could do much better for herself, she's clever, hardworking and she's even made herself more attractive recently."

"Aye," nodded Ross and then backtracked just in time, "in a masochistic sort of way I mean."

"That's a bit unfair, I think she's changed in many ways," he said and thought about everything that she had gone through, the things that Avalon knew about her that even *she* didn't know about. They were however, secrets and they would remain secrets no matter how many whiskies he'd had.

"She has," nodded Ross, "but she's still got that slice of 'unknown' about her, that little bit of scariness, but then again, some men probably like that side of a woman."

"Don't you?" asked Avalon, "I don't mean Megan specifically, but those qualities I mean."

"Not really," replied Ross, "I suppose I like predictability, I guess that comes from having to work with the unknown so much, I don't want to go back home to it." Avalon just nodded and made a 'hmm' sound. "Or are you still thinking about the lovely Miss Underwood?" Avalon smiled and then sighed.

"I have accepted the inevitable," smiled Avalon, "*She walks in beauty like the night, of cloudless climes and starry skies.*" Ross sighed and finished his drink.

"I bet you could hold a complete conversation in poetry couldn't you?" he said.

"No, the odd thing is," was Avalon's rebuff, I know very little, just odd lines here and there from just a handful of poets."

"Well it's a handful too much for me," said Ross as he stood, "I better get off and try to sleep some of this Glenmorangie off." Avalon saw him to the door and, as he walked down the short path, he said,

"*Farewell and when forth I through the golden gates to golden isles steer without smiling.*" Ross didn't stop walking, he didn't even look back but Avalon clearly saw the two raised fingers under the street lamps. As Ross continued up the street, Avalon continued quietly to himself, "*Through the sea of smiles, isle upon isle,*" he closed the door and walked to the kitchen. "*I have been young and I have counted friends, a hopeless sail I spread, too late, too late.*" He finished his drink, turned out the light and blew out the candles. As he came to the last one he said quietly, "*Why should I from isle to isle sail, a hopeless sailor?*" and he snuffed out the final candle.

# Chapter Twelve

Avalon walked into the office a little early, there were things he needed to get done before everyone arrived. DS Wilson and DC Boyd would be at court all day on a case where three youths had beaten and robbed a teenager so they wouldn't be in at all. The rest of the team would be arriving piecemeal around eight thirty and so he had twenty minutes or so to do what he had to do. Most of it was gathering the information he needed if he was dropped from the case, he made notes and photocopied a few images. By the time Frazer arrived closely followed by Mackinnon, he had just about finished. Rutherford was next, with Ross dragging behind as usual, as soon as the coffees were poured and everyone was seated, he laid out his plans for the day. The warrant for Lawrence Hilliard was due around lunchtime and so the 'bomb' would go up as soon as the Superintendent got word of the arrest. Avalon went into the fine detail with his team and he explained that Ross and Rutherford would conduct the interview. Frazer and Mackinnon would stay working on the case from the Cave and Avalon would be the first line of defence against Croker and the Superintendent. He then warned the team that if he was removed from the case they would have to make their own decisions from there on. He did, however, ask Frazer privately if she would be his contact on the inside.

"Yeah, course I'll do it, we've put too much into this case tae see some uniformed Rupert close et down because he's swimming in shite." Her use of the term 'Rupert' being a military word for an officer reminded him of her own issues with her private life. Being involved with an ex-special forces type must bring a set of problems she didn't know how to handle. He nodded to her with a slight smile and then said,

"I don't want you compromised though, there's no point in taking risks for either of us, is that clear?"

"Aye," she nodded, "but I can't see him doin' et, questions are bound tae be asked."

"Well I'm hoping it won't but I'm planning for the worst-case scenario," he sighed then they left the booth and joined the rest of the team. Ross explained that he had arranged for two uniformed officers to be present for the arrest and everything was in place. Avalon nodded and then said,

"Well, that's as much as we can do until the warrant comes into play, do what you need to do and we'll meet back here at eleven thirty." Avalon then walked over to the window and looked out. There had been fog overnight and though the sky looked bright, the mist was still lingering here and there. He tried to think himself outside the case, he tried differing subjects to introduce to his brain to force the case to go away for a few minutes, but it wouldn't. He wondered what Carol was doing at that moment but with lack of anything to base possibilities on, he drifted back into the room. He then thought about taking some time off, not the sort ordered by the Superintendent but a few days he could choose for himself. A trip to Edinburgh to take in the city and maybe a train journey to see Carol's parents. That would be good, sometime away from everything to do with police work, but gradually the details of the case came back into his head and one item came thundering in with an explosion. He didn't know why it was but he suddenly had an overriding instinct that made him shiver slightly. He turned to Ross who was over the other side of the room pouring another coffee. Ross glanced back and saw him looking, so he held up his cup and raised his brows. Avalon gave a nod and Ross poured another cup. As he walked over and handed Avalon the coffee, Ross joined him by the window, after taking a sip, he asked,

"Do you think the fog will clear up?"

"Dunno," said Avalon in monotone.

"I think it'll be sunny if it blows away." Avalon didn't answer, instead he asked a question of his own.

"What single thing in this case kept destroying any solid theories?" Ross thought for a moment and then shrugged.

"I'm not sure, there've been several reasons we haven't made good progress, I suppose the biggest one is not being able to find Buchanan or get his DNA."

"I mean, one single item," insisted Avalon as he glanced round to Ross, "a single part of the story that refused to fit into any hypothesis we came up with."

"The car you mean?" asked Ross looking directly at him.

"Exactly, the car," and Avalon took a drink of coffee then looked back out of the window.

"But forensics checked it, they found very little."

"I know, because we wanted to put it back to see if Buchanan would return so they weren't given much time. That theory is outdated now, but the car still sits in that container," sighed Avalon, "as if it's there just to make trouble for us."

"So you think it's a red herring, left there as a puzzle?" asked Ross.

"No, but I think there is something about that car that doesn't fit," insisted Avalon and then he turned to Ross once more, "for instance, why is it there?"

"Well," shrugged Ross, "it's an expensive motor, we thought that Buchanan wouldn't want to put a torch to it."

"But we've seen his company books, we've been through his bank details" explained Avalon, "he could buy a whole stable of them, that can't be the reason it's there."

"Mmm, true," mused Ross, "there is that, so have you got a theory?"

"No, but I think we need to get Hendry to strip that car down," suggested Avalon returning his gaze to the window.

"Do you want me to ring him?" asked Ross. Avalon thought for a moment, he slowly turned to face him and nodded.

"I can't think of a single reason we're keeping it there now, let Hendry know and then get the transport lads to move it over to him." As Ross picked up his phone and dialled, Avalon looked back out of the window, watching the swirling fog that was drifting in from the Moray Firth, dance and swerve around the lampposts and other objects it couldn't move out of its way. Why had that moment of impulsive intuition come over him? Was it that like the fog, thoughts move around things they can't move, until there is so much fog you can't tell what is moving and what isn't? Maybe, but it was more likely that in his heart, Avalon had known that the car was important, he just didn't know why.

~~~~~~

The text said simply, "H int 1" and it was from Ross. The DS never wasted time on his text messages, they were so abbreviated that they were probably harder to work out than the messages that came from the German Enigma machine during the war. If there was to be a Bachelor of Arts degree on text-speak, then Ross would be the man to set the exams. Ross put his abbreviated messages down to the restrictions of having large thumbs, Frazer had suggested he should use his penis instead but that had started a session of bickering that lasted the best part of an afternoon. As it was, Ross's text was reasonably easy to figure out as Avalon was expecting it. The message meant that Lawrence Hilliard was in interview room one. Avalon had instructed Ross to try and stall Hilliard in phoning his solicitor until he was at the station, the reasoning was to cause Cameron as many problems as he could and to see how quickly he could arrange his day to suit the new situation. It would be a measure of the importance of Hilliard speaking to the police. Avalon picked up the file he had prepared and made his way to interview room one. Ross and PC Kirk were outside and Ross raised his brows as he approached.

"Any problems?" Avalon asked.

"No, he's in there with Martin who's prepping him."

"Okay," nodded Avalon, "I'll watch from in there," and he pointed to the viewing room with his thumb. Ross entered the interview room and Avalon looked to Kirk. "Coming?"

"No," replied Kirk shaking her head, "it's not my idea of entertainment," and she spun on her heel and walked away.

"Ross began by instructing Hilliard that they would be recording the interview and did he require his solicitor? Hilliard said he wouldn't speak without first taking advice.

"I suppose you want to phone Mr Cameron?" and he pushed the phone towards him. Hilliard looked relatively unfazed by the affair and just stared at Ross for a few seconds. He then gave a quick glance to the two-way mirror and asked,

"Is DI Avalon in the building?"

"He is," nodded Ross.

"Can I see him?" Ross didn't look to the glass, he just stared at Hilliard.

"He's busy, but I can ask him," and Ross stood to leave, he then entered the viewing room.

"What do you think?" he asked in a quiet voice.

"Not sure," shrugged Avalon still watching Hilliard, "but he may be ready to talk." Avalon then picked up his folder and said,

"Fetch Martin out of there and I'll join you in a minute." Ross nodded and Rutherford soon joined Avalon. After a couple of minutes Avalon entered the interview room.

"Mr Hilliard, you wish to see me?" he said and sat at the side of Ross.

"DS Ross says I've been arrested for suspicion of murder."

"That's correct," nodded Avalon hoping that wasn't the only reason he had been asked for.

"You're making a big mistake DI Avalon, I have done nothing like that."

"That's for the jury to decide Mr Hilliard, we just give them the facts," insisted Avalon and he gathered up the file from the desk as if he was about to leave.

"But you obviously haven't got the facts or you wouldn't be implicating me," insisted Hilliard. Avalon stood and looked down at the man.

"I once asked you to tell me anything you knew, you refused to tell me anything whatsoever and so now it's in someone else's hands," and he began to leave.

"Then I want to see a solicitor," insisted Hilliard a little more agitated.

"I'll get DS Ross to ring Mr Cameron."

"No," demanded Hilliard, "erm, not Cameron, here's who I want," and he handed Avalon a card from his pocket. He had said 'no' with some anguish and then tempered his voice with a little hesitation and Avalon saw that the pressure could be working.

"Are you sure?" asked Avalon, "these are not of the same exalted company of Mr Cameron?" asked Avalon looking at the card.

"I'm sure," nodded Hilliard. Avalon placed the card on the table and left the room. In the viewing room he looked at Ross with wide eyes.

"What's that about?" whispered Ross.

"I would say he wants to talk but needs legal representation to do so," explained Avalon. They both looked out at Hilliard with his hands interlinked on the table, staring into space. Rutherford watched the man without moving, hardly blinking but occasionally glancing to the mirror. "Get him his brief, it's not going to be a quick job but hopefully this is a positive move, and..." Avalon paused for a moment, "it could mean that the Superintendent won't hear about it just yet."

Hilliard had been made as comfortable as he could be given the circumstances, as it was to be some time before the solicitor he had asked for could attend, so Avalon and Ross went down to the yard where the storage unit that contained the car was situated. They double-checked at the offices that no one had been trying to access the container and then they waited for the transport crew to remove the vehicle and place it on a truck. It was then going to the forensic team's compound so that Hendry or another of Sarah Underwood's team could perform a deep search of the vehicle. As the truck rolled away Avalon and Ross got back into the car and set off.

"Should we check on the Buchanan house to see if the wife is back?" suggested Ross.

"So you've still not found her?" asked Avalon.

"No," admitted Ross, "I think she's done a runner."

"I suppose we could have a look," said Avalon, "or we could have a word with the cleaner, she might know where she is."

"I think that would be a waste of time, let's try the house," suggested Ross.

The house seemed empty and as the two men walked round it trying to peer through the windows they noticed there was mail on the carpet by the front door.

"I wonder why she's run?" asked Ross as they walked back to the car.

"I really don't know," replied Avalon leaning on the vehicle, "she's either scared or an accomplice in this I'm guessing. I'd go for the former though as she didn't need to tell us about *her* and Cameron did she?"

"Maybe," shrugged Ross, "but then again, why tell us about it anyway?"

"Let's get back," sighed Avalon and they headed for the police station.

There was a bit of a flap when they arrived, Trevor Cameron had got word of Hilliard being arrested from Hilliard's wife and he had just arrived at the station. He was raising his voice to the desk officer and complaining about being kept in the dark.

"Mr Cameron, can I help you at all?" called Avalon as he entered the foyer.

"Ah, DI Avalon, I want to know what the meaning of this is, I have-"

"Shall we retire to somewhere less public, somewhere there is less need for you to shout?" Cameron seemed to calm himself.

"Yes, of course," he nodded realising he was causing a scene. Avalon led him to one of the interview rooms where he asked Cameron to take a seat.

"Now then, what seems to be the problem?" he asked.

"You know damn well what the problem is detective, I have not been informed of the arrest of my client, which means he has been denied that right."

Cameron was not shouting anymore but his tone was sharp and aggressive. "You have no evidence to support your claims and to arrest him and then deny him his legal rights means you have overstepped the mark, I thought you were more professional than that, DI Avalon." Avalon just looked at the man, he rested his hands on the table as he sat and just listened. When Cameron seemed to have finished, Avalon said in a calm voice,

"I will try to address all the points you have made Mr Cameron. Firstly, we *do* have evidence that Mr Hilliard has been involved in a crime and we *do* have a witness that can attest to him knowing the victim." Avalon paused for just a second as he watched the information sink in.

"Simply knowing someone, doesn't mean they are involved in their death, if that was the-"

"We certainly have not," interrupted Avalon, "prevented Mr Hilliard from seeing his legal adviser, I think you are mistaken about your involvement in this case, Mr Hilliard has sought his legal representation elsewhere, Mr Cameron." Both Ross and Avalon watched the reaction on the man's face. "So you see, you have no business coming here at all," Avalon stood and made his way to the door, "oh, and as to professional conduct Mr Cameron," said Avalon looking back to him, "seeing as you were having an affair with one of your clients' wives, I don't think you can claim any higher moral ground do you?" Avalon looked over to Ross, "Escort Mr Cameron from the building would you?"

Avalon waited for Ross at the top of the stairs.

"I want to see just how long it takes for the news to get to the Superintendent."

"Do you think he's that closely tied to this case?"

"He's getting his information from somewhere, I can't see any other option, this Black Clan seem to have a very extensive network," explained Avalon and he headed off towards the Cave. Ross followed closely and as they entered the room, Frazer and Mackinnon looked up from their computer screens.

"I'm guessing you sorted the problem out downstairs," asked Frazer with wide eyes. Avalon nodded as he reached for the coffee. "The desk rang us but then said you had just arrived."

"You should have been there," smiled Ross, "Cameron's face was a picture."

"It was satisfying but now the fun starts," frowned Avalon taking a sip of the coffee, "I'm guessing it won't be long before..." the phone rang in the booth. Avalon raised his eyebrows and placed his cup on the shelf, he then strode off to the booth. "Avalon," there was just a moments paused and then, "yes sir, on my way." He then walked straight out of the room without saying a word. It was Ross's turn to raise his eyebrows and there was an expectant tension in the room.

Avalon could hear raised voices before he got to Croker's office and so he gave a single hard knock and waited.

"Come in!" called out Croker obviously still engaged in an argument. Inside the office the Superintendent looked livid, his eyes were staring and his face was almost purple.

307

"When I give you an order I expect it to be carried out," the man was shouting. Both men were standing opposite each other at either side of the desk but they both looked over as Avalon came in. It wasn't a large office and three people in there made it feel uncomfortable when tempers weren't raised, but with the atmosphere thick with rage it was stifling.

"And you," growled the Superintendent when he saw Avalon, "I don't know what your little game is Avalon, but I'll tell you this, you have finished in the force."

"I beg to differ," said Avalon as calmly as he could, "I'm just doing my job. On the other hand, I'm not quite sure what you're doing." The Superintendent turned to him, all his venom was about to drop onto Avalon but the DI wasn't finished. "Is this about us bringing Lawrence Hilliard in?" he asked.

"Of course it damn well is, what the hell do you think I'm-"

"Then I have a question for you," interrupted Avalon in a loud voice, he had to shout to break the Superintendent's rant, "how did you know he was arrested?" The man didn't think about his answer.

"I was told and I don't see-" Avalon interrupted again.

"By whom?"

"That's none of your business," began the Superintendent but Avalon didn't give him chance to continue.

"By Trevor Cameron?" This slowed the man down, for the moment, the Super was off-guard and Avalon pressed the attack. "I find it hard to see why Cameron would directly contact the Superintendent to tell him that a client had dropped his services, unless Cameron's interest in Lawrence Hilliard goes way above that of a professional one." The Superintendent closed in slightly on Avalon.

"Tread carefully Avalon," he said with menace, "tread-very-carefully." And then he turned to Croker. "Get him off this case now, I want his whole team off the case, hand it to B Section if you have to but I want him off this now," he demanded pointing to Avalon.

"No," said Croker casually and he sat, "I'll do nothing of the sort." The Superintendent was taken aback for a second.

"Have you forgotten who I am?" he growled.

"No I haven't," frowned Croker, "but I think you have," and Croker glared at the man.

"I'll have your balls for this man," hissed the 'Super'.

"You're quite welcome to go through proper procedure and make a formal complaint," continued Croker in a matter-of-fact way, "but until I am told otherwise, I am still in charge of criminal investigations here and DI Avalon is still working for me."

"I am your superior," demanded the Superintendent.

"And as such you are within your rights to make a formal complaint about me, but as I said previously..." there was no reason to continue, the Superintendent stormed out so quickly he seemed to take most of the air out of the room. Avalon looked down at Croker dispassionately. The DCI removed his spectacles and tossed them onto his desk and then rubbed his forehead.

"How *did* he know you had Hilliard?" he asked quietly.

"As I said sir, there was only one way, I had just spoken to Cameron and told him that Hilliard had changed his legal representation." Croker looked up to him and then realising he couldn't see a thing, replaced his spectacles.

"So what is the connection between Cameron and the Superintendent?" asked Croker.

"I can't be sure but I believe they all belong to some sort of secret club, a club that has contacts in many high places."

"So the poison could go higher than the Super then?" he asked.

"Yes," nodded Avalon, "it's possible and likely."

"And you believe that this club is protecting Buchanan?"

"Yes," Avalon nodded again, "and now it looks like Hilliard may be ready to talk to us, that's why he's changed his brief."

"And the club has suddenly become jumpy?" asked Croker, but it was more of a confirmation than a question.

"It would seem that's correct." Croker nodded slowly at this, he stared into the distance for a moment and then looked up at Avalon.

"I'm not going to state the obvious Avalon, we're both in the firing line, will Hilliard come up with something do you think?"

"I can't see why he would drop Cameron and go with different representation if he didn't want to distance himself from the club. I think he's probably ready to try for some sort of deal."

"He's in a good position too," sighed Croker.

"But then again," added Avalon, "he isn't privy to what's going on here, I think he feels isolated now, and I'm going to reinforce that upon him." Croker nodded.

"Do what you have to do," said the DCI and Avalon decided it was time to leave. As he made his way back to the Cave, Avalon suddenly felt tired, maybe it was seeing how exhausted Croker looked, either way he just wanted to drive out into the hills and breathe some fresh air and lie on the heather for a few hours. He stopped and looked down the corridor behind him, did he have a few minutes to walk into the car park? It didn't have the rejuvenating properties of Glen Affric or the Kyle of Sutherland but it was what he needed. It wasn't to be, his phone gave that distasteful little shake and he knew he had to see who it was. It was another brief text from Ross, "WYR" it said, from past experience it was short for "When you're ready" and meant 'get in touch we have something you may be interested in'. He sighed as he looked down the corridor and headed to the office. To his surprise there was quite a bit of activity in the Cave, both Ross and Mackinnon were on the phones and Frazer was busily typing at her computer. Avalon looked at the coffee machine but decided against it and instead sat at the side of Ross's desk until he had finished on the phone.

"Have you got something?" he asked. Ross didn't answer at first, he looked at Avalon and out of the window before saying,

"Yeah, but for the life of me I'm not sure what it means." He looked back to Avalon and began to explain. "Hendry phoned me a while ago, they started to look deeper into Buchanan's car and his team started their processes while Hendry looked at the paperwork from

311

the previous search which wasn't filled in fully as we were in a hurry if you remember?" Avalon gave a quick nod. "Well he was looking around the car and filling in the identification numbers and he saw that the engine number didn't match the ones logged with the DVLA. It's not that unusual, but not common in new cars and so he checked the VIN number and that didn't match either."

"So the car has had a number plate swap?"

"Yeah," nodded Ross, "but why swap the plates and then hide it? It doesn't make much sense."

"It doesn't at the moment but do we know anything about the real ID of the car in the garage?"

"I've just been speaking to vehicle records and they say that the vehicle from the container had recently swapped owners, but the new registered keeper isn't Buchanan, it's his wife. The vehicle isn't taxed or insured."

"Well it seems pretty obvious then," said Avalon standing, "something happened to the original car and Buchanan bought a replica to replace it."

"So why hide it?" asked Ross.

"I don't know," shrugged Avalon, "but we need to find the original car."

"Boss," came Rutherford's voice, Avalon turned and saw the big man holding his hand over the receiver of the phone, "Hilliard's solicitor has arrived and he's with his client."

"Okay," nodded Avalon, "give them ten minutes and then move them to an interview room." Rutherford nodded and continued with the call. Avalon turned to Ross and added, "Let's hope that Mr Hilliard is in a talkative mood then."

Ross and Rutherford sat opposite Hilliard and his solicitor and Avalon watched from the viewing room behind the two-way mirror. The interview had begun with Rutherford explaining the details of the interview and recording those present, then Ross began the questions.

"Do you know a female called Margaret Elizabeth Storey?"

"Yes," nodded Hilliard.

"When did you last see her?"

"It would be about the middle of March but I can't be precise."

"When you last saw her, did you take her to your house up near Garve?"

"No, we went up the A9 to a little café, all we did was talk," explained Hilliard.

"Did you know her as Margo or as Margaret?"

"You mean did I know she was a prostitute?" asked Hilliard.

"Just answer the question Mr Hilliard," demanded Ross.

"I called her Margo, she didn't like her first name."

"Did you know her in a professional manner?"

"At first I did, but I actually enjoyed her company, the sex side of it wasn't why I continued to see her."

"You mean you began a friendship with her?" asked Ross.

"Yes, you could call it that. Margo was an odd person, she was intelligent but could be very base."

"Meaning?"

"Well, we could spend an afternoon walking and talking about the finer things in life and then she would switch and become someone else," explained Hilliard. Ross leaned forward.

"Can you be more specific Mr Hilliard?"

"She actually liked her job," the man hesitated for a moment, "she was very sexually motivated but she had, what I would call, a perverse streak, she was into things that I wasn't."

"Such as?" Hilliard was obviously a little embarrassed about explaining the details to Ross.

"She liked to have sex in public places and she liked it when it was rough. I'm the exact opposite and so I found some of her quirks distasteful."

"Is that why you killed her?" asked Ross taking the man totally by surprise.

"I didn't kill her," he insisted, "I know you will find this hard to believe but I was very fond of her, she had life and a spark that many women can't even dream of, it just came with a price."

"You talk about her in the past tense Mr Hilliard, you are obviously convinced she is not alive."

"I'm guessing that's why I'm here, Detective Ross, unless you just want to find out about her sexual proclivities?" Ross gave him a stern glare and Hilliard became aware that he probably didn't want to anger this detective and so he looked away.

"Do you know of an organisation called the Black Clan?" asked Ross. This time the solicitor spoke.

"Mr Hilliard doesn't want to discuss anything not relating directly to the charge."

"It is related to the charge," insisted Ross looking at the solicitor and then back to Hilliard, "because the

Black Clan helped you and your friend cover this crime up, isn't that correct Mr Hilliard?"

"Detective Ross," interrupted the solicitor again, "I must point out that my client will not answer questions that include reference to any third party organisation that you may believe he is associated with." Ross raised his brows to the solicitor and then looked back to Hilliard.

"Why did you change your legal representation Mr Hilliard?" The man didn't answer, he just glanced up to Ross and then back to the table. "Was it because you were under their influence and you wanted to break free from them?"

"I must protest Detective Ross, my client will not comment on such matters." Ross didn't acknowledge the solicitor this time, he kept his gaze on Hilliard.

"There is so much evidence against you Mr Hilliard, there is blood and DNA found at the house, earrings worn by Miss Storey on that night and it's your house Mr Hilliard, your house that all that blood was found at."

"I didn't do it," insisted the man glancing up at Ross.

"Then how would you explain it away, because me and many other detectives don't see any alternative unless you're not telling us everything," insisted Ross, "unless you're protecting someone, someone who's made damn sure you're backed into a tight corner."

"I didn't do it," repeated Hilliard. Ross reached into his pocket and pulled out a small evidence bag and dropped it on the table.

"This is one of the earrings she was wearing, it had blood on it. As you say, Margo loved the rough sex play, did it go too far? Had she raised the game to much higher stakes and it just went wrong?" Hilliard was looking at the earring in the plastic bag and then he looked up at Ross again.

"I didn't do it," he said again in a quieter voice.

"Then who did?" growled Ross. For a moment, Hilliard looked like he was about to say something, but his solicitor interrupted.

"May I have a word with my client alone?" Ross stared at Hilliard for some moments and then said,

"Interview terminated..." he looked at his watch, "at seventeen thirty-one, on the thirty first of May 2018," and he switched off the recording machines. Ross and Rutherford walked into the corridor and met Avalon outside.

"What do you think?" asked Ross.

"He probably didn't do it," nodded Avalon, "but he knows who did and the solicitor can see that too. Just keep at him, I think he wants to talk but this man is canny, he's looking for some sort of deal, and probably a way to pull from the clutches of the Clan."

"Et's a big step," added Rutherford, "he's got a wife that probably doesnae know much about this and a career that has given him a good life."

"Agreed," nodded Avalon, "it's going to take a big leap for him to let go of that, we have to be patient," and he turned to Ross, "keep the pressure on him, I don't think he's as strong as most people think he is." Ross nodded, interviews were one of the hardest parts of the job, they could strain the interviewer more than the interviewee. "I'll go and check upstairs, Megan may have found something about Buchanan's wife or the other car."

She hadn't, she was left running the Cave whilst everyone was out and as Avalon entered, both she and Rory were busy on the phones. Avalon poured himself a coffee this time and waited for them to finish. It was Megan who ended the call first.

"How's et goin' down there?" she asked.

"As well as can be expected," replied Avalon, "Got anything new yet?"

"Tae be honest I haven't had the time since you left, there's been break-in just outside Dingwall and there's no one in B Section to attend."

"Typical I suppose, the timing of crime is always bad. Is it anything big?" he asked.

"No but the place has been ransacked, loads of damage and the only thing that has gone missing es a worthless painting."

"I suppose you and Rory will have to attend then," sighed Avalon. She nodded and looked at Rory who had just finished his call.

"Come on Rory," she said, "late night for us tonight."

"Right," smiled Rory, "I better let Emily Blunt know I can't make it tonight then." Avalon had no idea who Emily Blunt was, he guessed she was someone famous but what he did know was that the 'Cave Humour' was rubbing off on the young DC. As the two of them left, Avalon took his coffee into the booth and checked his emails, he then stood by the windows in the main office and finished his drink before returning downstairs.

Avalon watched though the two-way mirror as Ross continued with the interview of Lawrence Hilliard.

It was clear there had been some discussion between him and his solicitor as it had taken some time. It was getting late in the evening and everyone was tired and Hilliard looked particularly haggard. Before the interview formally began the solicitor spoke.

"My client Mr Hilliard wishes to convey that he is ready to work with the police to resolve this matter to his full ability but refuses to answer any question regarding what you describe as The Black Clan. He does, however, have information that would forward your investigation considerably," and here the solicitor paused to give Ross a look that meant a great deal, "however, in consideration that this information could be crucial, he would like guarantees that he will be treated with due regard for his help and this information."

"You mean he wants a deal?" asked Ross.

"I believe that some sort of arrangement could be reached," nodded the man.

"That depends on several things Mr Dodson, such as how involved Mr Hilliard is and how 'important' the information is that he is ready to divulge."

"Of course," nodded the man.

"But as you must know," continued Ross, "we, as police officers cannot make those kind of decisions, we can only guide the sheriff and the courts on the matter."

"As long as everything is taken into consideration," nodded the man. Ross didn't know what Avalon was thinking but he guessed he would have words to say afterwards, for now the interview got under way.

"Mr Hilliard," began Ross, "did you kill Margaret Elizabeth Storey, also known as Margo?"

"No, I did not."

"Do you know who did?"

"Yes," said Hilliard in a quiet voice. In the viewing booth, Avalon wanted to punch the air but he didn't, he was waiting for the next question.

"Who did, Mr Hilliard?" asked Ross but for a moment Hilliard went quiet and looked over to his solicitor. The man looked back and gave a single slow nod.

"Jason Buchanan killed Margo," he then said.

"How do you know?" asked Ross.

"He told me and asked me to help him cover it up."

"And did you help him?" asked Ross.

"No," frowned the man looking constantly at the table, "I did not assist him in any way."

"And yet you didn't inform the police of his admission."

"No, Jason Buchanan was blackmailing me. At the time my wife and family didn't know that I sought other women for sex, he had threatened to expose me, it would have ended my marriage and my career."

"So what did you do?" asked Ross.

"I tried to forget about it, I was scared though, Buchanan is a thorough bastard, I actually think he killed her because he knew I was fond of her."

"Did he tell you how it happened?"

"He did but it wouldn't be the first lie he's told," explained Hilliard.

"Then tell us what he said, for the record, Mr Hilliard." Hilliard looked up and swallowed deep.

"I'm ashamed that I have been such a coward, I regret not coming to you with this knowledge so I will

319

tell you what he told me," he said calmly. He took a deep breath and related the story.

"Buchanan met Margo through me at a party I held six months or so ago, he was struck by her, she had no inhibitions and he loved that about her but I don't think she liked him. Eventually she agreed to meet him and they went up north somewhere and they had sex on a cliff top. He became addicted to her waywardness, he said it was always risky with her. This particular night he took her up to the house near Garve. I had forgotten he still had a key and there he tied her to the bed where he beat her as they had sex." He paused seemingly upset by the memory. "He maintained that she taunted him and to scare her he pulled out a knife. She panicked at this and he says she broke free and tried to leave, he grabbed her to try and calm her but she struck him," and he looked up to Ross, "she could be aggressive herself," and then his eyes sank to the table again. "That's when he stabbed her, as she tried to escape into the kitchen, he panicked and dragged her out to the garden. He then tried to clean up the blood but there was too much, so he put her body in the car boot and went to fetch his van. He pulled out all the carpets and put them in the van to burn them somewhere later. That's when he phoned me."

"To tell you what had happened?" asked Ross.

"Yes, but at first he just said he had hurt her, when I saw the blood at the house..." he broke off and held his head in his hands.

"Did you ask him what he had done?" asked Ross, Hilliard nodded.

"Yes, he told me the story but I said I wouldn't help, I said I didn't care what he did, I still wouldn't help."

320

"Did he threaten you?"

"No, he smiled and then laughed, he accused me of being a coward. He said he would make me suffer for the rest of my life. I walked out and left the house. I don't know where I went, I was mixed up. It was the following day when I went home."

"Did he tell your wife about your secret life?" asked Ross.

"No, if he had done that, he knew he wouldn't have any power over me, so I decided to tell my wife some of the story."

"But not about the murder?"

"No, of course not, she could see I was upset and I think she just thought it was owning up that had caused it."

"How did she take it?"

"Not well," replied Hilliard composing himself a little, "two days later she left me." Ross just nodded.

In the viewing room there was a slight knock at door and then it opened a little to reveal PC Kirk peering around it. Her brows lifted and Avalon nodded and met her in the corridor.

"What is it?" he asked a little impatiently.

"Sorry tae bother you sir but there's somebody here tae see you."

"I'm pretty busy at the moment," he said with a frown.

"Aye a' know that sir but he's insistent, says his name is Milne," explained Kirk as Avalon's frown changed to a look of surprise.

"I'll see him, where is he?"

"By the front desk," she spun and strode off as Avalon watched her distinctive action.

PC Kirk?" he called.

"Sir?" she said as she stopped and turned.

"Sorry I snapped at you," he said. She smiled.

"Don't worry sir, I'll get y' back," and she turned once more and left.

Avalon took Malcolm Milne into one of the small offices on the ground floor that was being used for storage. He pulled out a chair from under some boxes and sat on an ancient photocopier by the door.

"It's not as delicately furnished as your office Mr Milne but it will suffice, what can I do for you?" Milne smiled.

"Surroundings are superficial detective, I'm at home just about anywhere," and then the smile subsided. "I've come because on our last meeting I don't think we hit it off as well as we ought to have done, so I'm here to help you where I can."

"And how do you think you can do that?" asked Avalon.

"At our last meeting you asked if there was an organisation called the Black Clan still extant, there isn't but if there were, that organisation would be honour bound to help, not hinder the police."

"So," nodded Avalon, "if this organisation, which doesn't exist but if it did, found that we had one of its members in our cells, ready to spill all of the secrets of this non-existent group, would its non-existent leader come with cap-in-hand to see me?" Milne sighed.

"I really thought you would be more accommodating, there is little sense or reason for us to be enemies, our aims are the same, we are the same."

"We are certainly not the same and our aims are not the same, for instance," Avalon stood and pointed to Milne's chest, "I don't have a tattoo here, and neither do I think that having spies in the police force is a good idea." Milne stood.

"Then there is little more I can say, a great shame but there it is," smiled the man.

"Oh, and just in case you were wondering Mr Milne, if I get even a sniff of your involvement in this issue, I'm coming for you next." The man raised his bows for a moment and then gave a short laugh.

"*The best lack all conviction, while the worst are full of passionate intensity,*" said Milne as he reached for the door.

"Yeats," said Avalon.

"Yes it is," frowned Milne but Avalon just said,

"*Heavy the load we undergo, and our own hands prepare, if we have parley with the foe, the load our sons must bear.*" Avalon then added, "It's by Rudyard Kipling, it's called Justice, you should look it up sometime.

"An art critic, historian and poetry expert," smiled Milne, "I can see I'll have to keep my eye on you detective," and he left. Avalon wanted to follow him and beat the living daylights out of the man, but he soon calmed, he even managed a quiet laugh to himself. Not from the recent conversation but from something Ross had said to him.

"I bet you could hold a conversion using poetry," he had said. After the poetry duel he just had with Milne, he began to wonder if Ross was correct.

## Chapter Thirteen

By the time Avalon had returned to the interview room Frazer was standing outside talking with Ross. The DI took a look at his watch.

"No need for you to be here at this time," he said to her.

"I know boss," replied Frazer, "but I managed tae track down Mrs Buchanan," she paused, "well I know which town she's en."

"Where's that?" asked Avalon.

"Nairn, I tracked her by her mobile."

"How did you do that without getting permission to pull her phone records?" asked Ross.

"I rang her number from my mobile," explained Frazer, "and when she answered I just said 'hello is that Mrs Buchanan?' and then disconnected, I guessed she'd ring me to find out who I was."

"That still doesn't answer my question." said Ross.

"I just got *my* phone records checked tae see where the call came from," she explained, "and the company told me et was Nairn. I then did some research to see if she had connections en Nairn, she does, her sister lives there."

"Brilliant," smiled Avalon, even Ross was complimentary, in his own way.

"Very good, you'll soon be good enough to come out with me."

"I'd rather stay with Rory, he's good at his job," she said with a blank expression.

"So what's going on?" asked Avalon nodding to the door of the interview room.

"It's more or less over, Martin is getting the statement transcribed and then we'll get Hilliard to sign it, after that, it's up to you," explained Ross.

"Did he say any more, I had to leave part way through?"

"He confirmed that Buchanan was a serial blackmailer and Hilliard supplied us with several names he thinks Buchanan has info on," replied Ross.

"The superintendent?" asked Avalon. Ross shrugged and added,

"Looks like it." Avalon frowned as he nodded, at least he was beginning to understand why the Super had been so aggressive, not that he thought it an excuse.

"Okay," he said glancing at his watch again, "we'll get this statement sorted out and call it a day, sleep might help us to think."


For Avalon, sleep didn't come easily, after a shower and a sandwich he went off to bed, only to find that he was thinking about the case and coming up with theories. Even though he knew he couldn't act until he was back in the office it didn't stop him rethinking the options, staring up at the ceiling, so he got up. He thought about a drink to calm his brain but he didn't fancy the whisky. He pulled the lone bottle of beer from the fridge and sat in the conservatory looking out into the small garden, peering into the darkness. Next door, the outside light was activated and Avalon instinctively looked at his wrist to check the time. There was no watch there of course and so he walked into the kitchen where the clock announced it was midnight. No wonder he couldn't sleep, it was only just coming up to his usual bedtime. He walked back into the conservatory to see why the neighbour's light was on, his neighbours were a couple, the woman he had seen there on a couple of occasions had a small dog, so it made sense the dog had been let out into the small garden, but as he was about to sit he noticed a figure. It was the neighbour and she caught sight of him and waved. He lifted his glass as a sort of salute and she disappeared behind the fence so he sat to finish off his beer. There was a gentle tap on the glass to his right, it was the woman with a smile and a wave. He stood and opened the door, it was only then that he realised he was dressed in his pyjama bottoms, nothing else and he was slightly embarrassed.

"Oh, hello," she began, "I'm sorry to bother you," she continued in an Inverness accent, "but we haven't had chance to speak, you are out most of the time and well..." she hesitated, it seemed she had only just noticed he was in a poor state of dress too. She was older than Avalon, probably in her fifties with an engaging smile and a pleasant face. She was a little overweight but it didn't detract from her charms. "Oh, I'm sorry, I didn't realise..." she half pointed to his chest.

"It's alright, I went to bed but couldn't sleep," he smiled.

"Oh I'm the same," she smiled back, "Alan's off to bed as soon as the news has finished but I can never sleep before midnight." He noticed she was looking at his chest now and then, he felt conscious about it and didn't want to be impolite but neither did he want to invite her in just in case 'Alan' got the hump. Instead he changed the subject.

"Been letting the dog out?"

"Yes," she smiled glancing back to the garden, "Tyrant, or Ty as we call him, he likes to go out late, like me really." The name amused Avalon as the dog was about the size of a large hamster. "Anyway," she continued, "I came round to ask you if you'd like to come round this Sunday, it's Alan's birthday and we're having a few people over, nothing fancy but we could get to know you a bit more?" The last part of the sentence was spoken softer than the rest and her eyes flitted from his chest to the table and back to his chest.

"Well, er..." he hesitated this time, "I'd love to but I work for the police and we are pretty busy at the moment-"

"I know," she interrupted raising her brows, "I heard you're a detective."

"That's right but honestly, if I get time I'll pop round, how old is he?" asked Avalon trying to distract her.

"Too old," she smiled with a slight mischievousness in her eyes. Avalon knew he had to get out of this, the police officer in him knew that this was potentially a dangerous situation, but the man in him wanted to grab her hair, force her onto the conservatory table and pull her skirt up to a position where could make them both happy, but he didn't. Instead he looked at her for as long as he could and suddenly felt an unconscious movement in his pyjama bottoms. He had to get rid of her now, quickly and politely or it was soon going to become obvious what was happening down there.

"Well if I can't get, I'll make sure I send him something," and he held his arm out to grab the door, "and now I'll see if I can finally get some sleep." She left in good humour but it was worrying to Avalon, was his lack of personal, female company turning him into a pervert? He hoped not but by the time she had disappeared back through the gate into her garden he had an erection he could have beaten a bull elephant to death with. He finished off the beer and spent an hour reading poetry to get his mind off the whole affair. Nothing like poetry to cool the ardour.

Friday morning was busy, very busy, there were so many things to analyse and check, double check and cross reference until the Cave began to sound like a busy day at the stock exchange.

"So where's the original car?" asked Ross during one of the quieter moments of the morning.

"Don't know," replied Avalon shaking his head, "but it's likely it has a woman's body in it." The door opened and in came PC Dowd with a sheet of paper.

"We're closed," called Ross.

"*You* may be closed sergeant but the Cave seems very much open," he said scanning the room.

"Tell me it's not another incident," frowned Avalon looking at the sheet.

"It's not another incident," shrugged Dowd.

"So what is it?" inquired Ross.

"It's another incident," replied Dowd.

"But you just said-"

"I know what I said but the Inspector told me not to tell him it was an incident and I follow orders to the letter, it's what keeps me from becoming important," explained Dowd.

"So it *is* another incident?" asked Ross.

"That's correct it is..." he trailed off as Avalon snatched the paper from him and read it quickly.

"It's like listening to a Monty Python sketch for Christ's sake," he growled and then added in a softer tone, "straightforward stuff PC Dowd," and he handed the sheet back, "go down to Primark and get a cheap suit, then you're a detective so you can go and solve it yourself."

"When I say follow orders to the letter, it was more of a metaphorical statement," replied Dowd.

"A lie I would have said," frowned Ross.

"They couldn't make me a sergeant, I'm sure I'm not gonna sign up for a job in a suit," shrugged Dowd not quite sure what to do with the incident report. Ross looked back to Avalon who was staring out of the window.

"So if the body is still in the car, the vehicle must be hidden where no one can get to it easily, if at all," he speculated, Avalon nodded and turned.

"I would have said he'd dumped it in the sea but there isn't anywhere you would be able to do that," he insisted.

"What about the case in Drumnadrochit, that security van we found in Loch Ness?" questioned Ross.

"Yes but that was unusual, there was a deep drop there, probably one of the few places it could have been

330

done," insisted Avalon, "and even then they had to remove the barrier."

"Off a cliff?" offered Dowd.

"Where, it's all beaches and shallows?" asked Avalon, "you can't just drive a car into the sea."

"Off a cliff?" repeated Dowd. Avalon wasn't in the mood for humour and his words were tinged with anger.

"Neil, if you know where there's a cliff that we could consider then tell me before I get more irate."

"Above Helsmdale, it's mostly cliffs north of there," suggested Dowd, "and around Berriedale the land rises to about four hundred and fifty feet, I think that qualifies as a cliff."

"It's a bit north though," suggested Ross but Avalon pointed to nothing in particular and said,

"But hang on, didn't Hilliard say something about Buchanan taking Margo north to have sex on a cliff top?" Dowd spoke quietly as he turned away.

"If you're gonna talk smutty I'm going," and he left the incident sheet on a desk. Avalon was deep in thought but Ross caught the words.

"Thanks Neil, as hobbies go, terrain heights is a bit weird even for you."

"It's not a hobby," replied Dowd turning back before exiting the room, "I go sailing up that coast now and then."

"Megan," called Avalon across the room, "see if you can find any reports from the Helmsdale area and north of there, any reports that are odd or uncommon from the local police stations over the past month." She nodded and stopped what she had previously been doing. "Buchanan may have had a particular spot that he knew,"

331

continued Avalon to Ross, "and he may have known somewhere there that you could hide a car."

"Are we going to interview Mrs Buchanan again?" asked Ross.

"No," replied Avalon shaking his head, "I don't see the point at this stage, at least we know where she is if we need her." He looked up at the clock on the wall. "I wonder if I need to tell the DCI about the Superintendent?"

"Probably," shrugged Ross, "it might make a difference to how he feels about the situation, but then again, we don't know for sure the Super *was* being blackmailed, it could be something else."

"True," nodded Avalon, "I may have to tell him though just in case the Super does his nut again." Ross understood what his boss was getting at, if the Superintendent *was* involved with the Black Clan it could easily be the reason he had made an enemy of Avalon and C Section. For now, they had to find the missing car *and* Buchanan and though a 'Be On the Lookout Order' had been issued it was doubtful the man would surface for some time.

"Boss," came Frazer's voice.

"Yeah?" replied Avalon looking round to her.

"There are a few incidents logged en the north, most of et es pretty insignificant though."

"Anything at all would be good," he shrugged.

"Well," she began looking back to her computer screen, "ef I leave out all the stray sheep and 'unusual lights in the sky' reports, there are three normal reports," and she glanced up to Avalon before returning to the screen, "a white van seen parked in several areas, suspected of stealing garden items?" Avalon shook his head, "how about campfire out of control near Dunbeath?"

"No," said Avalon shaking his head once more.

"Then try locked gate to an empty field taken off hinges?"

"That may be worth checking on," said Avalon raising his brows.

"A locked gate to an empty field?" asked Ross incredulously, "why would someone want to get into an empty field?"

"Why would someone want to lock a gate to an empty field?" smiled Avalon, "because it was on the cliff top and was dangerous maybe?"

"Okay, I'll get on it," nodded Frazer understanding Avalon's point. The DI noticed the incident sheet that Dowd had left and picked it up.

"You better look over this Rory," he said handing it to Mackinnon, "attempted break-in at Culduthel, you better get over there and show your face." Rory nodded as he stood, he wasn't keen on leaving the Buchanan case now things were moving but they had to respond to everything and he knew that. The phone was ringing in the booth.

"Avalon."

"*DI Avalon, it's Hendry, we've found something in the car from the container, I'm not sure if it's of any significance but there is a dusty substance on one of the door cards.*"

"Do you think it's recent?" asked Avalon not sure what Hendry was getting at.

"*Well it could be, it's only on the driver's door and on the seat but nowhere else in the vehicle, I*

333

*wondered if it got there from the driver of the vehicle as he squeezed out through the window."*

"You mean as he got out of the vehicle in the container?"

"*Exactly,*" confirmed Hendry, "*it's microscopic and there isn't much of it but it could be worth looking at.*"

"So any ideas what the dust is?"

"*Not all of it, there are deposits of microscopic pollens and smoke but there are elements we are still examining, it shouldn't take us long, I just thought you may want to know about it.*"

"Yes of course, anything could make all the difference at the moment," explained Avalon, "in fact, I'm on my way, I need to know if there is anything identifiable."

"*I have to go out now but there'll be someone to explain when you arrive.*" Avalon put down the phone and went to tell the others.

"Don't get your hopes up is my advice," announced Ross, "dust is an exacting science I agree but the damn stuff is everywhere, which makes it unreliable as evidence."

"I don't want it as evidence, I'm just hoping for a clue to where Buchanan might be," explained Avalon pulling on his jacket. Frazer had just ended a call and looked up to Avalon.

"Boss I've just spoken t' the local officer who went out tae the gate off ets hinges," she began.

"And?"

"He says et was reported by the farmer, John Mackenzie, he says the gate wasn't locked as such but had a bolt through a chain, the whole gate was taken off and a few vehicle tracks could be seen en the field."

"Okay," nodded Avalon, "we better have a look around there, where is it?"

"Er," Frazer looked at the screen and read from it, "the place es en the middle o' nowhere so you'll have tae go to the local office at Wick."

"You and Martin better have a look around," suggested Avalon to Ross.

"To Wick?" exclaimed Ross, "this is May, it's still winter up there."

"Wrong on two counts," explained Avalon, "firstly this is the first of June and secondly, it's so far up there that by the time you reach the police station it will be autumn." Ross sighed sporting the expression of a petulant child but Martin stood and pulled on his jacket.

"Come on sergeant, I'll drive," he smiled.

"Oh great," added Ross dragging himself to his feet, "a three-hour journey in some non-descript Japanese car listening to Abba, I don't think so, we'll go in mine." Avalon turned to Frazer.

"You'll have to hold the fort I'm afraid," he said apologetically.

"Aye no bother, I can talk to Rossy's imaginary friend ef I get bored," she smiled.

"It's Sergeant Ross to you DC Frazer," insisted Ross as he left the room.

"Oh aye, sorry your magnificence," called Frazer as the door closed.

~~~~~~

Avalon was greeted by a new face at the forensic lab, a young woman he hadn't seen before. She was engaging and ebullient which wasn't usual in the labs and it made it obvious she was very new.

"I haven't see you here before," he said trying to confirm the fact.

"No, I've only just started," she explained as she led him further into the building, "I've just moved up from Cambridge," she added which accounted for the very slight accent that he thought he recognised.

"My old stomping ground," he smiled.

"Cambridge?" she asked.

"Yeah, I was there for a while, glad I moved up here though."

"I wasn't sure before I was offered the job but I love it here," she beamed and they entered one of the small rooms to the side of the building. Avalon saw several people he knew and in the centre was Sarah, Sarah Underwood and she was giving him a broad smile.

"You didn't have to come you know, I would have sent you anything we found."

"I know that," replied Avalon returning the smile, "but Hendry said you may have found something we could get a lead on." She pointed to one of the viewing screens and moved closer to it.

"I'm not so confident that it's going to reveal anything," she said bringing the image into focus, "this is part of the dust sample we found in the vehicle, you can see here and here several microscopic types of pollen," she pointed them out on the screen which showed as a light blue image. "These needle-like particles are the interesting bit," she continued pointing to larger shapes on the screen.

"So what are they?" he asked.

"Asbestos," she said looking straight at him.

"Asbestos? but I suppose there's going to particles all over the place in small amounts?" he offered.

"True," she admitted with a slight shrug, "but never in such concentrations, if you look here, they far outnumber the particles of pollen and other detritus."

"Yeah it seems that way but..." he looked closer at the screen, "with this much you would think that the environment this came from was pretty lethal," frowned Avalon looking back to Sarah.

"Well it probably looks worse than it is close up and we are close to isolating what type of material these came from but I wouldn't want to spend any time where that green fleece has been," she said.

"So the green fibres were from a fleece?"

"Yes, and there's a great deal of other debris in there too," she nodded, "I'd say whoever was wearing this clothing had been in a very dusty environment." Avalon stared at the image for a few moments and then said,

"How long will it take you to find out what sort of asbestos this is?"

"About an hour I would think, you can wait if you have the time," she smiled.

"I can hang around for a few minutes but I'll have to make a call," and he exited the little room.

"Megan, it's Avalon, we need to check if Buchanan had any connection to a company or individuals that had dealings with asbestos or asbestos products."

337

"*I don't recall seeing anything, but I'll do a check around,*" she replied. Avalon thanked her and put his phone away as Sarah joined him in the corridor.

"Do you think this will help?" she asked.

"Maybe, it all depends on us finding a connection between asbestos and our suspect," he explained and they walked towards the front office. "I'm now wishing we had brought the vehicle in sooner."

"That's the nature of the bigger decisions we make, sometimes they work out, sometimes not," she smiled as they reached the office, "would you like a cup of tea?" she added.

"Please," nodded Avalon, "and talking of big decisions, have you set a date for *your* big day yet?" Sarah's expression told Avalon the story before she even began.

"Well, that whole thing turned out to be one of those decisions that doesn't work out, it's all off I'm afraid."

"Really, why is that, I thought everything was settled?"

"So did I but then he told me he couldn't move from Edinburgh and I would have to move south."

"But hadn't you made decisions about that previously, you said that-" she held her hand up to interrupt.

"I assumed he would understand, in my opinion, it's easy for doctors to relocate, not so for specialists like me," she explained as she made the tea. Avalon was bemused by her attitude to it, this was a part of Sarah Underwood he hadn't seen or realised was there. Her tone was of ambivalence, as if it was of minor importance and not a decision you make to change your

338

life. Avalon began to wonder if she was one of those people who consider that the whole universe revolves around *them*, someone who thought that everyone else had to bend to their world. As he watched her preparing the tea he thought about his own position, would he relocate or change jobs for a relationship? Maybe if it was for her he would, but then again, maybe not. He was seeing her in a new light, this time without the rose tint to it. She handed him the cup, at least she remembered how he drank his tea.

"Philip told me you still hadn't found this man?"

"Philip?" asked Avalon.

"Philip Hendry," she said as she sat.

"Oh, I didn't know his first name, yes that's true, I'm hoping a clue might come from this dust, I've put DC Frazer on the hunt already." The tea was always boiling hot at the labs so Avalon waited for it to cool before trying it.

"Well, once this last test is finished we may be able to tell you more about the material." She didn't seem to feel the heat of the drink and sipped merrily at it. She leaned back and crossed her legs, her skin looking tanned against the white of the lab coat. Avalon didn't quite know what to think about her, he had been infatuated by the woman since he first laid eyes on her and now he wondered if she had a flawed character. He couldn't make a true assessment based on a single statement so he decided to ask a few subtle questions.

"I still can't believe the engagement is off," he began. She looked across the room for a moment and then back to him.

"I think I was running scared," and she sighed, "at my age you start to wonder if you'll end up single for ever. Most of the people I knew when I was a teenager have married, divorced, married again and had a tribe of children and though that life isn't for me, I do wonder how men see me now." Avalon almost burned his mouth trying to sip the hot tea as she made the statement. He daren't tell her what *he* saw, he just shrugged and asked,

"Does it matter how they see you?"

"I didn't think it did but I'm not sure now," and she sipped the tea again, "maybe I was destined to live my life this way." Avalon made a 'Hmm', sound and feeling brave he said,

"Does it have to be one of those long-term, serious relationships, maybe you're looking for something you don't really want to find?"

"Is that what happened to you?" and then she shook her head, "no sorry, it's none of my business."

"It's alright," he smiled, "married yes, divorced yes, regrets no. I'm still friends with my ex-wife, in fact she's recently been up here to visit but if I was honest, I don't think anything to do with relationships can be quantified."

"And neither should it," she nodded and then after a pause, "do you have children?"

"No luckily," smiled Avalon, "they're not one of my favourite lifeforms," and he looked into her eyes, was that her problem? He couldn't help but ask. "Is that what you think you've missed, children I mean?" She broke into a smile at this.

"I don't think I do, there have been times where I thought the idea of it was good but the reality doesn't fit with who I am," she stared across the room once more and with a sigh added, "too old now of course."

"That's not true and you know it," insisted Avalon. She looked over to him.

"Well, yes it's possible but not likely and I think when I say too old, I mean it's too late." She smiled again and Avalon found it difficult to think anything but good things about her. He probably stared at her for too long because she looked away and took another drink of her tea. Avalon was thinking of a subtle way to ask her out, for a drink or a meal and his thoughts were moving ideas around like tiny boxes, trying to put them into an order that made sense and gave him the ideal way to put the question to her. He felt his heart quicken, he felt adrenaline enter his blood stream and just as he thought he knew how to do it, that damn phone rang.

"Sorry," he said rolling his eyes, "I better answer it," and he pulled his phone out.

"Avalon," he said as calmly as he could.

*"Boss, et's Megan, Ross has just phoned in, he's got no signal so he's used a local's phone. You better come in, he's found somethin'."*

"Like what?" he asked being not too eager to leave just yet.

*"He thinks et's the other car."*

"I'm on my way," he instantly replied and put his phone away as he stood. "Got to go," he said placing the still half full cup on the table and as he reached the door he turned back with a weak smile, "We'll have to continue this conversation sometime," Sarah nodded but as Avalon left he wondered what the conversation had been about exactly.

~~~~~~

341

Rory had returned from his trip out but both he and Frazer looked a little out of sorts as Avalon entered the Cave.

"So what's going on?" he asked as he poured himself a coffee.

"Rossy and Martin have found something but can't get to et."

"Not so cryptic please, tell me straight." It was Rory who explained.

"It's complicated Boss," he began, "they went to meet the local PC at a field where a farmer reported his gate being removed, while they were looking around the farmer told them that there were vehicle tracks in the field after the gate had been moved that seemed to head to the cliff but nothing had been seen or been reported. The edge isn't a sheer drop apparently, it's a very steep slope to the sea so you can't see the very bottom."

"Ross and Rutherford decided to walk along the edge," continued Frazer, "onto a short headland and Martin said he thought there was something in the water. They backtracked and tried to find a way down but couldn't see over the edge, Rossy said after he tried and slipped, they gave up but the farmer showed them a ledge that was dangerous but allowed a sightline to the sea shore." She paused and then glanced to Rory before looking back to Avalon, "They reckon there could be a car down there."

"DS Ross said he couldn't confirm it from where they were," added Rory, "but he's sure it's a vehicle, in a gully where the tide rarely goes out."

"So what are they doing?" asked Avalon.

"They've called out the coastguard to have a look, I suppose they're just waiting for a boat or a chopper to arrive," suggested Frazer.

"So I'm guessing we can't contact them?"

"No boss," frowned Rory, "the signal is poor where they are, DS Ross said he would go back the house nearby to call in when he knows something." Avalon nodded and said,

"Okay, keep me posted," and turned to go to the booth but stopped and asked Frazer a question. "Anything on the asbestos search?"

"Not yet," she said, "I thought this was more important." Avalon nodded again and walked to the booth. He felt tired, really tired, he needed the case to move a little quicker but there was no hurrying these things. He drank his coffee and then went to tell Croker all he knew.


Avalon looked up at the clock, it was twenty minutes past three and over an hour since he had arrived back from the forensics lab. He considered the reason his phone was ringing was some confirmation from Sarah Underwood about what they had found.

"Avalon,"

"*It's Sarah, we've finished analysing the material I showed you earlier*," said the voice.

"Excellent, and the conclusions?" asked the DI.

"*Well*," replied Sarah, "*we've narrowed it down as much as we can but the thing is*," she paused and Avalon knew another problem was coming, "*there are many types of asbestos particles in this mix.*"

"So what are you saying?" asked Avalon.

"*It's the sort of mix that you'd expect from a manufacturing plant.*"

"No one makes that stuff now do they?" he asked.

"*I doubt it, but that's how it seems,*" she replied.

"Well thanks anyway, let me know if you find anything else," and he ended the call. He looked through the glass partition to see Frazer rise to her feet and look towards him, he stood and entered the main room. "You look as if you've found something."

"Maybe," she said raising her brows, "but et's tenuous to say the least."

"I don't care, anything will do at the moment," he frowned refilling his cup from the coffee machine.

"Well, it seems several years ago, a company called MRD was set up near Fort George to handle-" her phone rang, "oh, hang on boss that could be Ross," and she made two steps back to her desk and picked up the desk phone.

"DC Frazer," she said and then shortly after held up her thumb to Avalon as she listened, "the boss's in, do y' want to speak tae him?" and she handed the phone to Avalon.

"What've you got?" he asked.

"*The coastguard confirms there is a car in the water, badly damaged and on its roof. It's in about a metre of water at low tide and getting a thrashing from the waves.*"

"Can they ID it, I mean what sort of car is it?"

"*They don't know what make it is but the colour and style seem to fit the missing car of Buchanan,*" replied Ross.

"So we need to get to it as soon as?" offered Avalon.

"*Yeah, but that's a no go, we'll need a boat and a diver, it's pretty dangerous there.*"

"Okay, let the local police know about it and get back when everything is secure. We'll have to organise it from down here." Ross confirmed he would set off as soon as he could. Avalon handed the phone back to Frazer and sat on a near-by seat.

"Problems?" asked Frazer returning to her own chair.

"A few," nodded Avalon with a sigh, "it looks like it could be Buchanan's car but it's in several feet of water in a gully where the waves are fierce. We're going to need a boat and a diver to get to it and even then we don't know for sure it is the car."

"Shall I get on it?" she asked.

"Yeah," nodded Avalon looking over to the windows. He thought for a moment and then continued. "It's going to have to be a big operation to get that car out of there, we can't examine it where it is so we need recovery trucks as well as a boat with divers."

"Similar to the case at Loch Ness," added Frazer.

"Yeah, but in this case, visibility isn't the issue, the sea is the enemy this time. We probably need to co-ordinate with the coastguard too." He stood and walked towards the windows. Yes, he was tired, he really just wanted to go to sleep. "Why is nothing straightforward?" he asked himself but loud enough for Rory and Megan to hear.

"Because this is Scotland," said Megan.

~~~~~~

"The DI says to get back as soon as we can secure the site," said Ross as he exited the little house. Rutherford was sitting on a low wall finishing off the sandwiches the kind lady that lived at the house had provided. He nodded, pushed the remnants of the sandwich into his mouth and stood. "Did you enjoy those?" asked Ross looking at the empty plate.

"Yeah, I was ready for some food I admit."

"I got *one* of those, just the one."

"I'm bigger than you," smiled Rutherford patting Ross on the shoulder.

"Rank means nothing to you does it?" he asked as the big man ambled down the garden path to the road.

"Aye course et does, et means you don't need as much food as me."

"That's a very flawed logic," insisted Ross as he followed the DC to the car.

"So what now?" asked Rutherford with his hand on the car door.

"Let the local plod know what we're up to," replied Ross leaning his arms on the roof of the car and then his chin on his arms, "tell the farmer to keep the gate locked and then we take the A9 back to civilisation and a temperate climate."

"I like et up here, I've never been this far north, and what's with your hatred o' the countryside anyways?"

"I don't hate the countryside, it just smells like cow shit, it's wet and cold and has all manner of beasties roaming about," explained Ross in a casual manner.

"This es the wild Highlands man, there's bound tae be the odd wild animal here and there."

"I don't think I said anything about wild animals," said Ross with a squint. Rutherford shook his head and turned to face the direction of the sea.

"Och, et's sound man, just breath it en," said Rutherford and took a deep lungful of air, then began to cough.

"See what I mean?" smiled Ross, "I think that proves my point."

"I think breathed en a fly or something," spluttered Rutherford taking out his handkerchief and blowing his nose. He looked down at the result and said, "Jees what is that?" and showed it to Ross.

"Gods man," replied Ross turning his head away in a grimace, "I don't want to look at what comes out of your nose thank you."

"I think et's a blue bottle or maybe a wasp," continued Rutherford. He eventually settled down to the idea that his nose was clear of wildlife and replaced the handkerchief into his pocket. As he looked over to Ross, he saw doubt or something similar on his face. "What?" he asked with a deep frown.

"Oh," sighed Ross glancing to Rutherford, "I was just thinking what a pretty stupid place it is to dump the car, especially if there is a body in it."

"Don't know," shrugged Rutherford, "et seems a good place to me, even now we know et's there, we still can't get to et."

"Yeah, but think on this," added Ross "there is no way that it wouldn't be found one day, I mean, we could easily have missed it on the investigation but one day someone, maybe a climber, or a lobster fisherman would have found it."

"True, but by then the violence o' the sea could have torn et to bits, and with the salt water, et won't stay lookin' like a car for long," suggested Rutherford.

"Well in my opinion it's not been thought out all that well, almost like we were meant to find it," replied Ross standing up straight and sliding into the car. Rutherford squeezed into the passenger seat rocking the car as he did.

"Maybe this character doesn't give a shit, have y' though o' that? He's probably a psycho," he said.

"Probably, we need to remember that when we corner him then," and Ross started the car engine and drove back to the field.

The uniformed officer was still there but there was no sign of the farmer. Ross spoke to the officer who promised he would make sure the field was closed off and then he left to carry on with his other many and varied duties. Ross then walked back to the edge of the cliff top and looked down the severe slope to the blue water beneath.

"I wish we could ID the car," he said as Rutherford stepped beside him.

"We could try but ef we slip on that slope we're knackered, they'll be two more bodies down there."

"What about the gully, I wonder if we could get down there?"

"I'll give et a go ef you want," replied Rutherford.

"No, it's not worth it, let the experts get to it," replied Ross shaking his head and he turned to leave, "let's get back before we get attacked by a wild sheep or something."

"I don't think you have anything tae worry about from sheep," called Rutherford as he began to follow on.

"I worry about everything with satanic eyes," called back Ross.

"You've obviously not seen Wallace and Gromit, then, Shaun is a very clever sheep. He even has his own movie," explained Rutherford.

"Must be worth a few bob then."

"Aye but then again he's a special black-faced sheep," called Rutherford over the strengthening wind. Ross stopped and looked back.

"Isn't that racist?" he asked.

"Only if you're a sheep," replied Rutherford and Ross nodded and continued towards the car in silence. As they reached the vehicle Rutherford asked,

"Shall we go back to the house and see if we can get some more sandwiches for the journey back?"

"Jesus man it's two hours, you'll not lose any weight in two hours," and he got in the car. Rutherford looked out to sea and then joined Ross.

"Yeah, suppose so, there's a chippy in Golspie anyways."

~~~~~~

Avalon turned away from the window, he was listening to Rory talking on the phone, trying to arrange for police divers and the support team. Frazer was sending out emails and making the odd phone call now and then. The activity had brought Avalon from his thoughts; the case, Sarah Underwood, Ross up in the brisk air of the north and what they would find in that car. He didn't know it at the time but he was thinking the same as Ross, he was thinking that if Buchanan had rolled that car off the cliff edge, he was brazen and confident and that was good. Overconfidence breeds mistakes and Buchanan had made so few yet, but that car was a big mistake. If they could retrieve it without disturbing it too much, forensics would be able to examine it at their leisure, and if Buchanan hadn't considered they would find it, there *should* be evidence aplenty. He strolled over to the coffee machine and placed his cup on the shelf then moved off to the booth where he removed his jacket and looked through his emails and then he remembered something. He walked into the main part of the Cave once more and strode up to Frazer.

"You were going to tell me something, something about asbestos?"

"Oh aye," she said with wide eyes looking to some notes she had scribbled on a sheet of paper. "You asked about any connections between Buchanan and asbestos. Well, some years ago, a company called MRD set up to undertake a contract tae remove asbestos from installations all over the Highlands. Et later became clear they were constantly breaking the law on the disposal of the stuff. In the end they were prosecuted for health and safety breaches, some of the directors even got suspended sentences. A few got off with minor fines."

"And I'm guessing Buchanan was a director?" asked Avalon.

"Aye, he got off pretty lightly though," nodded Frazer.

"So how does this help, if it was years ago?"

"Probably because the building they operated at still exists," explained Frazer, "the council closed et down and were supposed tae have the place professionally decommissioned but, the council being the council thought et would cost too much and had the place fenced off instead."

"And you mentioned Fort George?" asked Avalon looking at a small map they had on the wall.

"Yes, et's not all that far from there on some wasteland."

"Get your coat, we need to take a look, hold the fort Rory, we'll be back as soon as we can." Mackinnon nodded and Frazer and Avalon left for the car park.

Once in the car, Avalon tried to think of a way to introduce the subject of Frazer's private life without making it obvious Ross had spoken to him. He tried to remember what she had told him some days previous.

"When we went out to interview the Buchanan's cleaner," he began tentatively, "you were asking about the way Carol and me drifted apart."

"Aye, that's true, I like Carol, she's nice," replied Frazer.

"Yes... well I got the feeling that all is not well-"

"Has Ross been shooting his mouth off?" she demanded. Avalon glanced over to her, she was glaring wide-eyed.

"That question makes me think you have told DS Ross more than you were prepared to tell me," he said looking calmly back to the road.

"I didnae want you tae think I wasn't working at a hundred percent," she replied apologetically.

"So there is something wrong, it doesn't matter if you don't want to tell me, it's none of my business?" She went quiet for a moment.

"We've split up," she eventually said in a calm voice, "I don't think it's ever going to go anywhere and et just seems so pointless."

"You don't care for each other, is that it?"

"No, yeah, well no, I suppose I don't care for him," she spluttered, "I mean he's been fine with me an' all that but we don't have conversations, we don't eat at the same time, we have separate beds and the only time we touch es..." she trailed off feeling embarrassed that she had said too much.

"It's fine if the only connection is sexual," insisted Avalon.

"That's not et though, I was about t' say the only time we touch es when he's showing me how tae look after myself," she paused, "you know self-defence an' all that. I thought I had a mixed up mind but he's just..." she trailed off once more.

"But you must have realised that when you first met?"

"Aye I did but back then I didnae want anything like tha..." she stopped talking, her embarrassment was obvious as she sighed deeply. Avalon kept quiet, he knew she would tell him in her own time and as they turned off onto the Nairn road she continued. "C Section has altered, it's sort o' become a distant family and I feel part of that like I never did before," she paused for a second, "I know I'm startin' tae sound like a sentimental Tracy but it's sort of changed the way I think, and changed what I want out o' life." Avalon's face stayed straight, devoid of any obvious emotion but inside he was smiling, it was what he had hoped would happen to Frazer, it was sad that it had come at the cost of a breakup with her partner but nevertheless, Megan Frazer was becoming balanced, and a happier person for that.

"No it doesn't sound sentimental at all, it sounds like you know what you're about at last."

"I wouldn't go that far," she said looking out of the passenger side window.

"So what's happening back at home then?" he asked.

"Oh, he's going to get a flat as soon as he can, I'm thinking o' selling the house and finding something a bit nearer to town," she replied.

"I meant in the shorter term," added Avalon.

"Nothing really, I'm sleeping on the sofa until we can sort something out."

"Haven't you got a spare room, the sofa seems drastic?" he asked.

"You've seen the house, there's plenty of land but et's not a big house." There was silence for a few minutes, Avalon was thinking that the size of the house wasn't the issue, there *was* room for a second bed. It was probably more to do with her going through the motions of a physical split, something she *had* to do rather than something she wanted to do. "We turn down here I think," she suddenly said pointing to the left. Avalon indicated and pulled off the main road onto a single-track road.

"Well," he eventually said, "if you need somewhere to stay you only have to let me know, I have two completely empty bedrooms."

"Er, oh, right," she stuttered and glanced over to him, "that's nice of you but I'll manage well enough," and she shuffled slightly in the seat. Avalon didn't really think it was a great idea but if she was truly in a fix he would accommodate her, he would do it for any of his team. As the road turned into a rough track he looked over to her and said,

"Mind you, you'd have to put up with some very odd habits," and he watched the look on her face as she tried to keep it neutral. "I keep very odd hours and I often bring my work home with me, I'm a copper you see," and he looked ahead again. Frazer smiled, if it wasn't for the fact that he was her boss, she might have taken him up on the offer.

## Chapter Fourteen

The austere brick building looked in poor condition and the few windows were covered over or filled in. It was flat roofed and grim to the eye. The area was surrounded by a chain-link fence and covered the greater part of three acres. The land had no other features save for a few shrubs and nettles and it gave the feeling of a post-apocalyptic film set rather than a piece of flat wasteland on the coast. 'Danger' and 'Keep Out' signs were fixed to the fence at intervals and a coil of barbed wire ran around the top of the fence. Avalon coasted the car slowly up to the gates where he stopped and climbed out of the vehicle. He strolled over and looked at the large lock which secured the gate by a sturdy chain. It was rusty and didn't seem to have been tampered with. Frazer came to his side and looked into the compound.

"Nice neighbourhood," she said in a flat tone. Avalon was silent, he stared into the area and looked over the building which stood mocking him in the middle of that bare ground. It resembled something from the second world-war than a more modern industrial unit and its utter remoteness taunted him. He walked away to the left along the line of the fence, pressing his foot here and there until a part of the chain-link fence gave way. He stood and looked over to the building for a moment and then felt in his pocket where he usually kept his tiny flashlight. It was still there but he headed back to the car as he thought his idea through. He opened the boot and took out the large flashlight he kept there and strode over to the place where the fence was loose seeing Frazer moving to join him.

"You're not thinking of going en there are y' boss?"

"I don't see an option," he frowned.

"But et's not a good idea seein' as there's probably loads of asbestos in there."

"No it's not but by the time it's decontaminated enough for forensics to go in, anything found in there will mean nothing," and he bent down to push through the fence, "stay here, I'll have a quick look around," and he checked the flashlight to make sure it worked. He paused for a second looking out towards the building and then purposely stepped off towards it. It wasn't long before he heard the sound of the fence being moved and he looked back to see Frazer walking towards him.

"I told you to stay there."

"Et's my job tae back you up, put me on report ef you like but I'm not letting you go alone," she replied and her face told him she meant it. He reached into his jacket and handed her the small flashlight and then continued towards the building. The structure was larger than it looked from the fence, single storey but large enough to have several rooms inside. There were three or four doors and two large shutter doors to one side. A small compound still held several gas bottles which must have provided heat at some time. The doors and windows were all covered and sealed shut with the exception of a single door at the back. It was a solid wooden door but there were signs that the bar that had secured it had been moved recently. Avalon looked at Frazer and raised his eyebrows. He tried the door and though it didn't move immediately, a sharp tug made it open outwards. Avalon switched on the flashlight and shone it into the gloom, the floor was littered with debris and an odd burnt smell came from inside.

"Stay close, and try not to dislodge any dust," he said and he stepped inside the building. He found himself in a corridor with several small but empty rooms to both sides and as he moved very cautiously along that corridor, the burned smell became stronger. In a larger room to the left he saw what he considered to be the source of the smell. In a pile in the centre was burned debris with some of the material round the edges still unburned. It was carpet and he looked around to Frazer. He couldn't see her expression but he knew she would guess the significance of it. This was probably where Buchanan had destroyed the carpet from the Garve house. There was no sign of what might be a body within the debris and so they continued deeper into the building. Some of the rooms had machinery in them but they found nothing of significance, just dust, debris, piles of asbestos and rubbish with the odd table and chair. A thick layer of dust covered everything and by now both Avalon and Frazer had decided to cover their mouths and noses with handkerchiefs. They doubted it would be of any help but it felt the right thing to do. As they reached the final door they stopped before entering the room. It was the only door inside the building which had been found in a closed position and both Avalon and

Frazer felt that there was something behind that door. Avalon shone his flashlight on the handle and depressed it until the door was free, he then stood back a little and gently pushed it open with his foot. The beam of his flashlight burst into the small room and picked out several objects, there was a table and a chair and in the corner a mattress with a sleeping bag on it. There were a few discarded food wrappers and tins and the whole place looked as if a tramp had been sleeping rough there. Frazer shone her lamp behind the door as they entered but there was nothing much of any significance anywhere else in the room. A newspaper lay on the table and Avalon raised it with the aid of the flashlight to check its date. It was fairly recent being from the twenty fifth of May and then he scoured the debris on the floor for anything else.

"Well, this could have been his bolt hole?" said Frazer as she looked at the other items on the table.

"It could be," nodded Avalon, "but there's something wrong if it was."

"What do you mean?" she asked shining her light under the table.

"If the Black Clan were hiding Buchanan, don't you think it would be a little more salubrious than this hole?"

"True," replied Frazer, "I suppose that doesn't make any sense."

"Malcolm Milne seems to have access to endless amounts of cash, I would think if he was hiding someone, that someone would probably be in a very luxurious safe house somewhere in a hot climate," insisted Avalon. He prodded the sleeping bag with the toe of his shoe but found nothing in there. Avalon sighed a little, this wasn't quite what he was expecting, not at all. He moved the beam of his flashlight around the room, it was clear if Buchanan had been the former resident of that room, his position within the Black Clan wasn't quite what he had considered.

"Boss," called Frazer and Avalon looked round. Her flashlight was illuminating a calendar on the wall, it was a current one with an image of a kitten which looked completely out of context with that room. Some of the squares on the calendar that held the dates had notes in them, coded notes probably because Avalon could read no sense into them, just numbers and or letters.

"It looks like a diary of things to do," he suggested and he placed his lamp on the table and took out his notepad placing his handkerchief in his pocket. Frazer provided him with light as he took notes of the dates and tried to copy the coded messages verbatim. They couldn't remove the calendar as it may constitute evidence if they could prove it was where Buchanan had been for a short while. One obvious note stood out on the calendar. It was for the first of June and it had a thick pencilled cross through it and the letter 'C' in the corner. When Avalon had done he put the handkerchief back to his face, picked up his lamp and said,

"Let's get out of here."

Back at the car Avalon looked at his notes as Frazer called back to the police station.

"They're sending a team over later but et could be some time before anyone can get en there," she said as she put her phone away. Avalon just nodded as he studied the notes. "So what do you think et means?" she asked looking over his arm at the notepad.

"I think it's a plan, I think the calendar was his way of keeping track of what he had to do. I can't work any of it out though."

"So you don't think it was written in real time?" she asked.

"I doubt it," replied Avalon looking back across to the building, "the first dates could have been but the final dates were planning ahead, looking at the dust in that room I don't think anyone had been in there for at least a week, probably two. This was probably where he came after he left the suicide note."

"So what do you think the cross and the letter 'C' means?" she asked. Avalon knew she was referring to the final date, it was *that* very day, the first of June. The large cross and the letter 'C' was significant but it could mean anything.

"I don't know and unless we know what 'C' is we're helpless," sighed Avalon handing her the notepad. He walked to the front of the car and leaned on the bonnet and folded his arms looking out across the wasteland.

"Is it the car?" suggested Frazer, "maybe today was the day he was going to pick it up."

"No," replied Avalon shaking his head, "I think the car was never in his plans for a pick up, it was there to throw us off the scent."

"His wife then, her name begins with 'C'?" she then asked.

"But he's had plenty of time to see her," and why the first of June?" asked Avalon standing up and walking back to the fence. Frazer thought about it, there was something nagging her, right at the back of her mind, something she remembered but it wouldn't quite spring to the front.

"Et's a birthday," she suddenly said, "I think et's Buchanan's birthday," and she was already pulling her phone out to ring up Mackinnon. Avalon looked back and joined her as she spoke with Rory at the office.

"Rory, et's Megan, can you have a look at Buchanan's date o' birth for me, I think et's the first of June." Avalon looked at her features as she listened to the phone.

"Even if it is," said Avalon, "I'm not sure of the significance." Frazer gave a slight nod and then he heard her say, "thanks Rory, I thought et was," and she ended the call, "so he's planning something for his birthday," she added replacing her phone into her jacket.

"It seems that way," nodded Avalon and with Buchanan we can guarantee it's not going to be jelly and trifle with balloons."

"So what the hell is 'C'?" asked Frazer to no one in particular.

"Cameron!" announced Avalon suddenly.

"Cameron? Why would he bite the hand that feeds him?" she asked.

"What if it's payback for his affair with his wife?" asked Avalon and then he put his hand on his forehead and spun on his heel, "Christ, that's it," he spat, "it isn't the Black Clan pulling Buchanan's strings, it's the other way around," and he turned to Frazer, "Buchanan had been blackmailing so many of them that they have turned on him and he's after revenge."

"Et's possible," replied Frazer with wide eyes.

"Possible? It's so obvious now, the body at the Garve house to implicate Hilliard, the second car in his wife's name to implicate her and now he has something lined up for Cameron."

"But what?" asked Frazer with a deep frown.

"I have no idea but ten to one it will involve something that implicates others from the Clan," said Avalon with an excited look. "That could be why Buchanan's house was as clean as a whistle, he really didn't want anything found there but at Hilliard's house, he *wanted* evidence to be found to implicate Hilliard himself."

"He's a crafty wee bastard then," sighed Frazer.

"Oh yes and he's had us running around looking at the Black Clan as being the ones protecting him, the truth is," paused Avalon, "the Clan have been looking for him too. Milne hinted as much but I was too blind to see the truth." Avalon was shaking his head. "What an idiot I've been," he added. Frazer was looking down at the ground and was shaking her head slightly, as if she wasn't totally convinced.

"But ef Buchanan es making much bigger plans for the Clan, why does that calendar in the building end today?" and she paused before adding, "on Buchanan's birthday?" Avalon looked into her eyes, he didn't know if she was thinking the same but if his own thoughts were correct, he had to move quickly.

"Because he's going to kill Cameron and make it look like someone else did it," he announced with a startled look, "you drive!" he shouted and he jumped in the passenger seat. Frazer was quick off the mark and set off at speed down the narrow track towards Inverness. Avalon was dialling his phone.

"Where are you now?" he called into the mobile, there was a pause and then he heard Rutherford say,

*"We're just past Tore roundabout."*

"You're too far away, we think we know where Buchanan is, coordinate with Rory at the Cave."

*"Watch yourself boss,"* replied Rutherford, *"we both reckon Buchanan must be a complete psycho."*

"I'm sure of it," replied Avalon and he ended the call. "Ross and Rutherford are still too far away," he explained, "we'll have to get uniform involved," and he began to dial again. "Rory, we're on our way there but you need to get some officers to Cameron's office, they need to get there quick but no sirens is that clear?" Rory answered and Avalon replaced his phone into his pocket.

"We'll probably get there before them anyway," said Frazer as they closed in on the A9.

"Yes," sighed Avalon considering Rutherford's last statement, he already considered Buchanan was dangerous but the reality of coming face to face with him brought many doubts into Avalon's mind. He also considered Frazer, she had showed many times she wasn't one to stay out of the action. He could order her to stay with the car but he doubted she would listen anyway and after all, it was her job to get involved. It just wasn't her job to stand up to a man who was willing to kill, without backup. Of course, he *could* wait for the uniform officers to arrive but that could mean they were too late to help Cameron, and although Avalon disliked the man, it was his job to protect him.

"We could be too late boss, et's late in the day," she said looking at her watch as they crossed the A9 and sped down Millburn Road.

"I thought that too but it's likely Buchanan would wait until just before closing time before entering the office," suggested Avalon. Frazer said nothing as she too began considering what they might find there. Inverness was still quite busy as they braked to a halt outside the door to the offices and Avalon made his way immediately up the stairs towards Cameron's area of the building. In the reception of the office suite the place seemed quiet and there was no receptionist to greet them which was worrying. Avalon held up his arm as Frazer entered behind him, she stopped as Avalon moved quietly to the wooden panelled, double door and pushed it slowly open. Avalon's eyes scanned the room quickly assessing where the most danger lay. There was the body of a woman to the right slightly obscured by a large desk and on the floor close to the other desk lay another body, this time a man, Avalon assumed it to be Cameron. Sitting on the desk was what seemed to be a male with his feet resting on a sumptuous swivel chair. As the door swung open the man looked up, he was dressed in dark clothing with a balaclava over his head and a poker in his right hand. There seemed to be blood spatter on his clothing and he dropped the poker and stood to face Avalon. The DI slowly entered the room and looked into the eyes of the man.

"Jason Buchanan? I'm here to bring you in for questioning in connection with several crimes we believe you are connected with." The man didn't react at first, his eyes just bored into Avalon with a dark fire that was unnerving and in a deep voice said,

"You need to get out of my way," and he reached into what looked like a protective jacket and pulled out a long bladed knife.

"I'm going nowhere Mr Buchanan, and neither are you," said Avalon as calmly as he could, "there are other officers waiting outside so just put down the weapon and make it easy on yourself." He noticed Frazer moving to his left, slowly and calmly and he saw the eyes of the man look to Frazer and then back as he assessed his options. Avalon began to wonder if he actually had any handcuffs or wraps to secure the man even if he was able. He was also wishing he hadn't asked for a quiet approach as the sound of sirens would have brought some comfort to him at that moment. As Frazer made her way further out to the left the man reacted and moved slowly towards her and so Avalon began to close on the man.

"So you both want to die today do you?" the man asked and brandished the knife.

"Put the knife on the table," said Avalon with a little more authority in his voice.

"No," demanded the man, "you come and take it from me," he added and a smile developed on the visible part of his mouth beneath the balaclava. "A skinny Englishman and a weedy tart? You two are dead meat."

"Add on a grumpy, mean Invernessian bastard," came a voice from behind Avalon, "who's pissed off because he was on his way home and another 'tart' who's an expert at taking down knife-wielding arseholes." Avalon recognised the voice as DS Wilson but before he had time to react the man lunged for Avalon, the knife heading for his chest but somehow he managed to move, just as Frazer came from the left and Wilson moved to his right. They wrestled the man to the ground, not before Frazer had kneed him in the groin and Wilson tried to wrench his arms out of the sockets. The knife was on the floor and DC Boyd straddled the whole melee and forced cuffs onto his wrists and tie-wraps onto his ankles. Avalon turned the man over and pulled off the balaclava.

"Caution him," insisted Avalon to whoever wanted to do it. It was Boyd, after all, it was she who had trussed him up. Avalon and Frazer looked at Cameron as Wilson checked on the female. Cameron was in a poor state but was still alive as was the female but it was doubtful Cameron could survive the head injuries he had suffered. Uniformed officers flooded the room and Avalon retired with Frazer into the reception. He looked at Frazer, there was a sparkle in her eyes, she was made for the exciting side of the job, it really brought her to life. As Wilson joined them Avalon asked,

"I thought you were out again today?"

"We were supposed to be but the court was adjourned so we went back to the office, we were about to go home when Rory told us about your call." Avalon smiled.

"Your timing was epic," he said.

"What's this about 'tart' and knife-wielding arseholes?" asked Boyd as she too entered.

"I was just trying to put him off guard," smiled Wilson but she folded her arms and frowned, "I didn't mean the bit about 'knife-wielding'," he grinned. Boyd shook her head then looked at Avalon and said,

"The uniform sergeant has called for an ambulance, but to be honest I think the male won't make it." Avalon nodded and stood.

"You two get off, we'll stay here," he said.

"Do you want us to take the suspect in?" asked Boyd. Avalon nodded.

"Yeah, can do, we'll follow on after," and Boyd and Wilson went to get their charge.

As Avalon brought the car to a halt in the car park he sighed deeply.

"Doubts?" asked Frazer.

"Not doubts but in some ways the hard work starts now," he replied.

"Et's always the same," nodded Frazer, "et's always hard work but we have that twisted bastard off the streets and that has tae be a good thing."

"Yes, it is but we still don't know what's in that car up north, we still don't know how deep the connection to the Black Clan is and it's doubtful that anyone will offer information freely."

"They might now they know Buchanan is in custody," offered Frazer. Avalon turned to face her.

"Thanks for the support by the way." She stared back into his eyes and a slight smile broke in the corners of her mouth and she nodded slowly.

"That's what I'm here tae do boss." He turned and looked out of the windscreen and sighed again.

"Come on then, let's start the monumental climb over the mountain of paperwork," and they got out of the car and made their way up to the Cave.

~~~~~~

Avalon was leaning on the metal fence looking over the River Ness watching a duck come in to land on the surface of the water like a tiny little seaplane. Its webbed feet splayed out on contact with the surface and it skied to a steady halt with a spray of water. The little bird seemed so happy with the landing that he fluffed up his feathers and gave a happy quack knowing he was both an accomplished aviator and a decent water skier. Avalon smiled and turned to walk up Castle Road and onto View Place and laboured up the hill towards the castle. It had been a week since the arrest of Buchanan and two days previously the car found in the sea near Dunbeath had been recovered along with the body of the woman known as Margo. Cameron had survived his injuries but the doctors predicted he would never fully recover. Certain people had begun to talk, others had refused to have anything to do with the case and the whole sorry episode had taken its toll on the team. Avalon felt more tired than ever and his feet seemed to be heavy and slow to react and the hill felt steeper than it had ever been previously. As he reached the top and turned to face the Castle Tavern he saw Ross waiting in the beer garden holding a half filled glass and wearing a puzzled expression.

"You look like my old man looked just before he croaked," said Ross.

"I feel like gravity has been turned up to its highest setting," replied Avalon.

"Did you speak with Croker?" asked Ross.

"I had a meeting with him yes," replied Avalon.

"And did you do as I suggested?"

"About having some time off you mean?" replied Avalon, Ross just gave a nod, "yes I did, I told him I would have some time off later in the summer."

"And what did he say?" asked Ross taking a deep pull on the drink.

"He said it's fine as long as it wasn't too busy," explained Avalon shoving his hands in his trouser pockets and looking over the Ness.

"It's always busy," insisted Ross, "and he knows it's always busy."

"Well it's up to me when I take time off and I'm planning a couple of weeks at the beginning of September."

"What are you going to do?" asked Ross. Avalon shrugged, pulled his hands from his pockets and said,

"Do you mind if I get a drink, I feel like a spectator at a sport called 'Rossy Drinking' at the moment."

"Course," nodded Ross, "what do you want?" and he finished his own drink.

"Just the usual," he said and Ross walked inside to fetch them both a drink. Avalon rested his forearms on the fence and looked out across the river to the other bank again. It was after nine o' clock but it was still full daylight and Avalon basked in the warmth of the day as he wondered what to tell Ross. He was indeed planning time off but he had no real idea what to do with that time, it somehow felt stupid to say 'I have no idea what to do', but that was the truth. Ross soon returned with the drinks and handed a glass to Avalon who drank eagerly.

"So?" asked Ross joining Avalon at the railings.

"So what?"

"What are you gonna do with the time off?"

"I'm not sure yet," shrugged Avalon, "I thought about Edinburgh for a few days and then a trip to see Carol's parents."

"With Carol?" asked Ross. Avalon shook his head, that wasn't in the plan he had just formulated, he got on well with her parents and they had become friends he didn't want to separate himself from. Carol's father saw Avalon as the ideal partner for his daughter, even though things hadn't gone well with the relationship he always thought they made a great couple. In Margaret, her mother's eyes, he was the son she had never had and Avalon thought a great deal of her. He would always go to visit when he was in the area and had always enjoyed it. "Well, I suppose there are worse places to go," added Ross, never having been there himself. Avalon stood upright and looked up the hill at the side of the pub, shielding his eyes with his hand, he then took a quick look at his watch before taking a drink. "Expecting someone?" asked Ross.

"Yes, I am actually," he replied, "a new member of the team."

"C Section?"

"No, the drinking team," smiled Avalon. Ross frowned a little, what was Avalon up to? Ross looked up the road and then he saw someone he recognised. Aspects of the vision seemed wrong, skin-tight jeans, feminine blouse and a small handbag all went at odds with what he would have normally expected. The hair was different too and with more makeup on her face, Frazer looked so very different. In more recent times she had changed her look but here she was looking like a normal, everyday woman and Ross was stuck for words as she closed in. She saw Avalon and gave a smile as she approached and as she entered the beer garden and walked past Ross the frown dropped.

"What are you gawping at?" she growled. Yes it was certainly Frazer but Ross was dumbfounded, from her immaculately prepared hair to her piercing blue eyes and a new fragrance that wafted on the air.

"You look nice," smiled Avalon, "do you want a drink?" She nodded and followed him inside the pub,

Ross followed carrying his drink as if it were a glowing orb lighting the way through the darkness that followed Frazer into the building. Inside they decided to sit by the table that hugged the window by the bar.

"Do y' want tae wind your tongue back en you numpty?" she said to Ross who sat opposite.

"You look so…" he paused, "nice," he eventually spluttered.

"Aye, so what's so wrong with that?" she asked taking a sip of her drink.

"Well, nothing," swallowed Ross, "I can't stop looking at you." Avalon smiled but had to concede that he hadn't seen her look so good before.

"Well you better stop et," she hissed, "unless you get don't get offended by a kick in the nuts that es." The look wasn't authentic Frazer but the attitude certainly was. She turned to Avalon.

"Not wanting tae bring up the subject of work, the forensics reports came en just before I left," she explained.

"And was there anything found on the girl's body?" he asked.

"Yeah," nodded Frazer, "just like on Cameron, Buchanan was planting evidence where ever he went." Ross managed to come out of his dream and join the conversation.

"So he carried forensic material of other people to plant where ever he committed crimes?" asked Ross.

"That was his modus operandi," nodded Avalon, "he used the same methods to ensnare people he was about to blackmail. He left a letter and a tissue with DNA on the body of Margo in the boot of the car to implicate another person believed to be in the Clan and

371

when he was arrested at Cameron's offices he was carrying hair and cuff link in a plastic bag."

"How did he get all that stuff?" asked Ross taking a drink.

"Probably from the parties up at the Garve house," suggested Avalon, he may have even paid Margo to get it."

"The DNA results match seven other crimes including the McVie case to prove Buchanan has been a busy little pervert too," growled Frazer.

"It's a pity that Hilliard won't testify against the Clan though, I don't think they're innocent in this case," insisted Ross.

"No, probably not," shrugged Avalon as he picked up his glass. Ross saw something in Avalon's eyes.

"You know something don't you?" he asked.

"Nothing we can use in court," replied Avalon raising his brows.

"Well?" insisted Ross. Avalon took a swallow of beer and placed the glass back on the table. He then looked around the room to be sure no one was listening to the conversation then explained.

"Hilliard wouldn't testify against the Clan but when I was alone with him I told him that without knowing *all* the story, I couldn't guarantee I could keep his connection to the Clan out of the trial. Being the craven, self-serving turd he is, he told me most of the story off the record." Avalon had another quick glance around the room and lowered his voice a little. "As we know Buchanan was a serial blackmailer and he got the dirt on his victims from the parties mainly, and so many of the local branch of the Clan were being fleeced by

Buchanan, not just money but favours too. When Hilliard found out that Buchanan was about to tighten his grip on the Clan, he went to the Clan leadership and told them everything that Buchanan had been up to. He was told that they knew about it and that the Clan had already decided to do something about it. They then told Buchanan they wanted to see him." Avalon paused for a moment. "They told him that they had an ultimatum for him, they said they would pay him off but he had to leave the country, they told him he had no choice and they explained they would make it look like a suicide. Buchanan suspected they were doing a 'Lord Lucan' on him and he went along with it until he was out of their sight."

"Lord Lucan?" asked Ross.

"Yeah, you know, hide him until everyone forgets about him and then top him and bury his body deep," explained Avalon, "well at least that's what we assume he thought, so he went on the run to get away from them. It was then he planned to take them all down. So he cleaned his house to be rid of any DNA to link him to anything, his medical records had already been fixed on a previous favour he called in and then he began his reign of terror, leaving the suicide note to implicate the Clan. He then began targeting Clan members whilst implicating others."

"So he killed Margo to get at Hilliard?" asked Ross.

"Yes, he knew it would be almost impossible for Hilliard to defend himself, his mistake was leaving a few spots of his own blood there. If not for that, Hilliard was a goner."

"So how was the Super involved?" asked Ross. Avalon lifted his glass and stared at Ross as he drank.

"Oh come on, we can keep a secret," insisted the DS with a frown.

"As far as I can see there is nothing to tell," shrugged Avalon replacing his glass on the table.

"So you've become a company man, protecting those above you no matter what?" asked Ross still frowning.

"Like I say, there is nothing I am aware of," insisted Avalon.

"Just being connected with that sort o' club would get him sacked," offered Frazer.

"It would certainly cause him problems but all I know of his involvement is that he was likely a member of the Clan," explained the DI.

"So his future rests in your hands," said Ross, "is that it?" Avalon didn't say anything, he just looked into Ross's eyes. "Well, we're different obviously," continued Ross, "I'd drop him straight in the clay, as far as I can see I let him swim in shite for a hundred years after his handling of the case."

"Maybe you would," said Avalon at length, "but the way I see it, *he* knows that *we* know something but he doesn't know how much we know. So just think about it, if he's lucky enough not to get pulled into this during the trail, how is he going to regard C Section?"

"With suspicion I'd say," replied Ross.

"I'd agree with that," said Frazer looking at Avalon.

"Certainly, but he will probably stay out of our way for the foreseeable future," replied Avalon.

"Or systematically remove us from the picture piecemeal," suggested Ross.

"I doubt that," smiled Avalon, "like I say, he doesn't know what or how much we know so it isn't worth the work it would take to get us all moved."

"He might get ripped apart at the trial by someone from the Clan anyway," added Frazer sipping her drink.

"I don't think anyone will ever admit to being part of the Clan," explained Avalon, "as far as anyone is concerned the Black Clan doesn't exist and I think Mr Milne will do his best to make sure that any reference to it is swept under the carpet."

"So how do we approach it at the trial then?" asked Frazer.

"However we need to," shrugged the boss, "we have no evidence that it exists and so the best we can do is say that an organisation dedicated to hedonism and mutual assistance was being manipulated by Buchanan. We can say we believe it was called this, that or the other but the defence may do more to bring it into the open in trying to defend Buchanan than we can. We can only supply facts and evidence."

"Defence?" growled Frazer, "et's pointless trying to defend that bastard, he's going down there's so much against him."

"He's going away for good, I think that's clear but I'm guessing a great deal more of his life and his crimes will come to light once this is ready to go to trial," insisted Avalon. The three went quiet for a few minutes until Ross sighed and turned to Frazer.

"So to what do we owe this pleasure?"

"Why can't you just grab the concept that a woman has the right tae change the way she looks and deal with et?" hissed Frazer.

"I meant coming down the pub with us?" added Ross quietly.

"Oh, sorry," replied Frazer apologetically, "erm, well," she stuttered a little, "I'm moving into a flat up on Old Edinburgh Road en a few weeks so I was down this way having a look at et, the boss said I may as well come down tae the pub after."

"So you're gonna be a local?" asked Ross.

"Aye, sort of, I'll still have tae sell the house though," she nodded, "an' then I might find somewhere just outside the town ef anythin' suitable crops up."

"So does this mean you're going to be a regular down here?" asked Ross with a slight frown.

"Why?" she frowned back.

"Because if you are we may as well get married," he said still wearing the frown. Frazer's eyes burst open wide.

"You must be fff..." she began in a loud voice but managed to hold it back and then calmly but with glaring eyes, "you must be joking, why the hell would I want tae go an' waste my entire life living the rest o' my days with a dick like you?"

"Well," began Ross counting down on his fingers, "One, you do waste your life with me seeing as we work together, two, we're going to be seeing each other in the day and then here at night, and three, we're going to be arguing so much that everyone is going think we're married anyway." She seemed stuck for words.

"He's got a point," agreed Avalon draining his glass.

376

"Don't you start, I thought you were on my side," she said pointing at Avalon.

"I don't take sides, I'm a copper," he smiled and stood.

"Well let's put it this way Rossy, if you were the last man on the planet, I still wouldn't live with you," she looked around the room for the most unattractive man but seemed to struggle a little, then she saw one of the customers at the bar. The unfortunate was Harry the Hat. "I'd rather marry him," she pointed indignantly. Avalon laughed and went to the bar to buy drinks and stood by the side of Harry while Frazer and Ross continued to argue at the table.

"Evening Harry," whispered Avalon.

"Oh, hello Jim, how're y' doin'?"

"Fine Harry, you see that young lady with Rossy at the table?"

"Aye, I see her fine," replied Harry.

"I just heard her say she would rather marry you than Rossy."

"Is that right? She's got common sense then" and he squinted towards her. "By Christ Jim, she's a real stoater, but I think my wife at home would ha' something to say about it." Avalon smiled at him and took the drinks to the table.

"Harry says you're on," he announced to Frazer as he placed to drinks down.

"What?" asked Frazer with confusion in her eyes.

"Harry, he's says he'll marry you as soon as you're ready," and he pointed to the bar. Harry looked over and winked at Frazer.

"You're as bad as him when you're away from the office," she frowned prodding her thumb towards Ross.

"Not quite but I have my moments," smiled Avalon lifting his glass, "Sludge," he announced.

"Sludge," agreed Ross.

"What's this some sort o' religious chant?" she asked chinking her glass on theirs.

"Just say it and enjoy the moment," insisted Ross.

"Sludge," she announced without conviction but took a long drink from the glass.

"To the Three Musketeers," added Ross lifting his glass once more.

"I thought there were four of them?" frowned Frazer.

"There were but there were three before there were four," replied Avalon confusing the matter, "but as it is there are only three sad bastards in the Cave."

"True," smiled Ross, "we'll just have to wait for Rory to get married and then divorced." He then turned to Frazer once more. "So I'm thinking a September wedding, and where do you fancy for the honeymoon, Spain, Greece or maybe Dingwall?" Frazer just glared at him as if he had just broken wind. "There's a lot to sort out," he continued, "bridesmaids, flowers, cars and what are you going to be wearing?" She shook her head slowly as she raised her glass and gave Avalon a fleeting glance then looked back to Ross.

"I'll be wearing black, and you'll be wearing my drink," she said as the remaining contents of the glass headed straight for Ross.

The Avalon Series, by Peter Gray.

# The Drums of Drumnadrochit
## By Peter Gray.

Introducing Detective James Avalon, a man in turmoil. Both his private and professional life is at an all time low and to make things worse he is seen as a liability to his senior officers. He has to make a change in both aspects of his life, but how? Though he is still on good terms with his ex wife she is beginning to despair with his lack of compromise in his life until a chance meeting with another officer shows promise of opening new doors to his future.

# Auld Clootie
## By Peter Gray.

James Avalon faces a new menace in the second book in the Avalon series. Change and upheaval within the police forces sees him struggle with the problems of a reorganisation of the team. Trouble visits once again in the shape of a major crime that seems to have no clues or motives and Avalon has to work with limited resources to solve a crime linked to religion, ritual and legend.

# The Brollachan
## By Peter Gray.

After just twelve months based in Inverness, Detective Inspector James Avalon now feels more at home than any other time in his career. With his personal life still a shambles, Avalon takes solace in the landscape and his work, but when a woman disappears from her car in plain sight, he wonders about the accuracy of the report. When a body is found, the case becomes more serious. Is the woman's disappearance linked to the body or does Avalon need to reassess his methods?

# The Black Clan

By Peter Gray.
When Avalon becomes embroiled in secret societies and Masonic rituals he soon finds out how far up the food chain the rot has climbed. Once again the Inverness detective is on the streets and this time he's angry.

# Caledonian Flame

By Peter Gray.
Out 2019

Also by Peter Gray

## A Certain Summer

## Sam's Kingdom

## With Feeling

Please visit:

www.petergrayauthor.co.uk
www.acertainsummer.co.uk
www.avalon-series.co.uk

www.trickyimppublishing.co.uk